Lilian Harry's grandfather hailed from Devon and Lilian always longed to return to her roots, so moving from Hampshire to a small Dartmoor town in her early twenties was a dream come true. She quickly absorbed herself in local life, learning the fascinating folklore and history of the moors, joining the church bellringers and a country-dance club, and meeting people who are still her friends today. Although she later moved north, living first in Herefordshire and then in the Lake District, she returned in the 1990s and now lives on the edge of the moor with her two ginger cats and miniature schnauzer. She is still an active bellringer and member of the local drama group and loves to walk on the moors. Her daughter lives nearby with her husband and their two children. Her son lives in Cambridge. Visit her website at www.lilianharry.co.uk

Storm Over Burracombe

LILIAN HARRY

An Orion paperback

First published in Great Britain in 2007
by Orion
This paperback edition published in 2008
by Orion Books Ltd,
Orion House, 5 Upper St Martin's Lane,
London WC2H 9EA

An Hachette Livre UK Company

A CIP catalogue record for this book is
available from the British Library.

Typeset by Deltatype Ltd, Birkenhead, Merseyside

Printed in Great Britain by Clays Ltd, St Ives plc

The Orion Publishing Group's policy is to use papers
that are natural, renewable and recyclable products and
made from wood grown in sustainable forests. The logging
and manufacturing processes are expected to conform to
the environmental regulations of the country of origin.

www.orionbooks.co.uk

To the memory of Doreen Mudge

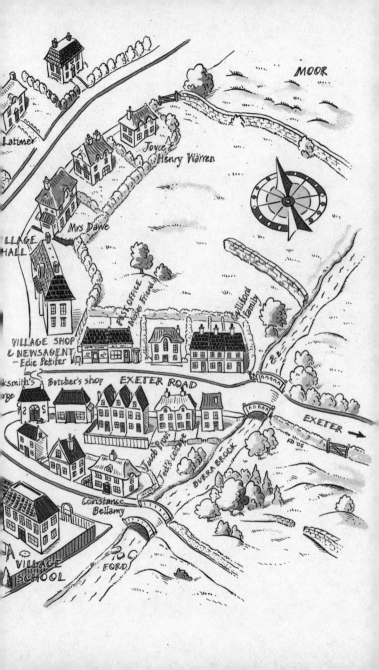

Chapter One

The storm began at about midday and raged all afternoon, and throughout the night. In the Dartmoor village of Burracombe, the Burra Brook rose higher than anyone could ever remember seeing it; first it covered the stepping-stones and then it broke over its banks to flood down the village street, swirling through gardens, right up to front doors, and threatening to find a way through any and every crack into the cottages themselves.

'Sandbags!' Jacob Prout exclaimed when he walked down to the bridge and saw the waters hurling themselves in a brown wave, swift and sinuous as an otter, over rocks that normally broke the current into a foam of white but were now hidden from view. 'Us'll need sandbags.' He hurried back to the school store-shed and began to drag out the supply that had been kept there since the war, and from there he lugged them to the church. On the way, he shouted through the doorway of the blacksmith's forge and hammered on the doors of the bakery and butcher's shop, and by the time he had started to pile the sandbags on the church path, Alf Coker, George Sweet and Bert Foster were there to help.

Together, they carried the bags to every cottage they thought might be at risk, and dropped them on the doorsteps, pushing them against the doors to keep the water out. They were only just in time; within twenty minutes, the flood had arrived and the gardens on the lower side of the street were awash, while people indoors peered through their windows in shock and dismay.

'The school!' shouted Mrs Purdy, the cleaner, throwing up her sash window and leaning out. 'That water'll be all through the lobby and into the classrooms – they'll be mired with filth. It'll take me a month of Sundays to get that lot cleared up.'

''Tis all right, Mabel, I've put bags all round the doors,' Jacob said. 'You won't have no extra cleaning to do.'

'Tidden that,' she retorted indignantly, ''tis the damage it can do. There's nothing worse than floodwater for ruining—'

'I knows that, and I done something about it,' he interrupted, jamming his sou'wester more firmly on his head. 'And I hope you'll forgive me if I don't stand here in this downpour chewing the fat about it. Coming down like stair-rods, it be, and I'm the one who'll be doing the clearing up after, when all the ditches and culverts is blocked. And if I don't get back to me own place soon, I won't be able to open the ruddy door!'

He stamped away through the water which was eddying around his feet, and pushed open his own front door. As he'd expected, the flood was already lapping at the sandbags he'd piled there and he stepped over them to get inside and slammed the door shut. The cat and dog were already in, Flossie on the windowsill staring out wide-eyed at the river that had appeared outside her home, and Scruff, who hated thunder and lightning, hiding under Jacob's armchair. Jacob gave him a scornful glance as he trod off his Wellingtons.

'Fine one you are. 'Tis only a drop of rain.' All the same, he knew that this was no ordinary storm. This, coming after a fortnight of almost continuous rain, was something very much out of the ordinary and, as he joined Flossie to gaze out of the window at the waters racing past along the village street, he told himself that he wouldn't be surprised if there weren't a lot of damage done in some places.

Inside the cottages of Burracombe that evening, it was more like winter than the middle of August. Wind raged around the roofs, howling down the chimneys, and rain hammered on the window panes. Darkness came early and the power went off, leaving people to search for candles or just go to bed early, where they lay listening and wondering, like Jacob, what the damage would be.

At some point during the small hours, the storm abated and they woke to a calmer, brighter day. To their relief, there was not too much damage, after all – Jacob's sandbags had held fast and there were only a few slates off the roofs that weren't thatched. A big elm was down across the lane that led out of the village towards the main road, Joyce Warren was bemoaning the loss of one of her apple trees and there were plenty of branches scattered about, but nothing more serious than that. Even the brook had receded and was running more or less normally along its usual channel, as if ashamed of its reckless behaviour the day before.

'Us has been lucky,' Jacob said, surveying the big elm. Ted Tozer and a few of the other men had gathered there too, to decide how best to remove it. 'Wireless says there's been a terrible lot of damage up North Devon. Lynton and Lynmouth got it real bad, so I heard.'

Basil Harvey, the vicar, had come out too, to make sure his parishioners were all right. He nodded gravely. 'It's a real disaster. The storm was even fiercer over Exmoor than it was here, apparently, and Lynmouth has been almost washed away. It seems that the two rivers Lyn piled up against each other above the town and surged down the hillside, tearing up huge trees from their roots and sweeping up boulders, and even wrenching houses from their foundations. They think nearly a hundred buildings have been destroyed, and goodness knows how many people killed or made homeless. All the boats in the harbour were washed out to sea, along with a lot of cars, and the main road bridges have been washed away. It's complete devastation.'

'My stars,' Jacob said, listening in awe, and he bent to rub

3

Scruff's ears. 'Those poor souls. You were right, boy. 'Twas more than a bit of rain. There'll be a sight of clearing up to do after that lot.' He thought about it for a few minutes, remembering a church outing they'd once had to Lynton and Lynmouth, when he and Sarah had gone up on the little rack railway to the top of the cliff and walked along to the Valley of Rocks. It had been a pretty place, but what did it look like now?

He shook his head and turned his mind to matters closer to home. 'There'll be a master clearing-up to do there, and no mistake, and I reckon us had better get on with our own. Look at this road, thick with mud. What a summer it's been, eh? What a summer it's been ...'

The whole village was shocked to hear of the disaster in North Devon, and there was talk of little else that morning. But for Hilary Napier and her father, Gilbert, once they had listened to the news and then turned off the radio, a storm of a different kind was about to break.

'Post's a bit late this morning,' Gilbert said, sorting through the pile of letters beside his breakfast plate. 'It didn't arrive until almost eight. Hello, here's a letter from Oliver Tutton. Haven't heard from him for quite a while. Wonder what he's got to say?' He picked up his silver paper-knife to slit open the envelope.

Hilary was pouring cornflakes into her bowl. 'Maybe there's going to be a regimental reunion or something.'

'Ollie would hardly be the one to write to me about that – it would come officially.' He scanned the sheet of thick, cream paper. 'Hm. Seems Arthur Kellaway's died.'

'And who's Arthur Kellaway?' She added milk and sugar and began to eat. 'Another Army friend? I don't think I've ever heard you mention him, though the name does seem a bit familiar.'

'He was Ollie's head gamekeeper. Just dropped dead in the

4

yard one day, apparently – fit as a fiddle until then. Heart-attack. Hm ...' He read on, tapping the back of his thumb against his chin. 'Arthur Kellaway ... That's Travis Kellaway's father. Seems the boy's been living with his parents and working as under-manager on Ollie's estate, and now the old man's dead he's losing his home – his mother's decided to go and live with her sister. Oliver says he's decided to make a break now and look for something more responsible.' He narrowed his eyes thoughtfully. 'Might be an idea to invite the lad over for a day or two. See what he's planning to do now.'

Hilary stared at him, bemused. 'Father, I don't know what you're talking about. Why should you invite him over here? And why should we be interested in his plans?'

'Because he's Travis Kellaway,' Gilbert explained, with an edge of impatience. 'Baden's friend – Baden's *closest* friend. Why shouldn't I invite him to stay? I'll be pleased to make him welcome.'

Hilary glanced involuntarily at the portrait of her brother, which hung above the fireplace. Although she had never met Travis Kellaway, she knew the story of how he and Baden had gone through the war together, how close they had been, how he had been with Baden when he died. She had seen the letter that Travis had written to her parents then – the letter that was now kept in a drawer of her father's desk, together with those written by Baden's officers, and all the other mementoes of his short life. She knew that Travis had visited Burracombe after the war, but for the past few years contact had been no more than a Christmas card.

'I still don't understand,' she said. 'We've hardly heard anything of him for years. Why do you want to invite him to stay now, after all this time?'

Gilbert Napier looked straight at his daughter. 'I've already told you. His father's just died. His mother's decided to go and live with her sister. And he thinks now would be a good time to better himself.' He put the letter back into its envelope and filled his own cereal bowl. 'I'd like to have a look at him. As I remember from when he came here before, he seemed a well-set-up sort of fellow, and he's got a few years' experience under his belt now.'

Hilary put down her spoon. Her stomach felt suddenly tight and her hand shook a little. 'And what's that got to do with us?'

Her father shrugged. 'Well, it's time we started to think what we're going to do with the estate. Who's going to take over the job of managing it, and so on. It's obvious young Stephen's never going to take a proper interest, even when he leaves the RAF, and there's no one else—'

'*No one*? Father, how can you say that? Ever since you had your heart-attack I've—'

'Oh yes, I know,' he said, waving a hand. 'You've thrown yourself into the breech and made a damn good job of it. I'm proud of you. But that was never intended to be permanent. You surely never thought I'd just sit back and let you throw your life away on this place.'

'I'm not throwing my life away! The estate *is* my life!'

'Don't be ridiculous, Hilary. Of course it isn't. You're a woman – a healthy young woman. You want a home of your own, a family of youngsters around your feet.'

'You're forgetting the essential requirement for those,' Hilary said grimly. 'A husband.'

'Well, of course you want a husband,' he said testily. 'That goes without saying.'

'Oh, does it, indeed?' Hilary's heart was thudding and she half-rose from her chair. 'Well, for your information, Father, a husband is the last thing I want! I'm perfectly happy as I am, thank you very much. I have a good life here – a lovely home in a village I've grown up in, where I have lots of friends. And I enjoy running the estate. I don't want any more than that. So invite this Travis Kellaway here if you want to, help him find a job if you feel you must, but leave it at that. We don't need to look for a new estate manager. *I'm* doing that job.'

'And isn't that rather up to me?' he asked in a dangerously quiet voice. 'Burracombe Barton and all that entails is still in my name, or so I understand.'

'Of course it is,' she said, sinking back again. 'But I thought you were happy to have things go on as they are. You say yourself I've done a good job. You said you were proud of me.'

'And so I am.' Gilbert leaned forward. 'Look, Hilary, all I want to do is have a look at this young fellow. See what he's made of. You never know—'

'I think I do know!' Hilary clenched her fist and thumped it on the table. 'I think I know exactly. You're going to go over my head – invite him here, see what you think of him and then offer him the job of estate manager. You're going to offer him *my* job!' Again, her voice quivered. 'How could you? How could you do this to me?'

'There's no need to get yourself into a state . . .'

'I'm not getting into a state! I'm just plain angry.' She rose again, so that she was looking down on the big man with his mane of silver hair, and wished that she could stop her body trembling. 'So would anyone be if they'd just been informed that they were being sacked.'

'Hilary, you're not being sacked! For heaven's sake, girl, don't be so dramatic. I've only just found out that the boy might be free.'

'What do you call it, then? You wouldn't do this if I weren't your daughter, you know. You wouldn't do it to a son – bring someone in over his head without warning.' Her voice broke. 'I thought you were happy with the way I've been working. We're working *together*. Why bring in someone else?'

'Together!' he exclaimed. 'Well, if we are, it's not without a lot of argument. You'd have kept me out of it altogether if you could – all these projects you've been coming up with, village archives, a book about the Barton, anything to keep me occupied. You don't want me to have anything to do with the estate. You want to run it yourself, your own way.'

'Father, that's not true. It's only because of your heart-attack. You know the doctors said you mustn't work so hard. Charles Latimer—'

'Charles is an old woman! I'm as fit now as I ever was.'

'You're not,' she said quietly, sitting down again. 'And we shouldn't be arguing like this. It's one of the things you need to avoid.'

They were silent for a few moments. Then she said, 'I admit it hasn't been easy to work out a sensible compromise, but I really thought we'd managed it in the last month or two. You've been coming round the farms with me, talking to the tenants, all that sort of thing. And I know you've been enjoying working on the book. Aren't you satisfied with the way I'm doing things? Is that what it is?'

Her father shook his head. 'It's not that, Hilary. You've done a very good job. But it isn't *right* – a young woman like you, spending her life tramping around the fields, thinking about rents and tenancies and future management. You should be enjoying life.'

'I *am* enjoying my life!'

'You should be looking after a husband and family,' he went on, ignoring her. 'Bringing up the next generation.'

'Father, we've already been through all this. We're going round in circles.'

'And we'll keep on going through it,' he drove on. 'Because that's the proper life for a woman. And don't tell me you had "responsibilities" during the war, as if that somehow makes you too good for a domestic life now. Don't tell me how capable you are – I know all that. You'll need all your capabilities once you're a wife and mother.'

'I can't just go out and find a husband under a hedge,' Hilary said impatiently. 'I can't buy one in the village shop.'

'And there's no need to be sarcastic,' he retorted. 'It doesn't become you. All I'm saying is, you'd have a far better chance of finding one if you weren't so tied up with estate work. Get out a bit more – go up to London, go to a few balls and dances, meet people again. The right *sort* of people.'

'Oh, for goodness sake, Dad! The world isn't *like* that any more. People are too busy getting the country back on its feet to bother about dances and balls and parties. Anyway, I'm too old now. If anyone does the Season at all, they're just young girls of eighteen or twenty. I'm thirty – from their point of view, I'm an old woman.' She picked up the coffee-pot and refilled both their cups, trying to calm herself, and softened her voice. 'You're not really serious about offering Travis Kellaway the estate manager's job, are you?'

'I think you need help,' Gilbert said stubbornly. 'Remember, I know what the estate work entails. I did it long enough myself and, as you and Charles never stop telling me, it made me ill. I don't want the same to happen to you.' He shot her a look from under the bushy brows. 'I've lost too many of my family to want to see you go that way.'

Hilary bit her lip and looked down at her plate, tears pricking her eyes. 'I'm not going to have a heart-attack, Dad.'

'Maybe not. But there are other ways of getting ill. Your mother was never strong ...'

'I'm not like Mother. I *am* strong – I always have been. And I enjoy the work, Dad. I don't want to give it up. Don't ask Travis Kellaway here. Or if you do, don't offer him a job. Please.'

Gilbert shook his head. 'I'm sorry, Hilary, but my mind's made up. I want you to have some help and I think he's worth considering. In any case, we owe him this. He's just lost his father, he's losing his home. After all he did for Baden—'

'Yes, all right,' she said hastily. 'I can see that you feel you ought to do something for him. But it doesn't mean you have to give him my job. Sir Oliver's still employing him, isn't he? He could become manager there in time.'

'Oliver's man's got years ahead of him yet and you can't blame the boy for not wanting to wait for dead men's shoes.' He glanced at her again. 'I didn't say I'd give him your job, Hilary. I simply said I thought you needed help. Why not let him come, show him around a bit, see what you think? You don't have to decide anything straight away.'

She cast him a bitter look. 'I'm not going to decide anything at all, am I? You've already done the deciding. And he won't be coming here to "help" me. You've already said he wants to move up. He won't want to come here as my assistant. Anyway, it's not help you think I need, it's time – time to find a husband and have children. Which, in your opinion, I can only have by giving up the job I've worked at and enjoyed so much in the past year.' She stood up again, forgetting her freshly poured coffee. 'You've made up your mind already to give this Kellaway man my job, and there's nothing I can do about it.'

'Not at all. I'm reserving judgement until I see him—'

'There! You see? You *have* decided! If you like him, you'll make him estate manager – don't deny it.' She turned towards the door, but looked back as she laid her fingers on the handle. 'And you *will* like him. That's something else you've decided. What I think and want doesn't come into this at all.'

'Hilary, it's you I'm thinking of.'

'It's *not*! How can it be? You're not thinking of me at all.'

'I simply want you to have the proper sort of life for a young woman. Managing an estate – that's no way for a girl like you to live. You've done very well up till now, but what about when an emergency crops up? Something that needs a man's strength?'

'There are plenty of men to deal with anything heavy. Ken Warne, Crocker, Furzey – the rest of the tenant farmers and their stockmen. When did you ever have to tackle any major heavy work? I'm administrating the estate, not working with the animals. You know that perfectly well.'

To her annoyance, she heard her voice tremble and knew that she was close to tears. Her father knew it too and his eyes narrowed.

'It's not just physical strength. You have to be able to deal with people too. Make decisions that are unpopular – sack people if they're not working properly. Keep your end up in an argument. It's no use bursting into tears when things go wrong. That's where a woman will never be able to make her way in a man's world, I'm afraid.'

'Oh, for heaven's sake!' She saw the glimmer of triumph in his eyes and knew that he was just waiting for the first tear to fall. Taking in a deep breath, she waited for a moment to regain her composure, then said, 'You're determined to do this, aren't you? You're determined to ask him here and offer him my job.'

'I'm determined to ask him here, yes,' he said, meeting her eyes implacably. 'And when I've seen him and talked with him, I'll decide what to do next.'

'*You'll* decide,' she said in a low, bitter voice. 'You. Not "we". Just you.'

Gilbert said nothing. They stared at each other for a moment more, then Hilary turned away. She opened the door and walked out, exerting all her willpower not to slam it behind her. For a second or two, she leaned back against the panels, breathing hard, and then looked up as Jackie Tozer came from the direction of the kitchen, bearing a tray of bacon and eggs.

'Are you all right, Miss Hilary?' Jackie asked anxiously. 'You look as white as a sheet.'

'Yes, thank you, Jackie. I'm just a bit off-colour, that's all.' She glanced at the tray. 'I don't think I'll bother with breakfast this morning. My father's in there, though – no doubt he'll manage some extra.'

He might as well have my breakfast, she thought sourly as she went upstairs to her room. He's taking everything else that matters.

Chapter Two

'But I thought you wanted to get away,' Val Ferris said.

She had spent nearly an hour clearing debris from the flood from her front garden and was now halfway up a stepladder inside the front room, a pot of yellow paint in one hand and a brush in the other. Since Hilary had arrived, half an hour ago, they'd been talking mostly about the Lynton and Lynmouth disaster, but then Hilary had told her about the argument she'd had with her father over breakfast.

'It's not all that long ago you were talking about getting a job as an air stewardess and living in London. Couldn't this be your chance? Not that I want you to leave Burracombe,' she added, slapping a dollop of sunshine on the wall. 'Especially now that Luke and I are settled here.'

'Yes, but that was before Dad's heart-attack,' Hilary said. 'As far as I knew, he was fit and well and would go on for years. I was no more than his housekeeper and it didn't look as if I'd ever be anything more. But since then I've found I'm good at running the estate. I *like* doing it. I don't want to give it up. And it's not just that. Even if Dad got the best manager in the world, I still couldn't leave him. He's got to have someone to keep an eye on him, make sure he doesn't overdo things. Suppose I went away and he had another attack. I'd never forgive myself.'

'No, I can see that. But surely he doesn't really intend to give this man – what did you say his name was? – Travers?'

'Travis. Travis Kellaway.'

'Yes, well, surely he doesn't intend to give him your job, just like that. What does he think you're going to do with yourself?'

'Oh, I'm meant to go out and find myself a husband,' Hilary said caustically. 'Just as if they grow on trees. I mean, look at me, Val – I'm thirty years old. Any man old enough for me is going to be either married already or ... well, not the marrying kind. There's not going to be much choice, is there?'

'You might find a widower.'

'Oh yes, with half a dozen kids already! I'm sure Dad would be thrilled about that. He wants me to carry on *our* family, not someone else's. Honestly, he's still living in feudal times. I can understand why Stephen didn't want anything to do with the estate.'

Val stroked her brush over the wall and gave her friend a mischievous look. 'It doesn't seem as if this Travis Kellaway's married though, or he wouldn't have been living with his parents. And if he was Baden's friend in the Army, he must be over thirty. Perhaps—'

'*No*! And you're in serious danger of having a pot of yellow paint thrown over you.' Hilary sat down on an old stool and propped her elbows on her knees. 'Oh, I don't know what to do. Once Dad gets an idea into his head, there's no shifting him. And I don't believe it's entirely to do with wanting to free me to go husband hunting. It's more complicated than that.'

Val glanced at her and climbed down the ladder, leaving her paint-pot at the top. She sat down on a lower step and said, 'What do you think it is, then?'

'I think it's a mixture of things. It's partly because he wants the family to carry on, and he's fed up with waiting for Steve to do anything about it – although any children he has will at least have the family name. Mine wouldn't, unless I went double-barrelled. Of course, Dad won't admit that – he just says I'd be happier being a wife and mother. He simply can't

13

bring himself to accept the possibility that I'll go on running the estate for the rest of my life. It seems all wrong to him.' She paused for a moment, then went on, 'And the other thing is that I think he almost looks on this Travis as a substitute for Baden. They really did know each other very well, by all accounts, and he was with Baden when he died. Dad's never got over losing him, you know. It wasn't just a son he lost – it was the whole future of the Napier family. That's the way he sees it, anyway.'

'A substitute for Baden?' Val whistled softly. 'That's a bit dangerous, Hil.'

'I know.' Hilary looked at her with troubled eyes. 'He could be facing a big disappointment if he puts too much store on this man. We don't really know him at all, and whatever he did in the war – well, it's not got much to do with the man he is now. People are different in wartime.'

Val chewed her bottom lip. 'Is he actually expecting to be offered a job, or is he just coming to visit?'

'I don't really know,' Hilary admitted. 'But he must be expecting something. Why would Dad suddenly invite him to stay after all this time? I think he did stay a night or so before, but that was six years ago.' She shook her head despondently. 'To tell you the truth, I think it's all cut and dried in my father's mind. He'd have to be a complete disaster for Dad to give up the idea now.'

'Maybe he will be. What did you think of him before?'

'I never met him. I was away when he came to tell my parents about Baden. They seemed to like him, but it was what he said that was really important. He could have had three heads and a green face, and they'd have liked him just then!'

'Three green faces,' Val murmured, and added hastily, 'Sorry, Hil. I am taking this seriously, honestly, but I really can't believe your father would do this to you. I think this man will just visit you and then go away again. I honestly can't see that you've got anything to worry about. Your father knows how valuable you are, and he'd rather have you running the estate than a stranger. Don't you think so?'

'I wish I did. But he's so certain that I'll toe the line and give in – and that annoys me too! It's as if he doesn't care at all about my feelings. He'll do whatever he wants, in the smug belief that little Hilary will just cave in and do whatever Daddy says. Well, if he thinks that, he's got a shock coming to him, because she won't. I'm the one who runs the estate now, and I'm not giving way to anyone.'

There was a long pause. Then Val said, 'Well, with that look on your face, I certainly wouldn't want to take it away from you! You're as obstinate as your father. The trouble with you and me is we've had such different lives, and it's hard for our parents to accept.'

Hilary grinned a little reluctantly. 'I know. The war, and Egypt and all that … And that's all part of it, Val. We know what we're capable of. Running a house, ordering a couple of maids and gardeners about and doing a little light flower-arranging, were all very well for our mothers – well, my mother, anyway,' she added, remembering that Val's mother was a farmer's wife and had not known the luxury enjoyed by Isobel Napier. 'But we've proved we're capable of doing so much more.' She sighed and shrugged. 'Let's talk about something else. How are you and Luke getting on with this place? It's looking better already.'

'Well, it couldn't look worse. Did you see it when we first came to look at it, after Jed's funeral? It was terrible – I don't think Jed had cleaned it or thrown anything out for years. And even that wasn't as bad as when Jennifer first came here, before she and Mum had a go at it. I don't know how anyone could live in such a pigsty.' She glanced around the empty room, scrubbed clean now after years of neglect. 'The walls are still pretty dreary.'

'That colour will brighten them up a lot. When do you expect to move in?'

'Probably about October. There are still some repairs to be done – the roof leaks a bit, and the plaster's all broken away in the kitchen. Jennifer's putting in electricity too, and the plumbing needs quite a bit of work. We're having a better sink and taps and a new WC. In fact, Jennifer's thinking of having a proper bathroom built at the back sometime.'

'That'll be good,' said Hilary, who had never had to manage with a galvanised bath hung on a nail in the back yard and brought in once or twice a week. 'I don't think I could live without a bathroom.'

'Oh, it's possible,' Val said with a grin. 'Anyway, we're not waiting for that. The tin bath in front of the fire can be quite cosy.' She flashed her friend a wicked look, and Hilary laughed.

'I don't think I want to know any more, thank you. Anyway, I'd better be going. I just came down to cry on your shoulder before starting work. It won't impress Dad if I start to neglect things now. He'll have every reason to bring in someone else if I do that.'

'I shouldn't worry so much,' Val advised her. 'You don't know that this Travis Kellaway will even want the job. He's probably got other irons in the fire and is only coming out of politeness, because of Baden or he may need a break, after his father's death.'

'I suppose that's possible,' Hilary agreed thoughtfully. She bit her upper lip. 'I have to be careful not to give Dad the chance to say I'm being a hysterical female, too …' She took in a deep breath and grinned at her friend, then went on with a deliberate change of subject, 'Listen, are you and Luke going to join this new Drama Group Felix is talking about getting up? There's going to be a meeting in the village hall next week for anyone who's interested.'

'And what does Mrs Warren think of that?' Val enquired, raising one eyebrow. Joyce Warren, who had a finger in all the village pies, had been self-styled Chairman of the Village

Drama Society for the past three years without so far managing to put on a single production. Her biggest success had been in persuading Stella Simmons, the village schoolteacher, to do most of the donkeywork involved in the children's performance of a scene from *A Midsummer Night's Dream*.

Hilary smiled. 'I think he's flattered her into being Stage Manager-in-Chief, or something. So are you going, then?'

'Yes, we'll be there. I like amateur dramatics – we did quite a bit in Egypt. And Luke says he'll help with the scenery.'

'That'll be a bonus – a real artist painting our scenery. Well, if you're going to the meeting, I will too. It could be fun, putting on a few plays and things in Burracombe. I expect Stella will be there as well.'

'Without a doubt,' Val said ironically, and they both laughed. 'Where you find one of those two these days, you find both. It'll be their engagement that's announced next, you mark my words.'

'And very nice too. The curate and the teacher – what could be more suitable?' Hilary stood up and stretched her arms. 'Well, I'd better leave you to your painting. I dare say Luke examines it closely to make sure you're doing it properly. I'm surprised he's not doing it himself.'

'He's an artist, not a painter and decorator,' Val said with dignity. 'Anyway, we're doing it between us. He's gone into Tavistock today to do some preparation at the school.'

She waved goodbye and started up the ladder again as Hilary let herself out into the village street. Before she began to paint again, however, she paused, a small frown creasing her forehead.

Hilary seemed quite sure that Travis Kellaway would be offered the job of estate manager. If he was, he'd need somewhere to live. And the most obvious place would be the house that had been given to the former estate manager, before Gilbert Napier retired from the Army and took over the management himself.

The only trouble was that the estate house, currently occupied by an optician from Plymouth whose own house had been requisitioned during the war, had been promised to Val and Luke when he returned to the city. This cottage, now owned by Jed Fisher's daughter Jennifer, was only supposed to be a stop-gap until that happened. Jennifer, who lived in Plymouth, hadn't made up her mind what to do with it next, but nobody would be surprised if she decided to come and live here herself one day.

And that'll be us back in the charcoal-burner's cottage, Val thought ruefully as she began to paint again. A tiny, two-roomed shack in the woods that had seemed a romantic place to start their married life, but was already feeling cramped. Obviously, this aspect hadn't occurred to Hilary, and Val wasn't going to increase her worries by mentioning it. And in any case, none of this might happen. As she'd pointed out to Hilary, Colonel Napier might not offer Travis Kellaway a job after all. Even if he did, Travis wouldn't necessarily want it.

We'll cross those bridges when we come to them, Val decided, slapping away enthusiastically with her brush. The important thing now is to turn this cottage into a nice little home. A few more coats of this lovely sunshiney yellow on the walls, and it's going to seem a different place.

With a new home and a new interest to look forward to, life was looking very good for Val and Luke Ferris. She wished she could be as optimistic about Hilary.

Chapter Three

With a week of the summer holiday still to go, Stella Simmons and Felix Copley were taking every chance they could to spend time together.

'Even with all the rain we've had, it's been a lovely summer,' Stella said, lying on her back on the soft, close-cropped turf at the foot of a tor a few miles from Burracombe and gazing up at the clear sky. 'It's almost impossible to believe that we've just had that terrible storm. I really do feel sorry for all those poor people in North Devon – but for us, everything's turning out right. We had a wonderful time in London, Maddy's started her new job with your uncle, Val and Luke are married, Jennifer Tucker's making herself a part of the village even though she still lives in Plymouth ... It's nice of her to let Val and Luke rent her cottage, isn't it? She could easily keep it for herself and stay in it at weekends. Come to that, she could live in it, and go in to work in Plymouth on the bus every day.'

'I suppose she wants to let some time pass before she makes any big changes,' Felix said thoughtfully. He was sitting up, his arms looped around his knees. 'Finding out that Jed Fisher was her father, and then looking after him before he died, must have come as quite a shock. And she seems happy enough to stay with Jacob when she comes to Burracombe. Those two seem more like father and daughter than she and Jed ever did!'

'It seems to have turned out well for both of them.' Stella was quiet for a few moments, then said in a different tone,

'The children did well with their scene from *A Midsummer Night's Dream* at the Summer Fair, didn't they! It looked just right, performed out in the open at the edge of the field. You could really believe they were in a forest clearing.'

'You made a good job of rehearsing them,' he said, smiling down at her. 'And that reminds me about the new Drama Club. You will come to the meeting, won't you? I'm relying on you to be my right-hand woman.'

'Of course I'm coming. I'm looking forward to it. Have you had any more ideas about the first production?'

'Depends who's interested, but I thought it would be nice to do a pantomime.'

'A pantomime! Isn't that a bit ambitious?'

'Well, perhaps,' he said with a grin. 'But it's a lot of fun, there are parts for plenty of people, including the children, and it doesn't matter too much if things go a bit wrong. The audience expects it.'

'But suppose not enough people join?' she asked doubtfully, and Felix laughed.

'Then we won't do it! We'll do something else instead.' He looked down at her. 'It's only meant to be fun, Stella. We're doing it to enjoy ourselves, and – I hope – help other people to enjoy themselves as well. All these things Burracombe does – the Gardening Club, the whist-drives, the Summer Fair and Christmas Bazaar – they're all part of what makes a village a good place to live in. They bring people together and help them to make friends. The Drama Club will do the same.'

'But will you have time?' she asked. 'You're awfully busy as it is, going over to Little Burracombe to take services for Mr Berry as well as doing your job here. A pantomime must need a lot of rehearsal.'

'A couple of evenings a week should be enough. To start with, anyway. I expect we'll need a bit more in the last two or three weeks, but by then I might have found a good assistant.' He grinned at her, his dark blue eyes crinkling at the corners.

'Oh no!' she said quickly. 'You don't catch me that easily. Christmas is frantic at the school. Parties, carol service, the end of term – you know what it's like. And it'll be just as bad for you. Worse, because it doesn't stop at the end of the term.'

'Suppose we put the panto on in November?' he suggested. 'That would get it all over and done with before the Christmas period starts.' He glanced at his watch. 'Heavens, look at the time! We'll have to go back soon – I promised to look in at the Mothers' Union meeting this afternoon. But first,' he leaned over and lowered his face to hers, 'there's something here I need to attend to.'

'Oh? And what's that?' she asked, feeling her heart quicken. She still hadn't got used to the idea that Felix really wanted to kiss her and hold her close. Their friendship had grown slowly over the past year or so, and for some time she'd believed that it was her sister Maddy who held his interest. But Maddy had laughed the idea away and gone to work for Felix's uncle, the Bishop of West Lyme, and at Val and Luke's wedding a month ago, Felix had made a private toast to Stella and himself. No more than that had been said, then or since, but he seemed to be taking it for granted that they would spend their free time together, and he nearly always found an opportunity to kiss her.

It had never gone further than that, and he was always discreet in public. As a curate, Felix had to be careful about his behaviour, and Stella's position as infant teacher at the village school meant that she must do the same. But it meant, too, that she could trust him, and she gave herself up to his kisses knowing that he would never take advantage of her.

At last they parted, regretfully, and stood up. Stella brushed herself down and followed Felix back to the little sports car his uncle had given him, which they had left at the bottom of the hill. They had been out for only a few hours, driving away from the interested gaze of the village to find a quiet place to walk and have their picnic lunch, and the time seemed to have flown. At least I'll see him at the Drama Club rehearsals, she thought, hoping that plenty of people would come. A pantomime would be fun, and the children could be involved as well ... She remembered her vow during rehearsals for *A Midsummer Night's Dream* never to let herself get involved in anything like that again, and smiled at herself. As if she could possibly avoid it! And it had been worth it, in the end. A proper, grown-up Drama Club would be even better.

'What are you laughing at?' Felix asked, glancing round at her suddenly. 'Did I do something funny?'

'I'm laughing at myself,' she told him, and walked into his arms, lifting her face for another kiss. 'And because I'm happy, too. Everything's going so well this summer.'

'It is, isn't it,' he said, resting his cheek against hers. 'Are you really happy, Stella?'

'Yes,' she answered softly. 'I've never been so happy in my entire life.'

News of the Drama Club spread quickly round Burracombe, aided by the notices Felix had put up – one outside the village hall, one in the Post Office window and one in Edie Pettifer's village shop. As usual, the villagers were divided in their opinions.

''Tis just another of that young curate's bright ideas,' Fred Purdy grumbled. 'Bound to make a lot more work for my missus round at the school.'

'How d'you make that out then, Fred?'

'Well, stands to reason, don't it, the little 'uns'll be dragged in one way or another, and that means more of those rehearsals like they done for that Shakespeare whatnot they done last term and at the Summer Fair, and that leads to more mess at the school. And since my Mabel's the cleaner there ...'

'All right, Fred, we get the idea,' George Sweet broke in. 'But this isn't for the children, and if it do get going, most of the practices will be at the village hall, not at the school at all.'

'And my missus is cleaner there too!' Fred retorted triumphantly. 'So it's going to mean more work for her, whichever way you looks at it.'

'Well, her gets paid for it, don't her?' George began, but at that point Edie Pettifer took charge.

'If you two are just going to stand there arguing, you might as well do it outside and let a few customers in. I'm here to sell newspapers and groceries, not set up a parliament.' She began to arrange the loaves and buns that George Sweet had brought round. He sold them from his own bakery across the village green as well, but both agreed that it was a good idea to have two outlets, rather than Edie getting bread in from someone else. 'I know it's not far for folk to walk across the village green to you,' she'd said when they'd first come to this arrangement, 'but 'tis handy for them to be able to get their bread along with their morning paper, and this way it doesn't take your trade away.'

'What d'you reckon about this new Drama whatsit then, Edie?' he asked now. 'Will you and Bert Foster be joining?'

Edie blushed. Bert Foster, the village butcher, had been setting his cap at her for years, yet nothing had ever come of it and Edie would never admit that there was anything more than friendship between them. The suppers she gave him on Friday nights, she would insist, were no more than a thank-you for the help he gave her in her garden, and if they listened to a bit of music on the wireless afterwards, what of that? He was always out of the house by a respectable nine-thirty, and if folk wanted to make something of it – well, let them. If you let spiteful gossip rule your life, you wouldn't have much of a life to live!

'I don't know about Bert,' she said tartly. 'It's up to him what he does. I'm not all that keen myself, never did like making a show of myself in front of other people. Anyway, I've got enough to do with the church choir, now they've decided to let women in at long last.'

23

'Well, Bert can't sing a note, so if rehearsals are on choir nights that'll keep you both out of mischief,' George said, with a wink at Fred, and Edie tossed her yellow head.

'Thank you for bringing the bread over, George,' she said pointedly. 'Is there anything else you want, Fred, apart from your *Daily Mirror*?'

'Packet of Players' Navy Cut,' Fred said, and dragged a scrap of paper from his pocket. 'And one of they tubes of fruit gums for the missus. Here's the coupon. About time we could do away with these, if you ask me.'

'It can't be much longer,' Edie said, regarding the crumpled scrap with disfavour. 'We've been cutting out these little squares for the past twelve years now. You wonder what they do with them all. And you're supposed to bring the book itself, Fred, not just the coupon. This could be anybody's.'

'What would that matter? You can only use it once, whoever it belongs to.' He pocketed the cigarettes and tube of sweets. 'Or d'you reckon I'm running some sort of black market?'

The others laughed and the two men left the shop together. George was on his way back to the bakery and Fred walked along with him.

'D'you think Bert Foster'll ever make an honest woman of her?' Fred asked after a moment or two. 'He've been after her long enough, one way and another. Mind you, she's a good-looking woman, for all my missus says that yellow hair comes out of a bottle.'

'You mean she dyes it?' The idea had evidently never occurred to the baker. 'It's always been yellow, all the years I've known her.'

'Yes, and that's a long time now. Longer than most women's hair stays yellow like that. I've had a look once or twice, when she's had her back turned getting something down off one of the shelves, and you can't see a grey hair anywhere, except round the edges sometimes, and then next time you look they'm gone as well. My missus says that proves it.'

24

'I dunno,' George said. 'I've never thought of anyone in Burracombe dyeing their hair. I wouldn't be surprised if it was someone in Plymouth, now, or even Tavistock, but in Burracombe ...' He shook his head. 'I don't see why anyone would *want* to.'

Fred grinned and said slyly, 'Your missus has got a fine head of hair too, George. Sort of coppery colour, I'd say, wouldn't you?'

'Yes, and I don't know what you'm implying, Fred Purdy, but it's as natural as mine,' the baker said indignantly. 'If you ask me, it's time you and your missus had better things to talk about than the colour of women's hair. Gossip like that can do a lot of harm in a place like Burracombe.'

'All right, all right, keep your hair on,' Fred said, and then roared with laughter. 'Here, that's good – keep your hair on, after what we been saying! My missus'll be tickled pink when I tells her about that. Well, don't you think it's funny, George?'

'No, I don't.' The baker wheeled sharply and went through his shop door. 'I don't think it's funny at all. You'd better watch your tongue, Fred Purdy, because if I hears any talk about my wife and her hair I shall know where it come from, and I shall know what to do about it.' He turned to glower at the other man, his burly frame almost filling the doorway, and Fred backed away, shrugging to show that he didn't take the threat seriously. George Sweet was all bluster, everyone knew that.

He walked away along the village street, on his way to the bigger houses on the other side of the village where he did gardening and odd jobs. It was funny, though, how George always lost his rag when his missus was mentioned, he mused. Maybe things weren't as sunny in that household as he liked to make out. It couldn't be to do with the strange hours he kept, working in the bakery half the night, because Ivy Sweet kept much the same times, working in one of the pubs in

Horrabridge. And she *did* have a fine head of hair, he thought, justifying his words to himself. In fact, she was a fine-looking woman all round, always dressed smart even if her taste was a bit showy for a little place like Burracombe.

George Sweet didn't realise how lucky he was.

'I'll join,' Tom Tozer said as the family sat round the big table in the farmhouse kitchen for supper. 'You won't mind, will you, Jo?'

'I wouldn't mind joining myself,' his wife Joanna said, 'but with the baby due in a month's time I don't see how I can.'

'You know me and Gran don't mind listening out for Robin,' Tom's mother Alice told her. 'After all, once he's asleep you don't hear a peep out of him till morning. But you're right, you'll be more tied with the little one.'

'I might join in a year or two, perhaps, if it lasts that long,' Joanna said. 'You may as well go along, Tom, if you fancy it.'

'So long as it don't interfere with ringing practice,' Ted told his son. 'Now Vic Nethercott's back from his National Service we're getting a half-decent team of younger ringers. I don't want to see them distracted.'

'Well, we'll have to see what the curate's got in mind,' Tom said. 'We don't know yet whether he'll even get enough interest to start this Drama Club in the first place. That Mrs Warren never had much luck with hers. I'll go along to the meeting anyway and see what's what.' He turned to his younger sister. 'You come along too, Jackie. It'll do you good.'

'Yes, that's a good idea,' Alice said at once. 'You spend too much time at home for a girl your age. You need more young friends to go around with.'

'Well, I'm not going to meet anyone I don't already know at a village Drama Club,' her youngest daughter pointed out. 'Still, I suppose I might as well. I quite liked the Nativity plays and things we used to do at school. I wonder if our Val will go? And Luke – he'd be a good actor. He looks a bit like Clark Gable.'

26

'More like Humphrey Bogart,' Tom contradicted.

'He doesn't look a bit like Humphrey Bogart!' Jackie exclaimed indignantly. 'He's much better-looking. You'd better not let Val hear you say that. She'll skin you alive.'

'If you want my opinion,' Ted said, holding out his plate for more sausages, 'it's best if he don't get ideas about going on the stage. 'Tis bad enough having an artist in the family without him turning out to be an actor as well.'

'Ted!' Alice protested as the others laughed. 'You know Luke's a good artist. And he'm a teacher, as well. You can't say he's not supporting his wife now.'

'No, I must admit I feel happier now he've got a proper job. And I'll be happier still when they're settled into Jed Fisher's cottage. I never thought to see my daughter living in an old charcoal-burner's shack in the woods. I'll have some of that mustard by your elbow, Tom, unless you'm keeping it for summat special.'

'Sorry, Dad.' Tom passed the pot of freshly mixed mustard and Ted spread some liberally on his sausages. They were the thick, solid ones made in Bert Foster's own shop, and known in Burracombe as 'Cokers' because of their resemblance to the blacksmith's huge fingers. 'Why don't you and Mum come along to the meeting as well? It says on the poster that everyone's welcome.'

'Don't talk daft – who'd want old fogeys like us in a Drama Club?' Ted said. 'Not that your mother's an old fogey,' he added quickly. 'Good enough for any drama club, you'd be, Alice.'

His wife shook her head. 'I've got enough to do, what with the church flowers and the choir and the Women's Institute and Mothers' Union, not to mention looking after you lot. If it weren't for Mother here …' she smiled at her mother-in-law '… I wouldn't be able to manage all that.'

'Wasn't there a Drama Club in the village years ago?' Jackie asked her grandmother. 'A proper one, I mean, not that one

27

Mrs Warren tried to get up. I'm sure I've heard you talk about it.'

'Yes, there was.' Minnie's old eyes brightened. 'Used to put on all sorts of shows, us did – plays and pantomimes, concerts and music-halls, there was no end to what we used to get up in the old days. It all stopped when war broke out – that were the First World War, of course – and the men went away. After those that were left came back, there didn't seem to be the heart for it, and us were just getting it going again when the Depression started.'

'It kept going for a few years though, didn't it,' Alice reminded her. 'I remember a few concerts. Val used to belong to that dancing troupe, you remember – the Sunshine Kiddies – and they put on a few shows. I can't bring to mind any plays being done, though.'

'No, you need someone who knows a bit about it to put on a play. But young Mr Copley must have some idea. I hope he gets plenty of people along to the meeting. It'll be nice to have something like that on in the village hall.'

'Well, I'll be going,' Tom declared. 'And I hope he decides to do a pantomime. I've always wanted to be the front half of a pantomime horse.'

'Back half of a donkey, more like!' Ted retorted, and the family burst out laughing.

Alice got up and began to clear the dishes from the table. 'Horses or donkeys, if he wants a few ideas for a pantomime he could do a lot worse than come round here and listen to you lot. I've never heard so much daft talk. Now – who's ready for a baked apple?'

'Of course I'll come to the meeting, maid,' Dottie said to Stella Simmons, clearing away the supper dishes at almost exactly the same moment as Alice was clearing away the Tozers'. 'Not that I'll be doing any acting, but if they want any sewing done I can do whatever they want. It'll be like old times.'

Dottie had once been dresser to an actress in London, recommended by Isobel Napier, the Squire's wife, who had known Fenella Forsyth at school. It was through Miss Forsyth's visits to her old friend Isobel that the actress had first met Maddy Simmons. Maddy, Stella's lost sister, had been separated from her when they were orphaned and sent to a Children's Home which was evacuated to Burracombe Barton. The actress had taken a fancy to the lonely little orphan and adopted her, leaving her to live with Dottie until the war was over, and it was only chance that had brought Stella herself to the same cottage after years of separation.

'It sounds as though there'll be quite a bit of interest,' Stella said. 'Everyone's talking about it. Felix will be really pleased if lots of people come.'

'Well; it's something new, isn't it,' Dottie said comfortably, pushing her cat Alfred off her armchair and settling herself on the warm cushion with a cup of tea. 'People either go all out for it like a bull at a gate, or they just ignore it. There's no happy medium. I dare say only a quarter of them as goes to the meeting will actually *join* the new club.'

'Oh,' Stella said, feeling slightly deflated. 'Well, Felix is so enthusiastic I'm sure he'll inspire them. Luke and Val are going, and Hilary too, I think.'

'So's Mrs Warren. I heard her say so when I was in the Post Office this afternoon, buying stamps to send my sister in Tiverton that cushion cover I embroidered for her birthday. I was going to make a parcel of it, but Jessie Friend said it would be better in a big envelope and she sold me one for threepence. Can you imagine – threepence for an envelope!' Dottie gazed at her indignantly over the rim of her cup.

'Do you really mean it?' Stella asked in dismay. 'I don't think Felix realises—'

'Why should he? He'm not posting cushion covers off to anyone, is he?'

'No, I didn't mean that. I meant about Mrs Warren. Only

you know what she's like …' Stella broke off. She tried hard to keep to her rule about never criticising villagers to other villagers, but it wasn't always easy, especially when it was someone like Joyce Warren, the solicitor's wife, who was liable to be criticised by everyone else anyway.

'Oh, we all know what she be like,' Dottie agreed. 'Curate'll have to watch her, but you know how keen she was on that little play you and the children put on about the donkey. Of course, she'm not a real village person, so us don't know what she might have done before her come to Burracombe.'

Stella laughed, partly at Dottie's words and partly at her reference to the scene from *A Midsummer Night's Dream* as 'a little play about a donkey'. 'You make it sound as if she might have a criminal record! I have to admit, she was quite helpful with the children in the end. Anyway, Felix knows her well enough by now. I expect he'll be able to cope. Now I come to think of it, he does know she's coming – he told me he'd offered her some important-sounding job to do. Perhaps we can get her to help you with the sewing as well, to keep her out of trouble.'

Dottie gave her a look, which made her laugh again. 'I think I can manage very well without Mrs Warren's help, thank you very much. Although her did put a very nice patchwork quilt in the craft display us had in the village hall last summer.'

'There you are, then,' Stella said. 'She has hidden talents. And she does work quite hard for the village. The Gardening Club would never have got going properly without her, and she runs the Bridge Club, and—'

'I know all that. It's just that her wants to be in *charge* of it all. Can't never sit back and let someone else take over. Wants her name at the top of every list, that's her trouble.'

Stella smiled. All that Dottie said was true, but there was another side to it as well. Anyone in the village could have done exactly the same as Joyce Warren did, but they seemed quite happy to let her take on all the various tasks and then complain about her bossiness.

'Well, I don't think Felix will let her take over the Drama Club,' she said. 'Unless she turns out to be a wonderful actress or something.'

'*Or something* – that'll be the size of it,' Dottie said darkly. 'That woman thinks she'm wonderful at everything.' She got up from her chair. 'I'll just wash these supper-things, and then I'll take myself off to the Bell. I'm doing a few extra hours behind the bar this week, as Bernie and Rose are extra busy with all these visitors about.'

'Yes, Felix says Mrs Madge has had different people in her spare room almost every night this past week or two. Mostly cyclists, but one or two have come in cars.' Stella spoke a little regretfully, thinking of the past few months when her sister Maddy had lodged in Aggie Madge's spare room. But Maddy was happy in her new job, and West Lyme wasn't all that far away – and the main thing was, they'd found each other again.

As Dottie wrapped a cardigan round her plump little body and set off for the village inn, Stella lifted Alfred on to her lap and sat stroking his soft fur, thinking of the day she had first come to Burracombe, two years ago, and all that had happened since.

I've been so happy here, she thought. I hope I can stay in Burracombe for the rest of my life ...

Chapter Four

'He's coming on Thursday,' Gilbert Napier announced, walking into the estate office where Hilary was going through that morning's correspondence. 'Says he'll be pleased to renew acquaintanceship. He'll be here sometime in the afternoon, so you'd better tell Mrs Ellis to get a room ready for him.'

Hilary put down the official form she was trying to decipher. 'He's actually staying here – in the house?'

'Well, you didn't expect me to throw down some straw in one of the stables for him, did you?' her father demanded testily. 'Have some sense, Hilary.'

She felt her face colour with annoyance. 'I thought you might have asked the Warnes to put him up. Or the Crockers. Or got him a room at the inn. I didn't think you'd actually ask him to stay with us.'

'He was Baden's friend—'

'Yes, I know that,' she interrupted. 'And I know you're very grateful to him for whatever he did for Baden, and for coming here to see you after the war. But that's nothing to do with offering him a job now. This is a business proposition. You wouldn't have asked anyone else in that position to stay in the house.'

'I don't see why not. I'm not thinking of taking him on as a gamekeeper, or a gardener. If I offer him a job at all – and it's by no means certain that I will, whatever you may think – it'll be a responsible position as estate manager. I'd extend the same hospitality to any other man I intended to employ in such a capacity.'

'Or woman?' Hilary enquired, and sighed as her father stared at her in some bewilderment. 'All right, I know you'd never dream of offering it to a woman. Perish the thought.'

'You're being childish,' Gilbert said coldly. 'In any case, the matter's not open for discussion. He's coming on Thursday and I want all proper arrangements to be made. A room prepared, and a decent dinner. And you'd better make sure you're available to show him around a bit, although I shall do most of that myself, naturally.'

'Naturally,' Hilary said, tight-lipped. 'And how long will Mr Kellaway be staying?'

'Haven't made any firm arrangement about that, but I should imagine he'll be here for the weekend. Probably go back on Sunday evening or Monday morning, though he's welcome to stay longer if he wants to. He's still got his job to do at Oliver's, of course.'

'Yes, of course. We wouldn't want him to neglect that.' She was aware of the edge of sarcasm in her voice and looked back at the official form in her hand. The print swam a little before her eyes and she cursed the tears that threatened to fall. Without looking up again, she said, 'I'll see to everything, Father, don't worry. It will all be done properly. I won't even make him an apple-pie bed!'

For a moment, she expected him to accuse her again of being childish, but instead he snorted, turned on his heel and slammed out of the office. Hilary sighed again. It would do no good to antagonise her father any further, she knew, but equally she saw no reason to hide her anger. Val's right, she thought, we're as bad as each other and neither of us is willing to give in. Well, maybe this Kellaway man will see that and decide he doesn't want to work for us anyway! We can but hope.

She went back to her work. At least she could express her anger by removing herself from the scene on Thursday afternoon. Her father couldn't force her to be present when

Travis Kellaway arrived. He wasn't coming by her invitation, and it would be just as well if he realised that from the very beginning.

'He's coming on Thursday afternoon,' she reported dolefully when she ran into Val that afternoon in Tavistock. She had gone in to buy some of her father's favourite cheese in Creber's, and to order some rib of beef at Palmer's, the butcher's shop close by. Val was doing some shopping too, and they decided to go into a nearby teashop to rest their feet. 'Dad's invited him to stay with us, of all things!'

'Well, I suppose that's reasonable,' Val said cautiously, not wanting to take Napier's side against her friend but unable to see quite why Hilary was so indignant. 'Or don't you think he'll be housetrained? Or not know which knives to use at table?'

Hilary favoured her with a scathing glance. 'I'm not a snob, Val! Of course I don't think that. It's just that – well ...' She floundered for a moment. 'I just think Dad's going overboard a bit. I mean, if it had been anyone else applying for a job, he'd have left them to find their own accommodation. Or at least suggested the village inn, or Aggie Madge's spare room. It seems so peculiar, asking him to stay with us. As if he's someone special.'

'But he is, isn't he? He was Baden's friend.'

Hilary sighed. 'Oh God. If I hear those words once more, I swear I'll scream.' She picked up her teaspoon and stirred her tea viciously. 'I know, I'm being mean and petty and suspicious. But haven't I got cause to be? He could be taking my job away. I'll be left with *nothing*.'

'Oh, surely it's not that bad—' Val began, but Hilary broke in angrily.

'It *is* that bad! He'll take over everything I do. I'll be back to where I was a year ago, looking for something to occupy my time. Looking for something to occupy my *life*. Something a bit more satisfying than arranging the church flowers and putting on little tea-parties and entertaining Dad's friends to dinner. I'm only thirty years old, Val – the thought of doing that for the next forty years is just appalling.'

'I can see it would be, if that really was all you had to look forward to. But—'

'Don't say I'm sure to meet someone and get married,' Hilary begged her. 'Just don't say it.'

Val grinned. 'Perhaps he's the one who ought to get married,' she suggested mischievously, and Hilary laughed.

'Can you see anyone taking on that old curmudgeon? No, I honestly don't see anything much changing at the Barton. It'll be just him and me together, for years and years and years. And that's why I've got to have something to do! That's why I want to run the estate myself.'

As they paid, Val said, 'You're still coming to the Drama Club meeting on Friday, aren't you? You can tell me about it then. Better still,' she gave her friend a wicked look, 'you can bring Mr Kellaway along too. It might be quite a good idea to show him just what he'll be getting into, if he decides to come and live in Burracombe!'

Travis Kellaway arrived at Burracombe Barton as the stable clock struck three on Thursday afternoon. He drove his Land Rover round to the stables, where Ernie Crocker, the gardener and stableman, took charge of the two Springer Spaniels that were bouncing about in the back.

'They can stay out here with me,' he said. 'I'll put them in one of the stalls for the night. Squire's got his own Labradors indoors, us don't want to set up a fight.'

Travis nodded cheerfully. He was a tall, well-built man in his middle thirties, with wavy, dark auburn hair and dark blue eyes. He gripped Ernie's hand firmly and gave him a friendly grin.

'They'll be OK. They live outdoors at home – better for

working dogs, keeps them hardy.' He looked around the stable-yard. 'Nice place. I came here once a few years ago, but didn't see much of the outbuildings. Got many horses?'

'Four,' Ernie said, moving towards the fence. 'They'm out at grass now. That's Sultan over there – Squire's black gelding, getting on for eighteen year old now – and the bay with the white blaze is Beau, Miss Hilary's. Gentlest beast you ever saw, though he's got some fire in him too, takes a strong rider to keep him under control, it do. And the strawberry roan is Master Stephen's – nice little mare, but her don't get ridden enough now, with the boy being away in the RAF. Miss Hilary takes her out as much as her can, but what with her putting in all the hours she do round the estate, her don't get the time for it. Val Tozer as was comes over and has a hack now and then.'

'And the other black?' Travis enquired, looking past the others at a solitary figure at the far side of the field.

Ernie Crocker waited a moment before answering. Then he said, 'That was Master Baden's. He'm an old chap now, nearly thirty years old, but Squire won't hear of having him destroyed. Not as long as he can still enjoy his life, any road.'

'Baden's horse,' Travis said quietly. 'He used to talk about him. Major, isn't that his name?'

'That's right,' Crocker said. 'Major. A fine horse. Miss Hilary still rides him now and then, and he'm as keen as ever; just gets a bit tired, that's all. It's going to be a sad day at the Barton when old Major goes.'

'Yes, it is,' Travis said. 'And not just because it's the loss of a fine horse.' The two men stood silently for a few moments, leaning over the gate and watching the four horses grazing in their field. Then Travis gave a little sigh and pushed himself away from the rails. 'I'd better go and make myself known at the house.'

He collected his suitcase from the battered Land Rover and walked round to the front of the house. It was a fine old

building, as grey as the granite tors that formed craggy out-
lines at the tops of the moorland hills, with a terrace running
along the front and along both sides so that there would always
be somewhere to enjoy either sun or shade. Travis walked up
the steps and pulled the handle of the bell. Somewhere deep
inside, he heard a faint jangle, and then footsteps.

'Good afternoon,' he said to the girl who opened the door.
'My name's Travis Kellaway. I believe the Colonel's expecting me.'

'Oh yes,' said Jackie Tozer, somewhat flustered. She'd
known Mr Kellaway was coming, of course, but she hadn't
expected this tall and extremely good-looking man with smiling blue eyes and hair the colour of a December sunset. 'Um
– the Colonel's in his study. I'll show you the way. Shall I take
your case upstairs for you?'

'No need,' Travis said with a grin. 'I'll carry it up myself
later. I'm not used to being waited on. But if you could just
show me somewhere to wash my hands before I go in?'

'Oh yes, of course. Through there.' She pointed to a door
off the hallway, and while he was occupied she went to the
study to tell Gilbert Napier that his visitor had arrived. By the
time she came back, Travis was standing in the hall, gazing at
one of the landscape paintings that hung on the walls.

'Would you like to come in?' she asked. 'I'll bring some tea
in a minute.'

'Thanks.' He smiled down at her. 'Don't run away, though.
What's your name? You're not the Colonel's daughter, are
you?'

'Goodness me, no!' she exclaimed, blushing. 'I'm just Jackie
Tozer, from the farm. I work in the house – helping Mrs Ellis,
the housekeeper, and all that sort of thing.'

'So you live nearby?'

Jackie nodded. 'We're the next house, really – I just cut
across the fields of a morning. My sister Val's one of Miss
Hilary's friends.'

They stood for a moment looking at each other, and then she said hastily, 'I'd better show you in. This is the study.' She opened a door and said, 'Mr Kellaway's here, Mr Napier,' and stood aside for Travis to enter.

Travis strode in, holding out his hand, and Gilbert Napier rose from one of the two armchairs standing each side of the fireplace. The two men shook hands and Jackie withdrew.

'Kellaway! Good to see you again. And good of you to come all this way.' He gestured at the other armchair. 'Sit down. Make yourself comfortable.'

'Thank you, sir.' The tall man folded his body into the armchair and Colonel Napier sat down more stiffly. They regarded each other for a moment, then Gilbert said, 'Sorry to hear about your father. Met him a few times when I came over for the shooting. He was a fine gamekeeper.'

'He was. A fine man, too. I'm proud to have been his son.'

Gilbert nodded. 'Baden always spoke well of you. You were a good friend to him.'

'As he was to me,' Travis said quietly.

It was almost like a dance, he thought, watching the big man opposite. A preliminary routine that had to be gone through, shifting and re-establishing their relationship – Gilbert Napier, the retired Colonel, friend of Travis Kellaway's employer; and Travis, wartime friend and companion to Gilbert's son, the only man to have been with him at the end, when Baden lay dying from his wounds. It was an important moment, and one which the bereaved families always wanted to know about. That was why Travis had come from Hampshire to visit Gilbert and Isobel Napier at the first opportunity after the war, and why they had kept in touch. It was why Gilbert had sent for him when he had heard about Arthur Kellaway's death.

The gratitude didn't have to go as far as offering him a job, though, and Travis wasn't sure he wanted to be under an obligation to the Napiers – or to anyone. His Army days, and his own ambition, had reinforced the streak of independence he'd had since boyhood, and he had no intention of accepting another post as an assistant. It was time for him to be in charge, to take responsibility and show what he could do.

For a while, the two men continued to discuss general matters – the state of the world as it gradually settled down after the devastating war, the state of Britain itself, the state of farming. From there they moved to more specific subjects and talked about the Tutton estate in Hampshire, where Travis Kellaway had grown up, and then Gilbert Napier's property here in Devon.

'Of course, you know Baden would have taken it over,' Gilbert said heavily. 'It wasn't to be, unfortunately, and young Stephen seems firmly set against it. And since my own bit of trouble a year or so ago, it's all come down on Hilary. She's made a good fist of it, mind you, I'm not saying she hasn't, but it isn't right for a young woman like her to be taking on so much. Ought to be concerning herself with a family, not worrying her mind over estate matters. It's not even as if she was ever trained for it, as Baden was.' He shook his big grey head. 'I'm telling you this in confidence, mind, because she's a proud young woman and will never admit it's too much for her – but I'd like to do something about it. Find some capable feller to take the burden off her shoulders.'

'I see,' Travis said carefully. He hadn't really wanted to get into this discussion so quickly – it would have been better to have had time to take stock of the place and the family he'd be working so closely with, should he accept the post he knew Napier was considering offering him. Nothing was certain yet – they were still assessing each other – and he didn't want matters to proceed too swiftly.

At that moment, the door opened and a young woman came in, carrying a tray. She was wearing dark green breeches and a cotton shirt, but the rather masculine outfit, similar to that worn by the Land Army girls during the war, did nothing to hide her slim, feminine figure. Her fair hair was drawn back to rest in a loose knot on her neck and her silver-grey eyes regarded him steadily.

Travis rose to his feet. This, he knew, must be Napier's daughter, Hilary – the sister Baden had talked about. There was little actual resemblance between them, for Baden had taken his father's dark, compelling looks, but there was something in that steely gaze that was Baden through and through, something vigorous and dynamic, that told him that Hilary Napier was no 'little woman' to be patronised. She would be resolute in her dealings and – depending on the circumstances – either a valuable ally or a formidable adversary.

Travis felt a flicker of interest. Hilary Napier didn't look the kind of woman to be easily brushed aside. He wondered just what she felt about her father's decision to take on an estate manager – the job she'd been doing for the past year. Was she aching to be rid of it, so that she could go back to the busy social life she'd no doubt given up to do it? Or would she want to have her own say on how the estate was managed?

Travis met her gaze and felt as if he already knew the answer. In that case, he thought, mine will be, 'No.' I could never work with a woman always looking over my shoulder. Not even one as interesting as Hilary Napier.

Chapter Five

Hilary had come in through the back door, shucking off her boots in the boot room and padding through the kitchen in thick socks. Mrs Ellis, the housekeeper, was standing at the big table making pastry and Jackie was taking a tray of freshly-baked scones from the Aga. She looked up as Hilary came in, her face flushed from the heat of the oven.

'He's here, Miss Hilary. I'm just going to take these in, and there's a fresh pot of tea ready as well. He wouldn't let me take his case up to his room – said he could do that himself.'

'I'm sure he can,' Hilary said dryly. She watched as Jackie split the steaming scones and arranged them on a large plate. 'Don't spread the butter on yet, or it'll soak in too much – put the butter-dish on the tray separately. I might as well take it in myself.' She pushed her feet into a pair of indoor shoes and went to the sink to wash her hands.

'Don't you want to change first, Miss Hilary?' the house-keeper asked doubtfully, but Hilary shook her head.

'He may as well see me as I am – a working woman. In any case, I've still got things to attend to outside.' She lifted the tray from the table and carried it to the door, which Jackie opened for her. 'Thanks, Jackie. If you wouldn't mind doing the drawing-room one too ...?' She smiled, even though she felt rather as if she were walking into a lion's den, and marched into the room with her head held high.

She saw him at once, rising from the armchair by the fireplace. He was a good six inches taller than she, and more commanding than she had expected, with his strong face and deep auburn hair. There was an air of authority about him, coming probably from his service in the Army, she thought, as if he were accustomed to being in charge, and there was no sign of servility in his expression as he moved towards her, his hand held out.

'How do you do? I'm Travis Kellaway.'

'Yes, I guessed you must be.' She took his hand and shook it, each giving the other a firm clasp. 'I'm Hilary.' She met his eyes and felt a tiny shock at their darkness. 'I've brought tea and some of Mrs Ellis's scones. They're straight out of the oven.'

'Heavens above, girl, this isn't a tea-party,' Napier protested grumpily, but Travis grinned.

'Tea and scones will go down very nicely. It's quite a long drive from Tutton.'

Hilary nodded and served the tea, then took her seat in the chair by the window. She wanted to be able to see Travis's face, and was quite well aware that this made it more difficult for him to see hers. She regarded him steadily, lifting her chin a little.

'It's good to meet you at last,' he said pleasantly, and she noted his voice, deep without being gruff, faintly tinged with a Hampshire country burr. 'You were away when I came before, but Baden told me so much about you that I feel I already know you.'

'You may have felt you knew me as I was then,' Hilary returned, 'but that's six years or more ago. I'm sure I've changed quite a lot in that time.'

He laughed. 'I dare say you have! I stand corrected, but I still feel I know at least a few things about you. Baden was very fond of you, you know.'

'I was his sister,' Hilary said briefly. 'Families do tend to have a certain affection for each other.'

'I've been admiring your horses,' he said. 'Fine-looking animals. You obviously look after them well.'

'Hilary's an accomplished rider,' Gilbert Napier said. 'Always been keen, from a child, just like her brother. Used to walk away with the prizes at the local gymkhanas.'

'Not all of them,' Hilary protested. 'There were plenty of other good riders, too. It generally ended up as a competition between Felicity Latimer and me.'

'I remember that name,' Travis said thoughtfully.'The doctor's daughter, isn't she?'

'That's right.' This time, Hilary was surprised by his memory. 'The eldest. She's just qualified as a doctor. The younger one, Tessa, is at Art College.'

'A painter?'

'No, she wants to do dress design. At least, that was her latest idea – she's had quite a few different ones while she's been there.'

'Lot of nonsense!' Napier snorted. 'Don't know what's got into young women these days – wanting to be doctors and artists, and have careers. Satisfied to have a husband and family in my day, and make a career out of that. And all the better for it, if you want my opinion.'

'Really, Father?' Hilary said sweetly. 'So were all those stories I've heard about the Pankhursts and Suffragettes just fairy-tales, then?'

Her father snorted again and Travis chuckled. Hilary stole a glance at him and found him watching her, his eyes dancing. She looked away quickly, and poured more tea into her cup, even though she hadn't finished the first.

'Have you been shown where you're to sleep yet?' she asked. 'We've put you into one of the rooms overlooking the stables, so you'll be able to watch the horses any time you like.'

'I was rather hoping you might offer me a ride,' he said, and glanced at Gilbert. 'Do you get out on your own mount these days?'

Gilbert shrugged. 'I'd like to, but Sultan's got too much fire in his belly. That old woman of a doctor says he'd be too much for me. And I refuse to demean myself by riding some staid old schoolmaster, kept for teaching children.'

'That's the trouble with all our horses,' Hilary said. 'They're all too spirited – even Major. We haven't had a quiet horse on the place since we grew out of ponies.'

'Nothing to stop you taking Kellaway out, though,' her father told her. 'Take your pick – Sultan or old Major. Either of them would be glad of an outing.'

'Major!' Hilary exclaimed. 'But he's Ba—' She stopped abruptly and bit her lip. She felt Travis's eyes on her but refused to look at him. 'He's getting very old,' she finished lamely.

'I know,' Travis said quietly. 'Crocker told me about him. He says he still likes an outing now and then, though.' He turned to the Colonel. 'What do you say? Would you like me to take Major out for a bit of a hack?'

'Don't see why not,' Napier said gruffly. 'You're here for a few days, anyway. Try 'em both. You've got the time.'

'Thanks,' Travis said. 'I will. I appreciate it.'

He reached for his cup and sipped from it, his eyes meeting Hilary's over the rim. She felt her cheeks colour and looked away again, wondering just how long he planned to stay. As she'd understood it, the arrangement was that he'd be here no more than two nights – one full day. Now here her father was, talking about 'a few days' and having time to try out both horses. She sighed, finished her own tea and then put down the cup and stood up.

'I'm afraid I'll have to go now. I've still got work to do. I'll get Jackie to show you to your room, Mr Kellaway. I'll see you at dinner.'

'Oh, but couldn't I come with you?' he asked disarmingly, his head tilted a little. 'It would be a good chance to see something of your estate. Unless you're just going to be doing office work, of course. I'd only get in your way there.'

'It will be office work,' Hilary said, immediately abandoning her plan to walk over to Home Farm and talk to Ken Warne about his sheep, a visit she'd purposely left till last. 'Anyway, I expect you'd like to wander about on your own for a bit.' As soon as she'd said it, she wished she hadn't. Letting Travis Kellaway wander about on his own might not be a good idea at all. 'I could leave the office work till tomorrow,' she offered lamely. 'There are one or two things I need to look at outside. You can come with me if you like.'

'That's fine, then,' Travis said cheerfully. 'I'll just get my boots out of the Land Rover.' He stood up and held his hand out to Gilbert. 'It's really good to meet you again. Very kind of you to invite me.'

Gilbert shrugged. 'Least I could do. Might as well come along with you now. Don't suppose Hilary's going all that far, are you, Hilary? Talking about going over to Home Farm, weren't you, to have a chat with Ken Warne about his flock?'

'That's right,' she said resignedly. 'I suppose you have South Downs in Hampshire, do you, Mr Kellaway? We're thinking of trying out a few Herdwicks on Ken's fields.'

'For heaven's sake,' he said, smiling, 'call me Travis. It's an odd sort of a Christian name, I know, but it's been in the family for generations and you do get used to it after a while. And since I feel I know you so well, even though, as you pointed out, I don't really, perhaps you won't mind if I call you Hilary? Your brother and I really were friends.'

'Yes,' she said, feeling suddenly ashamed. 'Yes, of course you must. And I don't think I've said how nice it is to meet you at last. Baden talked to me about you as well, you know. He thought a lot of you.'

They stood together for a moment, their eyes meeting. Hilary saw the smile begin in his eyes and spread over his face, widening the mobile lips. She looked away, sharply reminded of the brother who had died so young. Eight years since the telegram had come; eight years without him. And yet, just at that moment, it seemed as close as yesterday.

45

She blinked away the unexpected tears and moved quickly towards the door.

'We'd better be going, then. Ken's a great talker and once you get him on the subject of his sheep it's difficult to get a word in edgeways. Mrs Ellis won't be at all pleased if we're late for dinner. It's steak and kidney pie, and nobody does it better.'

They parted in the hallway while Travis went round to the stableyard for his boots and Hilary slipped through to the kitchen to let Jackie and Mrs Ellis know that they would be out for a while. 'I'll get Crocker to take Mr Kellaway's luggage up to his room,' she said. 'Make sure he's got everything he needs up there, won't you, Jackie.'

'Of course, Miss Hilary.' The girl paused and then said. 'He's ever so good-looking, isn't he? Is he staying long?'

'Not as far as I know,' Hilary said shortly, hoping she was right. 'But he's my father's guest, not mine. We'll just have to wait and see.'

She went through to the boot room for her own waxed jacket and boots, leaving Jackie to go on helping the housekeeper with preparations for the evening meal. She was annoyed – annoyed with Jackie for her naive interest, with Travis for his undoubted good looks, and with herself for the bad manners she hadn't seemed able to control. Acting like a silly adolescent, she scolded herself. How can you think you have the right to criticise poor Jackie, who's barely eighteen years old? If this is the way you're going to behave, Father will have every reason to give Travis Kellaway your job.

A wave of misery swept over her at the thought. At that moment, she would have given anything to turn her back and go upstairs to her room, pretending that none of this was happening. And *that* would be even more childish, she thought. Pulling on her boots and jacket, she marched out through the back door to the stableyard where Travis Kellaway and her father were waiting for her.

'Right,' she greeted them, 'let's go over to Home Farm and see what Ken's got to say. Which way would you like to go, Dad – over the fields or through the woods?'

Reluctant though she was to admit it, Hilary had to concede that Travis Kellaway certainly knew his stuff. Although Herdwicks were a northern breed, found almost exclusively on the fells of Cumberland and Westmorland, he seemed as familiar with their characteristics as he was with his own South Downs. He listened as Ken outlined his ideas and nodded thoughtfully.

'They're hardy enough – have to be, to withstand the conditions they get up there – but they're scrawny beasts and their wool's like barbed wire. I'm not sure they'd be worth your while.'

'I thought of crossing them with the Scottish Blackface we've got here now,' Ken said, and Travis pursed his lips and lifted his eyebrows as if half-agreeing with him. 'Get the best of both worlds then.'

'Or the worst!' Travis said with a grin. 'Still, it could be worth trying.'

'Think about it a bit more, Ken,' Hilary advised the farmer, determined that this was not going to become a discussion between the two men. 'Anyway, it's your decision – but my father and I will be interested to see how you get on, won't we, Dad?'

From the glance Travis shot at her, she knew that he had noticed her pointed exclusion of him and she narrowed her eyes and lifted her chin a little as she returned his look. He might as well understand the situation from the outset, she reflected grimly, and went on to ask the farmer about other matters. This time, Travis remained silent, though she had the uncomfortable feeling that he was taking note of all her words and storing them up for later analysis.

The steak and kidney pie they ate for dinner proved up to

Mrs Ellis's usual high standard. The pastry was light and flaky, softened on the inside by the rich gravy of the tender pieces of meat. There was a taste of dark brown stout as well, offset by the clean flavour of lightly-boiled cabbage and the sweetness of young carrots. Mashed potato sat like fluffy clouds on each plate and there was extra onion gravy in a large jug.

'Your Mrs Ellis is a magnificent cook,' Travis said, accepting a second slice of pie.

'She is,' Gilbert agreed. 'No better than Hilary, mind you. Fed me very well indeed when we were on our own except for one or two village women coming in to do the cleaning and the rough, didn't you, girl?'

'I did my best,' Hilary answered coolly. 'You would soon have complained if I didn't.'

'Yes, my daughter's an excellent little homemaker,' Gilbert went on, ignoring that remark. 'Make someone a fine wife one day – when she gets a chance to enjoy a bit of social life.'

'Father, I don't think Mr Kellaway is interested—'

'I thought we'd agreed that you'd call me Travis,' he interrupted with a smile. 'And of course I'm interested. What are you thinking of doing? Travelling, perhaps, now that Europe's opening up again?'

'I'm not thinking of doing anything,' she returned in a taut voice. 'And I travelled quite a lot during the war. I'm happy to stay at home now.'

'She means she's stuck in a rut,' Gilbert said. 'High time she got out of it and started to see life. Never saw much before the war, what with one thing and another, and now ...'

'Now it's too late,' Hilary said brusquely. 'Too late for the sort of life you mean anyway, Father. As a matter of fact, I'm not sure I'd ever have enjoyed the sort of life you're talking about – being presented at Court, going to endless balls and parties and so on. I'd have been miserable all the time.'

'Nonsense! All young girls enjoy that sort of thing. Lots of pretty dresses, plenty of attention.' Gilbert helped himself to more cabbage. 'Pass the gravy, would you, Kellaway ... Well, I admit you're a bit long in the tooth for all that now, Hilary, but there's still a decent social life out there if you care to look for it. We've got plenty of friends. Soon get you introduced to a few circles.'

Hilary kept a tight hold on her temper. 'Father, I don't *want* to be introduced to any circles. I've got plenty of friends and I'm very happy here. And I have an excellent social life.'

'Such as what?' her father asked, and she closed her eyes for a moment. She knew perfectly well what he was doing – trying to imply to Travis that she was only too keen to give up her work on the estate.

Determined not to allow him to get away with it, she said: 'Well, there's the new Drama Club for a start.'

'The *Drama Club*,' Napier echoed with sarcastic emphasis, but Travis looked up eagerly.

'A Drama Club? That sounds interesting. I've done a bit of that myself, from time to time. What are you putting on?'

'We don't know yet,' Hilary said, thankful for the change of subject. 'The first meeting's tomorrow evening.' As soon as the words left her mouth she regretted them, and her heart sank as she saw the spark in Travis's eyes.

'Tomorrow, eh?'

'Yes,' she backtracked, 'but I might not be going.'

'Oh, why's that?' her father enquired. 'Thought you were keen. You might as well take Kellaway along with you – be a good introduction to the village. You wouldn't mind going along, would you, Kellaway?'

'Not at all,' Travis said, his eyes meeting Hilary's. 'I'd like to.'

'That's settled, then.' Gilbert cleared his plate and put down his knife and fork. 'Another glass of claret? And then perhaps we can see what Mrs Ellis has provided for our pudding ...'

49

Chapter Six

School was due to re-open in the first week of September. Stella spent most of the last week of the holidays preparing for her new class – a mixture of last year's 'babies' who had now reached the grand old age of six, and the new intake of five year olds. Many of them had brothers and sisters already at the school and even those who didn't were familiar with the sound of the school bell, and the sight of the playground and the field where the children did their PT and sports. Miss Kemp, the headmistress, didn't anticipate any problems with the new 'babies'.

'Except for the Crocker twins, of course,' she said when Stella came to spend an evening at the schoolhouse with her to discuss their plans for the new term. 'You remember, we thought they'd be starting last year but their birthday is just one day too late, so they've had to wait. It means they'll be the oldest "babies" in the class, which may or may not be a good thing!'

'I haven't seen much of them,' Stella said. 'They live quite far out from the village, don't they?'

'Yes, in one of the cottages at Stannerton Farm. It's nearly two miles away – a few more hundred yards and they wouldn't be coming to this school at all. They come to church occasionally, but John Crocker isn't much of a churchgoer and Maisie looks permanently exhausted to me – not surprising, when you consider she's got two younger children as well as George and Edward.' She made a rueful face. 'I think if I'd started my family with those two, I'd have stopped there as well!'

'Oh dear,' Stella said. 'Are they that bad?'

'No, I'm sure they're not really,' the headmistress said optimistically. 'Anyway, I have every confidence that you'll be able to deal with them, Stella.'

Stella, who knew her headmistress well enough by now to be aware of her real feelings about the Crocker twins, smiled resignedly. It would only be for two years, anyway, she thought. After that, they'd be going into Miss Kemp's own classroom, where they would remain for the next four years. All the same, it was up to her to do the groundwork.

'Are they related to the Mr Crocker who works at the Barton?' she asked. 'He looks after the horses and the gardens, and I think he's one of the bell-ringers.'

'Yes, he's their grandfather. Nice man, and his wife's a very pleasant little body. Makes wonderful sponge cakes for the WI. Their son John's a stockman at Stannerton – he married a girl from Meavy. Janet Crocker's father is his son, too – another local family with branches everywhere. Now, who else have we got coming in?' The headmistress consulted the list on the table in front of her. 'Robin Tozer's not old enough yet – he'll be in next year's batch. How's his mother, by the way? Isn't the new baby due soon?' Miss Kemp had been away for the past three weeks and hadn't yet caught up with all the village news.

'Just under a month, I think. She looks really well. And Val and Luke are getting on with Jed's cottage – they're hoping to be able to move in by October. I saw them yesterday and Luke's quite looking forward to starting his new job in Tavistock.'

'That's good. He'll make an excellent teacher. Isn't there a new Culliford coming in?'

'Yes, the youngest boy, Billy. And Betty will be coming up into your class.' Stella smiled. 'We need never be afraid of running out of children while the Cullifords are in the village! There seems to be an endless supply. You know Mrs Culliford is expecting again?'

'No!' Miss Kemp put down her pen and stared at her. 'Though why I should be surprised, I really don't know. How many will that be – six? Or is it seven? I lose count.'

'Seven, I think. There are two or three older ones, aren't there?'

'Yes, one has left school altogether and the other two are at St Rumon's in Tavistock. You know, I'm hoping that we may get Shirley into the grammar school. She's a much brighter child than I realised at first. She's come on so well since she was made Festival Queen, and it could encourage the younger ones too.'

'She's worth helping,' Stella agreed. 'She has a real talent for recitation and maybe even acting. And she and Jenny Pettifer have become good friends too, so now that Jenny's gone to the grammar school, she might like the idea.'

They continued to discuss the children who had left, those who were moving up through the school, and the new ones coming in, and it was growing dark when Miss Kemp put down her pen, and declared that it was time for a cup of cocoa before Stella went back to Dottie's. She produced ginger biscuits as well and they sat companionably munching and sipping, while dusk fell on the garden outside the French windows and the birds settled down for the night.

'The nights are drawing in now,' Miss Kemp observed. 'And there's a distinct nip in the air in the mornings. That lovely September feel – "season of mists and mellow fruitfulness". I know this is a busy term, but it's full of enjoyable things – the Harvest Festival, November the Fifth and then all the preparations for Christmas. I never get tired of it, though I'm always exhausted by the time it's over.'

'And this year could be even busier, with the new Drama Group starting,' Stella said. 'Felix is really keen to do a pantomime.'

'Do you know which one he has in mind?'

'He won't say until the meeting tomorrow. I think he wants

to see how many are interested first. Will you be coming?'

'Oh yes,' the headmistress said. 'I don't think I'll volunteer for any acting, but I'd like to help behind the scenes. I could do some sewing, and of course if the children are involved … although perhaps they won't want their teachers taking charge of them then. It's supposed to be their time off!'

Stella laughed. 'Well, that'll make a good excuse if anyone takes it for granted that we'll look after them. I just hope it won't be too much for them, with all the other things we'll be doing. Too much for us, either,' she added.

'Time expands to fill the work available,' Miss Kemp said comfortably. 'Or is it the other way around? Anyway, we always seem to manage to fit in whatever we want to do. Now, would you like some more cocoa? There's some in the jug.'

'No, thank you.' Stella stood up and shrugged her arms into her jacket. 'I'm really looking forward to school starting again now. The holidays have been lovely, but I'm ready to start work again, and it's exciting to have new children coming in.'

'Even the Crocker twins?' Miss Kemp asked slyly.

'Even the Crocker twins! You never know, they may not be nearly as bad as we think.'

'That's quite true,' the headmistress agreed. 'And anybody who says pigs can't fly is just not looking in the right direction.'

'Oh well,' Stella said as she went to the door and looked out into the darkened village street. 'I expect we'll survive.'

She said goodnight to the older woman and set out on the short walk back to Dottie Friend's cottage. Above her, the sky was thick with stars and there was a crispness in the air. The summer was nearly over and to Stella it seemed as if this was where the new year really began, with a new school year opening, new children to get to know, and the new happiness that Felix had brought into her life. With her hand on the latch of

Dottie's gate, she paused and looked up as a sudden burst of song sounded from the tangled honeysuckle that clambered over the front door.

It was as if even the birds were offering her a welcome.

'It's marvellous to see so many of you here,' Felix said, looking round the ring of faces. 'Thank you very much for taking the trouble to come along. It looks as if there's quite a lot of interest in setting up a new Drama Club.'

'It's not exactly a *new* Drama Club,' Joyce Warren said at once. Despite Felix's efforts at directing her to another chair, she'd managed to appropriate the one next to him in the circle of chairs he had set out in the village hall. Stella herself was on his other side, feeling very conspicuous and rather glad to have Mrs Warren drawing attention away from her. 'There has been one in the village for some time, but for some reason nobody seemed very interested until now.'

'Well, if you asks me, I think us should call it a new one and start from scratch,' Alf Coker said. He was a big, burly man with thick dark hair that was beginning to turn silver – exactly what you'd expect a blacksmith to look like, Stella thought. She'd been surprised to see him at the meeting – surprised, in fact, by many of the villagers who had turned up. George Sweet was there with Bert Foster, both the Friend sisters with their brother Billy, Tom Tozer and his sister Jackie, Val and Luke Ferris, Dr Latimer's younger daughter Tessa, two or three other young men and girls she didn't know, and Hilary Napier, looking rather grim with an auburn-haired man sitting beside her. He must be a visitor, Stella thought, and wondered why he had bothered to come to the meeting of a club he was never going to join.

'I don't think it actually matters whether we call it a *new* Drama Club or not,' Felix said, not wishing to start a debate at the very outset. 'The important thing is that you've all come because you're interested, and to discuss what kind of dramatic production we'd like to put on.' He smiled round the circle of faces.

Silence fell. They all gazed back at him, evidently hoping to be told. Not unreasonably, Stella thought. Felix had, after all, called this meeting so presumably he had some ideas about what the Club should do.

After a few minutes, Alf Coker cleared his throat and said, 'Before the war, us used to put on a lot of things. Concert parties and pantomimes, mostly. Us did *Cinderella* once, with the Tozers' cart done up as a pumpkin and old Mr Bellamy's pony-trap for the coach.'

'That's right, I remember that,' George Sweet said. 'Weren't you one of the Ugly Sisters? And Abe Lillicrap from over Ash Farm, he was the other. Poor old Abe.' He shook his head and there were murmurs of regret from some of the others. 'Killed the day war broke out, he was,' George explained to Felix and Stella.

'Oh, how awful,' she said. 'He must have been one of the very first. Was he in the Army, or the Navy?'

George gave her a baffled stare, then shook his head. 'Bless you, maid, Abe never left the village. It was that old bull of his killed him – gored him to death, out in the field. Mind you, nobody was surprised; old Roger had a fearsome temper and we all knew he weren't to be trusted, but Abe wouldn't take no notice. Said he was as gentle as a lamb, and so he might have been, but he were a lot bigger than any lamb I've ever seen, and those horns of his ...'

'Yes, it must have been very sad,' Felix said solemnly, though with a slight quiver in his voice. Stella gave him a reproving nudge and, as she felt his body quiver too, immediately wished she hadn't. 'So can I take it that you'd be interested in performing in a pantomime?'

Alf Coker looked taken aback. 'Well, like I said, it were a long time ago,' he began, but Felix was already speaking again and he stopped, glancing around cautiously as if to gauge the reactions of his neighbours.

'Who else thinks it's a good idea to put on a pantomime? There's a lot of work involved – we need several who'd be willing to act, and plenty in the chorus. Not to mention scenery and costumes.'

'I could do costumes,' Dottie Friend said at once. 'And Miss Kemp says she'll give me a hand, although we could do with a few more that might be handy with a needle.'

'I could help too,' Tessa said. 'I could design some specially.'

'That's tremendous,' Felix said, smiling warmly at her. 'And how about our resident artist for the scenery?' He lifted his eyebrows at Luke.

Luke nodded, although Val looked doubtful. 'Are you sure? You'll hardly have time for your own painting as it is, now you're starting work at the school.'

'It's only for a few weeks,' he reassured her. 'It'll be fun. And you're going to be in it too, aren't you?'

'I'd like to,' she admitted. 'I did a bit of amateur dramatics during the war. But it depends if I'm good enough. We just did it for fun in the hospital.'

'Well, we're making great headway,' Felix said. 'I'm sure there are a lot more of you willing to act or help out in some way. Don't be shy – there's lots to do backstage as well. Mrs Warren has kindly offered to take over the stage management and props and she'll need help with that.'

The prospect of helping Mrs Warren didn't seem quite so attractive to the gathering, but their glances and shrugs seemed to indicate that they realised it would be necessary. George Sweet cleared his throat and said, 'I don't mind doing a bit of acting, as long as I don't have too many words to learn.'

'I'd like to do some acting, too,' Tessa Latimer volunteered. 'I was always in our productions at school. I was Cinderella

56

once.' She fluttered her eyelashes at the man sitting beside Hilary. 'Are you joining us as well, Mr ...?'

'That rather depends,' he said with a glance at Hilary, who cut in swiftly with an apologetic, 'Sorry, Felix, I ought to have introduced you. This is Travis Kellaway, who's staying with us for a few days.'

'I see.' For a moment Felix was slightly nonplussed; he'd assumed the stranger was someone from some outlying part of the parish that he hadn't met before, and had already marked him down as a possible 'baddie'. Slightly disappointed, he said, 'Well, it's good to have you here, Mr Kellaway. Perhaps you'll come back and see the pantomime when we put it on.'

'And that's summat us ought to sort out right away,' Alf Coker said. 'When's it going to be? And how much practising have us got to do beforehand? Us used to have rehearsals twice a week, backalong.'

'And I think we should do the same,' Felix nodded. 'Starting as soon as we've decided on the pantomime and who is going to be in it. Now, we all know how busy December is, so I suggest we make it the last week of November and perform for, let's say, three nights – that's Thursday until Saturday.'

'The twenty-seventh till the thirtieth,' Joyce Warren said, consulting her diary.

'That's right. We'll decide on two nights a week when everyone can come.'

'Not Friday,' Tom Tozer objected. 'That's ringing practice.'

'Not Wednesday, neither,' George Sweet said. 'That's whist night.'

'What about Tuesdays and Thursdays?' Felix asked. 'Or would Mondays be better?'

'The Gardening Club meets on Thursday nights,' Joyce Warren said. 'But that is only once a month. Perhaps we could find somewhere else to rehearse on those evenings. Our lounge is quite large and we could always bring extra chairs in from the dining room, just to practise words.'

'Our barn'll have a bit of room in it by then,' Tom Tozer said, grinning at Mrs Warren's look of distaste. 'We could send in one of the terriers to clear the rats out beforehand.'

'I reckon Tuesdays'd be best,' Alf Coker said. 'Give everyone a chance to get over the weekend.'

Stella felt Felix quiver again and knew that he was wondering just what the blacksmith got up to at weekends that needed two full days to recover from. As far as she knew from Micky at school, his father's weekend life followed a normal pattern of working in the garden to produce the vegetables for a Sunday lunch large enough to send him into a sound sleep until tea-time.

'Which pantomime d'you think we should do?' she asked, hoping to divert the discussion. Felix shot her a grateful glance but before he could reply, Joyce Warren spoke again.

'I've always thought *Cinderella* is the nicest one. All those lovely dresses, and the glamorous coach, and lots of opportunities for the children to be mice.'

'Well, that'll make a change,' Stella observed. 'They aren't much like mice at school.'

'Yes, but we done *Cinderella* before,' Alf Coker objected. 'If we'm going to start up again, it ought to be something different.'

'*Little Red Riding Hood*, then,' Joyce suggested. 'Although the wolf can be rather frightening for the little ones.'

'Go on, Burracombe kiddies aren't frightened of a wolf,' George Sweet said. 'They got more sense.'

'I think we should do something with a bit more action in it,' Tom Tozer said. 'Isn't there anything with some sword-fighting? Or a battle?'

'*Mother Goose*,' Joyce went on, still following her own train of thought. 'Or *Jack and the Beanstalk*. Or what about *Aladdin*? That's got lovely costumes.'

'They wouldn't be too hard to do, neither,' Dottie Friend said thoughtfully. 'Sort of pyjamas in bright colours, and the hats are easy enough.'

'I got some old lamps laying about in the forge,' Alf said, showing interest. 'And I reckon us could find some way of making smoke for the genie when it comes out of the bottle.'

The gathering was beginning to warm up and people looked at each other with something approaching excitement. Felix saw a chance to speak and said quickly, 'I was wondering about *Robin Hood*. The children did so well with the woodland scene in *A Midsummer Night's Dream*, and there are lots of parts for Merry Men to be the chorus. And Merry Children as well,' he added to Stella. 'The costumes shouldn't be too difficult and there's plenty of action, with bows and arrows and a sword-fight or two at the castle gate. And there's a dungeon scene as well, which the children would enjoy watching.'

'So you'd need scenery for greenwoods, outside the castle and in a dungeon,' Luke said, ticking them off on his fingers. 'That sounds interesting to do. I'd rather like to paint a dungeon.'

'Yes, and there'll be others too – a very grand room inside the castle, and a few others that could be in front of the curtain. It's a good story, with Robin as Principal Boy and Maid Marian as Principal Girl, and plenty of meaty parts for others – Will Scarlet and his girlfriend Lucy Locket, the evil Sheriff, of course, and Little John and Friar Tuck as a comic pair, and the Sheriff's two men Hangem and Floggem. And the Black Knight, who scares everybody. Oh, and the Dame, of course. You can't have a pantomime without a Dame.'

'And who might she be?' Alf Coker asked. 'I can't call to mind anyone like that in *Robin Hood*.'

'Why, Robin's mother, of course,' Felix said. 'Mother Hood! She's the one who really rules the roost, always nagging the Merry Men for wandering off into the forest and not coming back in time for their dinner – and she's the one who gets into the castle under disguise to rescue Maid Marian from the clutches of her father the Sheriff who wants to marry her to the Black Knight. That's why Robin and his Merry Men have to think of some way to rescue her as well, and when ...'

'Do I take it,' Joyce Warren asked a little frostily, 'that you already have a script for this pantomime?'

'Well,' Felix said, looking a little abashed, 'I did come across one, yes, and I thought it looked rather good. But we don't have to do it. If anyone would rather do *Aladdin* or *Mother Goose* or one of the others, you only have to say.'

'I reckon us oughter do it,' Alf declared. 'It sounds all right and if young Luke Ferris here can do the painting and Dottie can get enough green stuff for the costumes, I reckon I can knock up a few chains and instruments of torture for the dungeon. Might even be able to stretch to a portcullis, too,' he went on with growing enthusiasm. 'And I wouldn't mind having a go at being the Dame. Unless you got someone else in mind,' he added, belatedly remembering that Felix probably intended to be in charge of casting.

'I think we ought to have an evening reading through the script,' Felix said. 'Then anyone who'd like to be in it can come along and give different parts a try. We'll want all sorts, so please don't be shy.' He glanced at the young women – Hilary, Val, Tessa Latimer and Jackie Tozer – who had so far remained silent. 'There are some really nice parts for people like you.'

After a little more discussion and some minor wrangling between Joyce and Alf, who had never got on, it was decided that those who would like to take part would come along on two separate evenings the following week to read the script. The meeting broke up to a buzz of chatter, which sounded all along the village street as the various little groups made their way home, leaving Felix and Stella to close the hall.

'I thought that went very well,' Felix declared, stacking the chairs in one corner. 'There seems to be a lot of enthusiasm.'

'And you meant to do *Robin Hood* all along,' she accused him. 'Didn't you!'

'Well, perhaps. It really is a very good script, and it won't cost us anything to do. I mean, we won't have to pay royalties, as we would if we had to use a professional script.'

'Why not? Don't tell me you wrote it yourself!'

'Not entirely,' he said modestly. 'It was something a friend and I knocked up when we were at theological college. I've tinkered about with it a bit from time to time, but I can't claim to have written it myself. Not all of it, anyway.'

'Is there no end to your talents?' she asked mockingly.

'Probably. It's just that we haven't found it yet.' He pulled her towards him and hugged her. 'Maybe we never will.'

'I'm sure there's a weak spot in your armour somewhere.' She rested her head against his chest. 'Nobody's perfect, not even Felix Copley.'

'And will you be disappointed in me when you find it?' he asked, suddenly serious. 'Will you love me less?'

Stella looked up at him. His eyes were darkened and her heart gave a small shiver. She slipped her arms around his neck and stroked his hair.

'I don't think so,' she said quietly. 'I don't think I could ever love you less.' And then she realised what she had said, and burst out laughing even as Felix himself began to chuckle. 'I didn't mean – oh, Felix, stop it! You know what I meant!'

'I hope I do,' he said, his body shaking against hers. 'Because I know that I could never love you less either, Stella my darling. I'll never stop loving you at all. It's there for ever in my heart, and it will never, ever, change.'

'It's off to a good start, this Drama Club,' Travis observed as he and Hilary walked back to the Barton. 'Quite a lot of enthusiasm, and the curate seems to know what he's doing. Has he been in the village long?'

'Not quite two years. He settled in very quickly – people

61

like him.' Hilary liked him rather a lot herself, but not enough to accept his proposal when he'd made it. She was pleased to see him now genuinely fond of Stella Simmons. They'd make a good couple, she thought, and wondered when they'd announce their engagement.

'Are you planning on joining in?' Travis asked, but Hilary barely heard him, lost as she was in thought. Then, suddenly realising that Travis had spoken, she turned and looked at him. He was only a few inches taller than herself, yet she still had the impression that she was looking up. She straightened her shoulders, lifting her chin to make herself feel taller. It had been irritating to have to sit next to him all evening, pretending a friendliness she didn't feel, and she was still annoyed with her father for suggesting he come to the meeting. 'Sorry – did you say something? I was miles away.'

'I just wondered if you'd any plans to take a part in the pantomime? You'd make a good Principal Boy.'

'Oh no, I'm too old for that. Felix will want someone younger, like Jackie Tozer or Tessa Latimer. Or Val,' she added thoughtfully. 'She'd be good.'

'Val Ferris, who came riding with us? She's not any younger than you, surely?'

'No, but she's got that rather dashing look about her. I can just see her striding about the stage in tall boots, slapping her thighs.' Hilary stopped abruptly, realising that she was being drawn into conversation.

'But you'll go along to the reading, surely. There's bound to be another part for you.'

'Probably,' she answered shortly, and they walked a little further in silence.

'Do you mind if I come too?' Travis enquired, after a moment. 'I enjoyed this evening. And it's a good opportunity to get to know people better.'

Hilary stopped and faced him. The nights were drawing in now and it was almost dark, but she could just see his expression in the light of the rising moon. She felt her chest tighten and her voice sounded tense as she said, 'Why do you want to do that?'

'I told you, I enjoyed—'

'No,' she said sharply. 'I mean, why do you want to get to know people?' Travis did not answer at once and she said, this time with a bleakness in her tone, 'It's decided, isn't it? Dad's offered you the job of estate manager and you're going to take it.'

'Hilary ...'

'You *are*, aren't you? That's why you wanted to come with me tonight. You want to worm your way in – get to know the villagers, make them like you. It's not enough for you to take my job, you want to take my friends as well – the people I grew up with, the people I live amongst. You want to take everything!'

'Hilary,' he said quietly, and reached out to take her arm. 'Wait a minute. Let me—'

'Don't *touch* me!' she hissed, wrenching herself away. 'Don't come near me! It's no use trying to get round me – you may as well save your breath. I knew this afternoon, when you and Dad shut yourselves up in his study – I knew then what you were doing. I thought at least you'd have the courtesy to tell me, one or the other of you. I thought at least you'd be honest about it, and not just come along to the meeting, letting the villagers see us together, pretending to be my friend. But no. You arranged it all between you. Talked about me as if I were a child, decided the best way to "handle me". And I suppose there's nothing I can do about it. Not a thing.'

'You're wrong,' he said, in the same calm tone. 'There is something you can do about it. You can tell your father you don't want me here.'

'And he's going to take a lot of notice of that!' she exclaimed with a bitter laugh. 'I don't think!'

'Probably he won't,' Travis agreed. 'But *I* will. If you really don't want me here, Hilary, then I won't take the job. It'll be no more pleasure to me than it would be to you, having to work together in an atmosphere of hostility. All you have to do is say the word, and I'll leave tomorrow.'

Hilary stared at him. His eyes glimmered in the twilight and his mouth was firm and straight. She could see that he meant what he said, but she still had to ask.

'Would you really? Would you honestly turn down the job of estate manager at Burracombe Barton and go back to Hampshire? You wouldn't even try to persuade me?'

He shook his head. 'No, I won't. I promise. If that's your decision, I'll accept it. I want to enjoy my life, Hilary, not spend it fighting with my employer – because that's what you'd be. It wouldn't be just your father I'd be answering to, it would be you as well. But there is one thing you ought to think about before you decide.'

'And what's that?'

'It won't end here,' he said. 'If I turn the job down, your father will look for someone else. He'll find a new manager somehow – he's made up his mind. It might turn out all right – you might like the new man better, you might think you can work with him as you can't with me. But he may not want to work with *you*, and I doubt if another man would be as willing to walk away as I am. You're not going to get your way over this, I'm afraid.' He paused, then added simply, 'It may turn out to be a question of better the devil you know than the devil you don't.'

Chapter Seven

'So who's the good-looking man, then?' Tessa Latimer asked Jackie Tozer as they walked away from the village hall. After passing the village green, their ways lay in opposite directions and, since they'd never known each other particularly well, Jackie had been surprised when the older girl fell into step beside her. Tessa's question explained it.

'He was Mr Baden's friend in the Army,' she said. 'The Colonel wants him to take over the estate.'

'Really?' Tessa opened her brown eyes wide. She was about the same height as Jackie but well-rounded, with a small waist nipped in by a wide belt. Her beech-brown hair tumbled to her shoulders in a thick mass of waves and her skin was smooth and creamy. Jackie, who had been quite proud of her own slim figure and summer tan, felt ungainly and weather-beaten beside her. 'And what does Hilary think about that?'

'I couldn't say,' Jackie said shortly, unwilling to gossip about her employer. In any case, the Latimers and Napiers were friends. Dr Latimer often came up to the Barton to play chess with the Colonel, and now and then the two families entertained each other to dinner. But of the younger Napiers – Baden, Hilary and Stephen – only Stephen was of similar age to Tessa and her sister Felicity and, apart from the occasional party, there had been less contact between them in the past few years.

'Bet she's not pleased,' Tessa remarked cheerfully. 'She's enjoyed ruling the roost, hasn't she? She likes being in charge.'

'I think she's very good at running the estate,' Jackie said. 'It'll be a shame if she has to give it up. I don't know what she'll do with herself.'

'No, there's not much chance of her getting married, at her age,' Tessa said. 'She must be at least thirty. Well, I hope this Mr Kellaway does take the job. He looks rather interesting. I like older men! What's his Christian name, by the way?'

'Travis,' Jackie said, feeling a wave of annoyance. During the few days that Travis had been at the Barton, she'd found herself looking forward to arriving there each morning, hoping for a glimpse of him as he came down to breakfast or went out into the stableyard to see his dogs. He always smiled at her and often stopped to say hello, but hadn't shown any further interest. Still, you never knew what might happen if he came to live in the village. He didn't seem to be married ...

'And how's Roy these days?' Tessa enquired innocently. 'Any chance of him coming home from – where is it? Korea?'

'Yes, it is. And it doesn't look as if he'll be home for ages.' Jackie's voice was terse. 'He's not my boyfriend, you know, not any more. I just write to him, that's all.'

'Oh, I thought you two were practically engaged. Don't you have a boyfriend at all, then?'

'Not at the moment,' Jackie answered, wishing that Tessa would stop prying. They reached the corner of the church-yard, where Tessa would turn right to go to her own home and Jackie would continue through the village to the Tozers' farm, but instead of saying goodbye Tess paused, obviously wanting to continue the conversation, and Jackie automatically stopped with her.

'I wonder if Travis will join the Drama Club,' Tess mused, her eyes half-closed and lips pursed together. 'He'd be marvellous as the Black Knight, scaring everybody.' She gave an exaggerated shiver. 'I'd rather like to be scared by him!'

'I'll have to go now,' Jackie said abruptly. 'I told Mum I

wouldn't be late. I have to be at the Barton quite early in the morning to help with breakfast.'

'D'you like being a housemaid?' Tessa asked, as if it really interested her. 'I'd have thought you'd want something better than that. Not many girls go into service these days. I mean, you're never going to meet any really interesting men that way, are you?'

'Well, I've met Travis Kellaway,' Jackie retorted, and walked away, seething. She'd never liked Tessa Latimer all that much anyway. Her older sister Felicity was all right, but the doctor's younger daughter thought far too much of herself, drifting around the village like Lady Muck, speaking to you if she felt like it and ignoring you if she didn't, tossing you her coat without even a glance when she came to visit the Barton, treating you as if you were a piece of furniture. And she was man-mad. Jackie had seen it for herself, at the Barton when Stephen Napier was home, at the church whenever a new face appeared, and now at the Drama Club when her eyes had widened at her first sight of Travis Kellaway. It was a good job she'd been away at Art College when Luke Ferris had first come to the village, or Val wouldn't have stood a chance.

Or perhaps she would, Jackie thought as she passed the churchyard and came level with the Bell Inn. For quite a while, he'd seemed more interested in Stella Simmons, but that had fizzled out and now he was Jackie's brother-in-law. Even Tessa Latimer would leave a married man alone.

Her brother Tom came out of the inn as she passed. He grinned at her and they walked on together.

'You look a bit fed up, sis. Don't you like the idea of the pantomime?'

'Oh, I like the idea of that all right.' She shrugged away her annoyance. 'It's just some of the people who might be in it. That Tessa Latimer thinks she's the village's answer to Judy Garland. I bet she'll be after the part of Robin Hood.'

'Well, she's got the figure for it,' Tom said. 'What's the

matter, did you want it? I should think you've got just as much chance. You're not bad-looking.'

'Thanks a lot. How about you? Are you going to this read-through or audition or whatever it is?'

'Might as well. I think it's going to be fun. That's all it's meant to be, you know, Jack. We're not going on the London stage. It doesn't really matter who gets which part.'

'I suppose not. It was just the way she went on. It's a pity Felicity's not here to keep her in order.'

'I'm not sure anyone can keep Tessa Latimer in order!' Tom said with a grin. 'She's always been a bit of a rebel.' They turned to go up the track leading to the farm. 'Vic was asking about you, by the way,' he added casually. 'Says you've grown up a lot while he was away.'

'Well, since he was away for two years that's not really surprising,' Jackie said a little tartly. 'What did he want to know?'

'Oh, nothing really. He was wondering about Roy, I think. Asking if you and he were engaged or anything.'

'Oh, he was, was he? And what did you tell him?' Jackie enquired, trying not to sound too interested. Vic Nethercott was two or three years her senior and had been away in the Army for all of his National Service. She'd noticed him at the meeting and thought what a well-set-up young man he'd become. If National Service had done that for him, it might be doing the same for Roy Pettifer, but it would still be quite a long time before Roy came home, and although she wrote to him regularly she didn't think she was in love with him any more. It was time she had a new boyfriend.

'Oh, I told him you were utterly faithful and stayed at home every night writing long letters and knitting socks.' Tom grinned at her indignant expression. 'Well, what did you want me to say? That you went to Plymouth drinking and dancing every night?'

'It might have made me sound a bit more interesting,' she

retorted. 'Honestly, Tom, you are an idiot. You know I only write to Roy as a friend. It would have been better if you hadn't said anything at all.'

'I could hardly do that. He *asked* me. I couldn't pretend I didn't know you.' He looked at her sideways. 'Why? You're not interested in him, are you?'

'No! Well, I might be ... I don't know, do I? I haven't seen him for two years and I didn't really know him all that well before that. I don't want you putting him off me, that's all.'

'So if he asks again, I can tell him you're interested?'

'*No!*' she exclaimed. 'Don't tell him anything at all. You'll just make it worse.'

They arrived at the farm gate and walked through the yard where Joanna was shutting up the chickens for the night. Tom went over to his wife and kissed her cheek and Jackie went indoors where her mother, father and grandmother were listening to the wireless.

'You missed a good programme,' Alice told her. 'It was Wilfred Pickles in *Have A Go*. He had this old lady on, eighty-nine she was and sharp as a needle, knew the answers to all the questions. Everyone clapped when she told him her age.'

'Did he ask her if she was courting?' Jackie asked, and they laughed. Wilfred Pickles was well-known for asking all his guests that. His programme had been popular for years, touring the country and going to factories, hospitals, village halls – anywhere where ordinary people could gather and come on stage to tell him little things about their lives, answer a few general knowledge questions and win some money. They never won much – a few shillings, perhaps even a pound or two – but the excitement of meeting this famous man was a prize in itself. Quite a few people in Burracombe had grumbled at having to miss their favourite radio programme to go to the Drama Club meeting.

'He didn't have to ask,' Ted said. 'She told him she was walking out with the boy next door – he's ninety-two! You should have heard the audience laugh. Wilfred Pickles said "What's on the table, Mabel?" and wanted to give her all the money there and then, but she wasn't having it, said she'd come up to win it fair and square answering questions, and so she did.'

'You ought to go on that, if he ever comes down this way, Gran,' Jackie told her grandmother. 'You'd be good at it.'

'Maybe us ought to get the vicar to write and ask him to come,' Alice said, folding up her needlework. 'Put the kettle on, Jackie, and I'll make some cocoa.'

Tom and Joanna came in just as she was pouring hot water and milk into the big jug. Joanna lowered her bulky figure into an armchair and brushed back her hair with her wrist.

'I shall be glad when this is over. I seem to be bigger every day. I don't remember being this huge with Robin.'

'You were even bigger,' Tom disagreed. 'I had to sleep on the floor for the last three weeks.'

'You're going to have to again,' Joanna told him. 'I could hardly turn over last night. Not that I can turn over anyway,' she added gloomily. 'I'm like a beached whale. Once I'm lying down, I need a crane to get me up again.'

'It'll soon be over,' Minnie said comfortingly. 'And you know it'll all be worthwhile when the little dear's here.'

'It's here now,' Tom said, patting his wife's stomach. 'It's just not in the right place, is it, love?'

'It's in the right place for now,' Alice said, passing round the cocoa. 'Does anyone want one of these flapjacks Mother made this afternoon? 'Tis all goodness in them.'

Jackie sat in the corner, sipping her cocoa and nibbling at one of her grandmother's flapjacks. She thought about what had happened this evening – Tessa Latimer's obvious interest in Travis Kellaway, her questions about Roy and Tom's remarks about Vic Nethercott. I'm fed up with staying at home all the time, she thought. I don't know why I'm doing it. I'm not engaged to Roy – we haven't even got an understanding any more, not since that awful time when I thought I might have fallen for a baby. If I go on like this, I'll be like Hilary Napier, an old spinster of thirty with no chance of ever getting married or doing anything interesting with my life.

Maybe she should look for a different sort of job. She'd worked for the Napiers since leaving school at fifteen, and Hilary had told her several times that she ought to think about branching out. 'You're too bright to be working as a house-maid,' she'd said more than once. 'You could do something like hotel reception. I'd be happy to give you a good reference.'

Jackie felt tempted to take the advice she'd been given. Perhaps she could get a job at the Bedford Hotel, in Tavistock. Or even somewhere in Plymouth. She might have to live in, but that could be exciting, if her parents would agree. She felt itchy and restless, fed up with being treated as a child yet a bit scared of stepping out on her own.

Perhaps the Drama Club would help, she thought. There was Travis Kellaway, who smiled at her every day and asked how she was, and seemed interested in her replies. And if Tessa Latimer did get her hooks into him, there was Vic Nethercott. Even if she did decide to get another job, it would probably take a little while to find one. She might as well see if Burracombe did have anything to offer, while she was look-ing.

She finished her cocoa, brushed a few oat crumbs from her lap and wished the rest of the family goodnight.

Val and Luke were also drinking cocoa. They were curled up together on Luke's battered old settee in the charcoal-burner's cottage where they had lived since their wedding. The fire was lit and the tiny shack was cosy, but cold draughts were beginning to find their way through the gaps in the walls and Val had fetched a blanket from the bed to wrap around their shoulders.

'It's been fun living here,' she said, 'but I'll be quite glad to move into Jennifer's cottage. I should think we could go in next month, wouldn't you? The roof will be finished and the plumbing's almost done. It'll be getting really chilly at night soon and I'd like a bit more home comfort.'

'Maybe we ought to have waited ...' Luke began, but she broke in swiftly.

'No, I didn't mean that. You know I wanted to get married as much as you did. And I have enjoyed being here – it'll be something I'll remember all my life, living in a little log cabin in the woods. But we do need more room, apart from anything else. And running water would be nice!'

'It'll be a luxury for me,' Luke said. 'I've had over two years here now. I shall probably find it quite strange, being able to turn a tap on rather than go out to the stream with a bucket.'

'You'll get used to it before the first week's out.' She snuggled into his arms. 'This pantomime's going to be fun, isn't it? Are you sure you don't want a part?'

'Absolutely. I'll have enough to do, painting the scenery. And helping to shift it, during the performances. What sort of acting talent is there in the village, do you know?'

'No idea,' she said with a grin. 'All I remember doing is the nativity plays at school! I do vaguely remember the pantomimes they used to put on before the war, but they weren't very professional.'

'They're not meant to be,' Luke said. 'They're just meant to be village entertainments. Nobody minds if things go wrong – they expect it. It's all part of the fun.'

'Oh, I don't think we'll be allowed to make mistakes,' Val laughed. 'Not with Mrs Warren in charge. And I know Felix thinks *he's* going to be in charge, but he hasn't been in the village long enough to realise what she's like. The rest of us have!'

'So long as she doesn't interfere with my scenery, she can do as she likes.' He kissed her hair. 'Let's talk about the cottage.

Once we're there, we'll be able to think seriously about the future.'

'How do you mean?' Val asked, twisting her neck to look into his face. 'What future?'

'Our future, of course! The Ferris family's future.'

Val got up suddenly, the blanket falling away from her shoulders.

'It's time we thought about going to bed. I need to be up early in the morning to catch the bus to Tavistock. Did I tell you I'd changed to the morning shift at the hospital?'

'Yes, you did.' He watched her, a small frown gathering between his brows. 'Is anything the matter, Val?'

'No, of course not. What could be the matter?'

'I don't know,' he said. 'You just seem different, all of a sudden. Have I said something wrong?'

'No!' Her voice was sharp and she softened it quickly. 'No, you haven't said anything wrong, how could you? I'm just tired, that's all. It's been a long day, what with the meeting and everything, and thinking of all the things we have to do before we can move.' She turned and smiled down at him, holding out her hand. 'Come to bed, sweetheart. I just want you to hold me for a while.'

Luke took her hand and stood up. He drew her into his arms, still looking down into her face. Val met his eyes for a moment and then turned her head away.

'You would tell me if there was anything wrong, wouldn't you, darling?' he asked gently.

'Yes,' she murmured. 'Of course I would. There's nothing, Luke, honestly – I'm just tired. That's all.'

She moved out of his arms and stepped towards the tiny inner room where they had squeezed their double bed. Luke let her go, but his hand stayed on her arm until she slipped out of his reach. She smiled at him as she went through the door, but for a moment or two he stayed where he was, the troubled frown still creasing his forehead.

It wasn't the first time Val had refused to tell him when something was upsetting her. But the last time had been almost two years ago, before they had finally faced the truth of what had happened between them in Egypt during the war. A chill touched his heart, as he wondered if the ghosts of their past had returned once again to haunt them.

Chapter Eight

'I really didn't come here to take your job away,' Travis Kellaway said.

He and Hilary were sitting on the rocky tor above Burracombe, gazing across the wooded valley towards the burnished glow of the setting sun. They had walked up here after supper, each feeling the need to escape from the house – or was it from Gilbert Napier's restless gaze, and the sensation that he was waiting for something? A decision, Hilary thought, but whether it was his own or Travis's, she couldn't be sure. Not hers, she was certain.

She glanced at Travis but said nothing. Since his arrival, she had shown him around almost all of the estate; introduced him to the tenant farmers, walked and ridden with him on the moor. Her feelings towards him were still very mixed; the initial hostility, which had begun with her father's first announcement of the invitation he'd extended, had been severely jolted at their first meeting, when he'd looked at her with those very dark, intent blue eyes and had shaken her hand so firmly. Not since her fiancé Henry's death in the war had any man's look given her quite that strange twist inside, and she'd been conscious of an immediate warmth conflicting with the resentment that she had felt when she'd first heard he was coming.

That inner conflict had continued through the past few days. She still resented his presence and still felt angry towards her father for what he was trying to do, yet she couldn't help liking this man with his direct gaze and straightforward manner.

He seemed both practical and intelligent and, as they'd slowly relaxed in each other's company and talked of matters other than farming and gamekeeping, she'd discovered in him thoughts and interests that chimed with her own. It disturbed her: she didn't *want* to like him. It would have been much easier, she thought regretfully, if she could have disliked him on sight.

'I mean it,' Travis said. 'When your father invited me here, I had no idea of the situation. I expected to find you struggling to keep things together. An old, sick man and a daughter completely out of her depth.'

Hilary felt a fresh wave of anger. 'Is that what my father told you?'

Travis looked thoughtful. 'Not in so many words, no. It was just the impression I got.' He saw her face. 'Don't be angry with him – probably he didn't mean it to sound that way at all. Just me getting hold of the wrong end of the stick.'

'I don't think so,' Hilary said a trifle grimly. 'That sounds like Father all over. He's got this bee in his bonnet about me getting married and having a family. He's terrified that the family will die out and the estate be split up.'

'But surely Stephen would be the one to carry that on,' Travis said. 'He has the family name, too. And he's younger than you – there's plenty of time.'

'I know, I know. But Stephen doesn't really want it. He's too interested in what he's doing in the RAF. He loves flying. The last time he was here, he was talking about starting up a civil flying business when he comes out. He's talked about emigrating too – to Canada, probably.'

Travis stared at her. 'You mean he's not interested in the estate at all?'

'Not at all. He never thought he'd need to be, you see. It was always going to be Baden's.'

Travis looked at her for a little longer, then turned his eyes away, letting his gaze rove over the surrounding countryside;

the rolling moors, purple now with heather, the deep, wooded combes, the blue glimmer of the reservoir. He shook his head slightly and Hilary knew that he was having difficulty in imagining how anyone born to all this could possibly turn his back on it.

'We can't all be the same,' she said. 'You have to think what it was like for Steve, growing up in Baden's shadow. Baden was so much the son Father needed, and Stephen was so different that nobody ever thought of him even wanting to take over. The future seemed to be all mapped out – until the war came along.'

'The war changed a lot of lives,' Travis observed, and Hilary nodded. He gave her a quick look and said, 'I'm sorry – you lost your fiancé, didn't you? I didn't mean to bring back your own sad memories.'

Hilary shrugged. 'It's a long time ago now.'

'And there's never been anyone else?' he enquired, adding hastily, 'Sorry again – don't answer that if you don't want to. I don't want to pry.'

'It's all right,' she said, surprised to find that she didn't mind his question. 'No, there's been nobody else. Just friends, that's all, although one or two might have been more serious.' She thought of Felix, who had asked her to marry him yet seemed not too cast down when she'd refused. 'I think perhaps I'm one of those women who are doomed to spinsterhood,' she added with a laugh.

'I'm sure that's not true,' he said at once. 'But maybe your father's right. You're not likely to meet anyone buried down here in Devon.'

There was a short silence. Then Hilary said quietly, 'We seem to have come back to the same subject. And by the way, I didn't mean it when I said "doomed". As a matter of fact, I'm rather happy with things as they are – except for Father being ill, of course.'

Travis nodded, but didn't answer for a moment or two. At

77

last he said, 'It's not just one subject, though, is it? There are at least two parts to this discussion. There's the question of what you really want to do with your own life, and there's the question of the estate. They're not necessarily tied together, you know.'

'Aren't they?' Hilary felt her hackles begin to rise. 'What do you mean by that?'

'Well, if you don't want marriage, what do you want? You're not the sort of woman who'll be happy just to stay at home with Daddy and do as he tells you – coming in by ten o'clock, wiping your lipstick off before he sees it, all that sort of thing.'

'That's ridiculous! I'm thirty years old – we went through that stage when I was fifteen. Just because I still live at home doesn't mean I'm living under his thumb. And as for asking me what I want, I've already got my career – the estate. Isn't that what we're talking about?'

'And is it what you really want?' he asked quietly.

Hilary opened her mouth to retort, then paused. She thought of the weeks just before her father's heart-attack – how she'd planned to go to London, to share a flat with a friend and apply for a job as an air hostess. She'd been dismayed when she'd first realised that plan would have to be given up, yet how often had she thought of it since? Had she really wanted a career, or had she really just wanted to leave home?

'Yes, I think it is,' she answered at last. 'I love the estate and I love Burracombe. It's my place – and I want to help look after it. And I enjoy doing it. I'm good at it.' She met his eyes. 'It's a good thing you don't want to take my job away, because I don't intend to let you, or anyone else, do that.'

He nodded. 'That's what I thought.' There was a short silence, then he reached out his hand and laid it on hers, so that her fingers were sandwiched between his palm and the granite of the tor. The sun-warmed rock and the equal warmth of his hand formed a cocoon, and she looked down uncertainly. 'But your father does seem to think you need help.'

'I don't see why,' she said shortly. 'He did it on his own, after all.'

'And look what it did to him,' Travis said.

Hilary snatched her hand away. 'That's exactly what he says! But I'm not a man in his fifties who's been through a war as a soldier, and eaten too much good food and drunk too much fine brandy! I'm young and strong – I'm not going to have a heart-attack.'

'No, but you're not giving yourself time to do other things. You hardly ever go out or meet other people. You don't have any spare-time interests – you don't have any spare time, full stop.'

'Well, that's going to change. There's the new Drama Club. I'll meet people there.'

'But they're people you already know.'

'And what's wrong with that? They're the sort of people I *want* to know. They're my friends.' She sighed. 'You're talking exactly like Father, you know. He wants me to meet the "right sort" of people – people with estates and money. He thinks I'll find a suitable husband that way.'

'Maybe he's right.'

'Look,' she said, 'it may seem to you men that a woman isn't complete without a husband, but there are quite a few women who feel very complete, thank you very much. We want to make our own lives. We don't want to be kept by a man. We don't want to have to promise to *obey*, as if a man is always right. We don't want to hand ourselves over, body and soul, to someone who might not turn out to be worth it. And having money and an estate doesn't automatically make a man worthwhile. Quite the opposite, in some cases – and I have met quite a few, despite being *buried down here in Devon*.'

Travis laughed. 'All right, I'm sorry I said that! And naturally I agree with you. I don't think being born with a silver spoon in your mouth automatically makes a man a worthwhile

79

person, either. I think you have to earn respect, whatever walk of life you're in. But then I would, wouldn't I?'

Hilary looked at him again. His navy-blue eyes were steady but there was a glint of humour lurking deep inside. She smiled, a little unwillingly, and said, 'You seem to have earned respect – my father's respect, anyway.'

'He's biased,' Travis said lightly. 'What I'm more interested in, just now, is earning *your* respect.'

'Why should that be important to you?' Hilary asked after a moment.

Travis didn't answer at once. Then, with a little sigh, he said, 'Because I think, like it or not, we're going to be working together.'

Hilary stared at him. Her heart thumped painfully and she felt a wave of anger, disappointment and hurt sweep over her. There was a big, aching lump in her throat and she tried to swallow it, blinked and tried again. Even so, her voice was husky as she said, 'So you've decided to take the job after all. Despite what you said to me the other night.'

'Not quite.' His eyes were intent and she met them briefly, then looked away, not wanting him to see the glint of tears in her own. 'I wanted to talk to you first. It didn't seem either right or sensible to go over your head. But I do think you need to remember what else I said: if it isn't me, it'll be someone else.'

'So much for being trusted,' she said bitterly. 'He obviously thinks I'm totally incapable.'

'I'm sorry, Hilary,' Travis said, and she thought he did sound genuinely regretful, 'but that's the way his generation thinks, and I don't think he's going to change now. However good you are at running the estate, he sees it as a temporary measure – nothing more.'

'And if it were Stephen, who doesn't want to do it and would be hopeless at it, he'd be perfectly satisfied.'

'Well, maybe not *perfectly* satisfied,' Travis said, the glint of humour revealing itself again. 'Not if you're right and Stephen would be hopeless at it.'

Hilary laughed a little. 'But he'd find a way round that. Nag Steve into "pulling his socks up", as Dad would put it, or employ a manager to do the real work. Which is just what he's doing now,' she added, 'only Stephen would need it and I don't!'

'No,' he said, surprising her, 'you don't. Unless you want other things in your life. Suppose you do meet someone you want to marry. Suppose you find that's more important to you than the estate. It does happen. If you've had sole charge, devoted yourself to it, you'll never be able to walk out on it.'

'Of course I wouldn't walk out on it!' she exclaimed indignantly.

'You might find it even more difficult to hand over to someone else then. And who else would there be?' He leaned forward. 'Wouldn't it be better to have someone already in place – someone who understands the property, who knows the tenants and the way it all works? Someone your father trusted?'

Hilary stared at him. Then she got to her feet. She was trembling all over, her skin prickling with rage. It was a moment or two before she could trust her voice to speak.

'You're trying to manipulate me,' she said. 'What sort of a fool do you take me for? Did you think I wouldn't see straight through your scheming? You and Dad – you're as bad as each other. Only he goes at things like a bull at a gate, and you slither at them sideways, like a snake. Well, I can tell you which I prefer, any day, and it's not the snake!'

She wheeled away from him and set off down the grassy, boulder-strewn slope. Her eyes were filled with tears – tears of anger, of bitterness and of disappointment. I'd begun to like him, she thought, dashing the wetness from her eyes with the back of her wrist. I'd begun to *trust* him. And I thought he liked me, too.

Whatever he says, the truth is that he's after my job. He'll take it away, and I'll be left with nothing.

The school term started with its usual clamour of children arriving in the playground and settling back, like a litter of puppies, into their accustomed places and routine. After six weeks' holiday, it always took them a little while to claim their favourite spots, especially as the older children had now left to go to 'big' school in Tavistock and younger ones (the 'babies') arrived for their first day. Miss Kemp, experienced in these matters, advised Stella that it was a good idea to get the children organised as quickly as possible, to prevent any disputes.

'The babies need to come into their classroom as soon as they arrive. I'll look after the older ones in your class, as well as mine, and we'll do some drill in the playground first, to use up some of their energy and excitement.'

'I don't remember ever being excited about my first day back at school!' Stella said. 'But then I didn't come to school in Burracombe.' She thought briefly of her disrupted school-days – first at the primary school in Portsmouth, which was one of the first buildings in the city to be bombed, then the country school at Bridge End where the evacuees had to share classrooms with the village children, turn and turn about, and finally at the Children's Home where she had been taken after the death of her father. Really, it was a wonder she had decided to spend the rest of her life in schools – but perhaps she was still trying to cover the painful memory of those early years with more pleasant experiences. She certainly wanted to make school a happy time for these children, especially the 'babies' who were arriving now, clinging tightly to their mothers' hands and staring about them, wide-eyed, at the confident throng charging about the playground and shouting at the tops of their voices.

Miss Kemp stood on the small platform by the school door

and rang the bell loudly. After a few minutes, the sound penetrated the children's consciousness and they slowly stopped their mad rushing about and stood in uncertain, ragged little groups, looking at their head teacher. She clapped her hands for attention and said in a loud, clear voice: 'Now, I want you all to behave like big, sensible children and help each other. There are lots of little ones here today who are only just starting school and don't know what to do. I want all of those little ones to come into their classroom first. If you big children know who they are, I want you to bring them in and show them Miss Simmons's room, and then come outside again, quietly and sensibly, and make your lines in the playground like you used to before the holidays. I'm sure you all remember how you did that, don't you? Let's start now with all those who know one of the new children. The rest of you, stand still.'

As nearly all the children knew at least one of the 'babies', this instruction didn't work quite as well as it should have done. There was an instant rush of older children towards the nearest newcomer and it looked as if a battle might ensue over the privilege of escorting them to their classroom. Miss Kemp clapped her hands again.

'Children, please! Use a little bit of common sense. Just one person for each new child. And there's no need to argue over who it should be. I'm asking you to help, not start a fight. That's better. Thank you.' She watched as older brothers, sisters or cousins led the smallest children into the schoolroom – everyone seemed to be related in some way. Stella, who was already at the door, counted in her new charges and then shut the door, sat behind her desk and smiled at them.

Her heart twisted a little at the sight of their faces. Scrubbed clean, many of them with new clothes – the boys in grey flannel shorts and shirts, the girls in cotton frocks and cardigans – they looked little more than toddlers. Suddenly, the older children seemed enormous and she had a brief insight into what it must be like for these little ones, thrust so suddenly into a new world. Even though most of them knew the school well, passed it almost every day as they went through the village with their mothers, and many had older brothers or sisters there, they had never actually been inside unless to come to the nativity plays that Miss Kemp had started each Christmas, and then it had been as guests. From now on, they would be coming every weekday, until they were eleven years old – an almost unimaginable length of time for children who were only just five.

'Hello, everyone,' she said in her friendliest voice. 'It's nice to have you here with us at school. I expect you've been looking forward to it, haven't you?' The children gazed woodenly back at her and one little girl whispered, 'Yes, miss.' Stella gave her an extra smile and went on, 'We've certainly been looking forward to having you here. Now, I want you to choose a seat from those over there,' she pointed at a cluster of small desks, each with its own bench, near the front of the room, 'and that will be your seat, where you'll go whenever you come to school.' George and Edward Crocker, whose likeness made them instantly recognisable, marched over and commandeered the two desks at the front. Stella glanced doubtfully at them but decided not to say anything at this point. In any case, from what she'd already heard of the Crocker twins, it would be best to have them as close under her eye as possible. No doubt later on, when they grew a bit sharper, they'd be vying to sit at the back where they could plot mischief unseen by the teacher.

There were three other new children: Shirley Culliford's brother Billy, whose clothes were far from new but were at least reasonably clean, Linda Passmore, a delicate-looking child with wispy fair hair and very light blue eyes, and Elaine Batten, whose soldier father had been killed in Korea and who now lived with her mother and grandmother in a cottage near the outskirts of the village.

'Now, you all know why you're here, don't you?' she began. The children stared back wordlessly, and she added, 'You

84

are allowed to answer me, you know.' Probably it had been impressed upon them all that they weren't to talk in school. 'Billy, you've got lots of brothers and sisters who have been at school, I'm sure you know why you're here.'

'It's to get me out from under me mum's feet,' he said in a surprisingly hoarse voice. 'Her's got enough to be doing with, now her's in the family way again.'

'Please, miss,' Linda Passmore said, 'what's it mean, in the family way? Only I heard my Auntie Joan tell my mum that my cousin Susan's in the family way, and she was ever so cross about it.'

'Well, perhaps we'll talk about that later,' Stella said hastily. 'Or you could ask your mother what she thinks your Auntie Joan meant.'

'It means having babies,' George Crocker said scornfully. 'Like a cow does after she bin serviced by the old bull. Everybody knows that.'

'Well, *I* didn't,' Linda said, turning on him with unexpected ferocity, her pale features flushing with annoyance. 'And I don't reckon as you do neither, George Crocker. Or Edward,' she finished a little uncertainly, dashing Stella's sudden hope that there was, after all, a way to tell the two apart.

'Nobody's told me yet why you've all started to come to school,' she said firmly. 'Elaine, can you tell me?' Don't say something even more embarrassing, she prayed, but Elaine flicked back one of her dark brown plaits, looked at her with serious brown eyes and said, 'It's to learn things, miss, so that us can go to the big school when us is old enough.'

'That's right, Elaine,' Stella said thankfully. 'And you all know that you're going to come here every day, don't you—'

'Not Saturdays and Sundays,' one of the Crockers said belligerently. 'Us don't have to come to school them days, and you can't make us.'

'I've no intention of making you come then, George,' Stella said, reflecting that she was going to be only too pleased not to have to come on those days herself if this was how the new 'babies' were going to behave. 'But all the other days – unless we have a holiday, of course,' she added, forestalling his next objection. 'And you'll come just before nine o'clock each morning and have lessons until playtime, and then you can either go home for your dinner or have it here.'

'My auntie cooks the dinners here,' Linda said. For such a wispy-looking child, she seemed to have a remarkably strong character. 'Her's going to make sure I gets extra potatoes.'

'That ain't fair!' the other Crocker said immediately. He appealed to Stella. 'It ain't fair, is it, miss? Us all ought to get the same.'

'I'm sure you'll all get enough potatoes, Edward,' Stella said. 'Now—'

'Well, I won't, because we'm not stopping to school dinner, we'm going home,' he said, adding, 'And I'm George, not Edward.'

Stella stared at him. 'But when I called your brother George, he didn't say he was Edward.'

'Why should he?' the little boy asked, and Stella sighed. They were definitely going to have to find a way of telling these two apart.

'After dinner,' she said, determined to keep on track, 'you'll all come in here again for some more lessons. There'll be another playtime during the afternoon and then you can all go home to tea.'

'After some more lessons,' Edward Crocker said, to make everything clear.

'After some more lessons,' Stella agreed. Outside, she could hear Miss Kemp taking the other children through their drill. *'Arms stretched high above your heads. Higher – higher – and let them drop. Now all touch your toes . . .'* She glanced down at the register on her desk. 'Now, I'm just going to call the register, to make sure you're all here.'

86

'But you can see we'm all here,' George Crocker said, adding belatedly, 'miss.'

'I know, but when all the other children are in the room as well, I won't be able to see quite so easily, will I? Anyway, we'll do it now just for practice. I say your name, and you say Present. Elaine Batten?'

'Present,' the dark-haired girl said a little uncertainly.

'That's right, Elaine. Well done. Edward Crocker?' She watched to see which one replied. Not that it would make any difference; they only had to change places while she wasn't looking and she would be bemused again. 'George Crocker? Billy Culliford?'

'Present,' he said obediently. 'What's it going to be, miss? Can we choose or do it have to be a surprise? Only, I want a football like Micky Coker's got.'

Stella lifted her head and stared at him. 'Whatever are you talking about, Billy?'

'The present, miss. If we'm here, we gets a present and I wants to know ...' His voice faltered to a stop. 'Don't we, miss?'

'I'm afraid not, Billy,' she said gently, hating to see the disappointment in his eyes. '"Present" means you're here. It's just what you say when I call out your name. I'm sorry.'

'Oh,' he said, and subsided in his seat, the sudden excitement dying from his face. Stella looked at him for a moment and then bent her head to the register again. Unexpected tears stung her eyes. There had been something in Billy's expression, something lost and woebegone, that had reminded her for a brief moment of her sister Maddy – Muriel, as she had been then – when she'd lost her dolly, Princess Marcia, in the Blitz over Portsmouth. They'd lost everything when their home had been bombed that night, but it had been Princess Marcia who was the most irreplaceable. 'Linda Passmore?' she continued, pushing away the memory.

'Present, miss.'

'Thank you, children,' Stella said. 'Now, before the others come in, I'll give you something to do.' She went to a cupboard and took out a tin of beads and some thin twine. 'You can all make a necklace with these beads. You can either keep it for yourselves or take it home as a present for your mothers. Choose the colours you want to use, and try to do it quietly.' She gave each child a length of twine and put a little heap of beads on each desk. 'I'm going to call the register for the other children and then we'll start lessons.' She paused, looking down at Billy Culliford's expression. 'What is it, Billy?'

'We *are* getting a present,' he said, his face suddenly radiant. 'A present for me mum. That's better than any old football, miss.'

'Yes,' Stella said, feeling a lump in her throat. There was something very endearing about these Culliford children – none too clean, often dressed in little more than rags, from the poorest cottage in the village, yet so easily pleased. She felt glad that Billy had his present after all.

'How did it go, then, maid?' Dottie Friend asked, bringing a tray of freshly baked scones out of the oven. She set the tray on the kitchen table and slid the scones on to a plate with a knife. 'There you are, the cream's in that crock and there's a pot of my strawberry jam to go with it. I thought you deserved a little treat, first day back at school.'

'Dottie, you're a miracle-worker,' Stella said, sinking into the sagging armchair and laying her head against the back. Alfred leaped on to her lap and she stroked his thick fur. 'I'm exhausted! I ought to be used to it by now, but the first day of term always seems to come as a shock. Especially the autumn term, with the new children coming in.'

'Well, you've all got to get used to each other,' Dottie said comfortably, pouring tea into flower-painted cups. ''Tis strange for you all, and 'tis up to you to make them feel happy at school, as well as look after the bigger ones. I don't know how you do it, and that's the truth.'

Stella laughed. 'It's not really that hard. Look at the schools they have in towns, with forty-five or fifty children in each class. At least I only have twenty-two.'

'Yes, but in a town school they'd be all the same age,' Dottie pointed out. 'You've got three years in your class. You've got to do three different lessons at once.'

'A lot of them can be done all together. I can read a story to them all, or set the older children to do some work while I teach the little ones. It seems to work well enough.' Stella split one of the warm scones and spread jewel-bright strawberry jam on the flaky surface. She added a spoonful of thick yellow clotted cream. 'Dottie, this is lovely. To think they don't know what real cream is, up-country!'

'That's what they come on holiday for – proper Devonshire clotted cream. And the moors and the beaches, too. Us is a blessed county down here, for all that they Londoners might think we got no brains. It's they that haven't got brains, living in all that dirt and noise. I know – I had enough of it when I was with Miss Forsyth.'

'Didn't you enjoy living in London at all?' Stella enquired. 'I'd have thought it was really exciting, meeting all those famous people.'

Dottie wrinkled her nose. 'Well, I suppose it were, and I were a lot younger then so it seemed exciting enough to me. But famous people are just like anyone else when it comes down to it, you know. Some of them are as nice as pie, and some I wouldn't cross the road to say hello to. I was lucky with Miss Forsyth – she were one of the nicest ladies I ever met. Still is. But then, if I hadn't liked her to start with, I'd never have gone to London in the first place.'

'And then Maddy would never have come to live with you and I might never have found her again,' Stella said thoughtfully, starting on the second half of her scone. 'Life is very strange sometimes, isn't it, Dottie?'

'There are more things on heaven and earth than ... botheration, I've forgotten the rest of it,' Dottie said. 'Anyway, the main thing is she did come to live with me, and so did you, and if that don't prove that God works in mysterious ways, I don't know what do. Are you ready for another cup of tea?'

After tea, Stella went up to her room to prepare for the next day's lessons. She sat for a while at her window, thinking over the day. The older children had all settled down well, and the new ones seemed to understand the idea of school. (She had heard of children going home at lunchtime on their first day, thinking that was all there was.) Most of them knew older children already there, and brothers, sisters and cousins sought out their young relatives at playtime and took them under their wings. That would only last a day or two, she knew, before they got bored and went off to play with their own friends, but by then the 'babies' would have found their feet. The Crocker twins, especially, would be charging round the playground yelling at the tops of their voices and barging into other children's games before the next day was half over.

'I do wish there was a way to tell those two apart,' she had remarked to Miss Kemp as they had a cup of tea after supervising school dinner. 'I can't see any difference at all. And it's no use telling them to wear different coloured shirts or socks – they'd only change over the minute our backs were turned. You can see they enjoy muddling people up.'

'It needs to be something permanent,' Miss Kemp agreed. 'A different haircut – or a tattoo! But I can't see their mother agreeing to that.'

'Even the other children can't tell the difference,' Stella said. 'I've caught myself wondering if it actually matters; it would be so much easier in many ways to treat them as just one child! But that would be wrong. They're different people, even if they do look the same.' She smiled. 'Did you hear young Billy Culliford when his mother came to collect him? He told her he was sorry for them because they only had one face!'

'I don't think anyone need feel sorry for the Crocker twins,' Miss Kemp said, a trifle grimly. 'They'll make the best possible use of only having one face. I suppose we could try dipping George's finger in red ink and Edward's in blue,' she added thoughtfully. 'But I expect their mother would object to that, too. I think we're just going to have to hope they don't take too much advantage of it.'

A faint hope, Stella thought as she sat gazing out of her bedroom window. There was a look on the twins' faces – or face! – that told her that the head teacher was right, and they would take every opportunity to confuse. Sturdy, confident children of just six years old, they were almost a year older than Billy Culliford and several months older than Linda and Elaine. In some ways, they would be ahead of their classmates, but in others – reading and writing in particular – their extra year would make no difference, since no attempt had been made at home to teach them these skills. They would almost certainly feel this as a humiliation and try to redress the balance in some other way, and Stella had an uncomfortable feeling that they could all too easily become bullies. I'll have to watch them, she thought. And give them some encouragement too. It's not their fault they were born on 2 September and had to wait such a long time to start school.

Chapter Nine

By the time the day came for Travis to leave, Hilary was in turmoil. She had lain awake most of the previous night, turning over the various options in her mind. Not that I *have* any option, she thought bitterly. Travis is right – Father's determined to bring in a manager, and the next one might be a lot worse. He'd have to advertise and we'd have to go through all the misery of interviewing and making a decision, and a lot of choice I'd have in that! He's made up his mind that I'm no more than a stopgap. No matter what I've done over the past year, no matter what I've achieved, he never for one moment thought I was really capable of doing it for life. And whenever I've tried to convince him that it's what I want, he's simply brushed me aside and told me it's not the right life for a woman. I ought to be *married*.

'Father, it's not the only way to live!' she'd exclaimed one day, driven beyond endurance. 'Plenty of women don't get married and still manage to live fulfilling lives. Look at Florence Nightingale! Look at Elizabeth the First!'

'I don't want to look at them,' he'd retorted. 'I'm looking at my daughter. Who seems to be the only one of my children likely to give me grandchildren who will take an interest in their heritage.'

'That's ridiculous! Stephen's still in his early twenties. He's got plenty of time, and his children would carry the name.'

'So could yours, if you combined it with your husband's. And hasn't Stephen still got this idea in his head about emigrating, once he comes out of the RAF? I'm not asking you to leave home, Hilary. You could marry someone who'd be willing to make his home here. It's not out of the question.'

'Oh, for heaven's sake, Father! You can't just assume that I'll find a man who'll fit all *your* requirements. I might have a few of my own.'

'Which I should think would include making Burracombe your home, since you're so keen to run the place.'

Hilary sighed. 'And *he* might have a few of *his* own. Had you thought of that? Anyway, we're talking nonsense – the man doesn't exist. Or if he does, I haven't met him yet.'

'And never will, as long as you stay buried down here,' he retorted triumphantly.

Thinking of this, Hilary sat up in bed, drawing her knees up and resting her forehead against them. She should know by now that there was no winning an argument with her father. He would use any weapon that came to hand. Fortunately, he'd stopped short of bringing Henry, her dead fiancé, into the argument, but she suspected he would even do that if he felt he needed to.

If only I could be as ruthless, she thought, but I can't forget that he has a dicky heart and argument is bad for him. And he knows it too, blow him, and plays on it – and there's nothing I can do about it.

The early-morning light was beginning to creep in through the curtains. Sighing, she threw back the bedclothes and went to look out of the window. The garden stretched before her, the shrubs and bushes laced with gossamer; beyond them, the trees were shrouded in September mist and the purple heather of the rising moors hung like a shifting, shadowy backcloth against a pearly sky. It was a view she knew as well as she knew her own face in the mirror, yet it changed every day; the only thing that didn't change was her love for it.

Dad thinks if I got married I'd stay here, she thought. But how could he be sure? Any man I married would have to have

93

his own life, probably his own home. He wouldn't be prepared to come here and play second fiddle. I wouldn't want a man who was!

She turned away from the window and slipped along to the bathroom for a hasty wash, then came back and dressed in jodhpurs. Quietly, she crept down the stairs and let herself out of the back door to make her way to the stables to collect a leading rein. She walked through the yard to the fields where the horses were grazing and called Beau to her.

As he came over, she noticed a movement at the top of the field, by the far gate on to the moor. In the pale, shifting mist it was difficult to make out exactly what she was seeing, but it was definitely one of the horses, and it looked as if it was being led out through the gate. Her heart suddenly in her mouth, she caught Beau's mane and swung herself on to his back. Swiftly, though he must have been startled by her unexpected action, he responded to her signal to make for the top of the field, and as they galloped across the turf Hilary shouted at the top of her voice.

'Hey! You! What do you think you're doing? Leave that horse alone at once! *Leave* it, I say! Leave it!'

The horse stopped, and the figure leading it turned and lifted one arm. Hilary stared and then groaned. She slowed Beau to a walk and resignedly approached as Travis Kellaway stood politely waiting for her to reach him.

'Sorry, did you call?' he enquired civilly. 'I was thinking about something else – didn't notice you until the last moment.'

Hilary looked down at him. He had one hand on Sultan's neck, the reins gathered into the other. The horse was saddled and ready for riding. He met her gaze blandly, but she caught the spark of laughter deep in his eyes and realised that he knew exactly what had been in her mind. He was giving her a let-out, but if she took it, he'd know that she was being evasive, and she'd already decided there had to be honesty between them. She said coolly, 'I thought you were a thief, making off with one of our best horses.'

'An easy mistake to make,' he agreed solemnly. 'Especially on such a misty morning.'

'Yes. Well ...' she hesitated. 'I see you had the same idea as me. An early-morning ride to blow away the cobwebs.'

'I expect you wanted to be on your own,' he said. 'I'll go on, shall I? By the time you've got Beau saddled, I'll be out of your way.'

'No, it's all right.' She hesitated again, reluctant to say the words that were going to change her life. 'If you don't mind waiting for me, there are things we need to talk about. It might as well be now.'

He nodded, and she turned Beau and cantered down the field, taking him through the lower gate into the stableyard. It took her only a few minutes to saddle and bridle him and then she was trotting back to where Travis waited. As she came closer, she threw him a quick glance but his expression was inscrutable. Leaning over from Sultan's back, he held the gate open for her and then closed it as she came through. They set off up the track on to the moor, Hilary in the lead.

Neither spoke until they were on open ground. Then Travis drew alongside Hilary. His eyes were on her, thoughtful and appraising, and she felt the colour warm her cheeks.

'Are you ready to tell me what's in your mind?' he asked quietly. 'Or do you want a little longer to think? There's no hurry.'

'Isn't there?' She could not prevent the edge of sharpness in her tone. 'You said you needed to know by today.'

'But not necessarily at six in the morning,' he said with a twitch of his lips. 'There's a lot of today still to go.'

Hilary stared down at Beau's thick black mane. 'We may as well get everything out into the open. I've been thinking a lot about what you said. And about my father, and what's going to happen to the estate.' She raised her eyes to his, aware that her expression was still troubled. 'It's not just what's going to happen in the next year or two, or even the next ten years. I know this must seem very archaic to you, but people like us – we've had these estates for hundreds of years. They've been handed down to us, not just as a right, but as a responsibility. We get our living from them, it's true, but we also have to look after them. The land and the people who work it – the tenant farmers, the cottagers, everything. It isn't just a job.'

'I do understand that,' he told her. 'My father was head gamekeeper on just such an estate. And our family had been part of it for generations, too. We had our own responsibilities and our own pride in the place we lived in. But things are changing ...'

'They don't have to,' she said quickly, but he shook his head.

'They do have to, I'm afraid. We've had two World Wars in less than thirty years. Millions of people have been killed – many of them the generation who should be running the world now. All those young men killed in the 1914–18 war, who would have inherited their estates, or worked on them – think of the gardens of some of the great houses that have been neglected and lost because so many of the young gardeners went to war and never came back. The farms working with just a few men, where once they'd have employed dozens ...'

'But that would have happened anyway,' Hilary said. 'Farmers are starting to use so much more machinery now. Not that I want to lay off six men because we decide to buy a new tractor,' she added ruefully. 'But I can see it starting to happen. Father says we'll give up horses altogether, eventually.'

'He's right, and it won't be so very long, either,' Travis said. 'In another fifteen years, a horse-drawn plough will be a rare sight. We're all having to move with the times, Hilary.'

'So you're saying that I'll fail because I won't? That just shows that you don't understand me at all. I know about these changes as well as you do, Travis. For heaven's sake, I'm one of them! The world has changed for women, too, you know — we've got the vote, we can do men's jobs, we don't have to wait for some kind gentleman to come along and marry us so that we can stay home and raise children and not worry our pretty little heads about real life any more!' Her voice was growing heated and she stopped and took in a deep breath before continuing more calmly: 'I had a responsible job during the war. I didn't want to come home and spend my time arranging flowers and visiting the sick. I'd found out what it was like to be free to use my brain and my initiative, and I didn't want to lose that.'

'So why did you come home?' he asked.

'Because my mother was ill. There was no one else to take over the household, and she needed me. There was Stephen, too. He was still at school. And when Mother died, there didn't seem to be any choice but to stay on, at least for a while. I couldn't leave Father until he got over it. I thought – we both thought – that Stephen would take over, and then I'd be free to live my own life again. Although I realised pretty soon that he wasn't going to,' she added. 'He told me how he felt long before he said anything to Father.'

'And was that when you saw your chance at taking over the estate?'

'No! Not at all! I knew I'd never be allowed to do anything useful, so I decided to break away. I was planning to go to London and get a job as an air hostess, with one of my friends from the WAACs. I was ready to go, and then Father had his heart-attack, so that was that. It took me all my time to convince him that I could do the job, even then, but I did think he'd come round to the idea after I'd been doing it a year. It doesn't seem as if he has,' she finished a little dolefully.

Travis gave her a thoughtful look. They were high up on the moor, almost at the great pile of granite rocks on Burracombe Tor. The sun had climbed higher in the sky, melting away the mists that now threaded like pale chiffon scarves along the valleys. The browns and golds of autumn were beginning to touch the leaves of the trees on the lower slopes, while ahead of them the heather lay like a purple blanket thrown carelessly on the turf, grazed short by the sheep and ponies who roamed the moors.

'Would you really have been happy in London?' he asked, and waved one arm. 'Away from all this?'

'I was away from it during the war.'

'Yes, but we all had to do things during the war that we wouldn't have chosen. Choosing it in peacetime is rather different. When you live in a place as beautiful as Burracombe, and you have a job to do there ...'

'But I didn't have a job to do! I was just a housekeeper. I did what Mrs Ellis does. If I'd got my own family, maybe I would have felt differently, but I didn't. And I didn't have any more chance of having one than I do now,' she added bitterly. 'Father never seemed to realise that.'

'But when you knew Stephen was planning to leave, what then?'

'Oh, Stephen!' she said. 'He was talking about going to Canada – maybe he still wants to, I don't know – and he asked me to go with him.'

'Canada!' Travis said. 'Well, that would have been a good experience for you.'

'Oh yes? And what would I have been, there? *His* housekeeper instead of Father's! In any case, it wouldn't have been fair for both of us to leave the country. We're all Dad's got, you know. And he's never stopped missing Baden. It broke his heart to lose him.'

Travis nodded. 'I know. His eldest son – and Baden would have run the estate and given his life to it. He often talked to me about it.'

'I suppose if Baden had any say in things now, he'd want you to come here,' Hilary said after a moment or two.

Travis didn't answer at once. She got the impression that he was turning something over in his mind; then he said, 'But he doesn't. And things are different. It's for you to decide – you and your father.'

They reached the tor and paused, looking out over the undulating moor. Apart from the granite rocks that topped every hill, there was little ruggedness in the landscape. It was not like the craggy scenery of the Lake District or Wales. Yet it could still be bleak and cheerless, even rather menacing. Hilary had been up here more than once and seen stormclouds gathering, and had watched lightning rip the sky apart before common sense told her that such a high point was not a good place to be, and she'd turned for home. But whatever the outlook – gloomy and overcast, white with a blanket of snow, or bright with summer sunlight – it was the place that she had kept in her heart during those years when she had been away. And she knew that Travis was right. She didn't want to leave it. She never had.

'Father's already decided,' she said. 'He wants you here.' She drew in a deep breath. 'And so do I.'

Travis turned slowly in his saddle and faced her. She gazed back steadily as his eyes searched hers. At last, he said, 'Are you sure about this, Hilary?'

'Yes. It was what you said the other day – that if it wasn't you, it would be someone else.' She shook her head. 'I'm sorry, that sounds very ungracious. But it's true. He's not going to give up, and I could end up having to work with someone I really hated, who would make my life a misery.' She paused again. 'I could end up with someone who wouldn't want to work with me at all.'

'So that's your condition, is it?' he asked. 'That we work together?'

Hilary sighed. 'I'm not in a position to lay down conditions, am I? I'm still very much second-in-command around here – that's been made very plain. And when you come, I'll be third. But it's the best I'll get.' She looked at him again and her mouth twisted wryly. 'There I go again, being ungracious. Could you accept that, though? Would you want to work with a woman? With me?'

'It's not entirely unprecedented. There have been women farmers before, and very good ones too. I think we could work together, Hilary, but it will have to be with your father's agreement. If he thinks you ought to be going to London to attend balls and parties and find a husband—'

'If he thinks that, he's got another think coming! It doesn't matter who he appoints as estate manager, I won't be doing that. In fact, if the worst came to the worst and he did bring in someone who wouldn't work with me, or if Father won't allow me to go on working here, I'd have to go back to my other plan and move out. Find myself a job. There are plenty of things that women can do these days.' She threw him a look, half-defiant, half-despairing. 'I couldn't just stay here and watch someone else running our estate as if it were his, and not be able to have any say in it. I just couldn't.'

Travis held her gaze and, slowly, she felt her anger begin to subside. Tears pricked her eyes and she dropped her glance once more to Beau's mane. After a long pause, she drew in a deep breath, intending to apologise, but before she could say anything, he was speaking.

'I can see that, Hilary, and I can see how much it means to you. I wouldn't be able to stay, in your position, either. But it would hurt you just as much to leave, wouldn't it – even though you'd intended to leave, before your father was taken ill. It all means so much more to you now.'

'Yes, it does,' she said in a low voice. 'Or perhaps it's truer to say that I realise now how much it means to me. It would break my heart to leave it.'

'Then in that case,' he said, with a touch of humour in his voice, 'we'd better see how we can work together, hadn't we?'

Hilary lifted her eyes quickly. 'You're prepared to work with me? You think we could do it?'

'So long as it's *with*, and not *for*,' he said. 'It's your father who'll be employing me. We'd be joint managers – if he'll accept that. He might not, you know.'

'I think he will. He likes you, Travis. And besides, there's Baden.'

'Yes,' he said. 'Baden.' He waited a moment, then said, 'I'll tell you this now, Hilary, and it's something I couldn't tell you before because it could have influenced you – but when Baden talked to me about the estate, he used to say that if I ever needed a job, and not just a gamekeeper's job, a responsible job like the one I'm being offered now – there'd be one for me here at Burracombe.'

Hilary stared at him. 'You mean as estate manager? But—'

'But he'd be doing that himself,' Travis finished for her. 'Yes, that's what I thought. But I think he had other plans in mind – plans for the estate, for the future – which meant he'd need someone else to help him. And he wanted me.'

A slow suspicion crept into her mind. 'Have you ever told Father that? Is that why he asked you to come?'

'No!' he said immediately. 'No, I've never breathed a word. I never wanted to come here just because Baden wanted me – Baden's gone, and things have changed. The whole world has changed. I wanted to come on my own merit. But you said just now that if Baden had any say in it, he'd want me to come, and I thought you might like to know that you were right.'

Hilary's eyes filled with tears again. She looked out over the moors and the valleys, where the mist had now almost disappeared and the auburn tints of early autumn were bringing a deep, rich glow to the beechwoods. She had ridden up here so often with her elder brother, and they had paused here so many times to look at this same view. Now he would never see it again; but this man, who had been his friend, whom he would have wanted to come in his stead, was here, and she experienced a brief moment of insight, gone almost as swiftly as it came, and knew that whatever else might transpire between them, he was going to change her life.

'These horses will be getting cold,' she said brusquely, and touched Beau's sides with her heels. 'Let's give them a gallop before we go back.'

Chapter Ten

Luke Ferris had also started school this week, as art teacher at Tavistock Grammar School. He came home on the first afternoon to find Val preparing a meal on the little Primus stove that was the main source of cooking in the charcoal-burner's cottage.

'How did you get on?' she asked, kissing him. 'Are the children monsters?'

He laughed. 'Not at all. Well, not most of them, anyway. There are one or two I'm going to need to keep my eye on. But I haven't met them all yet. I've only had five classes today.'

'Five! That sounds a lot.' She slid half a dozen sausages into the frying pan. 'It's Cokers for tea tonight, if that's all right. And mashed potatoes and bubble and squeak from yesterday.'

'My favourite meal!'

'You always say that,' she said affectionately, and he grinned.

'Every meal you cook is my favourite. Is there any tea in the pot?'

'Yes, I've only just made it so it's nice and hot. Pour me one too, will you? And tell me about your day.'

Luke did as he was asked and sat back in the old settee. 'Well, we had Assembly first and I was introduced to the school. There's another new teacher too – Miss Marsh. She teaches maths. The children stared at us all through Assembly. I think they've already decided we'll probably get married.'

Val raised her eyebrows. 'And why would they think that?'

'Because she's young and pretty and I'm young and hand-some, of course. Anyway, they'll soon find out that I'm an old married man and there's absolutely no chance of any scandal there. I told every one of my classes that I lived in a shack in the woods with the most beautiful girl in the world. The girls thought it was really romantic.'

'You're a fool,' Val said. 'I don't suppose they believed a word of it. How did the classes go?'

'Not bad at all. I didn't ask what they did with their last teacher – I mean, what art they did, not where they buried him! I thought we'd start entirely fresh. So I gave out the paintbrushes and paints and told them to illustrate a nursery rhyme. I thought it might give me some ideas for pantomime scenery.'

'Did they enjoy that?'

'Yes, I think they did. There was some good work there, too. I think I may have one or two budding artists on my hands. And tomorrow I'll be having some different classes. It's going to be interesting.'

Val turned the flame down under the sausages and came to sit beside him with her cup of tea. 'I'm glad you're enjoying it, darling. So long as it doesn't interfere too much with your own painting.'

'It won't,' he said. 'It may even improve. I'll have to con-centrate on using my time well, instead of just loafing about painting the odd daub when I feel like it.'

'Luke! Your paintings are not daubs – and you don't loaf about. You're one of the hardest-working men I know.'

'I'm not sure your father would agree,' he said with a sigh. 'Still, I think I've redeemed myself a bit in his eyes by becom-ing a teacher. Anyway, talking of hard-working men, I met Jacob Prout while I was walking back from the bus stop.'

'Did you? I haven't seen him for a few days. He's been working over at Little Burracombe, so Dottie Friend told me.'

'That's right. Doing some tidying up in the vicarage garden.'

'How is the Vicar?' Val asked. John Berry, Vicar of Little Burracombe, had been ill for some time now and Felix had taken over almost all the services, much to the chagrin of Tessa Latimer, who had been a regular attender at Burracombe Church since coming back from Art College and noticing the young curate.

'Not well at all. I think he's got cancer. Jacob lowered his voice and looked both ways to see if anyone was listening, you know the way people do, when he told me. Same as the King, he said, so presumably it's lung cancer.'

Val nodded. 'It's been chest trouble all along. Bronchitis, pleurisy, pneumonia – I won't be surprised if that's what it turns out to be. What a shame. He's such a nice man.' They sat silently for a moment or two, then she asked, 'And how's Jacob? He was always cheerful but he's looking really happy these days, since Jennifer came back.'

'Yes, and he told me that she's coming out to see him this evening. I expect we'll see her if we go down there. You know, I think if we worked every evening this week we could get those bedrooms finished, and then we'll have done all we can. There'll only be the plumbing to do and we could move in.'

'That's earlier than we thought. Oh, if only we could! D'you think she'll get it done pretty soon? It's costing her money, after all. She must be using her own savings to do it – I don't suppose Jed left much money.'

'The sooner she's getting rent, the sooner she'll get her money back,' Luke pointed out. 'It's to her advantage to get the work done quickly. Just think, Val – we'll have so much space, we won't know ourselves!'

'It's only a two-up, two-down cottage,' she said, laughing. 'You're talking as if it was a mansion.'

'Well, so it is to me. Don't forget, I've been living in this tiny place for two years now. I'm not like you, living in luxury in a rambling great farmhouse.'

'A rambling great farmhouse full of people,' she reminded him. 'And more on the way. Joanna's baby's due soon.'

'And I'm sure everyone's looking forward to that.'

'Yes,' Val said, getting up to see to the sausages. 'Especially Joanna.'

There was a tiny silence. Then both started to speak at once. They stopped, laughed a little, and Val said, 'You first.'

'I was just going to say that if we go down to the cottage as soon as we finish our supper, we can get in a couple of hours' painting before it starts to get dark.'

'Yes, we could. But don't you have any preparation to do for tomorrow?'

'No,' he said. 'I'll just do something similar to today. It seemed to work well – gave the children a chance to relax as well as show me what they can do. There aren't many children who don't like messing about with some paints and a brush or two.'

Val turned back to the frying pan. 'These are done now. I'll put them on that plate and fry up the bubble and squeak; it won't take more than a minute or so. Put the knives and forks out, would you?'

Luke did as she'd requested, but there was a small frown on his forehead. He looked at her, undecided, and eventually asked, 'So what were you going to say?'

'Me?' said Val. 'Oh, nothing much. I've forgotten. Couldn't have been anything important.'

But she was evading his glance and Luke knew that whatever she had been about to say, it had been important.

However, she had evidently decided against saying it. Whatever was on her mind, he would have to wait to find out. He sighed and fetched the plates for their supper.

*

Jacob Prout was cooking sausages as well. He whistled to himself as he went about the preparations in his shining little kitchen, breaking off occasionally to talk to the cat and dog who sat nearby, waiting for scraps.

'You've got a while to wait yet,' he told them. 'You don't have your dinner until after we has ours, you ought to know that by now. Then you gets the leftovers – if there are any.' Floss and Scruff looked down their noses. It was as if they knew that Jacob always put a bit extra in, so that there would be leftovers. Floss shifted her paws a bit, and Scruff lay down with a sigh, his eyes following Jacob's every move.

'Us got a visitor coming,' the old man told them. 'Jennifer's coming to supper. You like Jennifer, don't you? Her's part of the family now, like her oughter've been all along.' He went on talking quietly and whistling as he scrubbed potatoes and carrots and set them to boil. Then he podded some late peas and sliced runner beans from the garden. ''Tis just a shame her poor dear mother never knowed she'd come back to Burracombe,' he murmured, gazing out of the kitchen window. 'A shame her never come back here herself. But there you are – that's life. God works in a mysterious way, so Vicar tells me, and I reckon he'm right.'

He set the kitchen table, laying it with a crisp white cloth and bone-handled cutlery handed down to him by his own mother, and placed a small fishpaste jar in the centre with a few flowers in, standing back to admire the effect. At that moment he heard a knock on the door and Scruff immediately burst into action, rushing through the tiny living room, barking at the top of his voice, while Floss leaped up on to the back of Jacob's armchair.

'For goodness sake!' he exclaimed, hurrying to the door. 'It be only Jennifer. I told you her was coming. There you be, my pretty!' he cried, flinging the door open. 'And how many times have I told you to come round the back? Us only uses our front doors for strangers, in Burracombe.'

'I know, I'm sorry,' Jennifer said, laughing. 'I always remember the minute I've knocked. How are you, Jacob?' She came in and kissed his cheek. He put his arms round her and held her for a moment, breathing in the clean, sweet smell of her. There was a slight aroma of roses about her hair, reminding him sharply of her mother, and he experienced a brief, sharp moment of sorrow, like a needlepoint in his heart. Then it was gone and he felt only thankfulness that Susan's daughter had come to him at last.

'Come you in,' he said, stepping back. 'I've got the kettle on for a drop of tea, and we'm having sausages for supper.'

'Cokers?' she asked with a smile, and he nodded.

'Be there any other sort? Not here in Burracombe, anyway. And the veg are all straight from my own garden, so 'tis all good natural food. Better than what you be getting down Plymouth.' He settled her in the better of the two armchairs and poured tea into a china cup from the set that had belonged to his grandmother. 'I wish you'd think about moving out here permanent, maid. You've got your little house, right next door. You could go into Plymouth on the bus, 'tis only a half-hour ride.'

Jennifer shook her head. 'I can't do that. I've promised the cottage to Val and Luke.'

'And you shouldn't have done it,' he said warmly. 'I know 'tis your kind heart that made you offer, but you weren't thinking proper. You were upset when old Jed died, though heaven only knows why ...'

'He was my father,' she said a little sternly, and he bowed his head.

'You don't have to tell me that, my bird. And I'm sorry, but I lived next to the old curmudgeon all me life and say what you like, he didn't have to be such a misery. Still, blood's thicker than water, so they tell me, and I'll not say no more. All I'm saying is that you weren't in your proper frame of mind when you found he'd left you the cottage – and I got to admit that

that *was* one decent thing he done – and you shouldn't have give it away so quick.'

'I haven't given it away,' she said, smiling again. 'Val and Luke are paying me a reasonable rent. And I don't suppose they'll want to be there for ever. It's not big enough for a family.'

Jacob snorted. 'Not big enough for a family! Folks used to raise ten or a dozen kiddies in houses this size, backalong. Mind you, they wouldn't all have been in the house together, what with miscarriages and babbies dying and the older ones being out in service or summat by the time the youngest ones came along. All the same …'

'It sounds awful,' Jennifer said. 'And even if Val and Luke don't have a dozen children, they're sure to want two or three. Say what you like, these cottages are too small. Now, if you took the wall down between them and knocked the two into one they'd make a very nice-sized house.'

'They would,' Jacob said, getting up to go and look at the stove. 'These veg are nearly done, maid, and so are the Cokers. Be you ready for a bite?'

'More than ready.' She came through to the kitchen and sat down at the table. 'Jacob, that looks wonderful. You've missed your vocation – you ought to have been a chef in a big restaurant.'

'Now you'm just making fun of me,' he said, dishing up the vegetables into a large crock and putting three huge sausages on to each plate. 'You help yourself now, while I boils up the gravy.'

'Ah, Bisto!' she said with a grin and he shook his head.

'Good onions from the back garden, fried down to a mash and a few mushrooms put in for good luck. And a little bit of Bovril for the flavour. Not that I don't use Bisto when it's just me,' he added honestly, 'but nothing but the best's good enough for you, my pretty.'

Jennifer felt her eyes grow moist. She watched the old man,

busy at his stove, and felt a deep regret that they had not been able to spend their lives together. But there was nothing to be done about that now, and they still had years ahead in which to enjoy each other's company. *Maybe he's right*, she thought. *Maybe I should sell the house in Plymouth and come out to Burracombe to live. And maybe I will – but not just yet. I'm not quite ready to make that final move. And I want to see Val and Luke with a more comfortable home than that hut in the woods. Maybe next year, when we're all more settled.*

Jacob came back to the table with a jug of gravy. 'My stars, whatever have you been doing – daydreaming? You haven't touched the veg. Now take as much as you want, my bird. You need fattening up.'

'I'm not so sure about that,' she said. 'I don't think Dingle's would be at all pleased if their senior fashion buyer suddenly put on weight. I have to look smart for my job, you know.'

'You'd look even smarter if you weren't as thin as a bean-pole,' he retorted. 'Most men likes a woman to be a bit of an armful.'

'But I'm not looking for a man,' she said gently. 'I'm trying to earn a living.'

There was a short silence as they both ate, and then Jacob finished chewing a mouthful of sausage and said gruffly, 'I'm sorry, maid. Talking out of turn, I was. You'll have to forgive an old man without the manners he was born with.'

'There's nothing to be sorry about. You can say anything you like to me, Jacob. Now, I've got a suggestion to make. I come out here to stay with you most weekends—'

'And very welcome you be,' he cried. 'Welcome as the flowers in May, and I hope you know it.'

'I do,' she said. 'But I'd like to suggest something. Why don't you come and stay with me instead, one weekend?'

Jacob stared at her, his mouth half-open, then he remembered his manners and closed it quickly. He blinked for a moment or two and then said huskily, 'What, in Plymouth?'

'Well, it is where I live,' she said, smiling. 'It would be nice. We could go up and sit on the Hoe and watch the ships, and you could come to Dingle's and see where I work, and we could go down to the Barbican early in the morning and watch the fishing-boats come in, and we might even go down to Cremyll and take the ferry across to Cawsands. What do you think?'

'I dunno,' he said in a bewildered tone. 'I ain't been to Plymouth for years. I've only been there three times in me whole life. When I come back from being in the Army, I reckoned Burracombe was good enough for me and I didn't never want to go nowhere else, except for Tavistock Goosey Fair and that sort of thing. And it's all been changed now, anyway. I don't suppose I'd know me way around.'

'You wouldn't have to. I'd be with you. You could come down on the bus on Friday afternoon and I'd meet you and take you home. I've got a spare room, so there's no problem there. And we'd have a nice meal to help you settle in – it's time I cooked a meal for you instead of the other way around – and maybe a game of cards, and on Saturday and Sunday we could do whatever you like. Go out and have some fish and chips, perhaps. And if you want to go to church, we could go to St Andrew's and I'll do a nice roast dinner with jam roly-poly for afters. What do you say?'

'I'd come back on the bus, Sunday night?' he asked. 'I'd have to be back in time for work Monday morning.'

'Of course you would! There are plenty of buses – I'll make sure you catch the right one. Say you'll come, Jacob. I'd really like you to see where I live.' She watched his face, seeing the indecision amounting almost to panic, and added gently, 'Just think about it. You don't have to come if you don't want to.'

'It's not that,' he said, rubbing his hand across his face. 'It's just a lot to take in all of a sudden. I thought you were quite happy coming out here and stopping with me.'

'I am, I love it. I just want to return your hospitality, that's all. Don't you want to see where I live? Don't you ever think you'd like to picture me at home or at work, as I can picture you?'

'Well, when you put it like that, I suppose I do,' he admitted. 'But 'tis such a big place, Plymouth, and 'tis all different now. I remember it as it was, and when I saw all them pictures of it, almost flattened in the Blitz, hardly one stone standing on another ... well, I told meself I never wanted to go there again. And I never have.'

'It's getting better now,' she said. 'They're rebuilding it, you know – they've done a lot already. There are lovely wide streets now, and big shops like Dingle's and Spooner's. It's a city for Devon to be proud of.' They both looked up as a shadow passed the kitchen window and someone knocked on the door. 'Look, you don't have to decide now. It can be any time, there's no hurry. That looks like Val Ferris at the door – shall I let her in?'

'Ah, bring the maid in here and give her a cup of tea,' he said, not hiding his relief. 'I dare say her and young Luke have come to get on with the painting. Getting a bit chilly up in that old hut of theirs, I expect.'

Jennifer got up and went to the door. She wasn't surprised by Jacob's reaction to her invitation; she'd known that he was firmly rooted in Burracombe and considered a day out to Tavistock an adventure. All the same, she hoped that he would accept. It was important to her that he should see the house where her mother, Susan, had lived and where she herself had grown up.

Perhaps that was the reason he didn't want to come. He knew as well as she did that Susan, the girl he had loved so much, had lived in that house. Perhaps he was afraid of the memories it might bring, and the pain it might cause his heart. She made up her mind to go very slowly. Eventually, she was sure he would overcome his reluctance.

She opened the door and felt the warmth of friendship

in her own heart as she saw Val and Luke standing on the threshold.

'Come in!' she exclaimed and stood back, throwing one arm out to beckon them into the kitchen. 'Come and have a cup of tea, and tell us how you're getting on next door.'

Chapter Eleven

Jackie Tozer usually walked home from the Barton along the track that led through the gardens and little wood before emerging into Top Field. Once there, she was on her father's farm and within five minutes of home. This evening, however, she decided to go the longer way round, down the drive of the Barton, past the main farm track and through the village before cutting up the hill and then back through the fields above the church. She'd been cooped up in the house all day and needed the exercise, and she could buy herself a bag of toffees with that week's coupons.

As she came out of the shop, she almost walked into a tall young man with brown curly hair who was on his way in. He held her at arms' length and grinned down at her.

'Jackie Tozer! Fancy meeting you here.'

'I do live here,' she retorted, feeling suddenly shaky and hoping the heat in her cheeks didn't mean she had turned bright red. 'You're Vic, aren't you?'

'That's right. You were just a kid when I went away. Not long left school, if I remember right.'

'Probably,' she said carelessly. 'I don't really remember. Did you do two years, or three?'

'Three,' he said with a grin. 'You get better pay if you do that.'

'And now you're home again.'

'Was demobbed a fortnight ago and got the suit to prove it. Green.' He wrinkled his nose. 'All the blokes got the same

– we looked just as much in uniform when we came out of the store as when we went in!'

Jackie laughed and he tipped his head slightly to one side and regarded her. 'So where are you off to now?'

'Home. I've just finished work, up at the Barton. I felt like a walk so I came through the village.'

'I wouldn't mind a bit of a walk myself,' Vic said. 'Mind if I come with you?'

Jackie shrugged. 'Can if you like. I'm not going far, mind. Just down to the bridge and back, maybe along the river a little way. 'Tis nice down there, with all the trees turning colour.'

They walked along the village street together, Jackie feeling self-conscious and awkward, certain that people were peering at them from every cottage window, and strolled towards the school and the little bridge with its ford and stepping-stones. They paused and leaned on the ancient stone parapet, gazing down into the tumbling brown water.

'I saw an otter here once,' Vic remarked. 'On that rock, he was, guzzling a big salmon he'd fetched up out of the water. I'd have had it off him, but he'd pretty well chewed it to the bone.'

'Is there anywhere like this that you've been while you were in the Army?' Jackie asked. 'You were in Germany most of the time, weren't you?'

'That's right. There were a few places a bit like it – woods and hills and bridges. But there's real big mountains too, and deep gorges. You wouldn't want to go swimming there, I can tell you – find yourself heading over a waterfall, like as not. A lot of it's pretty wild.'

'Were you out in the country, then?'

Vic shook his head. 'Round Berlin, mostly. They've been cutting it up into bits – a bit that we looked after, another bit for the Yanks and a bit for the Russkies. It was pretty grim a lot of the time – wire fences, dogs and guards, and all that.

And Berlin's a right dump, worse than Plymouth. Reckon we gave it a real hammering, and then when it was taken over we knocked down most of whatever was left standing. They're rebuilding it now, though.' He slanted a look at her. 'I hear young Roy's out in Korea.'

'Yes. He's fighting.'

'You keep in pretty close touch then, do you?'

'I write to him now and then,' Jackie said a little defensively. 'I mean, he used to be my boyfriend. He needs letters from home.'

'So he's not your boyfriend now, then?'

'Not really, no,' Jackie said, meeting his eye. 'We broke up before he went.' Remembering the reason brought the warmth to her cheeks again and she went on hurriedly, 'We're still friends, but that's all.'

'I dare say you've got plenty of other boyfriends,' he said, and she shrugged again.

'I'm not all that bothered, to tell you the truth. I'm thinking of moving away, anyway – getting another job, maybe in a hotel.'

'Leave the Barton, you mean? And Burracombe?'

'Why not? Miss Hilary says I ought to do something better than just be a housemaid. And there's not a lot of hotels in Burracombe.'

Vic laughed. 'No, there aren't. So where would you think of going? Tavistock?'

'Perhaps. Or perhaps Plymouth. Or Exeter. I don't mind, really.'

Vic regarded her speculatively and once again she felt her cheeks blush. His eyes were a very dark brown, she noticed, and since he'd left the Army he'd let his hair grow a bit, almost down to his collar. It gave him a slightly wild, rebellious look. His eyes narrowed a little and she felt a twinge somewhere deep in her stomach.

'Well, don't run away too soon,' he said at last. 'Not before I've had a chance to get to know you.'

Alice Tozer glanced up as her younger daughter came in for supper. She looked a bit different, Alice thought – bright-eyed and a bit flushed, and her hair was untidy. 'I hope you'm not sickening for something,' she said, tipping a bowlful of peeled potatoes into a big saucepan. 'There's a nasty cold going round, so they tell me. Jessie Friend's real poorly with it.'

'Always had a weak chest, she has,' Minnie said from her corner, where she was shelling peas. 'So's Billy, of course, but that's more to do with the way he is.'

'I haven't got a cold,' Jackie said, going through to the stair-case door. 'How long will supper be?'

'It'll be ready by half-past six as usual,' her mother said a little tartly. 'Why? You got something special on, then?'

'Might have,' Jackie said carelessly. 'Might be going out somewhere.' She started to go upstairs.

'Oh, and where might that be, then?' All Alice's senses were alerted. She'd seen that expression on her daughter's face and heard that note in her voice before, when she was getting too friendly with young Roy Pettifer. Talking about going to London to see the Festival of Britain, they'd been, on their own if you please, and staying a few days. The idea! But Roy was in Korea now, so it looked as if there was some other young chap putting that look on Jackie's face. 'And who with, might I ask?'

'Oh, for goodness sake, Mum!' Jackie exclaimed with an impatience that confirmed all Alice's suspicions. 'Do I have to tell you every little thing?'

'No. But you do have to tell me where you're going and who you're going with, and what time you reckon to be home. You're not twenty-one yet, you know, not by a long chalk.'

'Well, if you must know,' Jackie said furiously, 'Vic

Nethercott's taking me to Tavistock in his dad's van and we're going to see the film that's on at the Carlton.'

'Well, that's all right,' Alice said mildly. 'I don't know why you has to get all aeriated about it, if that's all you'm doing. Time you went out and enjoyed yourself a bit more.'

'Good!' Jackie snapped, deflated and angry about it. 'I'm glad you approve.' She stamped upstairs and Alice looked at her mother-in-law and chuckled. Minnie shook her head at her.

'You shouldn't tease the maid. You know how she flies off the handle.'

'Best if she learns not to, then,' Alice said, unperturbed. 'You'd think her could take a bit of chi-iking, after the years she's lived with our Tom. As if I'd mind her going to the pictures with Vic Nethercott. I saw his mother the other day, she says he's come back a real smart young man – polishes his shoes every morning, irons his own trousers, puts everything away neat and tidy. And he's getting a good job too, down Plymouth – going in the Civil Service, she said. That's a job for life. You don't get sacked from the Civil Service, not unless you gets sent to prison or something. Our Jackie could do a lot worse than Vic Nethercott.'

'Give 'em a bit of time,' Minnie protested. 'They haven't even been to the pictures together yet! You'll have them up the aisle before Pathé Pictorial's been shown.'

Alice laughed and looked in the oven to see how the casserole was getting on. There seemed to have been a rush on sausages at Bert Foster's this morning and she'd had to buy pigs' liver instead. Usually, she fried it with a bit of bacon but today she'd put it in a dish with some onions, carrots and tomatoes, half a dozen mushrooms gathered from the field that morning and a few butter beans to bulk it out. Ted was always one for butter beans.

'I don't think our Jackie's in any hurry to get fixed up,' she said, closing the oven door. 'She just wants to have a good time for a while, and why not? I've never liked her stopping at home writing letters to Roy Pettifer every evening, especially when they'm not even engaged.'

'You don't think she still carrics a torch for him, then?' Minnie asked.

Alice shook her head. 'They finished all that before he went the first time. It was only when he was going to Korea that she said she'd write, and I reckoned then it was more out of pity than anything else. But you know what they say, absence makes the heart grow fonder and I've been a bit worried just lately that she might be starting to hanker after him again. Young Vic'll take her mind off it.' She lifted the lid of the big saucepan to see how the potatoes were coming along. 'This'll be ready soon. Where are those men?'

At that moment, the door opened and her husband came in, followed by Tom. They both shucked off their boots at the door and padded across the floor in thick socks. Ted groped under the dresser for his slippers and Tom went to the sink to wash his hands.

'About time too,' Alice told them. 'I'm just about to dish up. Give our Jackie a call, will you, Tom? Joanna, too – she went upstairs for a rest.'

They all sat down together round the kitchen table with Robin, who had stopped using a high chair some time ago but still needed a thick cushion to raise him to a comfortable height, sitting between his parents. Alice served them all with liver casserole, mashed potatoes and cabbage.

'Jackie's off out to the pictures tonight,' she told them, 'so we don't want to take too long. There's blackberry and apple pie for afters. Joanna picked the blackberries this afternoon.'

'Yes, and I don't reckon her oughter've done it,' Minnie said. 'Reaching up like that. 'Tis bad for the baby – you'll get the cord round its neck.'

'That's an old wives' tale,' Joanna said. 'Anyway, I didn't reach up much. There's such a good crop this year, I could pick low down.'

'I'll go out tomorrow and get some more, for jam,' Alice remarked. 'Have you got enough potato, Ted? And Robin ought to have some more cabbage.'

'He doesn't like it,' Joanna said. 'It's no good giving him a lot. Just eat a tiny bit,' she said to her son. 'Just this little bit here, look.'

'Mix it in with his potato, he'll not notice it then,' Minnie suggested.

'He's not that daft,' Tom said. 'Anyway, who's our Jackie going to the pictures with? Got a new boyfriend, have you?'

Jackie coloured. 'If you must know, I'm going with Vic Nethercott, and he's not my boyfriend. We just happened to bump into each other outside the shop and we were both going for a bit of a walk, so we went down to the bridge and I happened to say there was this picture on that I wanted to see, and he said he wanted to see it too, so why not go together. And that's all there is to it.'

'Oh yes?' Tom said with a grin. 'I'll believe you, thousands wouldn't. So what's the picture, then?'

Jackie hesitated. 'It's the new Doris Day.' But her voice was uncertain, and her brother roared with laughter.

'You're both dead keen to see it but you can't remember what it is! Well, I can tell you – it's *High Noon*, with John Wayne! Nothing to do with Doris Day at all.'

'Well, perhaps that's next week, then. I'm sure I saw something about it in the *Tavvy Times*.'

'Never mind. You'll be able to go again next week to see Doris Day,' Tom said comfortingly, and she glowered at him.

'We might, and we might not. Anyway, *High Noon*'s supposed to be a good picture so it doesn't matter. Can I have my afters now, Mum? I've finished this and I haven't got much time. Vic's meeting me at the road at quarter to seven.'

'Quarter to seven? You'll miss *The Archers*,' Tom said in mock dismay. 'Don't you want to know if Phil's got a new girlfriend?'

'You can tell me when I get home.' The others had finished now too, and Jackie collected their plates while Alice brought the pie from the larder windowsill, where it had been set to cool, and put it on the table with a jug of custard. She began to serve portions and Joanna passed them round.

'Blackberry and apple's my favourite pie,' Minnie said. 'But the seeds do get under your plate, don't they, Ted? Not as bad as raspberries, mind.'

'Mum, if I can enjoy my grub the same as you do when I'm your age, I shan't complain about a few seeds,' Ted told her. He turned to his son. 'You won't miss ringing practice tomorrow night, will you? You know 'tis our turn for the Deanery Day this year, and us wants to put on a good show for the service peal, with all the other teams there to listen.'

'I'd better get the wives organised for the tea,' Alice said. 'Us needs to set out a good spread. You'll be wanting pasties as usual, I take it, and plenty of cakes.'

'They always goes down well,' Ted agreed. 'And gallons of tea, we'm always thirsty after all that travelling round.'

Deanery Day was a special day in the bell-ringers' calendar. Every church tower in the Deanery was open for ringers to visit and ring the bells, with one particular church playing host for a service and tea. Each team was also given a time to ring at that tower, but they could arrive at the others whenever they wished. Most teams made an outing of it, planning their route and getting together in vans, farm vehicles and cars to travel around, and they all met together in the evening to catch up on ringing gossip. There was no competition, and often two teams would arrive together somewhere, but nobody minded and it generally worked out with good humour. The hardest work was done by the wives of the ringers at the host tower, who provided tea for up to a hundred hungry and thirsty bell-ringers.

'It's a busy month for us this year,' Alice remarked. 'There's Harvest Festival the week after next, don't forget. Got to put on a good supper for that, and I dare say you'll be wanting to get the handbell team together for a bit of practice, Mother.'

Minnie nodded. 'People seemed to like us ringing the handbells for the Easter Day service, so Vicar's asked us to do it again. I thought us could do three hymns – "We Plough the Fields and Scatter", and "Come, Ye Thankful People Come", because everyone knows those, and maybe one of the others that folk don't know so well. I'll have to look at the music and work out the harmonies.'

Jackie finished her pie and got up from the table. She ran upstairs for her coat and came down looking bright-eyed and excited. Her father looked at her and said, 'You be in by ten-thirty, mind, maid. I don't want you out no later than that.'

'I don't know if the picture will have finished by then.'

'It finishes at ten,' Tom said. 'That'll give you plenty of time for a bit of spooning in the back seat.'

'Mr Nethercott's van doesn't have a back seat,' Jackie said, and flushed as he laughed. 'Oh, you're horrible, you are! I'll see you later, Mum.' She whisked out of the back door and slammed it behind her. The rest of the family laughed but Alice shook her head at Tom.

'You'll upset her one of these days,' she said, forgetting that she herself had been told not to tease her daughter. 'I'd be pleased for her to go around with Vic Nethercott. He'm a nice young chap. Decent, too.'

'Go on, Mum,' Tom said. 'He's been in the Army in Germany these past three years. He can't be decent! You should hear what our Brian says about what goes on over there.'

'And our Brian's a soldier too, I'll thank you to remember,' Alice said smartly. 'I hope you're not implying that your own brother's not decent.'

'He's married,' Tom retorted with a wink at Joanna. 'He's not allowed not to be decent!'

The family finished their meal and the women cleared up

while Ted and Tom went outside to finish off a last few jobs. Joanna sat down in the armchair with a sigh and Alice glanced at her sympathetically.

'Feeling tired, my bird? You'll be glad when it's all over.'

'It'll be worth it,' Minnie said. 'Another new little life in the house. Do you realise, there are four generations of us, under the same roof! Us ought to have our picture taken for the family album, once the baby's born.'

'Would you like me to put Robin to bed for you?' Alice offered, but Joanna shook her head.

'Tom'll do it when he comes in. And I'll read him his story now.' She reached to the dresser beside her for the storybook that Robin enjoyed every evening, and gave a sharp gasp. '*Ow!*'

'What? What is it?' Both older women stopped what they were doing and came quickly over to her. Alice bent over and put her hand on Joanna's, and Joanna gripped it hard and then relaxed.

'It's all right. It's gone now.' She looked up at her mother-in-law. 'It felt like a pain – you know. It felt like when Robin ... Mum, I think the baby might be starting!'

Chapter Twelve

Tom and his father came running as soon as they heard Minnie's shout. She stepped back to allow them to pass her and Tom crossed the kitchen swiftly to kneel at his wife's side. He caught her hands in his and looked anxiously into her face.

'Jo? Jo, are you all right? Is it the baby?'

'I think so. A pain caught me a minute or two ago. It was really sharp – not like with Robin when it started slowly and just sort of built up – oh! It's coming again! *Tom*!'

There was panic in her voice. Ted stood undecided for a moment, his hand on top of his head, then he said, 'I'll go for Nurse Sanders.'

'Ring her up,' Alice said, her hand on Joanna's shoulder as she creased with pain. 'It'll be quicker – she'll come straight away.' Ted had never quite got used to using the telephone for people in the village, most of whom didn't have a phone anyway. He nodded and went to the windowsill where it stood.

'She's out,' he reported a few moments later. 'Birth over Staddlecombe. Bill Sanders thinks it could be a long job.' He glanced uneasily at Joanna, resting again, her face pale and beaded with sweat. 'What are we going to do? She don't look too good to me.'

'And she don't need to hear you talking like that,' Alice said sharply. 'Call the doctor. For pity's sake, man, use your head!'

Abashed, Ted asked the operator to put him through to

Dr Latimer. A moment later he hung up and turned back to the others. 'He'm coming straight round. He said to get her to bed and get everything ready.'

'It's ready, most of it,' Alice said. Minnie was already filling kettles and setting them on the stove. She turned back to Joanna, who was leaning against Tom looking frightened. 'Come on now, my bird, let's get you up those stairs. Tom and me will help you. There's nothing to worry about, now. Everything's going to be all right.'

'It's too soon,' Joanna whispered, letting them heave her to her feet. 'It's not due for another three weeks.'

'Babies come when they'm ready,' Alice said. 'Anyway, it might be a false alarm. It might all settle down again in an hour or two.'

'It's not going to,' Joanna said. 'I know it isn't. These are real pains – oh my God, here it comes again.' She clutched her husband's hand and leaned heavily against him. He slid his arm around her and held her strongly, while Alice kept her steady on the other side. For a full minute they stood there in an awkward cluster, and then Joanna took a breath and murmured, 'It's going now. Let's get upstairs while I can.'

'They're coming awfully quickly,' Tom said in a worried tone. 'Last time, it was hours before they came this quick, and it wasn't long then before Robin was born.'

'Maybe this one's in a bigger hurry,' Alice said, but she was looking anxious too. Together, with Ted coming up behind them in case they all toppled backwards, they managed the narrow stairs and got Joanna into the bedroom. Swiftly, Alice stripped the bed and laid a rubber sheet over it, then remade it with old sheets and put towels ready. Joanna sank down with a sigh of relief and Ted went downstairs again and came back with a bowl of warm water.

'We'll leave you to yourselves for a bit,' Alice said to her son. 'Give us a shout the minute you need anything.'

Tom helped his wife undress and put on a cotton nightdress,

and washed her. He sat on the side of the bed, holding her hand and looking into her face.

'There. You'll feel more comfortable now. It's a few minutes since the last one, isn't it? Maybe Mum's right and it's a false alarm.'

Joanna shook her head. 'It's not. I can feel the baby moving. It's almost as if it's trying to push its own way out. Oh Tom, I'm frightened. Something's wrong, I'm sure of it. Why is it coming so early? Why is it so quick?'

'Surely that's a good thing,' he said, trying to cheer her up. 'Robin took ages to be born, don't you remember? You thought it was never going to end. It'll be much better to get it over quickly.'

'No, it's not. You ought to know that, you've seen enough calves and lambs being born. Tom, there was a girl I knew once who had her baby so quickly there wasn't even time to call anyone, and it died. Suppose that happened to ours. I don't know what I'd do.'

'It's not going to happen to our baby,' he said gently. 'There are plenty of us here and the doctor's coming. He'll be here any minute.' Footsteps sounded on the stairs. 'Here he is now. Don't worry, sweetheart. It's all going to be all right and we'll soon have our baby.' He turned as the door opened and said with relief, 'Here's Dr Latimer now. He'll look after you.'

'Good flick, wasn't it,' Vic Nethercott said as they came out of the Carlton cinema into Plymouth Road.

'Yes, it was.' Jackie had been surprised by the story of *High Noon*. 'I thought it was just going to be an ordinary Western.'

'It's a bit more than that.' They stood beside the van, hesitating a little. 'Feel like a drink before we go back?'

'What, in a pub?'

Vic grinned. 'Well, I don't think Good's or Perraton's are open at this time of night. You don't mind going in a pub, do you?'

'No, of course not.' She couldn't tell him she'd hardly ever been in one. Her father would have skinned her alive if she'd dared go in the Bell Inn, and she and Roy had seldom come to Tavistock, doing most of their courting around the village. Besides, they'd been too young and nobody would have served them. The only times she'd been into pubs were on the way home from village coach outings, when there had been a stop for a drink, and if her parents were there she'd had to sit outside with a lemonade. But she couldn't tell Vic that. He was too old – twenty-one, at least – and too sophisticated. He'd been abroad. He must have had lots of girlfriends who were happy to go into pubs.

'Come on, then,' he said. 'We'll go to the Tavistock Inn.'

'I've got to be home by half-past ten,' she said nervously, following him up Russell Street.

'I'll get you back, don't worry. Is your dad a bit of a tartar?'

'He is, a bit. He likes me to be in before he goes to bed. So does Mum.'

'My mum and dad are the same with our Brenda. She came in at a quarter to eleven one night and Dad wouldn't let her out of the door for a week. It wasn't even her fault – her bike had got a puncture and she had to push it home. All he said was, she ought to have left in time to walk, just in case!'

'Gosh,' Jackie said. 'So maybe we ought to go now, in case your van has a puncture and we have to walk home.'

Vic laughed. 'Nobody'd ever go anywhere if we all did that. We'd be coming home before we even set out.' They reached the door of the pub. The beery smell touched Jackie's nostrils and she heard voices and laughter. 'What are you going to have?'

'Oh, I don't know. What do you think?'

'Well, what do you like best? Gin? Port and lemon? Cherry brandy?'

'That sounds nice.' Something made of cherries couldn't be

too strong. She sat at a small table and watched Vic go to the bar. The other customers were mostly men, but she noticed one or two other girls, also watching him, and felt rather superior. He was much the best-looking young man in the room. He came back with two glasses, one containing a pint of beer, the other much smaller and filled with dark red liquid. He handed it to her and she took a sip.

'Nice?'

'Mm,' she said, feeling the heat trickle down inside to her stomach. 'It really tastes of cherries.'

He smiled and sipped his beer. They looked at each other for a minute and then he said, 'So what have you been doing with yourself while I've been away? Apart from growing up into a pretty girl, I mean?'

Jackie blushed. 'Oh, nothing much, really. There's not much to do in a place like Burracombe, is there? It looks as if this pantomime might be good fun, though. Are you going to be in it?'

Vic shrugged. 'I might be. The meeting was all right. Wasn't that the doctor's girl you were walking home with?'

Jackie had a sudden moment of fear that he might have brought her out and treated her to the pictures and now a drink, all to find out more about Tessa Latimer. 'Yes,' she said reluctantly. 'She was interested in Travis Kellaway – the man who came with Hilary Napier.'

'Oh yes – he's staying at the Barton, isn't he? I suppose you see quite a bit of him yourself.'

'A bit, yes,' Jackie admitted. She was still interested in Travis herself, but although he always smiled at her and asked how she was, she didn't think he'd ever look at a girl like her. Tessa Latimer, now – or even Miss Hilary herself ... although Hilary didn't somehow seem the sort ever to marry now.

'Well, I'll probably go to this audition or read-through or whatever the new curate calls it,' Vic went on cheerfully. 'He seems a bit of a live wire, doesn't he? Is he keen on that young schoolteacher – what's her name – Sheila?'

'Stella – Stella Simmons.' Jackie wished he would stop showing an interest in the other young women about the village. 'Yes, they've been going around together for quite a while now. Everyone's expecting them to get engaged.'

'Last I heard of you, everyone was expecting you and Roy Pettifer to get engaged,' Vic said, giving her a direct look. 'What happened to that, then?'

'Oh, you know, it just sort of fizzled out. I didn't really want to be tied down.' She avoided his glance, not wanting him to see that there was more to the story than that. 'I'm not one of those girls who just wants to be married with a couple of babies before I'm twenty-one. Though I think that's what my mum would like.'

'Mums are all the same,' he said. 'Mine's forever asking why I haven't found a nice young lady yet. She keeps telling me about all the single girls in Burracombe.'

'And am I one of them?'

'Of course you are. My mum and yours are friends, aren't they? They're probably planning the wedding at this very moment.' He grinned.

Jackie felt her cheeks flame. 'Crikey, I hope not! I mean, not that I don't like you or anything, but I don't – we don't – you might not even want – we've only just … Oh, I don't know what I mean!' She took a huge gulp of cherry brandy and started to cough.

Vic laughed and banged her on the back. 'It's all right, Jackie, I'm not proposing to you. Not tonight, anyway.' He waited until her coughing fit was over and said, 'I just want to have a bit of fun for a while. I reckon that's what you want too, isn't it?'

'Yes,' Jackie said, relieved. 'Yes, that's all I want.' She gave him a shy smile.

'Then that's all right.' He glanced at the clock over the bar.

'Here, drink up. We haven't got much time if I've got to get you home by half-past ten. But don't choke this time!'

Jackie grinned and finished her cherry brandy. She felt slightly light-headed as she followed Vic out of the pub, and he took her arm to guide her down the street. Once in the van, he turned and put his hand on her cheek, holding her face still. He leaned over to kiss her lightly on the lips.

'Here's to fun,' he said. 'It's been nice taking you out, Jackie. We'll do it again, shall we? That looks a good film on next week – would you like to come and see it with me?'

'Oh, yes please,' Jackie breathed, her heart thudding. 'I'd really like that.'

They drove back to Burracombe along the deep-cut, leafy lanes. A wind had sprung up while they were in the cinema and the first leaves of autumn lay scattered across the road. As they came out on to the moorland road, they could see shredded clouds flying beneath the half-moon, like foam-topped waves at sea.

'Did you do that poem about the highwayman at school?' Vic asked. 'You can see why he thought the moon looked like a ghostly galleon, can't you? It looks just like a ship sailing across the sky.'

'And the road looks like a ribbon of moonlight,' Jackie agreed. 'I liked that poem. We all did.'

Vic pulled off the road and on to the grass. He turned off the engine and the lights and they were in darkness, gazing out at the half-lit moor and the strange, brooding shapes of the tors. Jackie felt a twinge of alarm.

'I've got to get home,' she reminded him.

'By half-past ten. I know. But that doesn't mean we can't have a little kiss and cuddle first, does it? Come here, Jackie.' He pulled her into his arms and she leaned against him awkwardly. It seemed a long time since she'd last been properly kissed – not since she and Roy Pettifer had finished their romance. Once again, Vic turned her face to his and kissed her, but this time his kiss was firmer and deeper. Excitement and panic surged within her and Vic's arms tightened about her. He moved his lips along her cheek and then her neck, and murmured something in her ear, and she relaxed; he kissed her again, more lingeringly, and the panic drifted away as she felt her body grow soft.

After a while, she stirred and whispered, 'What's the time? It must be nearly half-past.'

'Gosh, I'm sorry,' Vic said, not sounding at all sorry really. 'It's a bit later than that. You're so lovely, Jackie – I just forgot all about the time. I didn't want to stop.'

Jackie hadn't wanted to stop either, but the spell was broken now and she wriggled away from him and sat up straight, a different sort of panic welling up within her. 'Take me home, Vic, please. You don't know what my dad can be like.'

'It's only quarter to eleven'.

'*Quarter to eleven?* That means it'll be nearly eleven when I get home! Oh Vic, what am I going to say?'

'Just say I had trouble starting the van.' He started it again, with no problem. 'D'you want me to come in with you?'

'No, better not.' It was bad enough having panicked like this, she wasn't going to have Vic witness her father telling her off like a naughty child. 'I don't suppose it'll be that bad – his bark's worse than his bite. Anyway, I dare say he'll have gone to bed by now.' She knew he would not have done.

They continued home, Vic whistling softly under his breath. It was all right for him, Jackie thought resentfully, he was over twenty-one and had been in the Army and no one could tell him what to do. She wished fervently she hadn't got into such a state. He would think she was still a kid, having to do whatever Mummy and Daddy said, and never want to take her out again. The pleasure of the evening evaporated, leaving her feeling cold and dismal. The next time she saw Vic Nethercott, she thought miserably, he would be driving by with Tessa Latimer.

They arrived at the farm gate. Vic turned to Jackie, obviously intending to kiss her again, but alarm welled up again and she pushed him away. 'Sorry, Vic, I've got to go in. Thanks for taking me out – it was lovely.'

'Next week?' he said, catching her hand as she scrambled out of the van. 'We'll go and see that picture, shall we? And maybe go for a walk or something over the weekend?'

Jackie turned and stared at him, hardly able to believe that he wanted to see her again after all. She felt a warm blush of pleasure touch her cheeks and gripped his hand in return.

'All right,' she said. 'Next week. And I've got Sunday off.'

'I'll borrow the van again,' he said. 'We'll go out somewhere in the afternoon. Pick you up here about half-past two, all right?'

'Yes,' she said, dizzy with relief. 'Half-past two. See you then.'

She turned and opened the farmyard gate. She still had to face her father's wrath for being over half an hour late, but it didn't seem to matter so much now. Vic wanted to see her again. He wanted to take her out again – twice in the next week. She almost skipped across the yard before reaching the door and stopping to take a deep breath. Her father was sure to be up and waiting for her, and he was sure to be angry.

But when Jackie walked through the kitchen door, it seemed that everyone was up, and nobody cared or even noticed that she was late. There was a strange mixture of animation and shock, worry and relief on her mother's face as she turned to see her daughter come hesitantly through the door, and to her surprise she saw a bottle of sherry on the table.

'What's been going on?' she asked. 'What's happened?'

'Oh Jackie, you've missed it all!' Alice exclaimed, coming over to kiss her. 'You've missed all the excitement. It's Joanna – she've had her baby. You'm an auntie again.'

'Had her baby?' Jackie stared at her mother. 'But how could

132

she have? I've only been gone four hours – there wasn't a sign when I went out.'

'She've had it, all the same,' Alice laughed. 'And there's more than that – she've had *two* babies! Twins! That's why she was so big. What do you think of *that*, then?'

Chapter Thirteen

'Twins?' Hilary Napier exclaimed when Jackie told her the news next morning as she brought a covered dish of bacon and eggs into the breakfast room. 'Good heavens, that was unexpected, wasn't it?'

'Nobody dreamed of it,' Jackie agreed. 'Even Nurse Sanders didn't have a clue. The doctor says one of them must have been laying behind the other one and she couldn't feel it. But Joanna was big, mind, and she often said she felt as if she were being kicked and punched by half a dozen babies instead of just one.'

'How are they? And how's Joanna?'

'Well, they're very tiny,' Jackie said. 'A bit scrawny, really, not like Robin when he was born. I only saw them for a few minutes – Joanna's worn out. It all happened so quick, you see. Everything was just the same as usual when I went out about seven o'clock and when I got back about eleven, it were all over.'

'Four hours! That's quick, especially for two babies.'

'So Mum says. She's a bit worried about them, to tell you the truth. Being early and so small, and everything. They're in two shoeboxes, all wrapped up in cottonwool to keep them cosy. The doctor says they ought to have gone into hospital, only Joanna's so tired and weak it wouldn't be fair to move her, and they can't go without her because of being fed.'

'Oh dear. I do hope they're going to be all right.' Hilary glanced round as Travis came in. 'Look, you'd better go home as soon as you've finished with the breakfast – they may want you there. Give Joanna my best wishes. I'll pop in and see her later on, when she's had a chance to recover a bit.'

Travis looked at her enquiringly. 'Somebody ill?'

'Not exactly. It's Joanna Tozer – you know, Ted and Alice Tozer's daughter-in-law. You met her the other day when we went round to the farm.'

'Oh yes, the one expecting a baby sometime soon. Is she having problems?'

'Not as many as she may have in the future,' Hilary said with a laugh. 'The baby was born last night, but it turned out to be twins! They're very small and apparently Charles – the doctor – would have liked Joanna to have them in hospital, but it all happened too quickly.'

'Mum won't hear of them going away now,' Jackie said, setting the dish in the middle of the table. 'She says she and Grandma and Joanna can look after them. Grandma says Uncle Joe – that was her first – was a premature baby. Seven months born, he was, and the doctor said he wouldn't live, but she kept him in a little box near the fire, all in cottonwool like the twins, and fed him with a fountain-pen filler because he were too small to go on the breast.' She glanced at Travis and blushed. 'And he grew up to be a big, strong man and went to America to seek his fortune, and he's still there now!'

'Goodness, yes, I'd forgotten your Uncle Joe,' Hilary said. 'I met him once, years ago, when he came over for a visit. He's done well, hasn't he?'

'Yes, he's quite rich, so it just shows what you can do with tiny babies. I reckon our twins'll be all right. I'll go and get some toast.' Jackie departed, standing back to let Gilbert Napier come through the door.

'What's all that about?' he asked, and Hilary told him about Joanna's babies. 'My God, more twins! There must be something in the water at Burracombe. Let's hope they don't turn out like Crocker's two grandsons, anyway. Little demons, they are, and going to get worse before they get better.' He sat down and helped himself to bacon and eggs, shooting a look from under his brows at Travis. 'It's today you're going back to Hampshire, isn't it? Come to any decision?'

'I thought we might have a talk about that after breakfast,' Travis said, and the Squire nodded.

'We'll go into my study. I dare say Hilary can find something to do in the office, can't you, girl? Always paperwork to catch up on, more's the pity.'

'I think Hilary should come too,' Travis said evenly, and the Colonel's bushy eyebrows shot up. 'She needs to be in on all our discussions, if we're going to be working together.'

'Hm.' Gilbert looked from one to the other, as if he were about to argue, then shrugged and took some fried bread and mushrooms. 'I'll have some coffee, if you don't mind, Hilary.'

Hilary hid her smile as she poured the coffee. She and Travis had had a long talk after their early-morning ride, and she felt that they were working towards an understanding. It wouldn't be roses all the way – they were both strong-minded people and had their own ideas – and it might not work out at all, but she realised that this was the best she was going to get. As he had said, with his sideways grin, better the devil you know than the devil you don't know, and he was right in saying that her father wasn't going to give up this idea. He had made up his mind to employ an estate manager, and nothing she could say would change that. At least this way she could stay on the land she loved.

And if it didn't work out? If she and Travis couldn't get along? Or if her father decided that someone else would conform more readily to his ideas, and gave Travis the sack? Well, she thought resignedly, in that case I'll have to think again. Maybe I'll end up going to London after all. Or maybe Dad will finally see that the estate is better in my hands than in a stranger's.

They gathered in the study at about half-past ten. Gilbert Napier sat behind his big desk, and Hilary and Travis took two chairs opposite him. He leaned his elbows on the leather top, rested his chin on his fists and stared at them both, his eyebrows drawn so low and so close together that they looked like an enormous, hairy caterpillar. His lips, pressed together, jutted above his chin which was thrust forwards. With his mane of iron-grey hair, he looked as fearsome as a male lion scenting a threat to his territory.

'Well?' he demanded. 'I take it you two have been having your own discussions about this.'

Hilary's heart sank. Already, they'd managed to annoy him by talking the matter over between themselves. She said, 'Travis needed to know how I felt about it.'

'Did he, indeed?' The formidable stare shifted to Travis. 'So you're prepared to put yourself under petticoat government?'

'Not at all.' Travis seemed unmoved by the suppressed annoyance in the Colonel's voice. 'It seemed only just, to me, to find out what Hilary's opinion was. If we're to work together—'

'There's no question of your working together! I've offered you the job of estate manager, not as second-in-command to my daughter. The whole point is to free her to live her own life.'

'But this *is* my life, Father! It's what I want to do. You're taking it away from me.' Hilary fought to keep the tears from her voice and her eyes. 'Look, do you really want me to leave Burracombe? Do you want me to go and work in London? Because if so, that's what I'll do.'

'Of course I don't. Have I ever suggested such a thing? Spend time in London, yes, or wherever else you like, but this is your home and always will be.'

'It won't,' she stated more quietly. 'If you won't let me have any hand in running the place, I might as well go away. I need to have something to do, Dad. I'm not a young girl looking for a husband, I'm a grown woman, and I want to make something of my life. If I can't do it here, I'll have to do it somewhere else.'

'That's blackmail,' he said, but she shook her head.

'It's not meant to be. It's just the way things are.'

There was a brief silence. Then Travis said, 'You may think this is blackmail as well, Colonel Napier, but I've come to the conclusion that if I'm to work here at all, I need Hilary to work with me. I'm afraid I can't consider accepting the post – if you still intend to offer it to me – unless she's part of it.'

Napier turned his eyes towards him again. 'Can you explain why? If Hilary can run the place without help, why can't you?'

'So you admit I *can* run it,' Hilary said quickly, but Travis lifted one hand and she fell silent, biting her lip.

'Because I know what Baden wanted to do here,' he said. 'He used to talk to me a lot about Burracombe – about his ideas for the place when the war was over and he came home. He didn't see himself taking over from you for years, but he knew you'd be working together and he knew you'd listen to him. He realised that things were going to change, you see. He realised that there would be different needs – the world was going to be a different place. We talked about it a lot.' He stopped. Gilbert was watching him intently, his eyes narrowed as if he were weighing up whether to believe him or not. Hilary looked at them both and made up her mind.

'Baden wanted Travis to come and work here with him,' she said.

Her father's head swung round and he stared her. *'What?'*

'He wanted Travis to come and work with him,' she repeated. 'He knew that it was going to be a difficult time. It *has* been, Father, you know that,' she went on, her voice rising. 'I know the war's been over for seven years now, but it lasted for six – and everything changed in that time. The country's still not properly back on its feet. We've still got rationing, for goodness sake! Baden didn't have a crystal ball, he didn't know how long it was going to last, but he could see well enough that whole cities, like Plymouth and Coventry, would have to be rebuilt, and he could see that there were going to be thousands of men who wouldn't come back.' She stopped, swallowed and went on more quietly: 'He must have known that he might be one of them. But he was still thinking about Burracombe.'

'He was,' Travis confirmed. 'It was in his mind all the time – the piece of England he was fighting for especially.'

There was another silence. The conversation seemed to have veered in a direction nobody had expected, and gone further perhaps than any of them had wanted. At last, Gilbert said to his daughter, 'Baden never spoke of any of this to you?'

'You forget,' she said, 'that we didn't see much of each other once the war had started. We were both away – we were hardly ever at home at the same time.'

He nodded. 'So it's only Travis's word that you have for this.'

A swift flare of anger rippled through her. Her head came up and she said indignantly, 'If you think he's lying—'

'All right, Hilary,' Travis said. 'I can answer for myself here.' He looked the Colonel in the eye. 'I only told Hilary that *after* we had discussed her feelings about my coming here, and after we had agreed to give it a fair trial. I didn't use it to influence her, and I would not have mentioned it to you. It was between myself and Baden.' He paused. 'I can understand your having doubts about it, but I assure you that those conversations did take place. If you do have doubts, you had better say so, because I certainly couldn't come here if I didn't feel you had complete trust in me.'

'And I wouldn't offer you the job at all if I didn't have that,' Napier said grimly. He looked at them both again. 'So. Do I understand that you have an agreement about the situation – that you're willing to work together?'

'I suggest we try it for six months,' Travis said. 'It's un-known territory for us all.'

Napier looked at Hilary. 'It's not what I wanted for you. You'll still be slaving on the estate when you should be enjoying your life.'

'But I *shall* be enjoying my life, Father. This is what I want – all I want.'

'God knows when I'll ever be a grandfather,' he muttered. 'But I suppose you'll not be forced. Wouldn't be a Napier if you could be.' It was the first glint of humour she had seen in him for weeks, it seemed, and she smiled at him with relief. 'All right, we'll give it a fair trial, as you say. We'll review it in six months.' He opened the big diary on his desk and flipped through it. 'March. Lady Day – that's a fitting time. Though I dare say we'll all have a pretty good idea of how things are going before then.' He closed the diary and regarded Travis. 'Better get down to brass tacks – a lot to be sorted out. Salary, for one thing, and accommodation for another. You'll be wanting a place of your own, no doubt.'

Hilary closed her eyes. This was another problem that had been haunting her all along. If Travis came to Burracombe, where was he to live? There were no vacant cottages on the estate, and the house that should have been his was currently occupied by her father's friend, Arnold Cherriman. And when he and his wife moved back to Plymouth, she'd promised it to Val and Luke Ferris.

Val was at the farm in the early hours of the morning, helping Alice tend the new babies. They lay in their tiny boxes, their minute faces wizened like old men, their arms and legs like little sticks. Alice's eyes were full of tears as she gazed down at them.

'Poor little mites. They haven't had a chance to fill out properly before they got born. Will they be all right, d'you reckon, Val?'

'I hope so.' Val felt a mixture of emotions as she looked at her two small nieces. 'We'll do all we can for them between us. But they really are very tiny.'

'Your grandma says your Uncle Joe were no bigger, but she raised him all right. Mind you, she only had the one. Poor Joanna's got to feed two. Still, once her milk's come through there's bound to be enough there. Nature provides.'

'They may not be strong enough to suckle. We'll need bottles for them, with especially small teats, or even pipettes to start with. I'd better go into Tavistock – there'll be something at the hospital.'

'Dr Latimer was talking about taking them in to be looked after there for the first week or two,' Alice said, her face anxious. 'D'you think that's necessary, Val? Can't us take proper care of them here? I don't like to think of our two little dears in a hospital, with strangers all around them.'

'Well, they don't know any of us very well yet, do they!' Val said with a rather wobbly grin. 'But I don't honestly think they'd be any better off, so long as they can feed. It's just that if anything went wrong and they needed special attention ...' She touched a tiny cheek with her fingertip. 'Not that they can do much more at the hospital than we could. Unless he says it's essential, I think they're just as well off here with Joanna. How is she now?'

'Asleep, poor soul. I know it were quick, but 'tweren't any the easier for it, and it were a shock to find herself with two little ones instead of one. And then to have them so small ... they don't amount to more than one good-sized baby between them. Do you think you'll be able to get the right-size teats for them, Val?'

'I'm sure I will. I'll go in on the eight o'clock bus – I'll catch it easily if I go now. I can slip up to the hospital and then get the next bus back.' She touched the little face again. 'Has Joanna thought of names for them?'

'Well, we did think she ought to, seeing as they were so

small. Doctor thought it might be a good idea to baptise them, you see, so Vicar's coming in as soon as he can.' Alice looked unhappy. 'It seems awful, almost like giving up before we've even started, but – well, you know how it is. And Joanna wants you to be godmother, but it seems more important for you to go now and get whatever we need. I don't really know what to suggest.'

'Why not decide when Mr Harvey comes? I'll probably get back before him anyway, if I can get a lift from the main road.' The village bus only ran a few times a day and she would have to catch the Plymouth bus to come back, and walk the last mile or so. 'But if the doctor thinks they ought to be baptised at once, you'd better go ahead. What are their names anyway?' Her fingers were tender on the small bodies. 'I'd just like to know – before I go.' She couldn't say what was in both their minds, that she might not see the babies alive again.

'This one's Heather Mary – Mary after your grandma, she's the eldest by half an hour – and this one's Suzanne Alice. Pretty names, aren't they?'

'Yes.' Val took one last look and then turned away, her eyes filled with tears. 'And they're going to be pretty little girls, Mum. We'll get them through this, don't you worry.'

'Well, if it's love that they need, there be plenty of that,' Alice declared. 'And with me and your grandma and their own mother to look after them, they won't want for care. Now, you ought to have a bite to eat before you goes off to Tavvy. I dare say you came dashing up here without so much as a mouthful.'

'Well, I was hardly likely to start frying bacon when Tom came rushing down to tell me the news,' Val replied. 'But I won't stop now, Mum. I want to get back and tell Luke – he'll be wondering what's happening.'

'Take a scone with you then, at least.' Alice went to the larder and hastily spread a few with butter and put them into a paper bag. 'Fresh made yesterday, they were, you can eat them on the bus. There's one for Luke as well.'

'Thanks.' Val kissed her mother hastily and opened the door. It was still early and the fields were pearled with dew, the sun filtering through the mist as if through a muslin curtain. She hurried through the farmyard, pausing to look in at the cowshed where her father and brother were busy with the cows. Tom saw her and got up from his milking stool.

'How are they?'

'They seem all right. I'm going in to the hospital to get bottles for them, as they may have trouble feeding from Joanna. Don't worry, Tom – they'll be fine.'

'You know we're having them baptised?'

'Yes,' she said gently. 'It doesn't mean they're not going to survive. It's just a precaution.'

'It means one of them might not,' he said. 'I've seen enough baby animals die through being too small. And even if they do live, they might have things wrong with them. It's no good telling me not to worry, Val.' He rubbed his face and she saw how exhausted he looked. He had been up all night with his wife and now he had to help milk forty cows.

'Where's Norman?' she asked. 'Couldn't he be doing this for you? You need rest yourself.'

'He did come up, but I sent him away again. I couldn't settle – I'm better off doing something. I might get my head down later on, when – when the doctor's been again. You won't be too long, will you, Val?'

'No,' she promised. The flippant, joking brother she knew so well had disappeared, leaving a tired, anxious man in his place. 'I'll be as quick as I can. You might bring the van and meet me at the road, if you like – that'll be a help. I should be on the half-past nine bus back.'

He nodded. 'I'll try. It depends when Dr Latimer comes, and the vicar. Oh, Val.' He sounded suddenly desperate. 'They are going to be all right, aren't they? My little girls?'

Val looked at her brother and felt her heart go out to him. She thought of the tiny babies in the cottonwool-lined shoeboxes by the stove, for all the world like lambs that had been brought in to be bottle-fed, and she thought of another baby, years ago, who had also been born too soon and not survived. There was a huge lump in her throat as she reached out and patted Tom's arm.

'We'll do everything we can for them,' she said. 'If love can keep them alive then they'll live to be a hundred. I must go now. I'll be back as soon as I can.'

'I'll meet you at the road,' he said, and turned to go back into the cowshed.

Chapter Fourteen

By mid-morning it was all over the village that Joanna Tozer had had twins, at least three weeks premature. It wasn't such a lot really, for just one baby who might be a good size – over five pounds, anyway – but for two, it meant they were very small and everyone was anxious. Joanna, who had come to the Tozers' farm as a Land Girl during the war, was well liked and the Tozers were a prominent family.

'Poor little toads,' Mrs Purdy said as she bought her newspaper and *Woman's Weekly* in the village shop. 'All the trouble of being born, just to slip away again. 'Tis cruel.'

'Who says they'm slipping away?' Edie Pettifer demanded as she handed over change from a two-shilling piece. 'Last I heard, Minnie Tozer was feeding them with a fountain-pen filler, and if anyone can rear an eight-month baby, she can.'

''Tis different with two, though. And you know what they say – if one twin dies the other soon follows. It's because they'm so close before birth.'

'Well, that's nonsense if ever I heard any!' Mrs Dawe, the school cook, chimed in. She and Mrs Purdy always took opposite views if they could. 'Look at old Abraham Bellamy, from over Lovaton. Seventy-five he'll be, come December, and his twin died at four years old.'

'Yes, but that were in an accident,' Edie pointed out. ''T'other little tacker fell into the threshing-machine. I know, because my dad used to talk about it; he were working on the farm at the time and he said everyone was in a terrible state about it.'

'I'm not saying Abraham had to fall into the thresher as well,' Mrs Purdy said with exaggerated patience. 'I'm saying that twins can't live without each other. They dies of a broken heart.'

'Well, Abraham Bellamy didn't, so—'

'Has anyone heard how Joanna Tozer is?' asked Maggie Culliford, coming into the shop at that moment. As usual, she was wearing a grubby pinafore over an old frock, and slippers on her feet. She was rarely seen without them and it was generally believed that she only had one pair of shoes, which she kept for 'best'. 'Ted Tozer sent over this morning for my Arthur to give a hand round the farm. Arthur didn't know much but he said she'd had her baby. I didn't think 'twas due for another two or three weeks.'

'She has, and it's twins,' Mrs Purdy said, pleased to be able to give the news. 'Two little girls, no bigger than kittens. Vicar's baptising them this morning so they don't die in a state of sin.'

'State of sin!' Edie Pettifer sniffed scornfully. 'How could two tiny mites like that, only just born, be in a state of sin?'

'Well, whether or no, they got to have their names given them proper to get into Heaven,' Mrs Purdy said obstinately.

'I wish you'd stop talking as if they'm dying!' Mrs Dawe snapped. 'Nothing but an old gloom-bucket, you be, and always have been. No wonder that hubby of yours is always round the Bell, drowning his sorrows. I'll have my *Western Morning News* now, if you don't mind, Edie. Can't stand here gossiping all day, there's work to be done.' She bustled out.

'Twins!' Maggie Culliford said. 'Well, that wasn't expected, was it?' She looked tired, and her own pregnancy was beginning to show. 'I hope to God I don't have twins. I got enough as it is.'

'You ought to tell your man to do something about it, then,' Mrs Purdy told her. ''Tis up to him to look after you. The school's over-run with Cullifords.'

'Well, they keeps you in work, then, don't they!' Maggie retorted. 'And you can't say my Shirley's any trouble, not since Miss Kemp realised what a clever girl she is. She never give any of my little 'uns credit before that. It'll be the same with my Billy, you mark my words – just because he's a Culliford, she'll expect the worst. All my kiddies have had the same trouble with teachers.'

'The only trouble your kiddies has is with their father,' Mrs Purdy declared. 'Out poaching again last night, was he? He'll find himself up before the magistrate again one of these days, if he's not careful, and he'll be lucky if he don't go to prison. You wants to tell him.'

She marched out after Mrs Dawe, leaving Maggie Culliford looking half-indignant and half-tearful. Edie Pettifer, who had a kind heart, smiled at her.

'You don't want to take no notice of she. Reckon her got out of bed the wrong side this morning.'

'Oh, it's not her I care about,' Maggie said, brushing back a straggle of lank hair from her forehead. ''Tis my little ones. Just because they come from a poor family, they gets picked on – nobody reckons they'm worth anything. But look at my Shirley, pretty as a picture she were as Festival Queen, and done well in her exams, and now Miss Kemp's talking about her going to grammar school next year. Never bothered with her at all before that. It's that new teacher, Miss Simmons, that's done it, you know. She treats all the kiddies the same, whoever they be.' She lifted her shopping basket on to the counter and took out her ration books. 'I'll have a few sweets, seeing as it's Saturday. How about these babies, then? Is it true they'm not going to live?'

'That's just Mabel Purdy looking on the black side. You know what she'm like. Mind you, it's true the Vicar's going up

147

this morning to baptise them, so it don't look too promising, do it?'

'Well, I call that a shame,' Maggie said. 'That young Mrs Tozer's a nice young woman, for all she'm a stranger to the village, and Ted Tozer often gives my Arthur a bit of work. Knows us needs the money.'

'Pity he can't find regular work,' Edie said, weighing out two ounces of toffee crunch. 'I don't want to be critical, Maggie, but with all those little ones to look after ...'

'He do try,' Maggie said defensively. 'He went into Tavvy last week and went round all the builders. They're talking about building some big new estates out at Whitchurch – he could get work there. But there's nothing yet. I reckon they're only interested in Plymouth, never mind us poor country folk getting left behind as usual.'

'You want to tell him to be careful what he gets up to at night,' Edie said, colouring as her glance fell on Maggie's pinafore, already looking tight across her stomach, and adding hastily, 'I mean, if he's going poaching he's going to get caught again, and you know what Squire said last time. It'll be a month behind bars if he comes up before him again.'

'He wasn't out poaching last night,' Maggie said instantly. 'Anyone who says he was is a liar. He was over with his mother; she's been poorly lately and he goes up to settle her down of a night. And I went to bed early so I don't know what time he come in, but it weren't late. I'll have twenty Woodbine as well, Edie, if you don't mind, and then I'd better get home. I left Shirley looking after the little ones and her wants to go and play with your Betty's little maid. Thick as thieves, those two are, even though Jane goes to the Grammar now.'

Edie handed over the cigarettes and took Maggie's money. She watched her go out of the shop and sighed.

Maggie Culliford wasn't a bad sort at heart, she thought. She might have made something of her life if she hadn't had to get married to Arthur after he'd got her in the family way.

Ever since then, she'd gone from bad to worse, one baby after another, and with no regular wage coming into the house it wasn't surprising she always looked poorly dressed and tired to death. Didn't have either time or energy to look after herself. And now, just when her eldest looked like doing a bit better, there was yet another baby on the way. There was no need for it these days.

Edie had never been married and didn't think she ever would, despite Bert Foster's pleas. Marriage was all right if you found the right person, but she liked her single life. At least I can have a cup of tea or go to bed whenever I feel like it, she thought, going out to the back room to fetch in another box of Woodbines and stacking them on the shelves. And I don't have to have babies!

The thought of being pregnant and giving birth made her shudder. And when you suddenly found you had two, like poor Joanna Tozer – well, it didn't bear thinking of.

She wondered if the twins were still alive, but she had great faith in the village grapevine. It wouldn't be long before someone came into the shop with some news.

Jackie arrived back at the farm just as the vicar hurried across the field path from the churchyard. They met at the gate and he gave her an enquiring look. 'How are they?'

'I don't know. I've only just got home.' Jackie stared at him, suddenly afraid. 'You're going to christen them, aren't you? Does that mean they're going to die?'

'Not at all. It's just a precaution – tiny babies need a lot of extra care, and it might be quite a long time before we can have the service in church. People want their babies baptised as soon as possible.'

'Robin was six weeks old,' Jackie remembered. 'But I've never really understood why. Surely God wouldn't refuse to have a tiny baby in Heaven, just because there hadn't been time to have it christened?'

'It doesn't seem very likely,' Basil Harvey agreed. 'But ours is not to reason why ... Anyway, it will be nice for Joanna and Tom to think that their little girls are in a state of grace, and if their mother and father feel happier, the babies have a better chance.'

Jackie couldn't quite believe this, but she opened the back door and followed the vicar into the kitchen. Minnie was in her chair by the stove with Robin on his stool beside her and Alice at the table, rolling out pastry as if it had insulted her, while Tom paced anxiously between the window and the staircase. As soon as she saw Basil, Alice dropped her rolling pin and started to wipe her hands down her apron.

'Oh, Vicar, thank goodness you'm here! The midwife's up there with her now, and our Val as well. They're feeding the poor little mites. Nurse Sanders says the first milk's the most important, not that it's proper milk, it's colostrum ... It's the same with calves, they've got to feed from their mother the first day. Only these two precious little hearts are so small, they can't ...' She stopped and reddened, unsure exactly how much of this was fit for a vicar's ears. Basil, who had ministered in slum areas and heard a good deal more explicit language than he was ever likely to hear in Alice Tozer's kitchen, smiled and laid his hand on her arm.

'I quite understand, Alice. I can wait here until they're ready for me, but perhaps you'd like to let them know I've arrived. Is the doctor coming again?'

Alice nodded. Her eyes were red-rimmed as if she'd been crying, and her grey hair was straggly, as if she hadn't had time when she got up to drag a comb through it, and had then forgotten. She brushed the palm of one hand up her face, leaving a patch of flour on her cheek. 'He said he'd be here by eleven. It's almost that now. Oh, I do hope they'm going to be all right. 'Twould be a tragedy if ...' Her eyes filled with tears again as she shook her head, unable to speak the fear in her mind. 'I'm sorry, Vicar,' she whispered. 'It just keeps coming over me. I was all right when it was all happening, and us was all so pleased they were both born and living, that us even had a drop of sherry to celebrate, but since then – oh dear.' She wiped her eyes with the corner of her apron.

''Tis the shock, my dear,' Minnie said from her corner. It had affected her too, Basil thought, glancing towards her. She looked smaller, almost shrunken, in her wooden rocker, a crocheted shawl around her shoulders. 'And you've hardly slept a wink nor ate a proper breakfast. 'Tis not surprising you'm feeling a bit leer.'

'It's a worrying time for you all,' he said. 'Alice, why don't you make us all a cup of tea? I could certainly do with one.' He thought God would probably forgive him for the lie, for Grace had given him a large cup of coffee not long before leaving the vicarage, but if he hadn't expressed a need of his own, Alice wouldn't have done as he suggested. He watched as she went to the sink and filled the big kettle, setting it on the stove, then went to lay her hand on Robin's head.

'Do you need any water for the service, Vicar?' she asked, hesitating.

'No, I've brought some holy water. I don't know if you've ever attended a private baptism, Alice?' She shook her head. 'It's a little different from the one in church. It's very short, and there are no godparents.' He smiled at Jackie, who had uttered a little sound of dismay. 'But you will be a witness – you all will – and when the babies are strong enough they can be brought to church so that everyone can see that they're baptised.'

'You mean you'll do it again? Properly?' Jackie asked, and he shook his head.

'No, this will be the proper baptism, the *only* baptism. When they come to church, it's so that I can say to everyone there that I myself baptised them, and then I shall ask for godparents and we have the service much the same as usual. And I'm sure Joanna and Tom will want that to be as soon as possible.' He looked up as footsteps sounded on the stairs. 'Ah, Val. How are they all?'

'We've managed to get them to suck the pipettes.' She looked and sounded as tired as the rest of them. 'They're asleep now. I think Joanna could sleep too, once she knows they've been christened.' She glanced across the kitchen to her mother, who was pouring boiling water into the big brown teapot. 'Do you want to have that first?'

'Oh no,' Alice said hastily, and then looked at the vicar. 'Unless you want a cup, Vicar?'

He shook his head. 'Let's have it afterwards as a celebration. Is Joanna ready for us?' Val nodded. 'Then let's all go up. Where's Ted?'

'He's in the barn,' Tom said, moving towards the door but casting anxious glances at the ceiling. Jackie caught his look and said, 'I'll fetch him. You go on.'

Alice caught Robin, who was just about to lift the cat in his arms, and hurried him over to the sink. She picked up a damp flannel and wiped it hastily over his face. 'You can't go to your sisters' christening with jam all round your mouth, young man. Let me just brush your hair back – there, that's better.'

'What's a christening?' he asked, squirming free and looking in disappointment after the cat, who had taken the opportunity to escape. 'Will there be presents?'

'It's to give your baby sisters their names,' his grandmother explained. She looked at the vicar. 'It's all right for him to come, isn't it? Us can't leave him in the kitchen by himself.'

'Of course he must come,' Basil said, and held out his hand to the little boy.

They mounted the narrow stairs, Tom first and then the vicar and Robin, followed by Alice, Minnie and Val. As they crowded into the bedroom, Jackie and Ted came into the kitchen, followed by the doctor who just had arrived in the yard, and Ted washed his hands hastily at the sink. They joined the others as the vicar was pouring water from his bottle into Alice's best jug and setting it on the washstand.

Joanna was in bed, propped up against half a dozen pillows and looking almost pale enough to see the wallpaper through her. The babies were in the family bassinet beside her; every baby in the family since Ted's father had been laid in that little cot and, although it had been made for one, there was room enough and to spare for the tiny scraps that occupied it now. Everyone peeped in and murmured softly about their size, or tried to see family resemblances, and then Basil said in a quiet voice, 'Let's start with the Lord's Prayer.'

As they repeated the familiar words, Val felt the beginning of a return to calm. The morning had been such a rush that her heart seemed to have been pounding in double time for hours. But here Joanna was, exhausted but safe, and here the babies were, tiny but successfully given their first important feed. The words of the prayer, spoken in that peaceful room by the members of her family, seemed designed to comfort; and with the word 'Amen' she took a deep breath and felt better.

Basil Harvey recited one of the Collects used at normal baptisms, then looked enquiringly at Tom. 'Will you let me have the elder of your babies, please, Tom, and tell me her name?'

Tom reached into the cot and gently lifted out his tiny daughter. He cradled her in his arms for a moment, gazing down at the crumpled face, and then handed her over to the vicar. Val saw her mother make a tiny, involuntary movement and knew that she was experiencing that sense of anxiety that all women feel when they see a man handle a small baby – the fear that the big hands will be clumsy, that the baby will be dropped or its head not properly supported. But Tom hadn't forgotten his own skills, and Basil had baptised too many babies to fumble now. He held the little bundle securely in one arm over the china washbasin and lifted the jug.

'Heather Mary,' he said, 'I baptise thee in the Name of the Father and of the Son and of the Holy Ghost. Amen.' He poured about a teaspoonful of water on the tiny, fuzz-covered head and looked down as Tom had done, into the baby's face; then he gave her back. Tom replaced her in the cradle and lifted out his second daughter.

'Suzanne Alice,' the vicar said, 'I baptise thee in the Name of the Father and of the Son and of the Holy Ghost. Amen.'

He poured the water again and the baby started slightly and let out a wail. It was surprisingly loud and everyone laughed a little, with surprise, although Alice's laugh was perilously close to a sob.

Basil handed the crying baby back and her wail subsided as if she were too tired to protest any further. He looked around at the small congregation and said, 'Would you like to kneel down? If you can't, just bow your heads.' After a moment while they did this, he went on: 'We shall now give thanks to God for these two precious lives, given into our care for whatever time He sees fit to grant. *We yield Thee hearty thanks, most merciful Father, that it hath pleased Thee to regenerate these infants with Thy holy Spirit, to receive them for Thine own Children by adoption, and to incorporate them into Thy holy Church. And we humbly beseech Thee to grant, that as they are now made partakers of the death of Thy Son, so they may also be of His resurrection; and that finally, with the residue of Thy Saints, they may inherit Thine everlasting kingdom, through the same Thy Son, Jesus Christ our Lord. Amen.'*

'Amen,' they all repeated, and then he smiled around at them and said, 'That's all for now. I think these three ladies need to rest quietly. Perhaps we could have that cup of tea now, Alice, and I'm sure Tom will bring one up for Joanna.'

'While you're doing that,' Dr Latimer said, 'I'll have a look at mother and babies to see if everything's all right. Nurse Sanders, you might stay and help me, please.'

'Can I help too?' Robin asked. He was standing by the bed, leaning against his mother and looking down at the two babies, now quiet in the crooks of her arms. 'Mr Harvey made them all wet, and they weren't even dirty.'

'You come down with me,' Alice said, reaching out her hand. 'We'll make Mummy a nice cup of tea and you can help bring it up.'

'With some biscuits,' he agreed, allowing himself to be led away. 'They'll all want biscuits.'

They trooped downstairs. Jackie was still looking disappointed. 'Is that all there is? I really wanted to be godmother.'

'And so you will be,' Alice promised her. 'You heard what Vicar said. We can have a church service as soon as they'm big enough. The main thing is, they'm now proper Christian souls. Now, fetch me some milk from the pantry, there's a good girl.'

'Bring out that fruit cake I made last week too,' Minnie called after her. 'None of us has had much to eat this morning, and 'tis good nourishment.'

'Sit you down, Vicar,' Ted said, pushing the cat off his own armchair. 'You've time to stop for a few minutes, I hope?'

'Indeed I have.' Basil glanced up at the ceiling, where they could hear footsteps and a low murmur of voices as the doctor and nurse moved about. 'I want to hear what Dr Latimer has to say, too.'

They were all holding cups of tea and plates with large slices of fruit cake when the doctor came downstairs. He accepted a cup from Val, but shook his head at the cake. 'I had a good breakfast and there'll be lunch waiting for me at one o'clock. Now …' He glanced round at the anxious faces, 'they're all doing very well. As well as can be expected, anyway,' he added hastily as they gave a collective sigh of relief. 'I can't make any promises. Everything depends on how things go for the next few days. But there's nothing wrong with Joanna that a good long sleep won't put right, and the babies seem to be holding their own. We must just hope and pray.'

They all nodded solemnly and Alice said, 'You'm not going to send them to hospital, then?'

'Not at present, no. They're being well cared for here in their own home and there's nothing much more that could be done for them in hospital. I'll come in two or three times a day, and if I do think they should be moved I'll make arrangements at once. But for now, I'm satisfied for them to stay here.'

'Thank goodness for that,' Alice said, wiping tears from her eyes. 'I'd hate to think of them taken away from us, the precious little souls. Oh, look at me!' She realised suddenly what she had been using to wipe her eyes. 'Still in my pinafore! And all through their christening too! Whatever will the good Lord think of me?'

'I don't think God will mind that,' Basil said with a laugh. He finished his cake – the fact that he'd eaten a hearty breakfast and would soon be going home for his own lunch hadn't stopped him from accepting a piece – and brushed crumbs from his cassock. 'Your pinafore is a badge of office, Alice, and one you can be proud of when you can produce cake like this. Oh, that was Mrs Tozer, wasn't it.' He would never, out of respect for her age, have dreamed of addressing Minnie by her Christian name. 'Well, the same goes for both of you. I only wish I could bake cakes. I did try once,' he added thoughtfully. 'It exploded in the oven. I never really knew why.'

As they all chuckled, he went out, promising to look in again very soon and Dr Latimer went back upstairs to give the babies a final check. Val said she'd go back to the cottage, where she had left Luke decorating again, and Jackie said she ought to return to the Barton.

'Miss Hilary said I could take as long as I liked, but there's not really much I can do here now, is there? And Mr Kellaway's going back to Hampshire after dinner – lunch, I mean – so there'll be all his room to do, and the bed to change and everything.' She didn't mention that she rather wanted to be around when he said goodbye.

'That's all right, maid, you go back.' Alice said. She looked at the mantelpiece clock. 'My stars, look at the time! All behind like a duck's tail we be this morning, not that there's any wonder about that. I don't know what you men think you'll be getting for your dinner, but 'twon't be much, I'm afraid.'

'Just give us eggs and bacon,' Tom said. 'We missed our breakfast, after all. A bit of fried potato and some tomatoes and mushrooms and we'll be set up for the afternoon.' He glanced at his father. 'I want to go and see if Jo's all right, Dad, if that's OK by you. I'll come out a bit later.'

'You take the rest of the day to be with her, boy,' Ted said gruffly. 'I've got our Norman on the tractor, and Arthur Culliford can give me a hand with that bit of wall that fell down last week.'

'That poacher!' Minnie said. 'I'm surprised you have him on your land, Ted.'

Ted shrugged. 'Say what you like about the man, he's not bad with a bit of dry-stone walling. Pity he goes and spends all the money on drink instead of giving it to that poor wife of his.'

'Her'd only spend it on fags,' Minnie said. 'They'm both cut from the same cloth, those two, and the children all growing up the same way. How many have she got now?'

'I don't know and I can't say I'm all that bothered just now,' Ted retorted, thrusting his feet into the Wellington boots he'd left by the back door. 'I'll be back in about an hour, Alice.'

'All right,' she said. 'Dinner'll be ready one o'clock as usual.' The door closed behind him and she and her mother-in-law were alone. Alice sank down in the chair. 'My stars, I feel as if I've been up for a week! I do hope those two little scraps are going to be all right. I didn't like to say when the others were here, but they don't look too good to me. They're so tiny! What do you think?'

'I don't know,' Minnie said, shaking her head sadly. 'I don't know at all. There's not an ounce of fat on either of them, is there? It don't look to me as if they were anywhere near ready to be born, not really. I'll tell you what I'm wondering – I'm wondering if Joanna had her dates right and they'm even earlier than any of us thinks. And I'll tell you what else I'm wondering – if the doctor knows they haven't got long, and that's why he hasn't sent 'em off to the hospital. He knows it wouldn't do no good, and he thinks we'll all be happier to have them at home for the time they have got.'

'Oh, Mother!' Alice exclaimed, staring at her. 'Do you really think that?'

Minnie shook her head again. 'I don't know what to think, Alice, and that's the truth. I don't think any of us do. All us can do, like the doctor said, is hope.'

'And pray,' Alice reminded her, and the old woman nodded. But before she could speak, hasty footsteps sounded on the stairs and Charles Latimer burst into the kitchen. Alice started to her feet and Minnie gripped the arms of her chair. They stared at him in alarm, and Alice cried out, 'What is it, Doctor? What's happened?'

'One of the babies,' he said, feeling hurriedly in his pocket for his car keys. 'Heather. She's not at all well – I'm taking her to the hospital at once.'

Chapter Fifteen

After she had seen Travis off in his Land Rover, Hilary set off on a walk round the estate. It was late afternoon by then and any office work could wait until tomorrow. More than that, she wanted to be away from her father for a while.

She had wished Travis goodbye with mixed feelings. She was still hurt and angry at what she couldn't help seeing as a lack of trust on her father's part. Surely he knew very well that she was unlikely to go to London, or anywhere else, in search of a husband! And if he really did believe that, why hadn't it occurred to him while she was at home keeping house for him, before his heart-attack? No, it was a lack of trust or, more likely, a dislike of seeing a woman do a job that he considered should rightfully belong to a man. His reaction to the proposal she and Travis had made – meaning, as it did, that Hilary would continue to work much as she had been doing – showed that it was not to his liking, and for a moment or two she'd thought he was going to reject it. But then, as clearly as if it had been written across his face, she had seen the thought that if he did so, he would lose his last connection with Baden, and his shoulders had sagged in acquiescence.

Hilary had felt a stab of guilt at that. It did almost amount to blackmail, she thought regretfully. However had she and her father got themselves into this situation? But there seemed to be no alternative. He wasn't being forced to employ Travis – he could find another manager, if he really wanted to. And he wasn't really being forced to employ Hilary either. He could 'sack' her, just as he could sack any employee, simply by cutting off the salary that she had insisted the estate paid her, rather than an 'allowance'.

He wouldn't do that either. And she knew it. So was that blackmail too?

Hilary sighed. She was climbing towards the Standing Stones. It was a place that many people seemed to make for when they wanted peace and quiet, or to think, or to do a bit of courting. In fact, she thought with a flicker of humour, it was surprising it wasn't always crowded!

There was nobody here this afternoon. She sat down with her back against one of the granite stones, drew up her knees and stared down at the village, huddled in the combe below.

It was a view she had always loved. The houses, straggling along the winding street, with the little cuts and alleyways in between, leading to cottages you'd hardly know were there. The church with its stumpy grey tower, standing proud on the little knoll above the village green. The massive oak tree, a thousand years old. The inn with its thatched roof and the half-barrels standing outside, still bright with flowers planted by Dottie Friend. The two little bridges over the Burra Brook, and the bright flash of water tumbling over the stepping-stones and the ford. The trees turning from green to gold and brown, with the occasional deep, burnished crimson of a copper beech.

And beyond and above all that rose the fields, the estate farms, the Tozers' farm, one or two others not part of the estate, and then the moors. The golden carpet of gorse which had clothed the rounded contours in spring had given way to the rich amethyst of heather and, grazing amongst it all, she could see the sheep and ponies which belonged to those Commoners who had the right to graze their animals there. And on top of every hill, like a heap of hastily dropped sweets on a birthday cake, was a tumble of granite rocks – the tors for which Dartmoor was famous.

Hilary felt a tug at her heart as she gazed out upon it all. This is my home, she thought, my place. I love it. I don't want to leave it. Even if Father told me to stop working on the estate – even if I got married – I'd never want to leave it. I'd find some way to stay.

She bent her head and rested it on her knees. After all the anxieties of the past few days, she felt exhausted, disheartened and close to tears. Who had won this battle, she wondered. Her father, who had got his way in bringing in a manager, and also in getting the man he wanted, or her? I'm staying, she thought but it's not on my own terms. I'm not independent any more. I'm having to share with this man, Baden's friend. So I don't feel as if I've won.

Does there have to be a winner, anyway? Why do Dad and I always seem to be pulling in opposite directions, when at the bottom of our hearts we both want the same thing; when Burracombe is the most important thing in our lives.

Perhaps that's why. Travis is right – the world is changing, even here in Burracombe. Stephen knew that, too; that's why he left, to live his own life somewhere else, because he knew he could never make it here. But I *want* to make my life here! And I don't want things to change – not too quickly, anyway. It all seems to be happening too fast.

'Hilary! We didn't see you come up here. Are you all right, love?'

She lifted her head and saw Val and Luke looking down at her in some anxiety. She gave them a weak grin and began to get to her feet, but Val dropped down beside her.

'Tell us to go if you want to be on your own. But you look as if there's something wrong.'

'No, it's all right. I was just thinking, that's all. About all this ...' She waved her hand at the scene laid out before them and Val followed her glance with understanding.

'It's lovely, isn't it.'

'Yes. And it's home. My home.' She bit her lip. 'I don't

'know how I could ever have thought of leaving it, you know.'

'Well, you didn't, did you, and you're not going to.' Val leaned against the same rock. 'At least, I hope you're not.'

'No, I'm not. It's all been decided, Val. Travis Kellaway is coming here as estate manager – but working with me. There's plenty for two to do. We'll divide things up between us and decide on new developments – the way things are going to go, all the changes that will have to be made.' She sighed. 'I know it's silly to wish there needn't be any changes. We have to move with the times, as they say, and the war changed so much. But at least I'll have a say in what happens.'

'But who's going to have the final say? You, or Travis Kellaway?'

'Oh, I don't suppose either of us will have that,' Hilary said with a slightly bitter laugh. 'Father will want to make any important decisions. But we're supposed to be working together, so I hope we'll be able to come to an agreement over most things.'

'Or a compromise,' Luke said, leaning against the nearest Standing Stone.

Hilary's eyes flashed. 'No! Compromise doesn't get anyone anywhere. Nobody gets what they want and everyone's resentful.'

'Or everyone gets some of what they want,' he countered. 'Compromise can work, if it's done carefully.'

'And can you really see that happening – with one woman against two men?' She shook her head dispiritedly. 'And yet, I do think Travis will try to work with me, rather than against me. If only he can satisfy my father as well. The first few months will probably be the most difficult, while we're all getting used to the new regime.'

There was a short silence and then she turned quickly to her friend. 'Listen to me, going on about my own concerns when you must be worried to death about your brother's babies. How are they? And how's Joanna? Poor Jackie looked as white as a sheet when she came back at lunchtime and told me they'd been taken to hospital. I told her she should have stayed at home.'

'There's nothing she could do,' Val said. 'She might as well be out of the house, and she thought Mrs Ellis would need help this afternoon. Well, Joanna's all right, just needs rest now, and we'll have to wait and see how the babies get on. They're so small, and the birth was too quick – it was a shock for them, poor little scraps. The doctor decided to take them all to hospital in the end – he said it was best for them to be together. It'll be touch and go for a few days, I'm afraid, especially for Heather.'

'That's dreadful. Jackie told me the vicar came to baptise them.'

'Yes. The doctor thought he should. The trouble is, it always frightens people – they think the babies are going to die before the day's out.' Her voice trembled a little. 'It doesn't always happen like that. It's just – just in case.'

Hilary gave her a quick, curious look. There had been a note in Val's voice which seemed to hint at some other thought, deep inside her heart. Probably a baby she knew in one of the hospitals she'd worked in, Hilary thought. Or out in Egypt. There must have been quite a few times when babies were baptised soon after birth, and not always because they were ill, but because they were in another kind of danger . . .

'These little ones aren't going to die though, are they?' she said gently. 'They're going to survive.'

'If love can keep them alive, they will,' Val answered. 'The trouble is, love isn't always enough. And Heather really is quite poorly.' Her voice shook.

Luke came over and laid his hand on his wife's shoulder. 'Val . . .'

'It's all right,' she said tearfully, laying her hand on his. 'I'm just tired – it's been a long day.' She turned to Hilary. 'Luke wanted me to get some sleep but I couldn't. That's why we came up here. It's always so peaceful at the Stones, it sort of seeps into your soul. We thought it would help.'

'And you found me here, brooding over my own troubles,' Hilary said. 'Such as they are. I'm sorry, Val.' She stood up and brushed grass from her skirt. 'I'd better go.'

'Not just because of us,' Val began, but Hilary shook her head.

'It's not because of you. I need to get back anyway. Mrs Ellis isn't cooking for us tonight so there's dinner to get ready, and I don't want Dad to think I'm sulking.' She smiled at them both. 'Come over for a drink sometime, when you feel more like it. And I'll see you at the pantomime auditions anyway, won't I?'

'The pantomime!' Val said. 'Good Lord, I'd forgotten about that. I don't know – it depends on whether they need me at the farm. If they don't, I suppose I'll be there. I don't know about Tom, though.'

Hilary gave them both a wave and set off down the hill. They watched her go and then Luke dropped down beside his wife and slipped his arm around her shoulders.

'And now,' he said, 'I think you'd better tell me what it is that's upsetting you so much. It isn't just Joanna's babies, is it? I know that's enough to upset anyone, but there's something else – something that's been worrying you for weeks.' He paused and went on gently, 'Tell me what it is, sweetheart – please.'

Felix and Stella were having tea in Dottie's cottage. As usual, she had produced a spread fit for a queen, as Felix frequently remarked, and the table groaned with sandwiches, buttered scones, home-made flapjacks and two kinds of cake.

'This is better than most people get at Christmas!' Felix said. 'You really shouldn't use your rations up like this, Dottie.'

'Go on, I'm hardly touching my rations. The butter and eggs come from the farm, the flapjacks are mostly Golden Syrup with a bit of sugar and some peanut butter and margarine and plenty of oats, and the cakes will last us all week. Anyway, you need feeding up, you're as thin as a rail.'

'I always have been,' he said, spreading strawberry jam on a split scone. 'It doesn't matter how much I eat, I never put on weight. And I wouldn't be too sure about these cakes lasting you all week, if I were you. Not if you keep inviting *me* to tea, anyway!'

'You eat up. I like to see a man enjoy his food. Anyway, you didn't come here to talk about cakes. We need to start thinking about the costumes for this pantomime of yours. There's not all that much time, you know.'

'I know. D'you think you'll be able to manage, Dottie? You'll have a few helpers, won't you?'

'My dear soul, yes. The vicar's wife and Mrs Latimer, and Edie Pettifer have all offered to give a hand. They'm all pretty handy with a needle. And young Tessa Latimer, too, she should be a help when it comes to making patterns, what with her college training and all. But we need to know what sort of thing you've got in mind, all the same. And who we've got to make them for.'

'Well, I can't really tell you that until after the read-through next week. But you know it's *Robin Hood*, so there'll be a lot of green – green tights and jerkins, and hats of some sort. And nice, country-style frocks for Maid Marian and Lucy Locket. I hope you'll be able to get enough material,' he added, gazing at her with sudden consternation. 'I don't suppose anyone's got any old clothes left, after the war. We just wore everything until it fell to pieces, didn't we.'

'That was seven years ago,' Dottie said firmly. 'Folk have had time to get new things and wear them out by now. I dare say there's quite a bit put away in cupboards. Old curtains are useful too – there's a good length and width in them.'

'Pity Robin Hood and his band didn't wear black,' Stella observed, cutting a slice of fruit cake. 'There must be hundreds of yards of blackout material still sculling about.'

'Well, they didn't, but it would do for the torturer in the dungeon,' Felix began, only to be shouted down by both the women.

'*Torturer*? This is supposed to be a pantomime! You can't have torturers in it!'

'Well, the prison warder, then,' he said. 'It comes to the same thing. I wasn't proposing to have anyone actually stretched out on a rack, or hanging from a beam. They'll be chained to the walls, that's all.' The women glanced at each other and nodded, accepting the necessity for chains. 'And maybe a few rats running about,' he went on, interrupted by further squeals. 'Not real rats! Dottie can knit some.'

Stella collapsed with laughter. 'Well, I've heard of some strange ideas, but knitted *rats* ...! Still, I suppose that's no worse than some of the animals you've knitted for the church bazaar over the years, is it, Dottie?'

'It's a lot worse,' Dottie said. 'But I expect I'll manage. So we want quite a lot of tights and jerkins in green. Well, I can start making them in whatever comes to hand and they can all be dyed. It doesn't matter if the jerkins are a bit big, they can be taken in when we know who's got to wear them. I don't suppose you know who's going to be Principal Boy and Girl yet?'

'I couldn't possibly say,' Felix said with dignity. 'Not before the read-through. But you might like to cast your eye over Val Ferris for Robin, just in case she decides to take part, and maybe our friend here,' he threw Stella a mischievous glance, 'for Maid Marian. And perhaps—'

'Felix!' Stella protested. 'You can't do that. You haven't heard me read yet.'

'I've been in the school plenty of times when you've been reading the children a story. You'll be a wonderful Maid Marian, Stella. You will do it, won't you?'

'I think you should wait until you've heard everybody else,' she said primly. 'Tessa Latimer might want the part. Or Jackie Tozer. Or Joyce Warren.'

Felix and Dottie hooted with laughter. 'Mrs Warren is going to be kept very busy stage managing,' Felix said. 'There are going to be so many props for her to find she won't have time even to consider taking a part as well. Anyway, I don't think there's one suitable for her. Unless she plays the prison warder,' he added thoughtfully. 'She'd be very good in that part.'

'Felix, you'm not fit to be a curate!' Dottie exclaimed. 'Talking like that about one of your parishioners! Suppose the vicar heard you?'

'He'd laugh till he cried,' Felix said unrepentantly. 'But we only say those sort of things in private, where nobody can hear us. And you're not going to tell, are you, Dottie?'

'Only because I wouldn't demean myself,' she said with dignity. 'Now, are you going to have some more tea, and another scone? They don't keep well, you know – if they don't get eaten up this afternoon I'll have to give you some to take back to Aggie's with you.'

'Is that a threat or a promise?' he asked. 'Well, I'll have one more now and not another crumb or I'll burst, and that would be a shame, just when you've washed all your cushion covers. And then I must go. I promised to go and see Mr Berry about Sunday's services.'

'Poor man, he'm no better, then?' Dottie asked sympathetically. Even though Little Burracombe was the village's greatest rival, the vicar was a popular man and his illness viewed with concern.

Felix shook his head. 'I'm afraid he's failing, Dottie. Dr Latimer looked in yesterday and told me to be on hand over the next two or three weeks. This is in confidence, of course,' he added with some haste, remembering rather belatedly that he shouldn't be passing on information given him in a professional capacity. 'But it can't be any secret. Everyone knows how ill he's been.'

'Poor man,' Dottie said, shaking her head. 'And his poor

167

wife too, I do feel sorry for her. Such a nice lady. And he's a good man, never had a bad word to say about anyone. It do seem a pity he can't have his three-score years and ten.'

'He's very close to it,' Felix said, trying to comfort her, but she shook her head again.

'Not close enough. And she'll be all on her own – they never had a family, you know. And to have to leave that lovely vicarage and all, once he'm gone. It don't seem fair, it don't really.'

'Life isn't fair, at least not by our idea of "fair",' Felix said, with a glance at Stella. 'But perhaps we set too much store by fairness, when really we should be reminding ourselves that there's a purpose in it.'

'Yes, that is all we can do,' Dottie agreed, but she still looked sad and Stella saw the look in her eyes and understood why.

On a day when two new lives had come into the world, perhaps only to be snatched away again, life really didn't seem fair.

Chapter Sixteen

'I don't know how to say it,' Val said.

Luke sat beside her, his arm still around her shoulders, and waited. There was no point in repeating his question; he had known for some time now that something was worrying her, and that she would eventually tell him about it, and in fact, he had more than a suspicion what it was. But he had to hear the words from her before they could talk about it.

'It's the babies,' she said at last, her voice trembling, and stopped again.

'Joanna's babies?' he asked gently, and felt her shoulders shrug in his embrace.

'Yes, of course. I'm so frightened about them. They're too small, Luke – they shouldn't have been born yet. You haven't seen them, but they look like tiny dolls packed in cottonwool like presents for a little girl. They shouldn't be having to struggle to breathe and suck, and do all the things we have to do once we're out of the womb – not yet.' She fell silent, thinking of the suffering children. 'But it's not just them. It's any baby. No, not any baby. Not exactly.' The breath she drew in was deep and ragged and he knew he would have to help her.

'It's our baby, isn't it,' he said very quietly. 'That's what's worrying you so much.'

At last, she turned and looked at him. They searched each other's eyes and he saw the fear and the pain in hers, and knew then what was really hurting her so.

'It's Johnny,' he said.

'Yes,' Val whispered, and burst into tears.

Luke held her tightly, laying his cheek against her hair and rocking her in his arms. He didn't murmur platitudes such as, 'There, there,' or, 'It's all right,' because he knew it was not all right. Val was still suffering over something that had happened years ago, something he had been responsible for but had not even known about, and she needed far more help than he had ever realised to overcome it.

'It's not just Johnny,' she said at last, when her sobs had subsided a little. 'It's the babies that haven't even been born yet.' She looked up into his face, her still eyes brilliant with tears. 'The babies you want us to have.'

It took a moment for her words to sink in. 'The babies *I* want? But – don't you want them too, Val? Don't you want us to have babies – children – ever?'

'I thought I did,' she whispered. 'I think I still do. I'm sure I do ... but I'm so frightened. Suppose something goes wrong. Look at Joanna, and the twins. Luke, I know just what she's going through – terrified she's going to lose them because they're so small. I know what that's like because I *have* lost a baby who was born too soon. Seeing them today, it's brought it all back. I couldn't go through that again, Luke. I just couldn't.'

'But it needn't happen again,' he said, feeling inadequate. 'Thousands of babies are born at the right time, strong and healthy. Ours could be like that. Would be like that.'

'We don't know that,' she said drearily. 'I've lost one baby. There may be something wrong with me. I may never be able to carry one to full term.'

'Val, you don't know that either! Lots of women have miscarriages, especially with their first baby. My own mother did, before I was born, and then she had me and my three sisters, all of us healthy. I'm sure there's nothing wrong with you.'

He could see that none of this was helping her. She knew all the arguments already – she was a nurse, for heaven's sake!

But Luke was aware that knowing something in your head did not mean that you believed it in your heart. He said gently, 'We don't have to have children, Val, if you really don't want to.'

'But I do want to!' she cried. 'Oh Luke, I'm sorry. I'm all in a muddle over it. Every time I think about babies, or see one, I want my own. And seeing the twins made it worse. I wanted my own – our own – so badly, but looking at those two little scraps, knowing that they might not survive, just scared me all the more. I don't know what to think. I don't know what to *do*!'

'I do,' he said. 'We just wait. We don't do anything in a hurry. We just give you all the time you need – all the time in the world – and we don't talk about it all the time, but we talk whenever you feel you want to. And if you don't ever feel ready to have babies, we still have each other. Isn't that the most important thing?' He lifted her face towards his and kissed her. 'I want a family as much as you do, sweetheart, but what I want more than anything is you.'

She closed her eyes and nodded, but he saw fresh tears seep from beneath the lids and slide down her wet cheeks. After a moment she drew in a deep, shuddering sigh and said, 'But I don't have all the time in the world, Luke. I'm thirty now – that's old for a first baby. And if we wait too long …'

'Darling,' he said carefully, not wanting to bring her more pain, 'it won't be your first baby, will it? There was Johnny.' He heard her sharp breath. 'It's all right – I know you hadn't forgotten him. You never will. *We* never will.' Even though Luke hadn't known of the baby's existence until a year or so ago, it was still his first child as well, and he mourned him now. 'And thirty isn't too old to have more babies. Lots of women have babies when they're over forty.'

'I'm sure you don't want to wait that long!' she said, with an attempt at a wry smile, and he shook his head.

'I'll wait however long it takes for you to be ready.'

'And suppose I never am?'

'Then, as I said just now, we still have each other.' He kissed her again. 'When I asked you to marry me, Val, I wasn't counting the children we might have. I just wanted you.'

'And I wanted you,' she whispered.

They sat quietly for a while, looking down at the village. Then she said, 'Let's go back now. We've still got some work to do in the cottage, and Jennifer said all the plumbing and wiring will be finished next week. We could move in at the weekend.'

'Yes,' he said. 'There's plenty to do. Let's go down and make a start.'

The babies lived through that night and the next. Prayers were said for them in church on Sunday and all the parishioners gathered round Alice as she and Ted came out, asking how the twins were.

'Poor little souls,' George Sweet's wife Ivy said. 'I remember when my cousin Ethel over at Sampford Spiney had her baby premature, he looked like a plucked chicken, he did, and only lived an hour. And you know the Barlows, who moved into Tavistock backalong, their Bertie was a seven-months' baby and he's never been right, even though they reared him. It's my opinion they're better to slip away quietly and—'

'Nobody's asked your opinion,' Ted said sharply, seeing Alice's face. 'Us don't need to hear about your Cousin Ethel, nor Bertie Barlow, neither. Anyway, if I remember rightly, he was dropped when he was a baby, fell on his head as like as not, and that's what made him simple.'

'Pardon me, I'm sure,' Ivy Sweet said in an offended tone. 'I were only trying to express my condolences.'

'Well, you needn't have bothered,' Ted told her, and turned away as Jessie Friend touched his arm. 'Oh hello, Jessie.'

'I just wanted to say we're thinking of you,' the little woman

172

whispered. 'And we'll pray for the little ones every night, won't we, Billy?'

Her brother nodded, his eyes soft with concern. 'I like babies, Mr Tozer. I'd like to come and see them.'

'I told you, Billy, they're not very well at the moment and they're in the hospital. Even when they come home, they'll be too small to have visitors. Wait until they're a bit stronger.'

He nodded again. 'I'll come when they'm stronger.'

Alice smiled at him. He too had been an 'early' baby, but she knew that his own problems were nothing to do with that. Children like him just 'happened' every now and then. Life was difficult for them, but with the love and care of their family they could live happy and useful lives, as Billy did with his sisters, helping at the shop and working a few hours a day for Bert Foster, the butcher. And Billy had the gentlest nature of any man she knew.

'I'll let you know as soon as they'm ready for visitors,' she promised, hoping with all her heart that she would be able to keep her promise, and his sweet smile broke out all over his face.

Basil Harvey and his wife watched their parishioners depart and then turned to go back to the vicarage. They always had an easy lunch on Sundays – salad in the summer, soup in the winter – and Grace cooked their dinner later, while Basil was at Evensong. In the afternoon, just like everyone else in the village, they gardened or read the newspapers or went for a walk.

'Do you think those two little ones are going to live?' Grace asked as they went through the gate leading to their garden. 'I feel so sorry for Joanna and Tom.'

'I'm afraid no one knows. They're in God's hands and as we all know, He works in mysterious ways.'

'But why should He want them to die?' she asked. 'Why let two little ones be born, only to take them away and leave a lot of suffering and grief behind? I don't understand.'

'We're not always supposed to understand, though, are we? That's what "having faith" means. And it may be that the grief itself has a useful purpose. It's not for us to question, Grace.'

'I'm not sure I agree with you there,' she said, frowning. 'I think we *should* question things we don't understand. There may be someone wiser who can tell us, or we may develop our own understanding by questioning and thinking. We shouldn't just accept everything we're told.'

'I'm glad you didn't live in Spain during the time of the Inquisition,' he said, smiling at her. 'You would have been condemned out of your own mouth! But you're right, of course. Questions are good and they do lead on to a better understanding.' He sighed. 'But what the answer is, in the case of the little Tozer twins, I really don't know ...'

Felix had been taking the morning service at Little Burracombe. He was spending more and more time there now and John Berry's wife had asked him to come to lunch afterwards. Stella had come with him.

'John's very tired this morning,' Mrs Berry said, handing them each a glass of sherry. 'He sends his apologies and says he really doesn't feel well enough to come down.'

'Perhaps we shouldn't stay,' Stella said anxiously. 'You must have enough to do without feeding us as well.' She began to get to her feet.

'Don't be silly, my dear. Sit down again and enjoy your sherry. John likes me to have visitors even if he doesn't feel up to seeing them himself. He knows I would hardly see anyone otherwise. And lunch is almost ready anyway. Mr Foster let me have a nice half-shoulder of lamb.'

'My favourite meat,' Felix said. 'With mint sauce too, I hope.'

'Yes, of course – I grow lots of mint in the garden. We'll have coffee out there afterwards, since it's such a nice, sunny day. We may not get many more.'

They drank their sherry and talked, mostly about the terrible flood damage in Lynmouth. Mrs Berry and her husband had known the vicar there and she had been particularly anxious on his behalf.

'And now there's this dreadful fog in London,' she said. 'They say you can't see your hand in front of your face and people are choking to death in it.'

'Smog, they call it,' Felix said, 'because it's partly fog and partly smoke. It's not like ordinary fog – that wouldn't choke anyone. It's got all kinds of nasty things in it that come from the smoke out of chimneys.'

Stella said, 'I learned at school that coal was banned in Elizabethan times, because they thought the smoke was dangerous. Perhaps they were right.'

'John was vicar at a London parish for years before we came here,' Mrs Berry said thoughtfully. 'I've often wondered if that had anything to do with his illness – all the smoke and fog we breathed in there. But Dr Latimer says nobody knows the cause, and if it had been that, then surely I'd have been ill, too. And all the other people who live there.'

After a while, she excused herself to get lunch ready. 'Go and have a walk around the garden,' she suggested, refusing Stella's offer of help. 'The dahlias and chrysanthemums are looking lovely.'

Stella and Felix went out through the French windows and crossed the lawn to the flowerbeds. They were bright with a rainbow of rich reds and golds, with white flowers like snowy washing in between the colours. They stood admiring them and Stella asked, 'Who does all this gardening? Surely Mrs Berry doesn't have time.'

'Who do you think?' he asked with a grin. 'Jacob Prout, of course! Not all of it – they have another man who comes in for half a day every week – but he looks after the lawn and hedges, just as he does for half the big gardens in Burracombe. And Mrs Berry does do quite a lot. She told me once it helps her, to come out and grub about amongst the flowers. John used to do quite a bit too, before he was ill.'

'It's such a shame,' Stella said. 'Is he ever going to get better?'

Felix shook his head. 'I don't think so,' he was beginning, when they both heard a sudden cry come from the house. They looked at each other in alarm.

'That sounded like Mrs Berry,' Stella said. 'It came from that upstairs window – look, there she is. Something's wrong, Felix, she's calling us! Quickly!'

They began to run back across the lawn. The vicar's wife was leaning out, her fingers gripping the windowsill. She called down to them again, her voice rising in distress.

'Call the doctor! Call him at once! It's John – I think he's dying. Oh, dear God, I think he may already have died!'

Chapter Seventeen

Mrs Berry had been right to say that he had already died when she called out of the window to Stella and Felix. He must have died almost as soon as she left him to go downstairs and let them in. 'His heart just gave out and he stopped breathing,' Charles Latimer told them after he had made his examination. 'It was a merciful end – better than it might have been if his disease had taken him. You might find some comfort in that, Mrs Berry.'

The widow wiped her eyes and nodded. 'I know, Charles. Cancer is cruel – I should feel grateful. But somehow all I can think is how I'm going to miss him. It's selfish of me, I know.'

'It's not at all selfish,' Felix said, taking her hand. 'It's natural, and it shows how much you loved him – how much you loved each other. I'm so sorry, Mrs Berry.'

'Why don't you go upstairs and have a rest?' Stella began, before remembering that the bed she and her husband had shared was now occupied by his body. 'Or sit down on the sofa, and I'll make you some tea.'

Mrs Berry shook her head. 'No. I'll just go and sit with him for a while. I suppose we'll have to notify the undertaker.' She looked at the doctor. 'I don't want him taken away.'

'I'll do all that's necessary,' Charles reassured her. 'I'll call Nurse Sanders to come and lay him out. You ought to have someone with you tonight, though. Is there anyone we can call?'

'I'll stay,' Stella offered at once, adding diffidently, 'unless there's someone else you'd rather have.'

Mrs Berry shook her head dazedly. 'No, I'd like to have you. But I'm sure you must have other things to do.'

'Where's your address book?' Felix asked. 'We could let someone know. What about your niece? She lives in Ashburton, doesn't she?'

'Pamela – yes, that's right.' She put her hand to her forehead. 'My address book ... it's in the desk in the sitting room ... oh dear, I don't know what to do.'

'You go up and sit with your husband,' Charles said gently. 'Felix will telephone your niece, and I'll see to the other matters. And Stella will look after you.'

Mrs Berry looked at them all as if not quite sure who they were, and then nodded and turned towards the stairs. Her shoulders were bent and she looked weary and bewildered. Stella went to her and took her arm.

'Lean on me, Mrs Berry, and we'll go up together. I won't come in – I'll come back down and make some tea. It'll do you good to have something hot and sweet to drink.'

'I don't take sugar,' Mrs Berry said, and Stella glanced at the doctor who nodded slightly.

'Put some in anyway. She won't even notice, and it's good for shock.' He turned back to Felix. 'You'd better get that address book and contact the relatives and anyone else you think should be notified immediately. Perhaps you could stay here tonight as well? I don't like to think of those two here alone.'

'Of course I will. I'll ring Mr Harvey as well.' Felix hurried into the sitting room, where the bottle of sherry and Mrs Berry's glass still stood. He realised suddenly that they had been about to have lunch, and raised his head and sniffed. 'Oh, my goodness – the lamb!'

'It's all right,' Stella said, coming down the stairs. 'I've just remembered it too. I'll see to it.' She stopped at the bottom stair, looking up at him with huge, distressed eyes. 'Oh, Felix, isn't it sad.'

'I know,' he said gravely. 'Even though we all knew how ill he was. And sometimes it happens to people who aren't ill at all. None of us knows how long we've got. Stella—'

'I've got to go,' she said, turning away from him. 'Everything will be burned. I may as well salvage what I can – she'll need food later. We all will.'

She hurried across the hall and went through the kitchen door. Felix stood watching her and remained there for a moment after the door had closed. Then he took in a deep breath and went towards the sitting room to begin telephoning.

Evensong in both parishes was a sad affair, kept as short as possible and with the same hymns sung in each church. There were more than usual in each congregation, for word had gone round the rapid grapevines of the villages, passing from garden to garden where people worked amongst their flowerbeds or vegetables, or through open windows where others sat reading the Sunday papers or listening to the wireless. The tranquil Sunday afternoon was disrupted by the news of sudden death, even more difficult to take in because it was not the news they had expected.

'I was sure you'd come to tell me they little babies had gone,' a number of people said, shaking their heads. And, 'Us knowed he was poorly, mind, but us never thought the end were that near.' And those who had already been to church that day and usually only went once, together with a good many others who hardly went at all, went to get out their best clothes to walk along that evening and say a prayer for the soul of the vicar of Little Burracombe, for he had been a kindly, gentle and well-liked man.

Ted Tozer went up the church tower as soon as he heard the news, to tie the leather muffles on the clappers of the bells. The ringers at Little Burracombe would be doing the same and the peals would sound across the valley, the muffled strokes hushed and sombre. Everyone in the area, whether churchgoers or not, would then know that someone important had died; men would take off their hats and women put their hands to their mouths, all observing a natural moment of silence for the soul that had passed away. It was almost certain that some of them would think the muffled sound was for one, or both, of Tom and Joanna's twins, but the grapevine would soon tell them the truth.

'It don't matter who you are,' Jacob Prout said to Jennifer as they walked to the main road together, for Jennifer to catch her bus back to Plymouth, 'hearing the bells ring like that always makes you stop and think. Last time was when the King died, you know, back in February. I rang for he that night, and I'll ring for Mr Berry too, when I go back after you've got your bus.'

'That was the day I first came to Burracombe,' she said. 'I was in the church when Mr Harvey came in to tell Alice Tozer. I remember how shocked they were. Well, I was myself. I just got on the bus and went back home.'

'Seems a long time ago,' he said. 'And a lot's happened since. If anyone had told me that day that I'd have found meself a daughter before the year was out, I'd have laughed in their faces.'

'Well, of course you would,' she said, smiling because she wasn't really Jacob's daughter and yet they both felt as if she was. 'And now here I am, in Burracombe. Part of the time, anyway.' They reached the main road and stood at the bus stop. 'You will think about coming to stay with me, won't you?'

Jacob stared up the long, straight road. The upper moors beyond Tavistock hung like a stage backdrop of purple and brown against the reddening sunset. To his right lay the combes and valleys that hid the villages of Burracombe, Little Burracombe, Clearbrook and Meavy, with houses and church towers peeping out from between the trees. He turned and looked the other way, towards Plymouth, remembering the terrible nights of the Blitz, when the German bombers came over in wave after wave to hurl down their bombs and you could read a newspaper in Burracombe by the light of the burning city.

He had scarcely ever been to Plymouth since then. It had changed so much, its cramped and narrow streets gone and wide boulevards taking their place. The rebuilding had started but it would never be the Plymouth he had known.

'I'll think about it,' he said at last. 'Maybe in a month or so, when we'm not so busy in the village.'

'That's right,' she said. 'Maybe to do your Christmas shopping.'

Jacob looked at her as if he'd never heard of such a thing. 'I does all that at Goosey Fair,' he said, and then, 'There's the bus coming – I can see its lights.' He took a step towards her. 'You'll come out again next weekend, will you?'

'Of course I will,' she said, and kissed him. 'It's made such a difference to my life, Jacob, finding you. But I'm not going to forget about your visit, you know. I won't hurry you, but I want you to come. I want you to see my home.' And my mother's, she thought, wondering again if this was why he didn't want to come. 'I want to see you in it,' she added, turning it around the other way. 'I want you to be as at home in my place as I am in yours.'

The bus stopped and she climbed aboard and blew him another kiss. 'Goodbye, Jacob. I'll see you next week.'

He stood staring after the green double-decker as it swayed off down the road. For a moment or two, he could still see Jennifer as she climbed the stairs and waved to him from the back window. Then he turned and began to make his way slowly back to the village.

As at home in her place as she is in mine, he thought. As if he ever could be. Knowing that Susan died there, and him not with her.

How could he ever feel at home in that house?

*

'There's really no need for you both to stay,' Mrs Berry said wearily as Stella brought her and Felix a cup of tea. Everything that needed to be done for the dead man had been done, and they were alone again. Evening was closing in; the burnished colours of the sunset had faded to a purple dusk, and the muffled pealing of the bells was just another sad memory. Through the open window came the solitary song of one blackbird and soon he too would fall silent, as the world had fallen silent for John Berry.

'We want to,' Stella said gently. 'There's no need to worry about us. We don't want to leave you alone.'

'I'm not alone.' The widow's eyes returned to the face of her husband. 'He looks so peaceful, doesn't he? As if he's simply gone to sleep. I can't believe he'll never wake up.'

Stella touched her hand, and Felix said, 'He is at peace now, Mrs Berry. There's no pain for him any more.'

'But does he *know* he's at peace?' she asked. 'Suppose we're all wrong about what happens next. Suppose he's just been snuffed out, like a candle. There may be nothing at all for him – nothing for anyone.'

Felix hesitated and repeated Basil Harvey's words about the baby twins. 'We just have to have faith, Mrs Berry. But even if it were so – he would still be out of his pain. Surely that must be some comfort.'

She sighed and shrugged a little. 'I suppose so. Yes, of course it is. I'm being selfish, thinking of myself.' Her eyes filled suddenly with tears and she put her hands to her face and began to cry, great sobs that seemed to be dragged up from the depths of her soul and wrenched at the hearts of the two who heard them. 'I'm going to miss him so much! We've been married for fifty years – I was just eighteen. That's my whole adult life. How am I going to manage without him? However am I going to *manage*?'

There was nothing they could say. They sat there with her,

Stella holding Mrs Berry's hand and Felix holding Stella's, forming a human chain of comfort. And with her other hand, the widow held that of her dead husband. At last, she withdrew and turned her head.

'Would you mind leaving me alone with him now?' she asked. 'I just want to stay beside him for one last night. I'll see you in the morning.'

Stella and Felix glanced at each other and stood up, still holding hands. Felix touched the older woman's shoulder and said, 'We'll be downstairs if you need us.'

'You can use the spare room,' she offered, her eyes on the still, cold face. 'At least, Stella can. You can use the sofa downstairs if you like, Felix.'

They nodded and let themselves quietly out of the room. Downstairs, they looked at each other and Felix said, 'Do you want to go to bed now, Stella? I'll do as she suggested and sleep on the couch.'

Stella hesitated and then said, 'No. I don't want to do that. I'll stay in the drawing room with you. I really don't want to be on my own tonight, Felix.'

He took her hand again and looked down into her eyes. Then he bent and kissed her very gently on the lips, and they went into the drawing room together and closed the door.

Chapter Eighteen

John Berry's funeral was held on the following Thursday. The small stone church at Little Burracombe was packed, with people crammed in the pews and standing in the aisles. There was barely room for the coffin to be carried in, and seats had to be saved for the chief mourners. As parishioners, friends and family filed into the church, the bells rang again in a slow peal, clear and soft by turn, and the notes of the organ sounded a sad threnody of sorrow.

There were plenty of people from Burracombe itself as well. The two villages had always maintained a friendly rivalry, but at times of both grief and celebration they came together. Felix assisted the Bishop at the service and Basil, also in the choir stalls, thought how well-liked the young curate had become. Mrs Berry herself seemed to turn to him almost as much as to her niece Pamela's husband Mark, a tall, thin man in his forties. It was good that she had some family members to support her, though, and Basil knew that there had been talk of her moving to live near them in Ashburton.

Ted Tozer, as captain of the Burracombe bell-ringers, had put on his black suit and tie and come with Jacob Prout. Alice, who would have come too, was staying at home with Joanna. Val and Luke were both at work and so was Stella. Hilary and her father were there, and Charles Latimer with his wife; so was Constance Bellamy, who had frequently played bridge with the Berrys. Edie Pettifer, Jean and Jessie Friend, George Sweet and Bert Foster had all closed their shops out of respect, and walked together down the little lane leading to the Clam and up the other side of the valley to the church, and a number of other Burracombe villagers stood in the side aisles, leaving the pews for the late vicar's own parishioners.

John Berry had been laid to rest at the side of the churchyard, his feet pointing away from the church as tradition demanded, so that his late parishioners, buried with their heads to the east, were still facing him. Jacob had come over that morning to help dig the grave but as the coffin was carried out, all but the closest members of the family drew back. When the coffin was finally lowered into the earth and the last prayer had been said, they turned and made their slow way back, either to the vicarage for sherry and a sandwich, or to their own homes.

'I reckon there were close on a couple of hundred there,' Ted said as he and Jacob plodded down the rough track to the river. 'And when you think how many folk were at work and couldn't come ... well, they'd never have got us all in, that's for sure. Us would have had to stand outside in the churchyard.'

They paused on the wooden bridge and gazed down at the hurrying waters, and Ted thought of the songs he knew about rivers – 'Old Father Thames', 'Old Man River', 'Way Down Upon the Swannee River' ... there must be hundreds of them. All making a picture of water on its inexorable way to the sea, water that caught at your feelings and tore at your heart and then went on its way, without a care in the world. He thought of the life just gone, and the two lives just begun; and the fear that touched his heart whenever he left the house clutched at him again. What had happened while he was away? Would he go back to find he still had two granddaughters, or would one or both of them have slipped away?

To everyone's relief, little Heather seemed to have rallied from her setback on the day of the christening and Joanna and both babies had come back to the farm. There, they were being treated as if they were made of glass although Joanna insisted that life must go on as usual. But nobody, least of all Ted and Alice, was fooled by this; the twins were not yet out of danger, nor would be for several weeks, at least.

'Let's go back, Jacob,' he said. 'I don't like being away from the farm just now.'

Jacob looked at him. For many years now he had believed himself to be childless, and in truth he still was. Yet since Jennifer had come into his life, he had understood something of what it was to have a child, a daughter, and he could feel a little of the terror that haunted his friend now. If anything happened to her ... if he'd known her as a baby, and felt that she was his, and she had been in danger ... even the smallest glimpse he could catch of the pain he would suffer was enough to show him what the Tozers were going through now. And having to come to a funeral when you were as frightened as that ...

'That's right,' he said. 'It's time for us to go. Your Alice'll be wondering where you be to.'

They crossed the Clam and walked up the sloping field to the village and home.

You could not go straight from a funeral to a read-through of a pantomime script, and so Felix had cancelled the meeting that evening. He put a notice on the door of the village hall, saying that there would be one on Monday and one the following Thursday.

'We really must start rehearsals soon,' he said to Stella. 'And Dottie needs to know which costumes are needed. There's an awful lot to be done.'

'Not to mention scenery and props,' agreed Val Ferris, who ran into them on her way to Jed Fisher's cottage. 'Luke wants to have a word with you about that some time, Felix. He's got a few ideas already from the script you gave him.'

'I should think he'll be too busy to do anything about that

at the moment, won't he?' Stella asked. 'You're just about to move in, aren't you?'

'At the weekend,' Val nodded. 'Dad's going to help, with Barley and the cart. We can get it up the field to the edge of the wood, but everything will have to be carried down to there. Not that there's all that much to carry – Luke never did have much furniture. There are a lot of paintings, though.'

'Well, if you want any other help, just call out,' Felix said. 'I could spare an hour or two on Saturday morning. I'm going over to help Mrs Berry in the afternoon – there's rather a lot to sort out.'

'Aren't her niece and nephew going to be staying for a while?'

'Until next week, yes, but these are parish matters. They can't really do anything about those. The Rural Dean will be taking over, but the Bishop asked me to make a start, just to get things into order.'

'I suppose there'll have to be a new vicar too,' Val said thoughtfully. 'Isn't the living in Colonel Napier's gift?'

Stella shook her head. 'I've no idea. Do you know, Felix?'

'No, I've never thought about it.' He finished pinning up his notice. 'Sorry, I'll have to go now. I'm spending the evening at the vicarage – got a lot to discuss there, too.' He laid his hand lightly on Stella's shoulder. 'I'll see you tomorrow.'

'Yes, after school.'

The two young women watched as he strode across the road to the vicarage gate. 'If you're at a loose end,' Val suggested, 'why don't you come and see the cottage? You haven't been in since it was all finished, have you?'

They strolled together past the shops towards the cottages, which had been occupied for generations by the Prouts and Fishers. No Fisher would live there now, nor any Prout once Jacob passed on, Stella thought. Yet the cottage where Val and Luke were to make their home was still owned by Jed Fisher's daughter, and probably she would inherit Jacob's as well one day, so neither would have gone to complete strangers.

'We're still trying to think of a new name for it,' Val said. 'Can't go on calling it "Jed's Cottage", but we haven't come up with one so far, and Jennifer'll have to be consulted too. All the usual things, like Rose Cottage, have already been used in the village, and anyway I think Luke would rather have something a bit different – something artistic.'

'Like "Rembrandt Cottage", for instance?' Stella enquired innocently, and Val laughed.

'No, you idiot, nor "Van Gogh Cottage" or anything like that! Well, I suppose we'll think of something eventually, but the longer we leave it the more difficult it will be. Everyone's always just called it Jed's Cottage – it'll take ages for them to change.'

'I don't honestly see why they should,' Stella said. 'It's a bit of history, isn't it? I mean, I think it's a shame when strangers move into a village and change the name of their house to something that doesn't mean anything to the village itself. Not that it's any of my business, of course,' she added hastily. 'And you and Luke aren't exactly strangers.'

'Well, I'm not. But maybe you're right – it's been called Jed's Cottage for about thirty years now, so maybe we shouldn't change it. I wonder what it was called before that?'

'Jed's Cottage,' Stella said promptly. 'His father was called Jed too – Dottie told me. The name must go back at least fifty or sixty years, maybe more.'

'Back into the last century, Queen Victoria's time,' Val said wonderingly. 'You're right, Stella, it's a piece of history. But I'll ask Jennifer what she thinks; she may want to change the name. It doesn't exactly have pleasant memories for her.'

They came to the front gate and pushed it open. Jacob Prout was in the front garden, digging over the ground he had cleared of its tangle of weeds. He paused and leaned on his spade.

'You wouldn't believe how much rubbish I've cleared out of this lot,' he said indignantly. 'I know us mustn't speak ill of the dead, but that old codger must have chucked everything he had out of the door and just left it. Old tin cans, bottles, bits of stuff I can't even recognise ... why couldn't the old fool have put it out for the dustmen, same as the rest of us? If you asks me, it were just cantankerousness, the evil-minded old crackpot.'

'Well, I'd hate to hear what you'd say if you did speak ill of the dead!' Val said, laughing. 'It's really good of you to do this for us, Jacob. I know how busy you are keeping the village tidy.'

'Why, 'tis a pleasure,' he said, as if his outburst hadn't occurred. 'Pleasure to do it for you, and a pleasure to get the place cleaned up and looking decent. I been wanting to get my hands on this bit of ground for years. Broke my heart, it used to, just to come out of me front door and look at it. Now, what do you want me to do when I've finished digging it over? Plant a few flowers? I can bring in some cuttings and such from my own place. I dare say you'll be growing your veg in the back.'

'I suppose so.' Val had never been a particularly keen gardener, but she had learned from her mother how to look after a kitchen garden, and it certainly saved money if you could grow some of your own food. 'I'm not keeping a pig, mind!'

Jacob grinned. 'They old pigsties haven't been used since the war. Me and Sarah used to have one, but Jed never. Couldn't be bothered, the idle old—' He caught Val's eye and stopped. 'Well, he were a lazy old man, you can't deny that.'

'I don't,' Val said with a grin. 'And dirty, too. I would never have believed anyone could live like he did here. I should think the pigsty was probably cleaner, even when it was in use. Anyway, we'll try to keep it all up to scratch now, Jacob, so you needn't be ashamed to live next door to us. And now I want to show Stella what we've done inside.'

They went indoors, leaving Jacob to finish his digging.

It was beginning to get dark and Val switched on the light. 'Ta-ra! Real electricity! Isn't it wonderful? I think that and the plumbing are the things I've missed most, living in the charcoal-burner's cottage. It'll be luxury, living here.'

Stella looked around her. 'It's lovely. So cosy.'

'Well, it will be when we get the furniture in. Did I tell you Hilary's giving us a three-piece suite? It's one they've had for ages in their small sitting room – she's decided to redecorate it and get new furniture – but it's in very good condition. Better than that old settee Luke's got in the cottage, anyway. And Mum and Dad are giving us a new kitchen table and chairs.' She led the way through to the kitchen and switched on another lamp. 'I can't get used to not having to fiddle about with a lantern. I just want to keep switching the lights on and off for the fun of it.'

'You'll be used to it in no time,' Stella said. 'I love the yellow walls. It's like sunshine all the time. I bet you can't wait to move in.'

'I'd like to sleep here tonight,' Val said. 'On the floor! Just to *be* here is going to be so lovely. Look at the new sink. Jennifer had the old one taken out and it's in the back garden. I expect Jacob will think we're as bad as Jed, keeping old rubbish, but I want to put it by the back door and plant flowers in it. Does that sound crazy?'

'I think it's a good idea. Can we go upstairs?'

'Of course we can. All the bedrooms are finished. Luke's going to use one as a studio, until . . .' She hesitated, then went on rather quickly, 'For the time being, anyway.' She led the way up the steep, narrow stairs. 'This is going to be ours.'

'Oh, this is nice.' Stella stood in the middle of the room, turning slowly to admire the soft green of the walls. 'When does the sun come in?'

'In the morning, I think, but not too early. It'll be just like being under the sea – you know, when you're swimming underwater and you look up and see the sun shining down through the waves. I used to love that when I was little and we went to Paignton on outings. And the other room is yellow, but not as bright as the kitchen. More of a cream colour, really.' They went into the next room, overlooking the front garden. 'Luke says it's better for painting.'

'Oh, *pictures*, you mean,' Stella said after a slightly puzzled pause. 'You haven't used wallpaper anywhere, then?'

'No. We did look at some but we thought the patterns would make the rooms seem cluttered. They'll be quite cluttered enough when we get all our stuff in! Well, that's it. The guided tour's over. Didn't take long, did it?'

'What about the little room? Is that going to be the nursery?'

Val hesitated again. 'I expect so. But we don't really want to stay here too long. If Luke's going to have a studio we'll need something bigger. Or with a garden we can put a good-sized shed in for him. And Jennifer's talking about turning that room into a bathroom one day.'

'A bathroom? How posh!' said Stella, who still took her baths in front of Dottie's fire, in a big zinc bath that hung on a nail in the back yard and was brought in on Tuesday and Saturday nights. 'You'll have to have a geyser then, won't you?'

'Don't let Jacob hear you say that!' Val laughed. 'It's one of his names for Jed – when he's not speaking ill of the poor old man. Honestly, those two were always at each other's throats, and now we know why,' she added thoughtfully. 'You can't really blame Jacob for feeling the way he does.'

They went downstairs again and Val switched off the lights. It was almost fully dark outside now and Jacob had stopped work and gone indoors. They stood at the gate for a moment, looking back at the little cottage.

'We'll make it look really pretty,' Val said quietly. 'Roses and honeysuckle round the door, and flowers all over the front garden. It'll be our first real home. Not that I'll ever forget the charcoal-burner's cottage, mind,' she added. 'That's special. And so will this be.' For a few moments, she looked pensive and then she turned away and said, 'I'd better go up to the farm now and see how Joanna and the babies are.'

Chapter Nineteen

The twins seemed determined to cling to life with every ounce of strength they possessed – not that there were many ounces there, Alice remarked wryly. At almost a week old, they had lost weight but this, Nurse Sanders said, was normal. It was worrying just the same, because they didn't have that much to lose, but they were feeding well and the midwife expected them to start picking up now.

'It really seems as if the little dears will be all right,' Alice said fondly, bending over their cot. 'I know it's still early days, but they'm getting stronger all the time. It'll be lovely to have two little girls running about the place.'

Joanna shivered. 'Don't tempt fate, Mother. I'm frightened to look ahead like that. There's still such a lot can go wrong.'

'I know, my flower, but us got to look on the bright side. 'Tis no good expecting the worst all the time. It don't help them to have us worrying ourselves sick. Now, is there anything I can get you while I'm up here? I'll have to go and start getting the pie made for dinner soon, and I've got all the baking to do for the weekend. Must have plenty of good country cooking to give your own mum and dad when they gets here.'

'They always look forward to your cooking,' Joanna said, laughing. Her parents were coming from Bristol to see her and the babies, and would be staying Saturday night. 'I just wish I could come down and give you a hand.'

'Now, you know what Margie Sanders said, not a foot out

of bed until they'm a fortnight old. You've got to build up your strength again.'

'I could come downstairs and sit in a chair, surely. I'll miss everything, stuck up here.'

'Well, us'll ask the doctor,' Alice said. Joanna was quite right, she would be left out of all the family chatter and company if she had to stay upstairs. It was all very well, her parents coming to stay – you could understand they'd want to, especially with the little ones so tiny and only just hanging on to life – but it would have been a lot easier if they could have waited until Joanna was up and about. Alice made up her mind to try to persuade Dr Latimer to allow the young mother downstairs. As Joanna said, what harm could it do for her to sit in a chair instead of in bed? And it would be so much better for Robin to have his mummy downstairs, too.

Charles Latimer said he couldn't see any harm in it at all and so Joanna braved the nurse's displeasure and was downstairs in the big rocking chair, swathed in blankets as if she were out in the cold yard, by the time her parents arrived. She stayed there the whole weekend, going back to bed early and getting up rather late, but otherwise making no concession to Margie Sanders's headshaking. And naturally, once the weekend was over, there seemed no point in not continuing to come down. As she said, the fortnight would be up in a few days anyway, so she might as well start moving about a bit. It couldn't really be good for you, sitting still all that time.

'That girl's so obstinate she might as well be a Tozer by nature, instead of just by name,' Alice declared, cutting up meat for a casserole. 'Do you know, I found her out in the garden this morning, picking blackberries from the hedge. Stretching her arms up, she was! I told her, if you can't behave yourself, my girl, you go straight back to bed and stay there. I was really cross.' She peeled a carrot and handed it to Robin, who was sitting on the rag rug.

'And what did her say?' Minnie asked, slicing runner beans.

'Laughed at me!' Alice said disgustedly. 'Said she wouldn't do nothing she shouldn't, because of the babies. I said, you'm already doing something you shouldn't, and I took the basket off her and sent her straight back in, but her wasn't a bit fazed. I don't know what's got into her, I don't really.'

'It's what's got out of her that's made the difference!' Minnie said with a chuckle. 'You must remember what it's like, Alice, when you first starts to get about after having a baby. You feel as light as air without that big lump you've been carrying about. And when it was two in there – well, we all know how hard she was finding it, the last two or three weeks.'

'I know. But I don't want her to overdo things, Mother. You're right about how a young woman feels at such a time, all full of energy and go, but that's just the trouble – it's too easy to overdo things, and she can't afford to lose her milk, not with two to feed.'

'I don't think you need worry, flower. She's getting plenty of rest, in between all that feeding, and a bit of fresh air won't do her any harm. And there's enough of us here to help look after the little dears.'

'Well, you'm certainly taking your turn, Mother,' Alice said with a smile. Minnie was rarely seen these days without a baby cradled on her lap. 'It's a good job there be two of them, or the rest of us would never get a chance of a cuddle.'

'No point in living to eighty-three if you can't get a few perks,' Minnie said, bending over the cot. She lifted Suzanne out and rested her cheek against her fuzzy head. 'This is my third great-grandchild and I want to make the most of her. And Heather's my second,' she added, 'in case you'm wondering how I worked it out!'

'And we hope it won't be too long before you have one or two more,' Alice said, just as Joanna came downstairs from the rest Alice had persuaded her to have.

'One or two more what, Mum?'

'Great-grandchildren,' Alice said, and laughed at Joanna's

expression. 'Not from you, my bird! There's our Val ready to start a family pretty soon, I reckon, now they're moving into Jed's cottage. There could be another dear little soul on the way by this time next year. Or even here.'

'Don't tempt Providence,' Minnie warned her. ''Tis unlucky to look ahead too much.'

'I've never understood that expression,' Joanna said, settling herself in her armchair and lifting Heather from the cot. 'Providence should be above temptation. Just *saying* things shouldn't tempt God to be unkind, should it? It's more likely to be – well, you know.' She stopped, as if simply mentioning the name was likely to bring bad luck.

The older women looked at each other, baffled. 'You'd better ask the vicar about that,' Alice said at last, gathering the pieces of meat into a pile and putting them into a casserole dish. 'He'll be looking in some time to see how the little dears are, I don't doubt.'

'Yes, and I want to do something about their proper baptism,' Joanna said. 'I know he told us that the one he did here was the proper one, but it says in the Prayer Book that babies baptised like that ought to be taken to church when they're strong enough, to finish the service off. They've got to have their godparents and all that. And we'll need a cake. We used the top tier of our wedding-cake for Robin's christening.'

'I was thinking that, too,' Alice said. 'I ought to be getting on with it – a good fruitcake takes at least a month to mature.'

'Well, let's make it in a month's time,' Joanna said, and stood up again. 'I'd better go and feed these two. Give me Suzanne, Gran, and I'll take them into our room, just in case anyone comes in. No, Robin, you stay here and help Grandma and Great-Granny.'

She departed with a twin cradled in each arm and Minnie went back to the vegetables she had been preparing. There was a short silence and then she said, 'You don't think Joanna's in a bit of a hurry over this christening, do you?'

Alice had begun to chop carrots. She stopped and looked at her mother-in-law. 'You mean she's still anxious about them? Well, I dare say she is – we all are. They'm still tiny and not out of the wood yet, and they've had three days in hospital already. But the doctor seems satisfied and Margie Sanders says Joanna's doing a wonderful job with them.'

'I know, and so she is. But I think she'd feel easier if she knew they'd been to church proper. And speaking of going to church ...'

'I know what you'm going to say, Mother. Joanna ought to be going herself, to be churched. I dare say that'll be one of the things Mr Harvey'll want to talk about when he comes.'

'Churching', the small service at which new mothers gave thanks for coming safely through childbirth, was indeed one of the things Basil wanted to discuss with Joanna. She wasn't as regular a churchgoer as Minnie, Ted and Alice, but she liked to observe the main occasions and she had asked for this after Robin's birth. She and the vicar arranged for it to be done one weekday morning when the twins were two weeks old, and Minnie and Alice went along as well while Val took Robin for a walk by the river.

'I hope now that's done everyone will agree I'm fit to be seen in public!' Joanna said as they came out. 'I can't wait to wheel the twins along the village street in that huge pram Miss Bellamy's given us. They'll look completely lost in it. Heaven knows how old it is.'

'I'm sure I don't remember any twins in that family,' Alice said. The pram was a double-ended one, especially made for twins. Constance Bellamy had come up to the farm the day after the babies were born and said it was in one of her out-buildings. Tom had been along to fetch it and spent several hours taking it to pieces and polishing and oiling it, until it looked as good as new. 'It must be well over fifty years old.'

'I remember them!' Minnie exclaimed. 'I'd forgotten all about them until now. It was one of Miss Bellamy's aunties that had them, but they were took off to America when they were about two years old. My stars, that was before the old Queen died – long before. They'd be about seventy years old by now.'

'Didn't they ever come back?' Joanna enquired, but Minnie shook her head.

'Not that I ever heard of, and I reckon us would all have known. The family didn't live in the village for long – they just came to stop at the Grey House for two or three years, I don't know why exactly. Miss Bellamy herself would have been a babby then, too.'

'And they left the pram behind because the twins had outgrown it,' Joanna said. 'Well, it was very nice of Miss Bellamy to let us have it. Those prams are really dear to buy.'

'Yes,' Minnie said, but there was an odd note in her voice. Alice glanced at her questioningly, but the old woman folded her lips and looked away. Joanna, who hadn't noticed anything, remarked on the amount of blackberries in the hedges and said she'd come out later and pick some more, and maybe some sloes as well, to make sloe gin for Christmas. She chattered on happily as they strolled up the farm track, and as soon as they were indoors she went to give the twins their morning feed.

Alice looked again at her mother-in-law. 'And now, perhaps, you'll tell me what was in your mind when us were talking about that pram. There's summat, I know. Come on, out with it.'

Minnie sat down in her rocking chair. Her face was troubled.

''Tis just silly superstition, I know, and I wish I hadn't remembered it. But thinking back to those times, I remembered those little twins and I remembered something else.' She looked up at her daughter-in-law. 'One of them died, Alice. Not long after they went to America. Miss Bellamy's mother was very cut up about it – it were her sister, you see, that had the babbies – and us all knew them in the village, of course, so everyone was pretty upset.' She paused. 'I didn't want to say anything to Joanna in case she thought the pram might be – well, unlucky.'

'Oh,' Alice said. She bit her lip and thought for a moment, then said, 'But the babby didn't die in the pram, did it? 'Twasn't until after it was taken to America. So I don't see how that could make it unlucky.'

'No. I told you 'twas me just being silly. Us'll think no more of it, Alice. But us won't say anything to Joanna, will us? I wouldn't want her to be worried.'

'No,' Alice agreed. 'Us won't say a word to Joanna. 'Tis only silly superstition, after all.'

They looked at each other for a moment, and then started to get dinner ready.

Chapter Twenty

'Here we all are at last,' Felix said, looking around the circle of faces. 'And thank you for coming along. I'm sorry we had to postpone last week's meeting, but you all understand why that was. However, it does mean that we've got some leeway to make up, so what I want you to do is look at these scripts ...' Stella began to go round and hand sheaves of paper to all those who had come to the pantomime audition, '... and we'll start reading. I'll ask you all to read different parts, so don't imagine that because I've asked you to read the Dame, for instance, that that's necessarily the part you'll end up with. You might not even want it.'

'And don't forget that I'm here to help decide who does what,' Joyce Warren put in. She glanced at Felix, to whom this had obviously come as news, and not very welcome news at that. 'It makes excellent sense, since I've been in the village so much longer than you, and know everyone so much better.'

'Well, that's true but—'

'Mother Hood,' George Sweet read out, looking at the top page. 'Is she the Dame?'

'That's right,' Felix said, abandoning for the time being any suggestion of a power struggle between himself and Mrs Warren. 'She lives in the greenwoods with the Merry Men, doing their washing and cooking their dinners and so on ...'

'Typical!' Hilary muttered to Val, who was sitting beside her, and Val giggled.

'What about Maid Marian, then?' Tom Tozer asked. He

had almost decided that with the twins needing so much attention, he ought to drop out of the production, but Joanna had encouraged him to go on with it. There were enough women at the farm to look after two tiny babies, she'd said, and he worked hard and deserved some relaxation. 'Didn't she do the washing and cooking?'

'Honestly!' Hilary exclaimed. 'Did the Pankhursts die in vain? Didn't getting the vote and helping win the war make any difference at all?'

'A woman's place is in the home,' Joyce Warren said severely. 'Of course we can come out when the men need our help, but otherwise ...'

'Yes, well, this is a pantomime not an electoral debate,' Felix interposed. 'So, if you don't mind, we'll get started on the readings, shall we?'

'I was actually joking,' Hilary said mildly. 'Didn't mean to start a war. Tell us who you want to read, Felix.'

'Yes. Thank you, I will.' He glanced around again. 'Mr Sweet, could you read the Dame, please – Mother Hood? And Mr Coker, you might try the Sheriff of Nottingham. The Black Knight – hm ... Tom, you could read him, and Hilary and Stella, you might read the Black Knight's sisters, Dusk and Dawn. Then we've got Friar Tuck and Little John, who will be the two comic ones who fall over themselves and get everything wrong. Vic, you can read Tuck, and maybe Tom could read John, as the Black Knight doesn't come in for a while. There's another comedy pair too, Hangem and Floggem, the two evil Sheriff's men, who are sinister but not very bright. Those two pairs are never on stage together, so if necessary they could be played by the same two actors.' His audience looked at each other and preened a little on being called 'actors'.

'Which one is the Principal Boy?' Tessa Latimer asked, turning her head a little sideways and drawing her fingertips down through her long blonde hair.

'Robin's the Principal Boy, of course, and Marian is the Principal Girl. The second couple are Will Scarlett and Marian's friend Lucy Locket.'

'I don't remember her being in the story either,' George Sweet interrupted.

'This is a pantomime,' Felix pointed out. 'You can have anyone in it. We could have Little Boy Blue if we wanted.'

'Oh, I don't think so,' Joyce Warren said. 'Little Boy Blue is about sheep and meadows. This story is set in a forest.'

'Seems to me us oughter hear what the story is before us starts reading,' George said. 'Just so as us don't get no surprises.'

'All right,' Felix agreed, thankful to have the diversion and wondering if he would get through the evening, and all those to come, without totally forgetting his calling and strangling the woman beside him. 'Well, the story is basically the one we all know, but because it's a pantomime, there will be some changes. Robin and his Merry Men are in the greenwoods when Maid Marian, the Sheriff's stepdaughter, and her friend Lucy Locket come by with their entourage – their maidservants and so on. They're lost and ask Robin for help and, naturally, she and Robin fall in love on sight. But she tells Robin she is going to be married against her will to the Black Knight, who will then grant the Sheriff a place at Court. At that point, Hangem and Floggem arrive and snatch her away. Robin vows to save her and marry her himself, and while this has been going on Will Scarlett and Lucy Locket have also fallen in love.'

'Has she been snatched away as well?' Jackie enquired. She was sitting beside Vic Nethercott, their chairs pulled slightly closer to each other than most of the others.

'Yes, they've all been snatched away by the Sheriff's men. There's lots of scope for people who don't want a speaking part, you see. Now, Robin and Will want to rescue the girls from the Sheriff's castle, but how are they to do it? Robin has heard the story of the Trojan Horse, and Friar Tuck and Little

John, who want to help but aren't really much good, hastily build a wooden horse, get inside and wait at the castle gate. Unfortunately their plan goes badly wrong when the Sheriff's men find them there, realise what it is and have some fun with them before chasing them back to the greenwood.

'Mother Hood comes up with another plan. She will gain entry to the castle disguised as a fortune-teller and tell the Sheriff's and Black Knight's fortunes, persuading them that this marriage will have dire consequences, thus setting Marian free to marry Robin and, of course, Lucy to marry Will.'

'I bet that all goes wrong,' Vic Nethercott remarked.

Felix grinned. 'But of course. The first thing that happens is that the Sheriff falls in love with Mother Hood! Without realising it, she has made a prophecy that he thinks means they're soulmates, and he assumes this will come true. Too late, she realises what's happened but he is besotted with her and won't let her go. And worse still, the Black Knight's sisters, Dawn and Dusk, who both fancy the Sheriff, realise the truth and tell the Sheriff she is a traitress and must be imprisoned. The Sheriff, who sees this as a way of keeping her until she agrees to marry him, agrees to this and she's hauled off to the dungeon and chained to the wall.'

'Is this really suitable for little children?' Joyce Warren enquired. 'Couldn't we just have her put into a room at the palace?'

'Castle,' Felix corrected her. 'And no, we couldn't. There's a scene in the dungeon, with prisoners chained to the walls and rats nibbling their toes, the odd skeleton or two ... the children will love it, won't they, Stella?'

'I'm afraid they will,' she agreed. 'So what happens then?'

'Lucy Locket brings her a meal and hears her story. She fetches Maid Marian and they try to think of a way to rescue Mother Hood. Maid Marian is, of course, in love with Robin and wants to escape as well. So Lucy, who is still allowed out, offers to go to the greenwood and find Will Scarlett and Robin, and tell them what's happened. Then they can get the Merry Men to attack the castle.' He stopped and looked around. 'I think that's all for now. Let's start reading, shall we?'

'Hello, everyone. I'm Mother Hood, Robin Hood's mother,' George Sweet read out in his deep voice. Felix held up his hand and he stopped.

'Can you use a higher voice, Mr Sweet? A falsetto, if you can manage it – as if you were an old woman, you know?'

George gave him a dubious look and tried again in faint, quavering tones. 'Hello, everyone, I'm Mother Hood ... Is that better?'

'Yes, quite a lot better,' Felix said diplomatically. 'But it does need to be a bit louder or no one at the back will hear you. Try again. Not quite so old-sounding perhaps – just a few tones higher.'

'Hello, everyone,' George said in a shrill voice, and Jackie giggled. He gave her a baleful look. 'I don't know why you think that's funny!'

'It's meant to be funny,' she said in an injured tone. 'Isn't it, Mr Copley?'

'Well, yes,' he said. 'And before we go any further, may I suggest that you all call me Felix? It makes things so much easier if we can all be friendly together. Do you want to have another go, George?'

'Not really,' the disgruntled baker said. 'I'd rather use me own voice, if it's all the same to you, Curate. Get Alf Coker to do it – he done the Dame in our old pantomimes before the war, didn't you, Alf?'

'All right, you read the Sheriff instead, then. He needs to be played by someone with a nice deep voice. Mr Coker – Alf – would you like to start?'

Alf Coker cleared his throat and began to read, his normal deep tones transformed into the falsetto voice of a pantomime Dame. Felix gazed at him enthralled, and George pursed his lips and nodded, as if he could have told them all to start with that the blacksmith was the man for the job. He had the build for it, apart from anything else.

'Hello, everyone. I'm Mother Hood, Robin Hood's mother. I live here in the greenwood with my son and his Merry Men. Well, they call themselves merry, but they're not very merry if I don't get their dinner ready on time, I can tell you. You ought to hear them then! Never a thought for the poor little woman at home, slaving over a hot campfire. And when it's not the cooking, it's the washing and ironing – those green doublets and hose have to be washed every other month, at least, to keep them fresh and smart. I do like a man to look smart, don't you, girls?'

Here Alf, who was obviously getting into his part, turned his face slightly sideways and stroked his bald head rather flirtatiously. 'I always try to look my best myself, just in case some handsome young man comes wandering through the greenwoods looking for a nice little wife. Well, I'm a widow now, you know. Robin's father – Rain Hood, he was called – was killed years ago. Tragic, it was. He was teaching young Robin how to shoot a bow and arrow and he held the bow the wrong way round. I went straight into mourning, of course, but I'm in the afternoon of my life now and looking for another man to take his place. There's nobody here who'd like to take me on, I suppose?'

Alf paused and shaded his eyes with one hand, as if peering out into the audience. 'Oh well, maybe tomorrow night, when we get a proper audience in. Now, what was I saying? Oh yes, we're an old greenwood family, we Hoods. I expect you've heard of us. There was my sister's granddaughter, Little Red Riding Hood, the one who got into all that trouble with the wolf, she's married to a woodcutter now, ever such a nice chap, and they've got a little baby, proper chip off the old block he is. And then there's Uncle Balaclava, he's from the Helmet branch – stuck-up lot, think they're a cut above us common or garden Hoods. Anyway, as I was saying ...'

He broke off and there was a stunned silence. After a moment, Felix recovered himself and said, 'Very good, Alf. Very good indeed. Now, who's reading Friar Tuck and Little John? Oh, it's Vic and Tom, isn't it? They come in at this point asking when dinner will be ready ...'

The reading proceeded, in fits and starts as people stumbled over their words, forgot to come in on cue or mispronounced words they weren't familiar with, even, in some cases, words they *were* familiar with. Slowly, they stumbled through the first scene and then Felix called a halt.

'We'll have a break now. Did I see some tea and milk being brought in?'

'It's in my basket,' Dottie said. 'I put the kettle on just now, while you were showing Hangem and Floggem how to say their words. It should be boiling.' She went out to the tiny lean-to kitchen and began to make tea in a huge tin pot. Stella followed her.

'How do you think it's going?'

Dottie shrugged. 'Sounds like any other rehearsal I've ever been to. Half of them don't seem to be able to read and the other half don't know how to say it. Apart from Alf Coker, of course, he'm a natural.'

'He is, isn't he! Did George Sweet say he used to play the Dame before the war?'

Dottie nodded and poured boiling water on to several spoonfuls of tea leaves. 'You'd never think it to look at him, but when he'm dressed up in a frock and got the bosoms in and everything, and some make-up on his face, he looks just the ticket. Knows how to put it over, too. Your man won't go far wrong if he puts Alf Coker in as the Dame.'

'I should think he will.' Stella didn't comment on Dottie's reference to Felix. After her worries at the beginning of the summer, when she had thought he was falling in love with her sister, she felt secure in their relationship and confident that, although it was progressing at a very gentle pace, it would eventually lead somewhere worthwhile. 'I was really surprised by Mr Coker,' she went on. 'I'd never have thought he would let himself go like that – putting on that falsetto voice and saying the lines so well. He'd never even seen them before.'

'I always reckoned Alf Coker could have gone on the stage,' Dottie said. 'He've got a lovely singing voice too. Baritone. Mind you, he were a boy soprano when he were a tacker. He was in the church choir then, and when he sang the first verse of "Once in Royal David's City" at the carol service, all on his own, it made you feel all funny inside.'

'Well, his son hasn't inherited that,' Stella remarked. 'Micky's not only flat himself, he makes everyone around him go flat. He quite likes acting, though. Remember him as Bottom in *A Midsummer Night's Dream*?'

'I don't reckon as I'll ever forget. The nights you spent sticking bits of newspaper together with flour and water paste, to make that old donkey's head!' Dottie loaded cups of tea on to a tray. 'I'll take these out, flower, and you can bring the sugar for them as wants it.'

Once the tea break was over, Felix announced that they would read the scene where Robin Hood first met Maid Marian. 'Hilary, would you read Robin, please, and Tessa read Marian. Jackie, you can read Lucy Locket, and Tom, perhaps you'll read Will Scarlett. Ready, everyone? We'll start from where Mother Hood is grumbling about the washing.'

Alf cleared his throat. He had been talking to George Sweet about the baker's carthorse, which needed new shoes, but he switched almost without taking a breath from his normal deep rumble to the high, affected tones of the Dame. 'I don't think you realise how difficult it is, Robin, trying to keep twelve Merry Men clean and smart in the greenwoods. If only you could provide me with better facilities – a proper well, with a nice bucket instead of that stream that dries up every summer. Can't you do something about it?'

'I'm sorry, Mother,' Hilary said, 'but we can't afford it. You know how poor we are.'

'I know how rich we'd be if you didn't keep giving all our money away to other poor people,' Alf retorted. 'I've seen the so-called poor people round the city walls – they're all better off than we are. Why, some of them have got two sets of clothes! Whenever I wash your tights, you all have to sit under a pile of leaves until they're dry.' He turned to the imaginary audience. 'His father was just the same, you know. He'd give anything away. He even tried to give me away once or twice!'

'That's terrible, Mother,' Hilary said. 'How could we have managed without you?'

'Oh, he wasn't taking much risk. He knew no one would have me. Now ...' Alf stopped abruptly and there was a silence. Felix looked down at his script.

'Marian and her entourage are supposed to enter now. Tessa?'

'I haven't got an entourage,' the doctor's daughter said.

'No, but you don't actually need one for the run-through. They're just your servants and friends, they're not going to say anything. Can you give us the cue again, Alf?'

'Now,' Alf Coker said.

The scene limped along, Tessa making it apparent that she might be a very pretty girl but she was not a good reader, so that it was difficult for Hilary to deliver her own lines effectively. After a while, Felix suggested some changes, asking Stella to read Marian, Val to read Robin and Vic to read the Dame. They started again.

'I don't think Vic Nethercott's at all right for the Dame,' Joyce Warren murmured in Felix's ear as Vic stumbled through the words, crimson to the ears at the idea of speaking in a falsetto voice. 'He's too young, for a start. The Dame needs to be a man of maturity, with stage presence. I don't know why you've decided against Mr Coker.'

'I haven't,' Felix said, reminding himself again that he was supposed to show charity towards his fellow men and women, and that this included Joyce Warren. 'I'm simply giving everyone a chance to show what they can do.'

'Well, not much as far as Vic's concerned,' she sniffed. 'If you want my opinion, he'd be better off backstage, shifting scenery.'

Felix didn't want her opinion – he had come to the same conclusion himself – but he merely smiled and put his finger to his lips to remind her to be quiet. She buttoned her lips together and subsided, but he knew from her expression that he had not heard the last of her helpful advice.

At last the rehearsal was over and Felix thanked them all for coming. 'I was going to suggest another reading, but I think everyone came along this evening and you've all had a chance to read something. Now, I'll go home and put on my thinking cap, and by Thursday I'll have an idea of who I'm asking to read the main parts.' He looked consideringly at his script. 'There's only one part I'm not sure I can cast, and that's the Black Knight. We really need someone menacing for that part – someone who looks really sinister.'

'That lets me out, then,' Tom Tozer said, trying to rearrange the perpetually cheerful expression on his face and look sinister instead. 'Mum says I look happy even at funerals.' Even when his own babies were ill, he thought ruefully.

'Me too,' Vic Nethercott said. 'I'd rather be one of those comic chaps – Hangem, or Floggem.'

'Oh well,' Felix said. 'I'm sure someone will turn up.'

At that moment, the door opened and they all looked round. A tall figure stood there, wearing a long khaki greatcoat, goggles and a black helmet. They stared, and Jackie Tozer gasped.

'Sorry,' Travis Kellaway said. He came inside a little further and spoke to Hilary. 'Your father told me you were down here. I wondered if I could join in.'

Chapter Twenty-One

'That all went very well, I thought,' Felix said, putting away the cups and saucers as Stella dried them. 'Thank you for bringing the tea and milk, Dottie. It was very thoughtful of you.'

''Tis always good to have a bit of a break in these things,' she said, tipping out the washing-up water. 'I know at whist-drives, things always seem to perk up a bit after a cup of tea. Folk enjoy it – seems a bit special, to have a bite to eat and a hot drink when they'm not at home.'

'Do you think we ought to bring something to eat as well, then? I don't want it to take too long.'

Dottie shook her head. 'A biscuit's enough when it's re-hearsals. I'll pop in a few of my own next time.'

Felix put away the last cup and Stella folded the tea towel and laid it in Dottie's basket. They took a last look round to make sure all the chairs were replaced against the walls and went out of the hall.

'And now I'm going to take both you ladies to the Bell for a drink,' Felix said, unhooking Dottie's basket from her arm and looping it over his own. 'You deserve it after all that hard work.'

'Not me, thanks all the same,' Dottie said, taking her basket back. 'I see enough of that place from the other side of the bar four nights a week, and then cleaning during the day. You take Stella along. 'Tis all right, maid,' she added, noticing Stella's dubious expression. 'I know young ladies don't go into pubs much, especially on their own, but you ought to know by now this is our village inn and 'tis a bit different. Anyway, you'm with the curate, so that makes it respectable.'

Stella laughed. 'All right. Just one shandy, and then I'll come home. Tomorrow's a busy day at school.'

They said goodnight at Dottie's gate and then strolled across to the Bell Inn. Some of the others were already there, talking about the pantomime or playing dominoes, darts or bar skittles, and Stella and Felix greeted them and then went to sit at a small table in a corner. Felix fetched the drinks and they smiled at each other.

'So, have you decided on the parts?' Stella enquired, sipping her shandy.

'Some of them. Alf Coker for the Dame, of course – he's marvellous. And George Sweet will make a good Sheriff with that deep voice of his. I think I'll ask Val to play Robin Hood, and I'd like you to be Maid Marian.'

'Oh no!' Stella exclaimed. 'I wouldn't be any good at that. It's much too big a part.'

'Not at all. You'd be very good.'

'I'd rather not. Honestly, Felix, there's too much to learn and I've got so much to do at school this term. We're putting on a nativity play, you know. Couldn't I have a smaller part? What about Tessa? She's so pretty, and I'm sure you could teach her to say the lines properly. I think she'll be disappointed at not being Robin.'

'Mm, perhaps,' he said. 'I was going to make her one of the Black Knight's sisters, with Hilary.'

'Well, I could do that, then. Please, Felix. I'd rather have a smaller part this time.'

'All right. You can be Dawn and Hilary can be Dusk. Then there's Little John and Friar Tuck – I thought Tom Tozer and Vic Nethercott for those parts – and Jackie Tozer for Lucy Locket.'

'And the Black Knight?' she asked a little slyly.

Felix grinned. 'If he always comes in as smartly on cue as he did tonight, I think Mr Kellaway will be ideal! He certainly looked the part.'

'If medieval Black Knights wore Army greatcoats and rode motorcycles, then I think he did,' Stella agreed solemnly. 'Or will you put him in a suit of armour for the pantomime?'

'Don't be cheeky,' Felix said sternly. 'Don't forget, I'm the producer and you have to do as I say.'

'And what will happen if I don't?'

'I'll tell you later,' he said, and waved a hand at someone just entering the bar. 'Jacob! Bring your drink over here. Haven't seen you to talk to for ages.' He waited until the old man had his own pewter tankard in his hand, the foam spilling over the top, and said, 'How's Jennifer these days? I saw her getting off the bus the other day, but I didn't have time to stop for a chat.'

'She'm doing fine,' Jacob said, sitting down and giving Stella a nod. 'Wants me to go and stop down in Plymouth with her, but I dunno.'

Stella stared at him. 'And leave Burracombe? Surely you wouldn't want to do that.'

'No, not permanent. Just for a weekend, like. Wants me to see where her grew up, that sort o'thing. Take me round the shops, I dare say, and up on the Hoe.'

He spoke as if he'd been sentenced to a weekend in Dartmoor prison, and Stella and Felix burst out laughing.

'What's wrong with that?' Felix asked. 'Burracombe will still be here when you get back. We won't run away.'

'How long is it since you've been to Plymouth?' Stella asked curiously.

'Donkey's years. I went once or twice during the war, but the whole place was a mess, all them bombed streets and buildings. Anyway, I never did like towns much. Tavistock's big enough for me.'

'But it's different now,' Stella told him. 'A lot of the damage has been cleared away and there are new shops. Dingle's, where Jennifer works, is a lovely shop. It's even got escalators.' She saw Jacob's face and decided that this probably wasn't a big attraction for him. 'Anyway, won't you like seeing where she lived as a child?'

He gave her an unreadable look. 'Her oughter've been in Burracombe. That's where her oughter've growed up, not Plymouth.'

'Yes, but ...' Felix was beginning, when Stella gave him a nudge. He cast her a quick, sideways glance and then fell silent. After a moment or two, she spoke, slowly, as if feeling her way.

'Perhaps she's trying to pull all the ends together, Jacob. Like sewing up a piece of knitting. You know, when she first came out here it was because she wanted to know her whole story. She found you, and you're an important part of it, so now she wants to tie some more ends together by letting you see where she lives in Plymouth. I don't know if that makes any sense,' she finished doubtfully.

Jacob pondered. He drank some beer from his tankard, licked foam from his lips and thought a little longer. They both watched, waiting for him to come to a conclusion.

'Maybe you'm right,' he said at last. 'But 'tain't just where Jennifer lived, you see. 'Tis where my Susan lived as well. I don't know as I want to see that.'

'You needn't go if you really don't want to,' Stella said gently. 'But you must have wondered what it was like. I expect there is a part of you that wants to know.'

'Ah,' he conceded, 'maybe there is. Sometimes, when I sits of an evening thinking it all over, I do wonder what sort of a place she had. I try to picture her there.'

'Would you feel better if you could?' Felix asked. The noise around them, of people laughing and talking, the shouts when someone scored a bull's-eye at darts, the low murmuring of the dominoes players, seemed to have faded, as if they were in their own private cocoon. 'Would you like to be able to picture her at home, with Jennifer and the other girls?'

'I dunno,' Jacob said. 'I just don't know. And that's another thing. Susan's other two girls. I dunno how I'd feel, meeting them as well.' He stared into his tankard, then looked up again. 'Maybe you're right, though. Maybe I do want to know.' They waited while he considered once more; at last he sighed and said heavily, 'Well, I suppose I'll have to do it in the end, so might as well get it over. I'll tell her next time her comes out here.' He nodded at them both and finished his beer. 'Reckon I'll go home now. Got a lot to think about.'

They watched him make his way out of the inn, then turned to each other. Stella had a tiny frown between her brows. 'I hope we said the right things.'

'I'm sure you did. I'm not so sure about myself.'

'Oh, you did! Once you realised he had a real problem ...'

'Yes,' he said, 'but I didn't realise it quickly enough, did I? Not like you.'

'Oh well,' Stella said, smiling a little, 'that's because I'm a woman.'

'Yes.' Felix looked at her and she met his eyes, then looked away, disconcerted by the intentness of his gaze. 'You know, you'd make a good vicar's wife.'

Stella caught her breath. 'Do – do you really think so?' she asked after a moment.

'Yes, I do.' He caught her hand. 'Oh damn, I didn't mean to say this here – not in a crowded pub! Let's get out.' He rose to his feet, pulling her with him, and pushed his way through the crowd. Once outside, he tucked her arm in his and walked swiftly across the green. He stopped and drew her into the shadow of the great oak tree.

'Darling, I'm sorry. I didn't mean to blurt it out like that. But you must know how I feel about you – and I've been trying to think of a way to say it ever since – ever since the night Mr Berry died. When we were together, downstairs in their sitting room.' He kissed her. 'I felt so close to you then, and I knew I wanted to be close to you for the rest of my life. I wanted to propose to you properly, something romantic that you'd remember all your life – and instead, it had to be in the Bell Inn after a pantomime rehearsal! I'm so sorry.'

Stella stared up at him, trying to see his face in the darkness. 'Felix, are you asking me to marry you?'

'Well, of course I am, you ninny!' he exclaimed. 'What else do you think I'm doing?' Then he caught himself up and added remorsefully, 'Oh Lord, just listen to me. I'm making it worse than ever. I'm sorry, sweetheart, I'm all in a muddle. Let's start again.' Letting go of her, he dropped dramatically to one knee and asked in ringing tones, 'Stella, my darling, my only love, will you marry me? Will you be my wife? Say yes and I'll be your slave for life.' He grabbed her hands and began to kiss them. 'Say yes! Yes! *Yes!*'

'Felix, get up, you fool.' Half-laughing, half-crying, Stella tried to drag him to his feet. 'You're kneeling in all the mud – Aggie will wonder what on earth you've been doing.' He straightened up and she put her arms around his neck. 'Of course I'll marry you. I think I'll have to – someone's got to keep you in order.'

'You will? You really will?' He caught her up against him and kissed her lips. The joyful kiss deepened and they clung together. At last, letting her go, he said a little shakily, 'I do love you, Stella. I love you so very much.'

'I love you too, Felix,' she whispered. 'I'll do my very best to be a good vicar's wife.'

'Well – a curate's to start with,' he said, a little ruefully. 'It might be ages before I get a living of my own.'

'Curate's wife, then,' she said. 'I don't mind what you are, Felix. I just want to be your wife.'

*

215

'Why didn't you let us know you were coming tonight?' Hilary demanded as she marched down the lane. 'And where's your Land Rover?'

'It wasn't mine. It belongs to the Tutton estate. I had full use of it, so of course I could drive here before, but now I'm not working there any more I had to give it back. I came on my motorbike.' His teeth gleamed in the dark as he smiled at her.

'Your *motorbike*?'

'Yes. There it is.' He shone his torch at the machine standing beside the hedge. It was large, with a dark green petrol tank and shining handlebars. A bulky pannier bag hung on either side of the rear wheel.

Hilary stared at it, then said blankly. 'So you'll be expecting to use our Land Rover, then?'

'I assume so. Doesn't it come with the job?'

'But *I*—' She stopped, biting back the angry words. 'Yes, obviously you'll have use of it. I just hadn't thought … We'll need to do something about a second vehicle.'

Travis regarded her for a moment, then said quietly, 'He didn't tell you I was coming, did he?'

'No, he didn't.' Hilary fought for a moment to control the emotions rising within her. 'He never said a word about when you were coming. I thought it wouldn't be for at least another couple of weeks.'

'I'm due to start work on Monday,' Travis said. 'Perhaps he thought you knew. Although to be fair, I didn't know myself until yesterday that I'd be coming today. I'd meant to make it Saturday, so that I could settle in first, but then Mr Tutton suggested I come down early. I'd handed everything over in good order, so it seemed like a good idea.' He grinned and cocked his head to one side. 'Don't be afraid to say if you don't agree. I could always go away again for a couple of days!'

'Of course I—' Hilary began, and then realised he was teasing her. 'Oh, don't be ridiculous. Of course it's all right.' It had to be, she thought, and made an effort to be more welcoming. 'Were your lodgings ready for you?'

'Yes, Mrs Warne's made me very comfortable.' It had been agreed that for the time being, Travis would lodge with the mother of Ken Warne, one of the tenant farmers, who lived in a cottage adjoining her son's farmhouse. There was an outbuilding for his dogs and plenty of room for any equipment he brought with him, and he would be close enough to the Barton to be able to reach it quickly in an emergency. Not that this would be necessary, Hilary had determined. She intended to remain firmly in charge, and quite capable of dealing with any emergency that might crop up.

Just now, however, she was more concerned with the immediate future.

'Well, anyway, you'll be welcome to use the Land Rover, of course, but it's going to be a bit difficult until I've done something about another one.'

'You don't have a car of your own, then?'

'I used to, but since Dad had his heart-attack I've never needed one. He's still got his Armstrong, and there's Stephen's car standing idle most of the time, but neither of those are really practical for driving round the estate or up on the moors. We really do need a second Land Rover.' She frowned. 'I can't see Dad being too keen on that. They're awfully expensive.'

'Well,' Travis said reasonably, 'he's the one who wants the estate manager.'

Hilary looked at him. 'Are you saying you should have first claim on it?'

'Not at all. I'm saying that he should have taken this into account, knowing that you intended to go on working. Can the estate afford it?'

'If it can afford to pay a manager,' Hilary said dryly, 'it should be able to.'

'Let's talk it over on Monday,' he said, and swung one leg over the motorcycle. 'I'll see you then, shall I?'

Hilary felt a vague, unexpected disappointment. 'You're not coming into the office tomorrow?'

'No, I thought I'd use the next few days to potter about and get to know the area a bit better. I expect that's why your father didn't tell you I was coming.' He smiled at her. 'As far as the estate's concerned, I'm not here until Monday.' He kicked the engine into life and settled himself on the saddle. 'Goodnight, Hilary. See you on Monday.'

'Yes,' she said, feeling a little flat. 'See you then.'

The motorcycle roared away down the lane and Hilary turned and began to walk home, the pleasure of the evening overridden by her irritation. Travis's unexpected appearance had taken her completely by surprise, and she felt wrong-footed. She was also disconcerted by his rather offhand manner, as if they had never had that conversation on the tor. Maybe that was the way he wanted it, though. Not exactly strangers, but on a more businesslike footing. He was no longer staying in her home, after all; they were colleagues now – not friends. And that, she thought fiercely, is just the way I want it too. Keeping our distance.

She was too absorbed in her thoughts to notice the two figures standing in the shadow of the great oak tree. But they saw her, and wondered for a moment at the dispirited droop of her shoulders and the slow pace of her steps.

Then they kissed again, and forgot her.

Chapter Twenty-Two

'We're in at last!' Val stood in the middle of her tiny, sunny kitchen and gazed in delight at the tea chests and cardboard boxes surrounding her. 'We can unpack our wedding-presents and start using all that lovely crockery and everything that we've been given. It's been stored in Dad's barn so long I've almost forgotten what we got!'

Luke hugged her, his face as flushed and excited as hers. 'Our first home! I ought to have carried you over the door-step.'

'No,' she said, 'the charcoal-burner's cottage was our first home, and you did it there. I hope we're as happy here as we were in that little shack in the woods, Luke.'

'No reason why we shouldn't be. We've got each other and that's the main thing. And a bit more room! Real bedrooms, Val. And a room for me to paint. I can hardly believe it. We ought to have a house-warming party.'

'I think we're going to,' she said with a smile. 'The whole family are coming round as soon as we're settled, and I thought we might as well ask a few others at the same time – Hilary, Felix and Stella, all our friends. And Jennifer and Jacob, of course. We can't leave them out. In fact, I'm not sure who we can leave out, without offending someone.'

'We may as well make it open house, that'll solve that problem.' He moved away from her and started to open a tea chest. 'Let's start unpacking. Where are we going to keep this tea-service that your granny gave us?'

Val unwound a sheet of newspaper from around a rose-patterned saucer. 'They'll all have to be washed first – look, this is covered with newsprint. You unwrap them and I'll wash them. These are our best so we'll keep them in that nice display cabinet Hilary gave us, in the front room.'

They worked cheerfully together, chatting about the cottage, Luke's job and Joanna's twins. 'They're looking a lot stronger now,' he observed. 'Are they out of the wood, do you think?'

'Not quite. We won't really be able to say that for weeks yet. They still haven't made up their birth weight, and then they need to start putting on extra. And it was touch and go with Heather for a day or two, though she does seem to have recovered from that. But it's always a worry with premature babies that their lungs haven't developed properly, or their other organs.'

'I wouldn't say there was much wrong with their lungs,' Luke remarked. 'Not from the way young Suzanne was screaming when I went up to the farm yesterday evening.'

Val laughed. 'They can certainly yell when they want to, can't they? Which is encouraging … Luke, you're supposed to be unwrapping things, not reading the newspaper they're wrapped in!'

'I know, but old papers are so much more interesting than today's, aren't they?' He held out a sheet of the *Daily Sketch*. 'Look, there's a report here about the last London tram running. I didn't know about that, did you?'

'I've never taken all that much interest in London trams, so I don't suppose I'd have noticed it.' She took the paper from him and scanned it. 'Luke, this is right back in July. See, there's a bit about Little Mo winning at Wimbledon. We saw it on Pathé Pictorial, don't you remember?' She read a bit further before recollecting herself, and screwed the newspaper into a ball. 'Now you've got me at it. Come on, let's get on with this or we'll never get sorted out.'

They worked companionably together, unwrapping, washing and putting away their crockery and kitchen utensils until the cottage began to look like home. Their blue and white striped Cornishware cups and saucers went on the dresser, and Val went out into the garden to pick a few late flowers to stick into a jug in the middle of the table. As she bent over the dahlia bed Jacob had planted for them, she heard a sound and looked up to see Jacob himself, leaning over the fence, beaming.

'That's a sight for sore eyes, I must say,' he told her. 'Next-door's garden being properly used at last, and good neighbours moved in. 'Tis going to be a pleasure to have you on the other side of the wall, Mrs Ferris.'

Val straightened up and laughed. 'It's going to be lovely for us to have you as a neighbour, too – but why have you suddenly started to call me Mrs Ferris? You've known me since I was a baby.'

'Ah, and now you be a married woman and entitled to your proper title. Nobody could ever say Jacob Prout don't know his manners.'

'They couldn't,' she agreed. 'So as it would be very bad manners to go on calling me Mrs Ferris when I've asked you to call me Val, you won't be doing it, will you?' She grinned at him and he scratched his head while he thought about it, then nodded his head. 'Is Jennifer coming out this weekend?'

'Just for tomorrow,' he said. 'Her's going to see her sister in Plymstock today.' He hesitated. 'Her wants me to go and stop in Plymouth with her some time.'

'You mean for a visit?' Val asked. 'Not to live there?'

'That's right. One weekend, maybe.' He folded his lips together in uncertainty. 'I dunno what to say. I got talking to the curate and young Stella about it the other night, and they reckoned I ought to go. Meet her sisters, too. But 'tis a big step for me. I mean, I don't doubt they'm nice enough bodies, but why should they want to be bothered with an old codger like me?'

Val regarded him thoughtfully. 'They're Jennifer's half-sisters, aren't they?'

'That's right. My Susan's girls.'

'Is that what the problem is?' she asked gently. 'Knowing that Susan was their mother?'

'I don't see why it should be.' He sounded bewildered by his own muddled reaction. 'I mean, why should that matter? She were properly married to their father, it's not as if ...' he tailed off and Val remembered the circumstances of Jennifer's birth. 'Well, I don't suppose they'm the least bit interested in me, anyway,' he finished in a mumble.

'Of course they would be,' Val said. 'You're important to Jennifer and you were important to their mother as well. Of course they must want to meet you.' She paused for a moment and then added, 'And once they've met you, they'll want to know you better, because you're such a lovely man, Jacob.'

The old man stared at her. His mouth worked a little and he said gruffly, 'D'you really reckon that's right, Val?'

'Of course I do. I wouldn't have said it otherwise.' She went closer to the fence and touched his arm. 'Go and stay with Jennifer in Plymouth and meet the rest of your family, Jacob.'

'Yes, but that's just it, isn't it? They'm not my family, not really. They'm no relation.'

'You think of Jennifer as your family, don't you?'

'Yes, but – that's different.'

'It's not,' she said quietly, hoping this wasn't too brutal a way of putting it. 'It's not really different, is it?'

The blue eyes looked into hers and then turned away. She held her breath, hoping she hadn't gone too far, and then he heaved a deep sigh and said, 'What you'm saying is more or less what the curate and Stella said. I reckon if that's what everyone else thinks, it's probably about right. I said I'd tell her this weekend, only I still weren't too sure it was the right thing. I reckon I will now, though. I'm only going to go on worrying about it, else. Now, have you and Luke got everything you want in there? You mind and knock on the wall if there's anything you need, won't you?'

'We will,' Val said, wondering a little nervously how much sound did carry between the two cottages. She and Luke had got used to having no near neighbours, up in the woods. 'And I'd better go in now or Luke will think you've kidnapped me.'

Jacob grinned and gave her a straight look. 'I meant what I said, mind. 'Tis a pleasure to have you living here. I hope we'll be neighbours for a long time.'

'Yes,' Val said, turning to go back indoors and thinking how welcoming the little square of yellow light looked, shining through the kitchen window. 'I hope so, too.'

'I wish the Cherrimans would decide when they're going to move out of the estate house,' Hilary said as she and her father sat down to Mrs Ellis's fish pie that evening. 'You were playing bridge with them last night, weren't you? Didn't Mr Cherriman mention if the work's started on their old house yet?'

Gilbert shrugged. 'Evelyn was talking about it. Getting a bit over-excited, if you ask me – wants to do some work on the garden. I thought she liked the garden at the estate house well enough.'

'She does, and she's made a lovely job of it, but she wants to be back in her own home. It's years since it was requisitioned for Government offices – ridiculous that they haven't had it back before now.' Hilary helped herself to cabbage. 'They've quite decided not to go ahead with building a new house, then?'

'Seems like it. Apparently there would be all sorts of permissions to get – lot of bureaucracy – and the builders in Plymouth are all on full stretch with the new shops and council estates and so on. Don't see what the hurry is, myself.'

'Well, I do. As long as they stay here, they're paying rent, and if their own home is being given back to them they'll lose whatever payment they were getting for that. And Evelyn isn't really the sort to enjoy living in the middle of the woods. Besides, it's not right for them to have two homes when there are other people with none.'

Her father nodded. 'Can't argue with that. We'd better see about getting young Kellaway settled in as soon as they move out.'

'Travis?' Hilary stared at him, her fork halfway to her mouth. 'But we promised it to Val and Luke.'

'*You* did. I don't remember being asked what I thought.'

'You agreed at the time.'

'We didn't have an estate manager at the time,' he pointed out. 'Be reasonable, girl. It's the estate manager's house – it's what it was built for and it's what we always call it. Of course Kellaway must have it.'

Hilary noted that he had become 'Kellaway' again instead of 'Travis', which her father had begun to call him while he was staying there. It seemed to make him more official, somehow – not so much a friend of her dead brother, more a trusted and responsible employee. She bit her lip, wondering what to say. Her father was right, of course, and she'd known this debate was bound to arise at some time. She'd meant to steer clear of the subject but had spoken without thinking and wished now that she'd been more circumspect.

'We don't know yet that he's going to stay,' she said lamely. 'We agreed on a six-month trial, both sides. There doesn't seem to be much point in moving him into the house if he's not going to stay there.'

'Nobody's suggested that. I told you, the Cherrimans don't even know when they're moving out. Anyway, Val and young Ferris have only just got into Jed Fisher's place, haven't they? They won't want to be moving out yet. There's plenty of time to decide all this, Hilary. What's the hurry?'

'None at all. I was just asking, that's all. D'you want any more, Father?'

'No, I've had enough. Very good too,' he added as Hilary got up to clear the plates. 'Plenty of cheese on top. Tell Mrs Ellis I enjoyed it.'

When Hilary brought in the blackberry and apple crumble, he gave her a sharp look from beneath his bushy eyebrows and said, 'How are you and Kellaway getting along now? Sorting out the work all right between you?'

'It seems to be working reasonably well,' she admitted, setting the hot dish on a tablemat depicting a foxhunting scene. 'He knows his stuff, I have to give him that, although all his farming's been done on downland rather than moor. I keep telling him, it's going to be a bit more tricky in winter. If things were different I'd be happy to consider him for the job.'

'What d'you mean, if things were different?'

'If I weren't going to be here,' she said, meeting his eye as she sat down. 'If we actually *needed* an estate manager.'

Gilbert Napier gave a sigh. 'Hilary, for heaven's sake, leave it! I've decided we do need a manager, and I believe I do still have a say in what goes on here. If you and Kellaway can work together, well and good. If not, you know what my opinion is.'

'Oh yes,' Hilary said quietly, 'I know what your opinion is. If I don't like it, I can bow out and live a life of idleness.'

'I didn't say that.'

'Oh, let's leave it, shall we, Father!' she exclaimed, forgetting that this was exactly what he had suggested. 'We keep on doing this, talking in circles. All I was doing was thinking of Val and Luke and where they were to live.'

'Which is not our responsibility.'

'I promised—'

'A promise you had no right to make. And it seems to me that they're very well-suited anyway.' There was a short silence and then he said more gently, 'Hilary dear, I don't want us to be at loggerheads over this. Let's give Kellaway his six months, shall we, and think about all this then. A lot can happen in that time. Things may be very different by next March.'

'Yes,' she said with a sigh. 'You're right. A lot can happen in that time, and things may be very different indeed ...'

On Sunday afternoon, Vic Nethercott took Jackie Tozer for a drive in his father's van.

They went across the moor to Teign Steps, where they parked and walked beside the river for a little way. There were a few other people about but it didn't take long to find a quiet spot, a grassy hollow between some rocks, and Vic drew Jackie down beside him. He began to kiss her and slid his hand inside her blouse.

'Vic, don't.' She tried to squirm away, though the touch of his hand made her heart kick. 'I don't want to.'

'Come on, Jackie. We've been going out for ages now and all you let me do is kiss you.'

'That's all I want you to do. And it's not ages, it's only a few weeks.'

'That's ages. You know you'd like it, Jackie.'

'Oh, do I? And how d'you know that?'

'Well, all the other girls did,' he grinned, and she sat up, flushing with anger.

'So I'm just going to be another scalp for your belt! Well, if that's what you think, Vic Nethercott, you can think again. You'd better take me home.'

'No need to get into such a tizzy,' he grumbled, trying to pull her back down again. 'Look, we'll just lay here and have a cuddle, or is that too naughty for Miss Prim and Proper?'

Jackie turned and looked down at him. He was very good-looking, she thought, with his curly brown hair all tousled and untidy, and there was nothing she'd like more than to lie down beside him and let him hold her in his arms and kiss

226

her and stroke her body. But even while she yearned for his love-making, her mind could not forget what had happened with Roy Pettifer. I don't want to go through that again, she thought. I just couldn't.

'If you promise that's all,' she said doubtfully.

'Of course I do. What sort of a bloke do you think I am?' He smiled lazily at her. 'I've never had to force a girl yet ...'

Jackie missed any hidden meaning in his words and, after a moment's further hesitation, lay down beside him, her body not quite touching his. He immediately shifted closer and raised himself on one elbow, placing his other arm across her body. His face was very close as they looked into each other's eyes.

'You know, Jackie Tozer,' he murmured, his lips brushing hers and sending a wild flame of longing licking through her, 'you're playing with fire, coming to a lonely spot like this and then saying no.'

She stiffened. 'You promised—'

'It's all right.' He gave her a quick, small kiss, then drew back. 'I'm not going to break my word. I won't do anything you don't like. Not a thing.' He stroked her neck gently with his fingertips. 'Is that all right?'

Jackie closed her eyes and whispered, 'Yes ...'

'I think so too.' His lips were soft on hers and the kiss lasted longer. His fingers strayed up to her ear, tracing its contours and stroking the creases behind it, and then into her hair. 'Mm, Jackie, you're delicious. You taste better than strawberries and cream, did you know that?'

Jackie laughed shakily. 'Don't be daft.'

'I'm not. I mean it, I really do.' He kissed her again and she felt her body melt. They lay for some time, their kisses slowly growing deeper, and Vic let his hand slide down her neck again, one finger touching the top of her breast as delicately as if he were hardly aware he was doing it. Jackie trembled a little but he murmured reassurance into her ear and she relaxed once more. As his fingers explored further she wanted again to tell him to stop, but the words wouldn't come. A little bit won't matter, she thought hazily. Just a little bit longer. It's so nice. Oh, Vic ...

Suddenly, he broke away and sat up. Startled, Jackie opened her eyes and stared up at him. He was on his feet, smiling down at her and holding out his hand.

'What's the matter? Is someone coming?'

'No, I don't think so. I just thought it was time to stop.'

Jackie sat up, brushing the hair out of her eyes and feeling dazed. 'But – why? I thought you wanted ...'

'I do,' he said with a smile that made hot colour run up her neck. 'I want to a lot. But you don't, and I promised, so – well, it's time we stopped, that's all.' He gripped her hand and pulled her to her feet and into his arms. Holding her close against him, he murmured, 'There's only so much a red-blooded bloke can stand, you know. Another few minutes of that and I couldn't be held responsible. Come on. Let's go and find some tea.'

Still dazed, and washed by a turmoil of emotions, Jackie followed him along the path. She hadn't wanted to stop. She'd wanted Vic to go on doing what he'd been doing – no more than that – for hours. She wanted him to do it again. Her body ached and throbbed with wanting him, and she felt disappointed and hurt that he'd called a halt. Men weren't supposed to do that. It was the girls who were supposed to say no. Miserably, she trailed behind him, aware that the longing that had been set up inside her was mingled with guilt. Guilt because he might think she was too 'easy', and guilt because of Roy Pettifer.

That's daft, she told herself crossly. Roy was over long ago, they were no more than friends now. It was nothing to do with him, what happened with Vic.

Vic swung along in front of her, whistling cheerfully, apparently unaware of Jackie's gloom. As they climbed the stile and walked up the footpath to the road, he chatted about his job in Plymouth and the motorbike he was hoping to buy. 'We'll be able to go wherever we like on that. Mind you,' he stopped and glinted a wicked look at her over his shoulder, 'it's not as cosy as the van on a dark winter's night.'

Jackie looked at him dolefully. At that moment, she gave nothing for her chances of being invited to go out with Vic again, either on the new motorbike or in his dad's van. He'd find some other girl – a girl like Tessa Latimer, who was bright and flirtatious and had been away from home, a girl who knew what was what.

Tessa Latimer wouldn't say no, Jackie thought as she and Vic went to have tea.

Chapter Twenty-Three

'So when shall we announce our engagement?' Felix enquired.

They were standing together on the little bridge, looking down at the ford and stepping-stones. Stella remembered when they had stood here once before and Felix had been just about to kiss her for the first time when half a dozen of her pupils came chattering down the lane and interrupted them. It had had a special place in her heart ever since, and perhaps in his too since this was the spot he had brought her now.

She looked up at him. 'I'd like to keep it to ourselves for a little while longer. It feels so new – I need time to get used to the idea.'

'Oh, come on,' he protested. 'You've known for months that I want to marry you.'

'Not really, not until you actually asked me.' She smiled at him. 'I *hoped*, that's all.'

'And what were you going to do if I didn't ask?' he wanted to know. 'Wait until the next Leap Year so that you could ask *me*? Another four years?'

'Well, if you could wait that long, I'm sure I—'

'And you know very well that I couldn't!' He silenced her with a firm kiss. 'Now, let's get back to this important matter of when we're going to make it official. If you don't want to shout it from the top of the church tower this very day, which is what I was planning to do – I've got the key and everything – when *do* you want to tell everyone? I warn you, I'm not prepared to wait for ever.'

'I thought perhaps Christmas,' she said demurely.

'*Christmas?* But that's months away!'

'I know, but it's such a nice time to get engaged. Val and Luke got engaged at Christmas and I thought then that if ever ... well, if ever anyone wanted to marry me, I'd like to do that too. And it would save you buying me a present,' she added with a wicked grin.

'Well, there is that, of course,' he nodded. 'All right then, we'll make it Christmas ... And there's no need to pinch me quite so hard. I was just agreeing with you. Now, the next thing to discuss is the wedding.'

'Felix!' she protested. 'That can't be for ages yet. We've got to save up, and find somewhere to live – and all sorts of things. And we can't rush into it, you know what people would say.'

'I should hope they wouldn't,' he said with dignity. 'The curate and the schoolteacher – the very idea!'

'Exactly. We don't want any scandal. And I'm sure Mr Harvey doesn't, either. Is it all right for curates to get married, by the way?'

'Why shouldn't they?'

'I don't know. You just don't seem to come across many married ones, I suppose.'

'That's because they can't afford it,' he said gloomily. 'The curate's stipend is pitiful. I don't know what I'm doing even thinking of getting married. It's mainly because I'm afraid that if I don't grab you quickly, someone else will.'

'Well, there you are, then. We can get engaged but we can't get married for ages. It's not that bad,' she added bracingly. 'As long as we're not married, I can go on working. I'd have to stop afterwards, so it's a good thing we have to put it off for a while.'

'Ah,' he said mysteriously, 'but that's where you may be wrong. It's possible that I may not be a curate for much longer.'

Stella turned and stared up into his face. 'What do you

231

mean? What's happened? Felix, you're not moving away, are you?'

'I don't think so. Not yet, anyway.' His face was serious now. 'Look, darling, this is just between ourselves. Nothing may come of it. But I've talked it over with Mr Harvey and he thinks there may be a chance that I could be given the living at Little Burracombe.'

Stella took a moment or two to digest this. Then she said, 'As their vicar, do you mean? Oh, *Felix*!'

'That's right. It's not certain,' he added warningly as her face lit up. 'Not by any means. But I've been a curate long enough now, and this is my second curacy so I could be expected to be looking for an appointment. Mr Harvey said something to me about it a few weeks ago, as a matter of fact, but I just told him I wasn't keen to leave the area and would sooner stay on a bit longer. But with Mr Berry dying ...'

'It seems so sad,' Stella said. 'Almost as if we wished him—'

'No! Don't say that – neither of us wanted that. I certainly didn't – I thought a lot of Mr Berry. And I know it never even occurred to you. But we have to deal with the situation as it is now. Little Burracombe will have to have another vicar, and it could be me.'

There was a moment's silence. They stood watching the water tumble over the rocks. A grey wagtail appeared and perched on a round stone, ducking its yellow head and flirting its tail. At last, Felix said, 'What do you think about it, Stella? Would you like to live in Little Burracombe?'

'Of course I would. You know how I love it around here. Ever since I first arrived, I've known that this is where I want to be. It felt like home from the start.'

'But that was Burracombe itself,' he said solemnly. 'Would you really want to move across the river?'

Stella laughed. 'Do you think they'd let me in?'

'They'd welcome you with open arms.' He proved it by

wrapping his own arms around her. 'Darling, I don't want to raise false hopes, but it would be marvellous, wouldn't it?'

'Mm.' She relaxed against him. 'How soon will you know?'

'Well, there's a lot to go through yet. For the time being, the Bishop is responsible for the parish but it's the Rural Dean who'll look after most of it – and he's got his own parish as well. Then they'll have to consider possible appointees. I don't think they would just offer it to me without giving other men the chance. In fact, they might not offer it to me at all. The Bishop might decide I'm too close.'

'But you've done a wonderful job, helping out while Mr Berry was ill.'

'You may think so,' he said with a smile, 'and perhaps others do too, but I dare say there are plenty who don't agree. And even those who've liked what I did while I was standing in for Mr Berry, might not want me as their vicar.'

Stella frowned. 'That doesn't seem fair.'

'It's the way things are. It wouldn't be *fair* simply to give me the job, out of hand, without considering who else might be better for the parish. There's a lot to think about.'

She sighed. 'I suppose so. But doesn't the Squire have any say in it? Someone told me the living was in his gift.'

'Yes, it is, but in practice he's not likely to do much about it. These days, those things are normally passed over to the Bishop to deal with. I don't think we can go canvassing at the Barton!'

'I wasn't suggesting—' Stella said indignantly, then saw his expression and laughed. 'All right, I shan't go leaving baskets of Dottie's home-made cakes on their doorstep as bribes. But it really would be lovely, wouldn't it? Living so close to Burracombe and all our friends – and in that beautiful vicarage. It seems too good to be true.'

'It very well may be,' he said. 'No chicken counting! And remember, whatever happens, it's for the best. If I don't get this appointment, we'll just stay here until something else turns up.'

'And wait years to get married,' she said despondently, and he laughed again.

'No, we definitely won't do that! One way or another, our engagement won't be too long – a year or two at most. And as you say, we'll need time to save up. Beautiful vicarages don't come fully-furnished, you know.'

He drew her arm through his and they wandered off the bridge and along the riverbank. The grey wagtail was left behind and instead they saw a dipper, bobbing on a large rock, his dark back and wings and white breast almost invisible against the flashing waters. A flurry of movement low down on the opposite bank betrayed the presence of a water vole, its bright eyes peeping at them from behind a frond of green fern, and Stella caught the darting movement of a small brown trout. Above them, leaves were beginning to turn yellow and brown and the ground was scattered with those that had already fallen.

'I love walking through leaves in autumn,' she said. 'Kicking them up and making them crunch underfoot. I hope we can stay here for ever, Felix.'

'I do too,' he said. 'But we may not be able to, you know. My job could take me anywhere. We might find ourselves in the middle of a city – Bristol or Portsmouth, London or even somewhere in the north. Would you mind that?'

'I wouldn't like it as much as Burracombe,' she said honestly. 'But if it's where you had to go, of course I'd go with you.' She stopped and looked up into his face. 'I think what I'd say is, that I'd rather be anywhere in the world with you than in Burracombe without you.'

'And the same goes for me, too,' Felix said.

Despite Hilary's reservations, she had to admit that Travis was a good manager. If they'd actually *needed* one, she thought, they couldn't have done better than pick him. Their main disagreement was over Arthur Culliford.

'I don't know why anyone gives him any work,' Travis declared one morning as they sat in the office going over some of the forms that had to be filled in. Some of the restrictions, still in force from wartime, seemed to be going on for ever, as if farming and its importance had been forgotten. 'The man's a liability. Have you seen the state of his cottage?'

'Of course I've seen it,' Hilary said impatiently. 'I've lived here rather a long time, in case you've forgotten.'

'And it's always looked like that?'

'As long as he and Maggie have lived there, yes. And he's not a complete liability. There are some jobs he's very good at. Dry-stone walling, for instance. There's not another man in the village who can touch him for that – except for Jacob Prout, of course.'

'Yes, we could do with a few more like Jacob Prout. But as for Culliford – well, he may be a good stonewaller when he's sober, but as far as I can see, he hardly ever is. And he's an incorrigible poacher. How many times has he been up before your father?'

'Quite a few,' Hilary admitted. 'But Furzey only takes him to court if he has no alternative.'

'*No alternative*? So when does he think he *does* have an alternative? Who's Furzey to decide these things? How long's he been your head gamekeeper, anyway?'

'Fifteen years. We were lucky to keep him during the war – he'd just turned forty when it started, so he didn't have to go and fight.'

'So he's in his early fifties now. And how old is Culliford?'

'He must be about forty. What's that got to do with—'

'I was wondering if they'd known each other as boys. Played in the woods together, snared the odd rabbit – that sort of thing.'

'You mean you think Furzey turns a blind eye because

they're friends,' Hilary said coldly. 'I think that's a disgraceful accusation. Furzey is as honest as the day is long.'

'And by your own admission, lets a notorious poacher get away with his crime.'

'For goodness sake!'

'*Isn't* that what you said?' he challenged her. 'Either Furzey is letting the man get away with it by not bringing him before the magistrates every time he catches him poaching, or he isn't. Which is it?'

Hilary sighed. 'For a man whose father was a gamekeeper, you seem to understand remarkably little about country life. For a start, rabbits are a pest ...'

'It's still poaching. And who says he stops at rabbits? I doubt if there are many winters that go by without a few pheasants finding their way into Mrs Culliford's larder.'

'... and for another, we try to get along with each other in this village,' she went on, ignoring him. 'Obviously we can't let him or anyone else get away with too much, but if Furzey brought him up before the magistrates every time he snared a rabbit, he'd never be out of jail.'

'Which might not be a bad thing,' Travis said bluntly.

'Which would mean his wife and children would starve,' she countered.

There was a short pause while they measured each other with their eyes. Then he said, 'So what you're saying is that the estate tacitly subsidises this man and his family.'

'I suppose it does, if you put it that way,' she admitted.

'Even though what money he does earn goes on drink? I don't see his wife and children benefiting from that, much.'

'No, they're more likely to benefit from the odd rabbit.'

'If you ask me, they'd be better off without him. He's a liability to them, as well as to the estate. And if he spent a bit more time in prison, where he belongs, his family might not be quite so big. She's expecting again, isn't she?'

Hilary sighed again. 'Yes, she is.'

'We can't let this go on, Hilary,' he said after a moment. 'I'm new here – an unknown quantity. I have to show people they can't take advantage.'

'By making an example of Arthur Culliford?'

'Is there anyone better?' he asked. 'Look, if I let him get away with it, not only will he get worse but others might follow his example. He's not the only poacher in the area, I'm sure.'

'No, he's not. So why not go after them? And he's just small fry, Travis. Furzey was telling me only the other day, there are gangs coming out from Plymouth to take game birds and salmon in huge quantities. They're the ones we should be aiming for.'

'Oh, I shall,' he said grimly. 'I certainly shall. But I want it to be quite clear to you, and to Furzey, that I'm not letting Arthur Culliford off the hook. The next time I catch him poaching, he goes before the magistrates, and I hope he gets a proper sentence. I shall do my best to make sure he does, I'll tell you that. And I'll also see that they're evicted from that cottage.'

'*Evicted*!' she exclaimed. 'And what about poor Maggie? And the children? Where are they to go? Little Shirley's just beginning to make something of herself. Stella says—'

'You can do what you like about his wife and children,' Travis said. 'They could apply for one of those new council houses in Horrabridge.'

'Horrabridge! But that's out of the village.'

'I do realise that,' he said, and she stared at him, angrily.

'You can't do this, Travis. The Cullifords may not be a credit to Burracombe, but they're part of it, just the same. And Arthur's not at all bad when he's sober. He's a member of the darts team, and he—'

'I'm sorry,' Travis broke in, sounding bored. 'I don't think your father employed me to encourage poachers simply because they're in the village darts team. But I'll tell you what

I'll do. I'll give Culliford one warning – *one* – and if he ignores that, it will be at his own peril. Does that satisfy you?'

Hilary opened her mouth to make an angry retort, then closed it again. Against all her own instincts, she knew that what he was saying was reasonable and no more than any other estate manager, especially one new to the job, would say. After a moment, aware that she sounded petulant, she muttered, 'I suppose you've got to show your authority somehow. The new broom, sweeping clean, and all that.'

'Exactly,' he said in an irritatingly cheerful tone. 'Now, let's get on with the rest of this paperwork, shall we? Ken Warne's sheep – how are they getting along?'

The subject of Arthur Culliford was dropped, but Hilary continued to smart for some time. Travis had won the argument, and she didn't like it. Worse still, she knew that if she had taken her grievance to her father, he would have sided with the new estate manager.

I don't have any say at all, any more, she thought resentfully. He's going to have everything his own way, and I won't be able to do a thing about it.

Travis didn't see Arthur Culliford for a few days after that, but he did see Arthur's daughter Shirley. Along with Micky Coker and a few other children, she had started to attend some of the pantomime rehearsals. Micky was to be a page and Shirley a maid in the castle, while the others were village children, performing short dances under the leadership of Tessa Latimer.

'I did quite a lot of ballet at school,' she told Felix when she offered to take on this task. 'I thought about being a dancer myself at one time, but it makes your legs too muscular.' She fluttered her eyelashes at him. 'I didn't want to look like a footballer so I decided to do dress design instead.'

'I'm sure you'll be able to get the children to dance very well,' Felix said, noticing the eyelashes with some amusement.

Tessa knew perfectly well that he and Stella were 'going out' together, although not, of course, that they were engaged. Even if she had, he doubted that it would have prevented her from the flirting which seemed to come as naturally as breathing. He had met quite a few girls like Tessa Latimer during his two curacies and managed to withstand most of them.

'I'm not doing ballet!' Micky Coker declared in outrage when he heard about it. 'That's girls' stuff, that is – soppy!'

'No, it's not, or there wouldn't be men ballet dancers,' Shirley told him. 'And there are, 'cause I've seen pictures.'

'They'm soppy too, then. Anyway, I'm not doing it. You got to wear tights and stuff, and it looks rude.'

'Nobody's going to ask you to do ballet dancing,' Stella interposed. 'You're a page. It's only the small children who will be dancing, and I don't think they're going to do actual ballet, are they, Tessa?'

'Oh, I shouldn't think so,' the doctor's daughter said. 'They may do a few simple steps, perhaps, but I shouldn't think they're up to anything complicated.'

'They do some very nice dances in school,' Stella said, feeling affronted. 'Not ballet, but some lovely folk dances, and the children were very good on the maypole at the Summer Fair. I expect you saw them there.'

'Oh yes,' Tessa said dismissively. 'It was very pretty. I'm sure you teach them quite a lot of little dances.' She turned away, leaving Stella feeling irritated. She was further annoyed when she noticed the other girl lay her hand on Felix's arm as she talked to him, but before she could go over and interrupt them she found Shirley Culliford gazing up at her.

'What is it, Shirley?'

'Please, miss, can't I do ballet too? You said it's only the village children, not me and Micky.'

Stella looked down into the large grey eyes. 'I'm sure you can do ballet as well, Shirley,' she said. 'Ask Miss Latimer if you can.'

'I don't know as she'll let me, miss,' the little girl said, her lips trembling slightly. 'And I did want to do ballet. If I'm a villager, could I do it then?'

'Well, yes, but I really want you to be the maid because you've got a nice little bit of poetry to say, and you're good at that. Remember how you recited Puck's song in *A Midsummer Night's Dream*? You spoke it beautifully.'

'I did want to do ballet, though,' Shirley repeated, and looked at her with woebegone grey eyes.

'I'll ask Miss Latimer for you, shall I?' Stella said, not too sorry to be given an excuse to break up the intimate chat Tessa seemed to be having with Felix. With Shirley in tow, she crossed the hall to where the pair were standing, and touched Felix's arm. 'Sorry to break in, but Shirley's a bit worried about her part.' She smiled at Tessa. 'She's desperately keen to do some ballet dancing, but as she's not a villager but has a part as the maid, she's afraid she may not be able to. You will include her, won't you?'

Tessa looked at the poorly dressed child with some distaste. 'I suppose so. She can go at the back.'

Stella opened her mouth indignantly, but Felix gave them a quick glance and spoke first. 'I don't think that would work, Tessa. The audience will hardly be able to see her there, and as she has a speaking part she ought to be at the front. She's quite important to the story – you realise that, don't you?' He gave Tessa his most charming smile. 'I don't think Tessa knows how fond we all are of Shirley,' he added to Stella. 'She didn't see her as the Festival Queen last year, did she, darling?'

'I don't think so,' Stella agreed, torn between annoyance and laughter. 'You were away then, weren't you, Miss Latimer?'

'Yes, I was in Rome,' Tessa said shortly. 'Oh, very well, I'll make sure she does a few steps of ballet, and I'll make sure the audience sees her.' She gave Shirley a look of veiled dislike, then laid her hand on Felix's arm once more. With another flutter of eyelashes, she said, 'I'll see you later, then, and remember what I said, won't you?' before moving away in the direction of Travis Kellaway who was talking to Constance Bellamy.

Stella gave Shirley a smile and a gentle shove back towards the other children, and then turned to Felix, a question forming on her lips.

'Thank goodness you came along then,' he muttered before she could ask it. 'That girl was about to eat me for breakfast. I hope she got the "darling" – I tried to put some emphasis on it.'

'I don't think she's the sort to take notice until there's a ring on my finger,' Stella said. 'And what did she mean by "seeing you later" and "remembering what she said", hm?'

'Goodness knows. She said rather a lot.' He gave her arm a squeeze. 'It's all right, sweetheart, you've nothing to fear from the Tessas of this world. I'm not so sure about Hilary, though.'

'Hilary?' Stella followed his glance to where Tessa was now standing rather close to Travis Kellaway, gazing up and fluttering her eyelashes in exactly the same way as she had done with Felix. 'Why, you don't think Hilary's interested in him, do you?'

'Of course she is! Haven't you noticed the way she looks at him, when she thinks he's not watching her? There'll be two engagements announced at Christmas, unless I'm very much mistaken.'

'I think you are. I'm not sure she even likes him much. And the Squire would never approve – he's not a "gentleman".'

'Neither was Lady Chatterley's lover,' Felix said wickedly, and Stella looked at him in surprise.

'You haven't read that book, surely? I thought it was banned.'

'Well, there are ways and means, and Lawrence *was* one of the great literary figures of the century.' He grinned at her shocked face. 'Clergymen have to be prepared to listen to all kinds of things, you know. We've got to be unshockable, despite what most people seem to think. So it's not surprising that we sometimes read a bit more than books of sermons.'

Stella had no real idea what *Lady Chatterley's Lover* was about, or why it was not allowed to be published or sold in Britain, but there surely had to be some good reason. How had Felix acquired a copy, and had he been committing an actual crime by reading it? She decided it was better to change the subject. 'Anyway, I don't think there could be anything between Hilary and Mr Kellaway. You're quite wrong there.'

'We'll see,' Felix said. 'I rather hope I am, come to think of it, if it means he'll keep young Tessa Latimer occupied. Ah, I can see some of the mothers arriving to collect their children. We'll be able to get on with the main rehearsal now.'

'Not just mothers, either,' Stella said, following his gaze to the door of the hall. 'There's Mr Culliford for Shirley.'

'So there is. I wonder why.' Felix strode across the hall, holding out his hand. 'Hello, Mr Culliford, how good to see you. I hope your wife's well.'

'She'm a bit poorly, if you wants to know. I come for our Shirley, seeing as it's getting dark these evenings. Maggie frets about her being out by herself.'

'I'm sure someone would have made sure she got home safely,' Felix said kindly, 'but I'm pleased you're here. Shirley's looking forward so much to the pantomime.'

Arthur Culliford grunted. 'Lot of play-acting nonsense, if you asks me. Still, it keeps the kiddy out of mischief.' He held out his hand to his daughter. 'Come on, my bird. It's getting near your bedtime.'

'Daddy, I'm going to be allowed to do ballet!' she told him, her voice bright with excitement. 'I'm doing a dance all by myself, at the front of the stage. Miss Latimer's going to teach me.'

Her father looked down at her and his rough face softened. His voice also was gentler as he said, 'Ballet, eh? That sounds handsome. Us'll have to come and see you doing that, won't us?' He led her out of the hall, still listening to her eager chatter, and Stella and Felix watched them go.

'He seems really fond of her,' Stella said, a slight note of surprise in her voice.

'Why shouldn't he? He's her father, whatever his faults.' Felix turned back to the others and clapped his hands. 'Right, let's get on with the next part of the rehearsal. We'll start on page three – the beginning of Scene One. Mother Hood is in the greenwood, cooking dinner for the Merry Men ...'

The actors began to take up their positions, all holding their scripts, and Stella moved to stand beside Val. She glanced across the hall and saw Travis Kellaway.

He was watching the door through which Arthur Culliford had just departed, and he was frowning heavily.

Chapter Twenty-Four

'He just came to collect Shirley, that's all. There's nothing more than that in it,' Hilary said impatiently.

'Yes, and where had he been before that? Checking his snares? He doesn't strike me as being the sort of man to make a point of fetching his little daughter home. It's not as if she had a long way to walk.'

'It was dark!'

'And it's her own village street, that she knows like the back of her hand.' Travis shook his head. 'Sorry, I don't believe it. I don't trust the man – he's a poacher, and leopards don't change their spots.'

'First he's a poacher and then he's a leopard. Make up your mind,' Hilary said sardonically, and looked round as the office door opened and Gilbert came in. He glanced from one to the other, frowning.

'What's going on here? I could hear you two arguing right along the passage.'

'It's Arthur Culliford,' Hilary said. 'Travis has decided he's got to be made an example of.'

'Culliford? Has he been up to his tricks again?' Napier lowered his heavy body into a chair by the desk. Travis was behind it, and Hilary to one side. The surface was covered with papers, all in neat piles awaiting attention.

'No, he hasn't,' Hilary said at once. 'But Travis is expecting him to at any moment. He's got his sights set on Arthur and whatever he does is suspect.'

'Every village has an Arthur Culliford,' the Squire observed. 'They need to be kept in check ...'

'Exactly what I'm saying,' Travis said swiftly.

'... but there's not much point in making an example of them,' Napier went on, frowning at the interruption. 'It's their way of life. You're not going to change a man like Culliford.'

'Which is also exactly what you were saying,' Hilary told Travis. 'And we have to think of his family too. Poor Maggie and all those children.'

'He's the one who should be thinking about them,' Travis retorted. 'I'm sorry, but I can't agree with all this sentimentality. My father was a gamekeeper and I know the trouble characters like Culliford caused him. Up at all hours of the night, out in the woods in all weathers – it's no wonder he had a heart-attack. I don't intend to let the same thing happen here.'

'So you're going to make Arthur a scapegoat for what happened to your father!' Hilary exclaimed. 'That's unfair. Besides, it's not really your business. Furzey's our gamekeeper – it's his job to deal with poachers.'

'It's my job to manage the estate. If people think I'm soft now, I'll never have any authority.'

'You don't have to be a bully, though.'

'Applying the law is not being a bully,' Travis said, and she snorted.

'That's just pompous.'

'Perhaps, but it's the way I intend to proceed. If Culliford sticks to the law, he has nothing to fear. It's as simple as that.'

Hilary knew that it was *not* as simple as that, but she could also see that Travis was immovable on this point. She looked at her father. 'You don't really want to send Arthur Culliford to prison, do you?'

Gilbert sighed. 'I don't like sending anyone to prison, much less a man from my own village who has a family to support.

But if I'm on the Bench when he comes up, I won't have much choice. He's offended too often in the past.'

'Quite right too,' Travis said, and Napier gave him a sharp look before inclining his head.

'Thank you, Kellaway,' he remarked with just the slightest hint of sarcasm in his voice, and Hilary was pleased to see that Travis looked discomfited. 'Now, can we leave this subject, please? Until Culliford is actually caught offending again, there doesn't seem to be much point in pursuing it. I want to have a word with you about Home Farm.'

'Why, what's the problem there?' Hilary asked and again her father sighed.

'Did I say there was a problem? Please try not to meet troubles halfway, Hilary ... All the same, I'm not entirely happy with some of Warne's decisions just lately. Those sheep of his, for a start ...' He went on to discuss his concerns about the new flock at Home Farm, and eventually rose from his chair. 'I think it would be a good idea for you and me to go over and have a look, Kellaway. You've got plenty to be getting on with here, haven't you, Hilary?'

She looked at the piles of documents. 'Yes, but—'

'You did say you'd deal with those Government forms this morning,' Travis reminded her. 'Since they're concerned with last month's returns, before I came.'

'I know, but—'

'That's all right, then,' Napier declared, stamping over to the door. 'I'll be back for lunch. Kellaway may as well stay at the farm, I dare say Mrs Warne will have something ready for him there. I'll see you at twelve-thirty.'

Hilary nodded resignedly and moved round the desk to begin attacking the paperwork. She watched the door close behind the two men and bit her lip, feeling outmanoeuvred. Is this what it's going to be like from now on, she wondered. The two of them, ganging up on me, leaving me to do the office work while they go round the estate together?

For two pins, she could have thrown down her pen and walked out. But that wouldn't help her cause. That would simply confirm their belief that, as a woman, she was incapable of rational behaviour.

The trouble was, she didn't feel at all rational.

On the first Wednesday in October, the school was closed so that the children could attend the annual Goose Fair in Tavistock. A bus was laid on specially and they rushed to board it, pushing and shoving each other in their excitement.

'Get out of the way, Micky Coker! I was in the queue before you!'

'No, you wasn't! I was here already when you come down the lane. Anyway, I wants to sit next to Henry.'

'It's all right, Micky,' Henry Bennetts called from halfway down the bus. 'I've saved you a seat.'

'Well, that's not fair,' Billy Dodds grumbled. 'People didn't ought to save seats for people that aren't on the bus yet. It ought to be first come, first served. I was here before Micky and I ought to get a seat before him.'

'Nobody'll be getting a seat if we don't have a bit of quiet,' the bus driver shouted. 'Now, stop pushing and get on properly. Haven't you lot been taught no manners at all? And that'll be threepence each, and I want the right money. I'm not giving change.'

'I haven't *got* the right money,' Betty Culliford wailed. 'I've only got sixpence, and a shilling to spend at the Fair.'

'Me too,' came a chorus of disappointed voices. 'Threepence there and threepence back – my mum gave me sixpence specially.'

'Well, form up in twos then,' he said. 'You can give me sixpence between two of you. Make sure you keep the other one for coming back, and make sure you come back with the same person so that you can pay their fare.' He gazed doubtfully at them, not at all sure that they understood this complicated instruction. 'Don't spend the fare back,' he finished, wondering if he could manage to swap shifts with another driver before the afternoon.

Felix and Stella, also waiting for the bus, looked at each other and grinned. 'Aren't you glad you're not in charge of them today?' he whispered.

'I never know what I should do,' she confessed. 'Should I be the officious teacher and take charge or pretend I've never seen them in my life? I usually take the coward's way out and try to avoid them!'

The children scrambled aboard and sat three to a seat, chattering like starlings. The Goose Fair was the highlight of their year, after Christmas, and they looked forward to it for weeks, planning which rides they would go on and hoping to win valuable prizes to bring home. Henry Bennetts was intent on winning a goldfish in a jar of water, while Shirley Culliford wanted a teddy-bear for the new baby when it arrived, and Micky Coker was planning to spend all his money on the rifle-range, where last year he had set his heart upon a model railway engine which he had not won. It had still not been won on the last night of the fair, and he was convinced it would not have been won yet. He had been practising all year with his cousin Derek's airgun so he was sure it would be his.

'Go on, nobody never wins those good prizes,' Henry scoffed. 'The rifles is all bent, see, so you can't aim straight. My uncle told me about it.'

'I'll aim bent, then,' Micky declared. ''Tis easy enough, you just point a bit to one side. I bet I'll win it.'

'Don't suppose it'll be there,' Henry said, shrugging.

'Bet it will.'

'Bet it won't.'

'Will.'

'Won't . . .'

Their argument continued until they both got tired of it and stopped to listen to Shirley and Betty Culliford, in the seat behind them.

'I'm not going on anything till I've got some more money,' Betty declared. 'Then I'll be able to go on anything I like.'

'How are you going to get more money?' Micky demanded, twisting round to peer between the backs of the seats. 'You ain't going thieving. You'll end up in prison, like your dad.'

'My dad's not in prison!'

'No, but he will be, I heard my dad say so. And that's where you'll go if you thieve.'

'Well, I'm not going thieving, so there. I'm going to win it on those roll-a-penny things.'

'Go on,' he sneered. 'Nobody wins money on them.'

'Well, I do,' Betty retorted. 'Our mum took us to the fair last year and I won nearly two shillings.'

'That's right,' Shirley confirmed. 'Whenever her rolled her penny down the wooden holder, it landed in a square. There was a whole crowd of people round us, watching, and the man was ever so nice to our Betty. A lot of people had a go after that. I don't think they won much, though.'

'I bet they didn't,' Felix muttered to Stella. 'He was obviously using her as a crowd-puller. I hope she's not going to be disappointed.'

'I don't suppose the same man will be there anyway,' Stella murmured back. 'Once she gets there and sees the round-abouts, she'll forget all about it.'

'To tell you the truth,' he said, 'I'm surprised that such young children are allowed to go to the Fair all by themselves. It's all right for bigger boys like Henry and Micky, but those Culliford children are likely to get trampled underfoot. Why don't their parents come with them?'

'Do you need to ask?' Stella enquired ironically. 'Maggie's worn out with having babies, and isn't too well with this new one coming, and Arthur – well, Arthur's a law unto himself. Anyway, the children will all go round in a group. They'll be all right.'

Tavistock was already busy when the bus arrived. It was unable to get all the way along Plymouth Road to the bus station and stopped by Sir Francis Drake's statue, where coaches and charabancs from other towns were already lining up. The children raced off down the long, straight road, screaming with excitement, and Felix and Stella went into the Meadows, across the canal and the river, and up Pixon Lane towards the cattle market to see the sale of sheep and cattle and even the geese that gave the Fair its name.

'The pony sale was a few days ago,' Felix remarked as they wandered between the pens and listened to the auctioneer's patter. 'You ought to go out next year and see the Drift – when they bring the ponies in off the moor. They do it on horseback, just like cowboys – it's quite impressive.'

'I saw it last year,' Stella said, 'when I was out walking with Luke one day. Oh, look at those lovely little Jerseys! Surely those must be false eyelashes they're wearing.'

After a while, they strolled towards the town for some lunch, but as they came across the bridge they saw that the entire square was filled with a solid mass of people, moving slowly past the stalls and sideshows erected along both sides. There were displays of all sorts – plants, household goods, china, clothes, toys, you name it – cheek by jowl with people telling fortunes, guessing ages or showing off tiny monkeys which gazed around with wide, sad eyes at the milling crowd. The square itself was almost unrecognisable, and once you were in the throng it was difficult to make out just where you were.

'We'll never get through,' Stella gasped, clinging to Felix's arm.

'We'll just have to go with it,' he grinned. 'Luckily they all seem to be going the same way ... We'll get there eventually, darling.'

Where 'there' was, she wasn't too sure, but after some time they did indeed find themselves outside Perratons, the big café close to the Midland Bank. Like all the other cafés in the town, it was crammed with visitors, townsfolk and farmers and their wives from all over the area. Stella and Felix found a table in one corner and squeezed themselves between a large, red-faced farmer who looked as if he had been a Toby Jug in a former life, and a matching wife. They were tucking into large plates of roast goose and laughing uproariously, but when they tried to explain the joke to Stella she found their speech so broad that she couldn't understand a word.

'I'm sorry,' she apologised. 'I thought I'd got used to the Tavistock dialect.'

'Us be from Okehampton, midear,' the man said kindly. 'Us don't speak like they Tavistock volk, that's why you can't understand, I dare say. And how be you enjoying the Goosey Fair, then?'

'We haven't seen much of it yet. We've just been to the cattle market, and now we're going to look round the rest. I didn't realise it would be so crowded.'

'Ah, us always comes to Goosey Fair,' the wife said, beaming. ''Tis the best day out in the year. And us always meets the same people, in just the same spots, as if they've been stood there all year.' They both roared with laughter again and pushed away their empty plates. As well as roast goose and all the trimmings, they had each had a large slice of blackberry and apple pie and several cups of tea. No wonder they looked so hearty, Stella thought, smiling at them.

The farmer took his wife's arm. 'Come along, midear, 'tis time us was moving on. Us hasn't met half the volk yet, and I've just seen old Bill Hannaford go by the window. I wants a word with he.'

They pushed their way out, leaving Stella and Felix to deal with their own substantial plates of roast goose, after which Stella declared that she couldn't eat another thing and Felix ate her helping of apple pie. At last, fortified for the afternoon, they staggered out of the café and surveyed the seething mass in the square.

'It hasn't eased off at all while we were in there,' Stella marvelled. 'In fact, if anything there are even more people. Wherever are they all coming from?'

'You heard the man – Okehampton, Hatherleigh, Holsworthy, Plymouth and all stations west,' he said. 'It's a big event. It should be – it's been going on for hundreds of years.'

'Has it? When did it start?'

'I've no idea,' he confessed. 'I just know it has ... Come on, let's throw ourselves into the fray again and go on some of the rides. I've been looking forward to sitting on one of those roundabout horses with my arms round your waist.'

'I think it had better be the other way around,' Stella said as they made their way through the throng. 'I'll never be able to hold on tightly enough for us both. I wonder how the children are getting on? I hope Betty Culliford wasn't disappointed over her roll-a-penny.'

'We'll probably spot them somewhere about,' Felix said, and gripped her hand tightly. 'Oh look, a switchback. And bumper cars. I love bumper cars, don't you?'

'You're supposed to call them dodgems,' she said as he dragged her towards the whirling vehicles and their screaming occupants. 'You're meant to avoid the others, not bump into them.' But it was obvious, as Felix settled them both into a little scarlet car and put his foot down hard, that he had other ideas, and she was helpless to do anything more than cling to the handle and close her eyes, trying not to scream too loudly as they hurtled around the floor, crashing into every other car there.

'I told you,' she said, when the operator had refused to take a second payment from Felix and evicted them. 'Honestly, Felix, you're no better than Micky and Henry. I just hope none of the children saw us. In fact, I hope nobody from Burracombe saw us.'

'I'm afraid that's too much to hope for,' he said with a grin, and nodded his head towards a corner of the dodgems, where Ted and Alice Tozer, with Val and Luke, were holding each other up, tears of laughter streaming down their faces. 'And I've a feeling I saw Mrs Warren on the other side, with the Harveys.'

'Mrs Warren? I wouldn't have thought she'd even come to Goosey Fair!' Stella said. 'And don't tell me Mr Harvey saw us too. Well, there go your chances of ever becoming a vicar, Felix.'

'They probably weren't that great anyway,' he agreed with a shrug. 'Let's go on the switchback next.'

'Wait a minute.' She was staring between two of the tents. 'I'm sure that's the Culliford girls over there. They look as if they're crying. Come on, Felix, we'd better go and see what's the matter.'

'It was the roll-a-penny man,' Betty wept, hiccuping with grief. 'He took all my money. He didn't let me win *anything*. And he didn't even remember me. He knew my name last year, didn't he, Shirl, he called me his little princess, and everything. And today he – he …' She could not go on. Her shoulders shook and she buried her face in her hands and cried as if her heart would break.

'Oh, Betty.' Stella stared at her in dismay. 'So you haven't been on any rides at all?'

'No, miss, and neither have I,' Shirley said. 'I give Betty my money too, see, 'cause we thought she'd win some, and she lost that too.'

'But what have you been doing all this time?' Stella and Felix gazed down at the dirty, woebegone faces. 'It's hours since the bus arrived.'

'We just been walking about, looking.' Shirley's voice trembled and tears spilled from her huge grey eyes. 'And please, miss, we don't know how we'm going to get home because we lost our bus money too. We didn't know what to do, miss.'

Her voice broke at last and she wept as inconsolably as her sister.

Stella looked at the two little girls in their worn dresses, dirty and tear-streaked, clinging together in their misery. She crouched down and gathered them both into her arms. 'Oh, Shirley. You poor little mites. And you must be hungry, too, and thirsty. Have you had anything at all to eat?'

'We had some sangwidges, miss, but we ate them on the bus,' Shirley said. 'We thought it would save carrying them.'

'Well, we'll find you something to eat and drink.' Stella stood up, taking a grimy hand in each of hers. 'I saw a stall selling sausage rolls just now. And we can get you some lemonade as well. Will that do? And afterwards, we'll take you on some of the rides, won't we, Felix? Which ones do you like best?'

'Please, miss, the horses,' Betty whispered. 'And Shirley wanted to go on the switchback, only that's sixpence.'

'Only for grown-ups,' Felix told her. 'It's threepence for you. Anyway, if that's what you want to go on, that's what we'll do. It's one of my favourites, too. And Miss Simmons and I have been wanting to have a go on the horses, so that's all right as well. Now, where's that sausage-roll stall ...?'

By the time they had fed the two children and taken them on every ride they could think of, or dared, it was almost time to catch the bus back to Burracombe. With the girls between them, happier now and each clinging to a hand, they walked back down the road to Drake's Statue, meeting and greeting other Burracombe people as they went. Everyone, it seemed, had had a wonderful day, although Micky had once again failed to win the model railway engine, and he and Henry had both been turned off the dodgems for bumping into the other cars too much. Both were loudly indignant.

'It's not fair,' Henry declared. 'They'm *bumper* cars. They'm meant to be bumped into. That's what they'm for – isn't it, Mr Copley?'

Felix opened his mouth to explain to the boys that they

were actually meant as a test of skill in avoiding each other, when he caught not only Stella's eye on him, but those of Basil and Grace Harvey, Ted and Alice Tozer and Val and Luke Ferris, and remembered that they had all witnessed his own ignominious eviction.

'Well, I always thought that myself, Henry,' he said humbly. 'But it looks as if we were both wrong, doesn't it? Perhaps we'd better remember that for next year.'

'Yes,' Stella said as they climbed aboard the bus, 'perhaps we had!'

Felix grinned. 'I'll tell you something else that will be remembered next year,' he murmured, guiding her to a seat. 'Those two little Culliford girls have been put off gambling for life. That experience really shook them – they won't try winning money again in a hurry. So, on the whole, it's been rather a good day, don't you think?'

'I do,' Stella said, clasping his hand. 'It's been a very good day indeed.'

Chapter Twenty-Five

It was two days after the Goose Fair that Jacob Prout went to Plymouth to stay with Jennifer. Looking as if he were about to attend his own funeral, he caught the late afternoon bus from the village green, his belongings packed into two bulging shopping bags. At the main road, he waited for the Plymouth bus and boarded it feeling as if he were departing from Burracombe for ever. He climbed to the top deck and sat there, staring out at the moorland they were leaving behind and told himself that it was only for two nights. He'd been away for much longer than that during the Great War, when he'd served in the Royal Navy, and seen far worse than he was likely to see in Plymouth this weekend, and he hadn't known then whether he'd ever come home again. So why had he found it so difficult to agree to this visit? Why did he feel as if he were leaving a part of himself behind?

I'm too old for this, he thought. Gallivanting round the country, staying in strange houses. I ought to have said no. She wouldn't have tried to make me go. She'd have been disappointed though, I knew that. I could see it in her face.

Disappointing Jennifer was something Jacob found impossible to do. Every time he looked at her, he thought of her mother. It wasn't that Jennifer resembled Susan much – she was more like Susan's own mother to look at – but she was Susan's girl and, if everything had gone as it should, she'd have been his as well. Her arrival in his life had been like a miracle, but he had an uneasy feeling that it depended partly on Burracombe. They had only ever been together in the village. Going to Plymouth might somehow break the spell.

Suppose it don't work out, he thought miserably. Suppose I seem different there, away from the lanes and the hedges and the moor. I'm a countryman – I don't feel right in the city. I might not behave right. Suppose I let her down and she's ashamed of me.

The bus was trundling through the streets now and he looked out of the window, depressed by what he saw. Bombsites still not cleared, houses being built to replace those destroyed during the war, great estates of those prefab things they'd put up to house all the homeless. And as they got further into the city, he could see the new streets Jennifer had told him about and the big shops – Dingle's, Spooners and the rest. Huge places, where you'd never be able to find what you wanted and it would all be too expensive anyway. It was as bad as London.

Jennifer met him at the bus station, her face alight with pleasure, and he felt ashamed of his gloom. The girl wanted him to see her home, she wanted to give him a good time and he ought to be grateful. He gave her a smile and a kiss and shook his head when she offered to take one of his bags.

'Haven't you got a suitcase?' she asked. 'I could have lent you one of mine.'

'Never needed one,' Jacob said. 'I had a kitbag during the war – the First War, that is – but that's out in the shed now. I keeps potatoes in it. Anyway, I didn't reckon to bring much. Left me dinner-suit at home.'

Jennifer laughed. 'That's all right, then. Now, we need to catch another bus and we'll soon be home. You'll be ready for a cup of tea, I expect.'

'I wouldn't say no,' he allowed, and followed her across the bus station. They boarded the bus for Devonport and trundled through more depressing streets until getting off again not far from St Levan's Gate. Jacob looked around him.

'However do you find your way about, maid? They all look the same.'

Jennifer glanced at the rows of terraced houses which had miraculously escaped the Blitz. 'They do, rather, but I suppose it's like the country lanes – we just get to know our way about. My house is along here.'

'There's no grass,' he said, looking at the houses with their front doors opening straight on to the pavements. 'There's no trees. There's not a bit of green anywhere.'

'We've got gardens at the back,' she said apologetically, 'but they're not what you'd call gardens – just back yards, really. But there are some nice parks, where we can go to see grass and trees. And there's the Hoe, and the swimming pools along Tinside, and we can get the Cremyll ferry over to Cawsand for the beach, or catch the train out to Shaugh Prior. It's not so bad really.'

Jacob didn't reply. He was chastising himself for being critical. This was Jennifer's home, the place where she'd grown up, and it had been his Susan's home as well. He'd got to remember that.

As if I could forget, he thought, following Jennifer along the narrow street. As if I could forget that my Susan lived here all those years, not an hour's journey away from Burracombe and me, away from where she belonged. And he knew then that this was why he hadn't wanted to come.

He didn't want to think of Susan living in these mean streets, without him. He didn't want to think of the life she'd had, married to another man. For over thirty years he had believed her dead and, as he stood at the brown front door, watching Jennifer put her key in the lock, he felt almost as if he'd rather he had never known the truth. He wanted to go back to where he'd been a year ago, with Susan and all that had happened, left in the past. He didn't want to step through the front door and into the life she had really lived.

But when Jennifer opened the door and went inside, he took a deep breath and walked in after her.

'I thought we'd have a quiet supper together, just the two of us,' Jennifer said when he came down from his bedroom and stood awkwardly in the back room. She had put a match to the fire and it was burning brightly, filling the room with the scent of woodsmoke. But she could see that Jacob was ill at ease and tried to think of ways to help him relax. 'Betty and Audrey are coming over to tea on Sunday so we'll have all day tomorrow to do what we like. I expect you'd like to see the new shops.'

'I don't reckon I'm one for shops, much,' Jacob said uncomfortably. 'Tavistock's always seemed to have enough for me, if you needs anything you can't get in the village.'

'Well, we don't have to go to the shops. You might like to see Dingle's, where I work, though. And then we could go up on the Hoe. I dare say you've been there before.' She was beginning to feel as if she was trying to jolly along a small child. 'Anyway, we don't have to decide that now. Sit down – this chair's nice and comfortable – and I'll make us a cup of tea. I've put a steak and kidney pie in the oven for supper.'

Jacob sat down gingerly, as if he feared the chair might bite him, and looked around as Jennifer went out to the small kitchen. The room was about the same size as his own living room, with an armchair on either side of the fireplace, a brightly coloured rag rug on the lino-covered floor, and a square dining table and four chairs in the middle of the room. Against one wall was a sideboard and on it stood a radio set that looked quite new, a vase of chrysanthemums and a bowl of shiny red Quaranden apples. There were pictures on the walls, two of some people in old-fashioned clothes playing chess, and one of a farm cart which appeared to be crossing a ford. He liked that one and got up to have a closer look.

'I've seen this before,' he said as Jennifer came back with a tray of tea. 'Got it on a biscuit-tin once.'

'It's quite famous,' she said, setting the tray on the table. 'I've brought a couple of slices of cake as well, since it'll be a while before supper's ready. I made it myself.' He sat down again and she handed him a plate and put his cup and saucer down in the hearth beside him. 'You always give me such good food, I wanted to show you I can cook as well.'

'I knows that already,' he said, taking a bite. It was good fruitcake, full of sultanas. 'You brought enough out for Jed when he was alive.'

'Well, now I'm cooking for you.' She sat opposite him and smiled. 'It's lovely to have you here, Jacob. It really is.'

Jacob regarded her. He was beginning to feel a little better now. He drank some tea and said, 'You've made this place nice and cosy.'

'I haven't done all that much to it,' she said. 'It's more or less the same as it was when Mum was here.'

There was a small silence. Jacob put down his cup and looked around again. There were some photographs on the mantelpiece – two or three of children he didn't recognise and one of a couple at their wedding. He stared at it and realised the bride was Susan. He looked at Jennifer and met her glance.

'You've never showed me that one before,' he said a little huskily.

'I know. I thought you ought to see it here – where she lived.' Her heart was beating fast. She had realised why he was so reluctant to visit her in Plymouth and had been just as nervous as he, afraid that it might upset him too much, that it might spoil their relationship, which had become so precious to her. By confronting him with the reality of Susan's life without him, she might be bringing his memories back too sharply, too painfully, for him to bear, and he might turn away from her as a result. Yet she knew it was a stage they had to go through. Their relationship was such a strange one, based on a moment of someone else's violent and regretted passion, and the only way to security was to face the truth.

Jacob got up. Slowly, he reached out his hand and took the photograph from the mantelpiece. He gazed at it, his eyes moving from one face to the other, and then, gently, he put it back.

'She looks happy enough. And he looks a decent sort.'

Jennifer let out a tiny breath of relief. 'He was. And I think they were happy together.'

Jacob nodded. 'Ah. I were happy enough with my Sarah, when we found each other. Don't do no good to hanker over what you can't have.' He took one of the other photographs from the mantelpiece. 'And who be these little tackers, then? You and your sisters?'

'Yes.' She got up and stood beside him, pointing. 'That's me, of course – I'm the biggest, I was three years old when Audrey was born. This is Audrey, in the pinafore, and the baby is Betty. She's a few years younger than we are because Mum had a miscarriage in between.' She stopped suddenly as Jacob turned to her.

'Susan lost a babby? You never told me that before.'

'Well, we haven't talked like this much, have we?' she said gently. 'I'm sorry – I said it without thinking. It's all right, Jacob, it was very early on and Mum wasn't ill or anything. But it just took a while before she felt ready to have another one, I suppose.'

He nodded and looked at the photo of the three girls again. 'You would have been about eight when this was took.'

'Yes, I was. Audrey was five and Betty's one. I think it was her birthday, as a matter of fact.'

'Nice little family,' Jacob said, and sat down again.

Jennifer looked at him. There had been a wistful note in his voice and she wondered if he was thinking that it ought to have been his family, not that of some other man. With the loss of Susan, Jacob hadn't wanted to marry; it wasn't until many years later that he had taken Sarah Lilliman as his wife, and by then both had been in their forties.

'You'd have made a wonderful father,' she said quietly. 'It's

261

a shame you never had any children. But you've got me now, and I feel as close to you as any daughter could.'

He sat silent for a moment or two, staring into the fire, and again she feared that this visit had been too much for him. Then he said thoughtfully, 'I dunno, maid. If I'd had other kiddies, 'twould all have been different when you come back to Burracombe. I mean, there would have been they to think about, and how they might feel about it all. It might not have been all that easy.' He raised his head and looked into her eyes. 'Seems a funny thing to say, but I ain't sorry it's turned out the way it has. As things stand now, mebbe it's not a bad thing Sarah and me didn't have none of our own. I reckon you'm good enough for me, now.'

Jennifer felt the tears come to her eyes. She brushed them away and laid her hand on Jacob's arm.

'Thank you, Jacob,' she whispered. 'Thank you.'

Somehow, it seemed easier after that, as if an invisible bridge had been crossed. The ghost of Susan which had been lurking in a dark corner of Jacob's mind, had come out into the open and, when he was alone again, he had another look at the wedding photograph, holding the frame tenderly in his big hands. It had been taken a few years after he had last seen her but, despite all she had been through, she looked little older; she was still, he thought, the girl he had loved and remembered all these years.

He replaced the photograph and turned to the one of the family. It was a studio portrait, like so many that families had taken, with Susan sitting on a chair and her husband behind her, one hand resting on her shoulder. Jennifer and the older of the other two sisters – Audrey, wasn't it? – stood one on each side, and the baby was on her knee, wearing a frilled dress of what looked like creamy satin. I bet it didn't look like that for long, he thought, smiling a little. One chocolate biscuit at her birthday tea, and she'd be just as much a little ragamuffin as any other twelve-month old.

On Sunday, he would meet these two little girls – grown women now – who had been so big a part of Susan's life. Two women who would not have existed, had he and Susan married. He wondered what their feelings were about him. It was a strange and complicated situation. Too complicated for him to think about too deeply now, he decided and, as Jennifer came back into the room with another tray of tea, he gave her the first real smile he had managed since his arrival and said, 'Reckon it'll be a good idea for me to see that big shop where you spends your days, maid, and then us'll go up on the Hoe. That'll be another trip down Memory Lane – seeing the ships out in the Sound. Many's the time I've been aboard one of they, when I were in the Navy. I reckon 'tis one of the best views in the world, coming back into Plymouth and looking out for all the green, with Dartmoor beyond, and Brentor Church up on its hill. I tell you what, maid, on Sunday, if 'tis all the same to you, I'd like to go to morning service at St Andrew's. And now let's have a game of crib before us goes to bed.'

Jennifer put down the tray and gave him a hug. She too knew that a bridge had been safely crossed.

'My stars,' Jacob said slowly, 'I wouldn't never have believed it.'

Saturday had passed more successfully than either of them had expected. Jacob had slept well, despite being in a strange bed and knowing that Susan had slept in the next room, and woken to the smell of frying bacon. Downstairs, Jennifer had given him as good a breakfast as any he would have had in Burracombe, and afterwards they had gone into the city centre to look at the new roads and shops that had been built over the ruins left by the Blitz. Jennifer, who often worked on Saturdays, had arranged to have the whole day off and stopped to talk to almost all the salesgirls, introducing Jacob as a family friend with such pride that he protested that he was being shown off like a pet dog.

After they had looked at all the departments, none of which had appealed to him greatly since there were no tools or gardening equipment, they went to a restaurant and had lunch, which Jennifer insisted on paying for. At this, Jacob put his foot down. 'I may be your visitor but when a man takes a young lady out, he pays. I'd never be able to look meself in the eye again if I let you do that.'

'All right,' Jennifer said with a laugh. 'So long as you let me buy you a cup of tea or an ice cream up on the Hoe.'

'Well, that's different,' he allowed, and he accepted a large strawberry cornet with good grace as they sat at the foot of Smeaton's Tower an hour or so later, gazing out across the sparkling blue sea towards the dark line of the breakwater and the faint pencil-shape of the Eddystone lighthouse on the horizon. It was a perfect October day, and the air was clear and crisp. The trees on Drake's Island were turning to red and gold, and beyond them could be seen the glowing colours of Mount Edgcumbe Park. The Sound was dancing with white sails, and when Jacob and Jennifer wandered down to the railings they could hear the laughter of children playing amongst the rock pools on the cliff terraces.

'Really, it's a shame the Tinside swimming pool's closed for the winter,' Jennifer remarked. 'It's like a summer's day.'

'Luke's little summer,' he nodded. ''Tis a pretty sight.'

They stayed on the Hoe for a long time, as Jacob recounted some of his experiences in the Navy during the First World War, and then they strolled down to the Barbican where the fishing-boats were drawn up beside the jetties, ready to go out for the next night's fishing. The streets here were more or less as Jacob remembered them – quaint and narrow, with half-timbered houses reaching across towards each other – and the water wound its way between the quays almost into the heart of the city. When the two finally left the sea behind, they were once again opposite Dingle's and beside St Andrew's Church, where Jacob had asked to attend the morning service.

'It was almost destroyed during the war,' Jennifer said, looking up at the tall tower. 'But they never stopped holding services here, and the very first day after the Blitz someone nailed up a piece of wood with *Resurgam* painted on it to show that we wouldn't give in.'

'I remember that,' he said, gazing up at the doorway. 'It were in the paper. Showed 'em what Devon folk are made of.'

Jennifer cooked belly of pork when they reached home, with cabbage and mashed potatoes. 'I'll do a roast tomorrow – it can stay in the oven while we go to church. And Betty and Audrey will be here about three o'clock.'

'I'll have to catch the bus by seven o'clock,' Jacob said. 'Don't want to be too late getting back.'

'That's all right. They usually go at that time, too. We can go to the bus station together. They're looking forward to meeting you, Jacob.'

Jacob made no reply. He didn't think Jennifer would tell him lies, but he couldn't really see why her two half-sisters should look forward to meeting him. Why should they be interested? He was nothing to them, after all – no relation, not even half a one. He slept less well that night, thinking about them and wishing the weekend could have been just for Jennifer and himself. So far, he'd enjoyed it more than he'd expected. Now, it was as if a shadow had suddenly fallen.

The service at St Andrew's next morning helped a little. It was very different in the big church from the services he was accustomed to at Burracombe, but he enjoyed listening to the choir and the music of the organ, and the prayers and responses were the same. The roast beef that Jennifer served at one o'clock was as good as anything he'd tasted at home, and she'd done the potatoes to a turn. He enjoyed the stewed plums and custard they had for pudding, and by the time they'd washed up it was nearly three o'clock and he'd almost forgotten to be nervous.

When the knock came on the door, however, all his fears rushed back and he looked at Jennifer with sudden anxiety.

'It's all right,' she said, smiling reassuringly. 'They're not going to bite you.'

She went to the door to let them in. Jacob, standing in the living room as awkwardly as when he'd first arrived, heard a hubbub of voices, male as well as female. The two sisters had brought their husbands, of course, and Audrey, the elder, had two children. He could hear them as well, chattering with excitement. Feeling like an exhibit in a circus, he braced himself and watched the door open. The two women came in together, the younger first, and stood gazing at him and smiling.

'My stars,' he said slowly. 'I wouldn't never have believed it. You'm the spitting image of my Susan – both of you.'

Chapter Twenty-Six

'I've had a letter from the Bishop,' Felix said.

He had hurried over to Dottie's cottage just in time to catch Stella before she left for school. It was Monday morning and, as usual, everything seemed more difficult to get ready even though she had taken care to lay all her work and clothes out the night before. She stood at Dottie's front door, looking at him uncertainly, not sure what this news meant.

'He's not angry with you over something?'

Felix pretended to look hurt. 'Of course he's not! What touching faith you have in me, my darling. What do you think I could have done to make the Bishop angry?'

'Well, someone could have complained to him about the way you behaved at Goosey Fair, for a start,' she retorted. 'What has he written to you about, then? You'd better tell me quickly, I haven't got long.' She bent to pull on her Wellington boots. The fine October weather – 'Luke's little summer' – had disappeared in a lashing downpour, and the tiny stream that ran beside the road had overflowed its runnel and spread itself in a large puddle all over the road.

'He doesn't actually say,' Felix admitted. 'He just wants me to go and see him on Thursday. But that's encouraging, isn't it?'

'Is it?' Stella had had a disturbed night. Two half-grown calves had broken through the fence into the field behind Dottie's cottage the evening before and their father, Ted Tozer's bull, had spent the entire night bellowing from the other side of the hedge. When Ted had finally come to return the escapees to their family, the bull had taken them into a corner and given them what was obviously a good telling-off, nodding his great head up and down while they gazed up at him with wide eyes. Just as if their mothers didn't care about them at all, Dottie had remarked, watching from the kitchen window but, interesting though this behaviour was, it didn't make up for the loss of sleep Stella had suffered.

'Why is it encouraging?' she asked now. 'You do go and see him now and then, don't you?'

'Yes, he likes to keep in touch with all his clergy, even minor cogs in the wheel like me. But I was hoping it might be something to do with Little Burracombe – you know, the living. He must be thinking about who to appoint.' He helped her on with her mackintosh, getting her arm into the wrong sleeve. 'Sorry. Let's try again.'

'I'll do it myself!' Irritated, she pulled the garment away from him and dragged it on. 'I'm sorry, Felix, I really can't stop now, I'm late as it is, and all the children are going to arrive wet. That means coats dripping in the lobby and Wellington boots, and half of them will have come without shoes to put on. I hate wet Mondays!'

'I suppose everyone does,' he said humbly. 'Sorry. I was just so pleased, I wanted to tell you right away.'

Stella paused and looked at him. 'Felix, *I'm* sorry. I'm in a bad mood this morning. Look, why don't you meet me after school and tell me about it then? Come to tea.'

'I can't. I promised to go over and help at the vicarage. Mrs Berry's moving out soon, to go and live with her niece, and there's an awful lot of stuff to clear out. Actually, I was hoping you'd come too. She's thinking of leaving some of the furniture, and if there's anything we like . . .'

'But we don't even know if we'll be living there!'

'I know, but it wouldn't hurt, would it, to pick out any bits that might be useful? After all, it's a big house, and even if things don't work out there, we'll need furniture sometime. Will you come?'

She hesitated. 'We haven't told anyone yet. We said we'd wait till Christmas.'

'I think most people will have guessed long before then,' he said with a grin. 'And Mrs Berry's not going to gossip, anyway. Say you'll come, darling. I'll meet you after school and we can go in Mirabelle.'

'Oh, all right,' she said ungraciously. 'So long as you make sure the hood doesn't leak. I'll have seen enough rain by then!'

By three o'clock the rain had stopped and the clouds rolled away, leaving an innocent blue sky and an almost summery sunshine. Stella came out of school to find Felix standing beside the sports car his uncle had given him, the hood up and an umbrella held ostentatiously over his head. He was wearing a full-length mackintosh, a yellow sou'wester and Wellington boots.

Stella burst out laughing. 'Felix, you are a fool! Put that lot away, for goodness sake, before someone writes and tells the Bishop you're mad.'

'Well, I thought I'd better do as you said,' he answered humbly. 'Didn't want to get my head bitten off again.'

'I'm sorry.' She held the umbrella while he divested himself of the mackintosh and boots and rolled back Mirabelle's hood. 'It's just that we had an awful night, and the rain just about put the lid on it. Now you know what a horrible temper I've got.'

'Oh, I knew that before.' He stowed the coat and boots behind the seats. 'Remember that time when you fell in the bog when—'

'Yes, I do remember, and I didn't fall, you pushed me. I know you didn't mean me to fall in the bog, and I know it had its funny side, but I just couldn't see it at the time.' She squeezed into the passenger seat. 'Do you really think I'll make a good vicar's wife, Felix?'

'With the right sort of training, yes.' He started the motor. 'The more immediate question is, whether I shall ever make a good vicar. And how I'm to convince the Bishop that I could.'

'Not by crashing into all the cars you can at Goose Fair and dressing yourself up like an advertisement for cough sweets,' she said. 'Honestly, Felix, do you really think that the parishioners of Little Burracombe are going to accept you as their vicar, after John Berry?'

'I don't see why not. Apart from his wisdom and experience, what did he have to offer that I haven't got? And even he had to start somewhere.'

'Let's hope the Bishop has a sense of humour, that's all.' Stella leaned back in her seat, letting the soft air brush her face. 'Do you suppose that's what he wants to talk to you about on Thursday?'

'I don't know. To be honest, I'm not sure if he'll think it's a good idea to appoint me to the living. He may think I'm too close – not just because I've been helping out during the past few months, but also because I've been in Burracombe itself. It's not always a good idea to appoint someone who knows the parish, or whom the parishioners know. It's harder sometimes to make changes, you see. A completely new person, with their own ideas, can find that easier to do, simply because they don't know the village hierarchy.'

'Isn't it better if they do?' she asked doubtfully. 'Then they know who is likely to be offended by what they suggest.'

'But that's the point! The vicar *shouldn't* be afraid to offend people. Not by wearing silly clothes, or going to the pub, but by doing what he believes to be right within his church and parish. He can't allow the parishioners' prejudices to rule him, and it's much easier for a new man, who doesn't know what they are in the first place, to set his own rules. For instance, suppose I wanted to go in for High Church practices. It would create quite a lot of debate: some would want it, others wouldn't. Much easier if I came in fresh.'

'You don't, do you?' she asked. 'Burracombe's not High Church.'

'That doesn't mean I might not want to do it, once I got my own parish. At present, I have to work according to Mr Harvey's rules. Once I'm in charge ...'

'I've never been to a High Church service,' she said doubtfully.

'I'm not saying I do want to – it was just an example. And that's another thing – the parishioners have to be willing to accept me, too. They have quite a big say in the matter.'

'Well, that's all right. They like you. You know that.'

'They might not like it if they agreed to my appointment and then found I wanted to make huge changes. Like going High.'

'No, I don't suppose they would. But you'd have to tell them that beforehand, wouldn't you?'

'Anything as big as that, yes, I would. But there would be all sorts of other things I'd do differently. They might feel cheated if they agreed to my appointment and then found things weren't going exactly the same as when Mr Berry was vicar.'

Stella sighed. 'It's more difficult than I thought. Perhaps it would be better if you didn't even apply, and we waited for something else to come along.'

Felix glanced sideways at her and took his hand from the wheel to lay it briefly on hers.

'You know neither of us wants to do that. No, I think we should go ahead and hope for what we want. If it's the right thing, it will happen. If not – well, we'll know there's a good reason for it. And meanwhile, we'll do all we can to help Mrs Berry.'

The car pulled into the vicarage drive and they sat for a moment, looking at the gracious house before them. The front was covered with climbing roses, still with a few late blooms to catch the afternoon sun, and the crab apple tree at the edge of

271

the lawn seemed lit with tiny orange lanterns. The big, blowsy flowers of hydrangeas were as blue as the sky, and the borders were bright with asters and dahlias.

Stella gazed at it and thought of the vicarage where she had spent a few months of her childhood, when she had first been evacuated during the war. She and her sister, and the two Budd brothers, had been like one happy family, living there with the somewhat eccentric vicar and his housekeeper. She was swept by a sudden passionate desire to live in this house, to try to re-create that feeling of contentment and security for herself and for Felix and, she hoped, for their own family. This is where I want to be, she thought. This is my home.

The door opened and the frail figure of the vicar's widow appeared, waving and beckoning them in, and Stella felt ashamed of her sudden longing. It's not my home, she told herself, it's hers. I mustn't forget that. I mustn't let myself hope too much.

Yet, as she followed Felix into the house, prepared to help with the sad business of packing up the old lady's life, she still couldn't rid herself of that sensation that this was where she belonged. And as she laid her hand on the doorjamb just before she entered, she had again that overwhelming feeling that she had come home.

The downpour meant that Jacob was kept busy clearing culverts and ditches that had suddenly become clogged with leaves and other rubbish and were causing floods across the lanes and into the fields. He was still hard at work when Val came home from her afternoon shift at the hospital, and she paused to say hello and ask how the weekend in Plymouth had gone.

'Well, 'tweren't as bad as I expected,' he said, leaning on his long-handled shovel. 'I never been one for big towns, as you may know, and how anyone ever finds their way home in that maze of streets I can't understand, but 'tis cosy enough in

Jennifer's house, I got to admit that. And that shop she works in, Dingle's – well, 'tis like a palace, got everything under the sun for sale, except anything useful. I mean, there's not a wheelbarrow or a garden fork in the place, nothing but fancy stuff – necklaces and bits and pieces for women, and flashy clothes. But apart from that, 'tis all right, I suppose, for them as likes that sort of thing.'

'Did you go up on the Hoe?' Val asked, hiding a smile.

'Oh ah, us did that, sat for a long time watching the ships. That were all right.'

He hesitated. 'And she had her two sisters round for tea, with their hubbies. Audrey and Betty. And a couple of little tackers – Audrey's, they were.' He stopped and shovelled hard at a pile of leaves. 'My Susan's grandchildren, when you comes to think about it.'

Val waited a moment, then said quietly, 'Did you find that hard, Jacob?'

He straightened up again and looked at her. 'I thought I would. I'll be honest with you, Val, I weren't looking forward to it. It were bad enough going to the house and knowing my Susan had lived there – almost as if it was haunted. And then having to meet her two other girls – well, I dunno, it just seemed all out of kilter, somehow. I couldn't seem to come to terms with it. But once I met them, well ...' He stopped again and Val waited once more. 'They was the spitting image of my Susan,' he burst out at last. 'Both of 'em. They could have been her as she'd have been when she was their age. That's queer, ain't it? Jennifer don't take after her, she looks like Susan's mother, but these two ...' He shook his head. 'It was like seeing her come to life again. I just hadn't expected it. Took me right aback, it did.'

'Oh, Jacob,' Val said, feeling helpless. 'That must have been so sad for you.'

He thought for a minute and then said, 'It were and it weren't. It were a shock, I don't mind admitting that, but once

I got over that I was – well, I was pleased, in a funny sort of way. Pleased that my Susan had someone to take after her. And it was as if I knew them already. It wasn't just that they looked like her, they *were* like her. And they were pleased to meet me.' He shook his head in wonder. 'They said they'd been *wanting* to meet me.'

'Jacob, that's wonderful!' Val exclaimed. 'It must be almost like having two more daughters, as well as Jennifer.' She stopped and bit her lip, remembering that Jennifer wasn't actually Jacob's daughter. But he didn't seem to notice the slip and nodded.

'It's a whole new family,' he said. 'Them and their menfolk, and the two little 'uns. And they'll be coming out to Burracombe to see me, too, and see where their mother lived.'

'I'm so pleased,' Val said. 'I really am. A whole new family,' she echoed his words.

'Ah,' he said. 'And that's what life be all about, when it comes down to it. Families. That's what holds the world together. People having babies and bringing them up to take their place in the world. Us old 'uns, watching them grow. That's what's important. And I thought it had passed me by.' He lifted his shovel again, then gave her a sharp look. 'Don't you hang about too long, young Val. Don't you and Luke leave it too late.'

'No,' Val said, a little faintly, 'we won't.'

She went on her way, leaving Jacob shovelling his leaves and musing on the meaning of life, and walked slowly through the village to Jed's Cottage. They had finally agreed to keep the name, as part of village history, and Luke had painted a sign to nail on the gate. As Val reached it, she laid her hand on the fence and looked at the little front garden, cleared of its tangle of weeds and neatly planted, and at the roses already beginning to arch over the door.

It's time to put the past away and look to the future, she thought. It's time to think about our family.

Chapter Twenty-Seven

'*'Tis now your fortune I will tell,*' Alf Coker said in the tremulous, wheedling tones of an old gipsy woman, '*of marriage and a wedding-bell. A lady strange will come your way, and this will be your happy day. For at a stroke, you'll fall in love. For evermore she'll be your dove.*'

He stopped and looked winningly at George Sweet, who was sitting on the other side of a small round table, in the middle of which an old tennis ball stood on one of the village hall saucers. Alf cupped his hands round it and peered closely at the worn surface.

'*There is one warning I must state, unless you want a grisly fate. The wedding of Maid Marian, must not go as you all plan. If she is forced to wed this knave, the consequences will be grave.*'

'That's very good,' Felix said. 'Now, George, remember that you're falling in love with Mother Hood. You think that what's she's just said is about herself and you. You've been searching for a wife, and here's just the kind of lady you've been dreaming of.' There was a ripple of laughter as the rest of the cast regarded Alf, in his flannel trousers and old waistcoat. 'Well, she'll look more like it when we've got Alf into his costume, anyway. But she'll have to do a bit more wheedling before you can bring yourself to interfere in the Black Knight's plans, so don't look too eager too soon.'

'I don't reckon I'm going to look eager at all,' George said. 'I've never much fancied meself walking up the aisle with Alf Coker.'

'Gladys Coker must have done, once,' someone remarked not quite quietly enough, and everyone laughed again.

'Go on from there,' Felix said, and the two actors shifted their shoulders as if preparing for a boxing match, and bent their heads over the tennis ball again.

'*The thing you ask cannot be so,*' George said. '*Although it fills me full of woe. The Knight must wed where e'er his heart is, or he will have my guts for garters.*'

'I don't think that's a very nice line,' Joyce Warren said. She was sitting in a corner of the hall with a group of women, sewing costumes. 'And it's rather silly, too. Can't you change it to something a little more suitable?'

'It's a pantomime,' Felix said. 'It's got to have silly jokes in it.' He was holding on tightly to his patience; Joyce had already objected to half a dozen other jokes, none of them in his view at all offensive. 'Perhaps you would like to rewrite all the lines you don't like and discuss them with me before the next rehearsal. I'm sure we can come to some agreement, but remember we've got to give people something to laugh at.'

'They'll get that all right,' George Sweet observed. 'Once they see Alf here in his frock, with his chest stuck out like the balcony in *Romeo and Juliet*, they'll split their sides.'

'Well, at least I know I'm meant to be funny,' Alf retorted. They'd had a lot of trouble with George, who fancied himself as an actor and wanted to play the Sheriff as if he were Laurence Olivier. 'Look, can we get on with this, only some of us got to be up early in the morning and I was hoping for a pint at the Bell before I goes home.'

The rehearsal proceeded. Joyce, who was in charge of props, left her sewing and came to sit beside Felix, murmuring in his ear as she made a list of what was needed. 'Bows and arrows for all the Merry Men, and smaller ones for the Merry Children. Cooking equipment for Mother Hood – oh, and we'll need a bonfire too, with a rear bicycle lamp hidden in the sticks. And we'll need a proper crystal ball for the fortune-telling scene. And—'

'I think it would be a good idea for you and me to have a proper meeting, away from the rehearsals,' Felix suggested. 'I know I'm awfully stupid but I really can't concentrate on two things at once. I expect it's because I'm a mere man.' He gave her his most charming smile and Stella, looking up from her script, felt her lips twitch and turned away hastily.

'Yes, well, that probably would be the best thing,' Joyce said tartly, not swayed at all by his efforts. 'I can see you have a lot to learn about village dramatics. They're rather different from the little things you did at Cambridge, you know. There's a lot to take into account – all the little feuds and fussing that goes on, you've no idea.'

'I think I have some idea,' he said, wondering if she had any inkling as to how the villagers felt about her. 'Being a curate does bring me into contact—'

'But only with the churchgoers,' she broke in triumphantly. 'Whereas I have contact with *everyone*, one way and another. The Bridge Club, the Gardening Club ...'

'Be you going to listen to us or not?' Alf Coker demanded, coming abruptly out of his Dame persona and looking at them with some belligerence. 'How are you ever going to know if George here is saying his words proper?'

'I like that!' the baker said indignantly. ''Tisn't me that needs listening to, it's you with that silly voice of yours. I'm sure you don't have to make it go deep and look at the audience when you says that bit about not letting anyone see your garters.'

'It's an aside,' Alf said with dignity. 'It's meant to be said to the audience. Ain't it, curate?'

'Yes, it is,' Felix agreed. 'And I'm sorry I wasn't listening properly. You're quite right.' He glanced at Mrs Warren. 'We'd better leave this discussion until later.'

'Well, there won't be time this evening,' she said, sounding affronted. 'You'd better come round to my house tomorrow night and we'll go through everything. We need to sort out what we'll be doing about tickets, as well. Come after supper, about eight o'clock, and we can spend a couple of hours sorting it all out. There are a number of things I'm not happy about.'

Stella, peeping back, saw that Felix was now looking rather startled, and felt her smile break out again. That'll teach you, she thought smugly, and looked down at her script again.

The rehearsal lurched on, with the Dame's realisation that the wicked Sheriff had fallen in love with her, and her desperate and comical efforts to escape his embrace. This was interrupted by the arrival of the Black Knight, played to sinister perfection by Travis Kellaway who swaggered in, swirling an imaginary cloak around his broad shoulders, and deepening his voice until it almost fell through the floor. His scepticism was soon dispersed by the Sheriff, now completely enamoured of Mother Hood, and by Mother Hood's reading of his own fortune, which – as was only to be expected – foretold terrible disaster for the whole of Nottingham and especially Sherwood Forest itself, should he marry Maid Marian.

'*Your prophecy is hard to bear,*' he declaimed powerfully, swirling his cloak again. '*Yet responsibility I share. For this great forest we must cherish, not a single tree shall perish.*'

It looked as though all was going well, but just as Mother Hood gave the Sheriff a small, celebratory kiss ('It better had be small, too,' George Sweet told the blacksmith threateningly) the Black Knight's sisters, Dusk and Dawn, played by Hilary and Stella, burst in and denounced the fortune-teller as an impostor, tearing off her disguise to reveal who she really was, and demanding that she be thrown into the castle dungeon immediately, if not sooner. At this, George had another objection to raise.

'I don't see why the Sheriff would agree to that, not if he's fallen in love with the old woman. He wouldn't want her in the dungeon with all they rats and torture implements and such.'

'It's a way of keeping her in the castle,' Felix explained.

'I know it doesn't make sense, but we have to remember it's pantomime and nothing really makes sense. Nobody expects it to. Anyway, he can't risk the Black Knight thinking he's not on his side. He's a very powerful man.'

The scene ended with Hangem and Floggem being summoned to hustle Mother Hood off to the dungeons, protesting loudly. At this point, Felix called a halt.

'I think that's all we can do for tonight. It's coming along very well. We do need to get rid of these scripts, though. You'll find it much easier to act when you're not trying to read from them, so please all try to learn as many words as possible by next week. We're meeting again on Monday.'

'I can't come then,' George Sweet said. 'My missus wants me to take her over to see her sister in Buckland Monachorum. Her's been in bed with her leg.'

Felix bit back the obvious reply and said merely, 'Well, we'll do some of the other scenes, then. Is there anyone else who can't come on Monday?'

One or two others put up their hands and he nodded and made a note of the names. Dottie said, 'I'll need everyone's measurements by next week, remember. I've nearly finished the Dame's costumes, and these other ladies are doing the Merry Men's jerkins, so I'll be wanting to get on with the others pretty soon.'

The actors departed, some to the inn and some straight home. Hilary stopped to have a word with Val, and Travis sauntered out of the hall, closely followed by Tessa Latimer.

'So how d'you think you'll like living in Burracombe?' she enquired, falling into step beside him as he strolled along the lane to where he had parked his motorcycle. The moon was three-quarters full and very bright. 'You don't think we're a lot of country bumpkins?'

He laughed. 'I'm a countryman myself, remember. Grew up in a very similar village. I think I'll settle in quite happily, thank you.'

'Isn't that funny?' she said. 'You seem so much more sophisticated than most of the men round here. I suppose it's because you were in the Army.'

'And weren't most of the men of my age round here in the Army too? Or one of the other Services?'

She shrugged. 'Some of them, but they're either married or gone away. They're not interesting, like you.'

'And what makes you think I'm interesting?' he asked, stopping beside his motorcycle and taking hold of the handlebars.

'I can see you are,' she said, a smile in her voice. 'I bet you've done all sorts of interesting things.' She paused, then said, 'I bet you've had lots of girlfriends, too.'

'Do you, indeed? And why should that make me interesting?'

'It just does, that's all.' She laid her hand on the handlebar as he swung his leg across the saddle. 'You're not going already, are you? I thought we might have a talk.'

'That would be very pleasant,' he said evenly, 'but I'm afraid I have work to do. Another time, perhaps.'

'Work? At this time of night?'

'That's right,' he said, and kick-started the engine. It roared into life and Tessa jumped back. 'I'm sure you've noticed all the half-grown pheasants there are in the lanes just now. And I'm sure a few other people around here have, too. Furzey and I have a busy time ahead of us.'

'Oh, you mean poaching. But you're not a gamekeeper.'

'No, I'm a gamekeeper's son. And Furzey needs a bit of help.' He sat back on the saddle, regarding her in the moonlight, then revved up the engine and let out the clutch. 'Sorry I can't stop and talk, but I'm a busy man.'

The headlight cut a bright white path ahead of him as he roared off towards Home Farm, and Tessa stood watching for a moment, a frown on her face as he disappeared into the darkness. Then she turned and stalked back towards her father's house.

*

'Don't let's go straight home,' Vic said as he and Jackie came out of the hall. 'It's a nice night, let's go for a bit of a walk.'

'I mustn't be late,' she said. 'I'm going to Plymouth tomorrow, on the early bus.'

'Plymouth – what for? Started your Christmas shopping already?'

'What, in October? Don't be silly. As a matter of fact, I've got an interview for a job.'

'A job!' Vic stopped dead in the middle of the road. 'What sort of a job? Why Plymouth?'

'It was Miss Hilary's idea. She's been saying for ages that I ought to do something better than just being a housemaid. She thinks I'd be good at hotel work and I thought I might as well give it a try. I'm going to see the head housekeeper at the Duke of Cornwall.'

'The Duke of Cornwall? That's the best hotel in Plymouth! Setting your sights a bit high, aren't you?'

'I don't think so,' Jackie retorted, annoyed by his tone. 'And neither does Miss Hilary, or she wouldn't have suggested it. She knows one of the high-ups there.'

'So she's pulled some strings for you,' he said, still with a trace of a sneer in his voice.

'No! She's just put in a word for me, that's all. It's no different from giving me a reference. And it'll be up to me to prove I can do it, anyway. What's the matter with you, Vic? Don't you want me to get on?'

'Don't see the point. You've got a perfectly good job at the Barton, you don't have to travel to get there, and you can live at home and eat your mum's good cooking. And you can go out with me in the evenings. Why change?'

'Because I'd like to do something else! I'd like to make something of myself. Miss Hilary says all women should be able to have careers if they want them. They shouldn't just think they've got to get married and have children and be kept by a man. They—'

'Oh, she's one of those, is she?' Vic broke in. 'That explains a lot.'

'One of what? What are you talking about?'

'One of those women who can't get a man of her own and doesn't want anyone else to get one. I've met her sort before. We get them in the office – dried-up old spinsters with faces like boots. You don't want to get like that, Jackie.'

'Who says I would? And Miss Hilary isn't like that anyway – she's a lovely-looking woman. I know she's getting on, she's over thirty now, but you can't say she couldn't get a man. She was engaged during the war. It's not her fault he was killed.'

'She hasn't managed to get another one though, has she? And I don't reckon she ever will. Anyway, why do we have to talk about her? It's this harebrained idea of yours to go and work in Plymouth that we ought to be talking about.'

'That's what I was doing,' Jackie said haughtily. 'It was you who brought Miss Hilary into it.'

'No, it wasn't! It was you – "Miss Hilary this, Miss Hilary that"! I tell you what, it might not be such a bad thing if you got a job somewhere else, after all, not if it gets you away from *her*.'

Jackie gave a puff of exasperation and turned away. 'I think I'll go home. I don't feel like a walk after all.'

Vic grabbed her arm. 'Don't you go walking off like that! We've got to talk about this. What—'

'Let go of me!' Furious, Jackie twisted her arm away. 'Who do you think you are, Vic Nethercott? And what's it got to do with you where I work? You work in Plymouth, so why shouldn't I? Why shouldn't I have a decent job in a nice hotel and better myself? What harm's it going to do you?'

There was a brief silence, then he shrugged and dropped his hand. 'All right, Jackie, I'm sorry. I shouldn't have gone off at half cock like that. It's just ... well, you know how fond of you I am. I suppose I like to think of you all safe and cosy here in Burracombe. There's no knowing what might happen to you in the big city. Or who you might meet.'

'Oh, that's what you're afraid of, is it?' Jackie said, only slightly mollified. 'You think I might meet someone else and chuck you.'

'Well, it could happen, couldn't it?'

'Might do, I suppose,' she said carelessly. 'Depends how you treat me, doesn't it? But telling me what to do isn't going to do any good. I've got a dad to do that.'

'You'd have to do what a husband told you,' he remarked.

'Yes, and maybe that's why I don't want one! I'm not even twenty-one yet. I want a few years doing what *I* want to do before I let some man tie me down. Like girls did in the war. Look at our Val, she went all over the place, even Egypt. And Miss Hilary, she drove Generals about in a big car. You don't think I'm going to just settle down and be a housemaid until some nice man comes along and marries me, do you? I want to see the world – well, a bit of it, anyway – before that happens.'

'Starting with Plymouth?' he said, the sneer beginning to find its way back into his tone.

'The Pilgrim Fathers started there!' she retorted. 'So did Sir Francis Drake, and heaps of other people. It's all right for you, Vic, you've done your National Service and been around a bit. I've never been out of the village, except to go to school in Tavistock. And don't tell me that's because I'm a girl, or I'll hit you! Girls ought to be able to do as much as men. Like they did in—'

'In the war,' he finished for her, sounding bored. 'All right, I know, I've heard it often enough. But it doesn't work like that, Jackie. Girls *can't* do as much as men. They don't get paid as much, for a start. And they can't go around on their own like men can. Look, what's going to happen if you get this job at the Duke of Cornwall? What are you going to be? A housemaid – a waitress? What'll you be doing all day? Making

283

dozens of beds instead of two or three, carrying heavy trays about to people who won't even notice you're there, wearing yourself out and then coming home on the bus every night too tired to have any fun. What's the point of that?'

'The point is, to get on,' she said. 'I want to work my way up. I might start low down but I don't have to stay there. I could end up as head housekeeper myself – in charge. And I needn't be coming home on the bus every night. I could live in.'

By now, they had passed the last cottage and were in the dark, narrow lanes, bordered on either side by high Devon banks with hedges growing on top. Jackie's words echoed in the silence and then Vic said, 'Live in? At the hotel, you mean?'

'Well, I didn't mean live in a dustbin,' Jackie said with a nervous laugh.

'And what do your mum and dad think about this?'

'I haven't told them yet. I don't know it's going to happen, do I? But it'd be fun, living in Plymouth.' She turned to him, though it was too dark in the deep-cut lane to see his face clearly. 'You could stay in town after work and we could go to the pictures, or dancing. We could do all sorts.'

'Oh yes, and then *I'd* have to come home on the bus! On my own. A lot of fun that'd be. Look, can't you see what a daft idea it is? By the time you've paid your fares, or had money docked out of your pay for your board, you wouldn't be any better off than you are now. Worse, probably. And we wouldn't be able to see each other almost every night, like we do now. And all this talk about "getting on" – you don't really want to end up like some boot-faced old manageress, do you? That's not what's right for you.'

'I don't know why you think anyone who makes a career for herself has got to look like a boot,' Jackie said peevishly. 'I dare say this person I'm going to see tomorrow is really smart.'

'So she might be, but she still hasn't got a man, has she?

Believe me, Jackie, I've met a few and they *all* end up looking like boots! It does something to you, not getting married and having a family. It makes women go funny.'

'I didn't say I didn't want to get married – eventually. I just don't want to do it yet. I want to have some fun first.'

Vic stopped suddenly and pulled her into his arms. 'Married people can have fun as well, you know,' he murmured, kissing her face. 'More fun than single people, so I've heard.'

'Until the first baby comes along.' Jackie pulled away. 'Let me go, Vic, I'm not in the mood. Listen, you can't tell me anything about marriage. I've seen it with our Tom and Joanna. I'm not saying they don't love each other, they do, and they have fun too, but they have a lot of hard work and worry too. Especially with these new babies. Poor Jo looks about a hundred some days.'

'Is that what this is all about, then? You want to get away from the babies? They've put you off getting married?'

'No! Anyway, nobody's said anything about getting married. Not to me.' She looked him in the eye, as if challenging him, and after a moment, Vic glanced away and shrugged.

'That's probably because they know they'd get their face slapped. And suppose I did say—'

'Let's go home,' Jackie cut in, suddenly afraid that he was about to take the conversation a step too far. 'I'm tired and I've got an early start tomorrow. And I'm fed up with arguing.' She turned to walk back the way they had come. 'I'll come out for a bit tomorrow evening if you like, and tell you how the interview went. That's if you're interested.'

'Of course I'm interested.' But no hand felt for hers, no arm slid around her waist as they walked back along the lane, and they said goodnight at the farm gate as politely as if they'd been strangers.

Jackie went indoors, feeling depressed and heavy. Her mother was the only one in the kitchen as she came in; all the others had gone to bed. Alice gave her an enquiring glance but, just for once, asked no questions and Jackie went to put the kettle on.

'I'll make some cocoa, Mum. I'm feeling a bit tired. It was a long rehearsal.'

'That's right, maid,' Alice said, breaking off the wool she was using to darn Ted's socks. 'Make me a cup too, would you? An early night won't do none of us any harm.'

Chapter Twenty-Eight

Travis Kellaway parked his motorcycle outside the farm cottage and opened the door quietly. Old Mrs Warne was always in bed before he came home, leaving a pan of milk, a mug and cocoa and sugar ready for him, along with a slice of home-made cake or a sandwich. Tonight, he ignored them all and went outside again, to the little lean-to where he kept his boots and waterproofs. He put them on, picked up a large flashlight and walked soundlessly through the farmyard and into the woods.

Home Farm, being the principal farmstead of the Burracombe estate, was the one favoured with the best land, including fields running beside the river and some extensive woodland sweeping up both sides of the valley. In spring, the woods were a carpet of bluebells and in autumn they were alive with young pheasants for the shoot which was the Squire's pride and joy.

Travis and Bill Furzey, the gamekeeper, had had long discussions about these pheasants. There was always a degree of poaching, of course, but this year, Bill said, it had got worse. And you didn't have to look far to see who was doing it. That Arthur Culliford, the idle layabout, that's who. If he put as much effort into a proper job as he did into his poaching, his poor wife would be a rich woman and all those kids of theirs could be at posh schools.

'I suppose he must make quite a bit out of selling the birds he takes,' Travis observed.

Bill Furzey snorted. 'Where could he sell 'em? He'd have to go into Plymouth to get a decent price, and he can't hardly carry a bag full of pheasants on the bus. No, it's a back-door job at any cottage he can trust not to give him away, and they'm not going to give him much. 'Tis just another way for him to scrape along, and like everything else he earns, most of it goes in the pub.'

Travis sighed. 'The man's a fool, but he's got to be stopped. Are you sure he's the one taking all these birds?'

'No, I don't think he is,' Furzey admitted. 'The whole village would be dining on pheasant if 'twere just he. To tell you the truth, I think there must be a gang of 'em, coming out from Plymouth as like as not in a van and taking back a whole clutch of birds. And I wouldn't be at all surprised if Arthur Culliford ain't in cahoots with 'em. He knows the lie of the land better'n they ever could. Now, to my mind us needs to make an example, to show the rest us means business. There's a moon tonight and I reckon they'll be out. If they are, and us catches them, then 'twill be a good night's work. And if us catches Arthur as well, that'll be all to the good. What do you say, Mr Kellaway?'

'I say yes,' Travis had agreed. 'I'll come along to the gate after rehearsal. He won't be out before then. He's taken to fetching young Shirley home – to put us off the scent, as likely as not. You're right, we've got to make an example and if he really is helping a gang it's time he was stopped.'

As Bill had said, the moon was particularly good tonight – just past complete fullness and shining from a clear sky. It was cold, with a touch of frost turning the grass and fallen leaves to a crunchiness that made silent walking difficult, but Travis was accustomed to putting his feet down carefully, and any sound that he did make could readily have been mistaken for the scrabblings of animals in the undergrowth. Amongst the trees, the shadows were dark and deep, pierced by an occasional thin sword of moonlight and, as he approached the gate where he had arranged to meet Bill Furzey, his sharp eyes caught the movement of a badger, the white streaks on its head a perfect camouflage against its dark, hairy body. He paused for a moment, waiting for it to pass and making a note to mention it to the gamekeeper. Badgers were as big a menace as poachers when there were young pheasants to look after.

Furzey was already there, leaning on the gate. The two men nodded an acknowledgement.

'Seen anything?' Travis asked in a low voice.

'Not yet. Did he fetch young Shirley?'

'Yes. He should have taken her home by now and be out again. Can't believe he won't take advantage of this moon.'

'We'll go up to Top Cover,' the gamekeeper said. 'That's where most of the birds be, and that's where Arthur'll go. He knows every inch of the place, as well as I do meself.'

They walked quietly together, with no need for speech, climbing the slope towards the higher part of the woods, where Furzey had his rearing pens under a clump of conifers. He enticed the young birds in there each evening with a trail of seed and locked them in for the night, away from foxes and, he hoped, poachers. But on too many mornings lately he had found the pens broken into and the birds let loose, and there were never as many to entice in again the next evening.

They arrived to find the pens intact, and took position in the shadows nearby. Travis heard the gamekeeper cock his shotgun and felt a momentary qualm. 'You'll be careful with that thing, won't you,' he muttered. 'Don't want any accidents.'

'There'll be no accidents,' Furzey replied with an unnervingly grim note in his voice. 'Don't you worry, Mr Kellaway. I knows what I be doing.'

Travis was not especially comforted by this, but said no more. Furzey was right – he was too experienced a gamekeeper to take foolish risks with firearms. All the same, there was considerable enmity between him and Arthur Culliford, and he would have preferred there to be no chance at all of accidents. With a loaded shotgun, there always was a risk.

He was just opening his mouth to tell Furzey to put the gun down when he heard a sound. He froze, straining ears and eyes, and thought he saw a shadow moving by the pens. It was almost pitch dark, with not even a shaft of moonlight penetrating the thick canopy of the conifers, but Travis had good night-sight and his eyes were accustomed to the darkness now. He nudged Furzey with his elbow and received an answering pressure. They stood very still, barely breathing.

The shadow became slightly more distinct, a solid mass against the broken, varying greys of the trees, and then it seemed to split into several parts. Travis drew in a breath and Furzey whispered in his ear, 'There's two or three of 'em!' He lifted his gun.

'For God's sake, be careful,' Travis muttered. 'We want to catch them, not kill them.'

'I'll catch 'em all right, the thieving buggers,' Furzey mumbled, and moved away. In the next instant, before Travis could do anything to stop him, he fired the gun and began to shout at the top of his voice. 'Stop where you are! If any of you moves, I'll shoot again – and this time I'll take proper aim. Shine that flashlight, Mr Kellaway, if you will, and let's see what vermin us've caught.'

Travis switched on his torch. It cut a swathe of light across the clearing and there was a shout from one of the group near the pens. A dark shape launched itself at him, knocking the flashlight from his hand, and he heard a scream that startled him so much he froze. In that moment, Furzey's gun went off again, there was another terrified scream and the crashing of bodies making rapid escape through the undergrowth and along the track. In another second, they had gone and Travis could hear nothing except his own rapid breathing and a pitiful sobbing.

290

'What the devil?' He groped for the flashlight and found it. Thank God, it was still working. He shone the light around the clearing. 'What the hell's going on? What the blazes do you think you're playing at, Culliford? And what – oh, my *God*! Is she hurt?'

Arthur Culliford stared up at him, his face ghastly and distorted in the harsh light. He was kneeling over a small body lying crumpled on the trampled ground. He drew back his lips in a snarl and roared, '*You've killed her!* You and that bloody gamekeeper of yours – *you've killed my Shirley!*'

Travis was on his knees beside the whimpering child. He shone his torch on her body, shading the bright light with his fingers. 'For God's sake, stop that noise, man. She's not dead. But she's obviously hurt. What the devil were you doing up here with her, anyway?'

'Walking home, what d'you think? And if she ain't dead, 'tis no credit to you. Shooting off guns in the dark – don't you know no better than that?'

'Never mind that now,' Travis snapped. 'We've got to find out what's happened to her. Shirley, can you hear me? Can you tell me where it hurts?' He moved the light over her body. 'I can't see any blood.'

'It's my arm,' she whispered. 'It hurts. I think it's broke.'

Travis felt both her arms very gently. As he touched the second, she gave a yelp and he quickly directed the torch beam on the sleeve of the old coat she was wearing. It was bent oddly and he sighed. 'I think she's right. How the hell did that happen?'

'How should I know? 'Tis you and that pesky gamekeeper of yours ...'

'Furzey!' Travis looked round quickly. 'Where is he?'

'Saw what he'd done and ran off, I wouldn't wonder,' Culliford retorted. 'Or went off after them others.'

'What others?'

'Why, they poachers, of course, who else? That's who you come up here to catch, weren't it?'

Travis stared at him for a moment, completely nonplussed until another whimper from Shirley brought him back to his senses and he bent towards her again. 'Is it just your arm? You're not hurt anywhere else?'

'Ain't that enough? Ain't you satisfied with—'

'Oh, shut up, man! Look, we've got to get this child to a doctor.' He turned his head as footsteps crashed through the bushes. 'Who's that? Furzey? Where the hell have you been?'

''Tis no good, Mr Kellaway,' the gamekeeper began in a depressed voice as he entered the clearing. 'Got clean away they did in an old van – couldn't even see the make. But I don't reckon 'twas anyone local. If you ask me, they must've come from Plym—' He broke off abruptly. 'My stars, what's going on here? Is that Arthur Culliford's maid?'

'You may well ask,' Travis said grimly. 'Yes, it is, and she's hurt. Broken arm, I think. We've got to get her down to the village. Can we rig up some sort of stretcher?'

'I'll carry her,' Arthur said. ''Tis my little maid, I'll say what's got to be done. You done enough damage already.'

'Don't be ridiculous, man. She needs to be taken to the doctor at once.' Travis stood up and shrugged off his jacket. He laid it on the ground, tucked the sleeves inside and threaded his stick through one of them. 'Either of you got another one? Good. Shift her on to it – gently, now, mind that arm, and there might be other injuries. Are you all right, Shirley? We're not hurting you anywhere else?'

'No,' she whispered. 'It's just my arm.' She cried out as they moved her on to the jacket and lifted it between them. Then, with her father beside her and shining the flashlight, Travis and Furzey carried her down the rough woodland track.

It was a slow journey. Even with the light, it was difficult to see the stones and roots on the path, and every now and then one or another of them would stumble slightly, causing

Shirley to cry out again. At last they were at the gate and on more evenly metalled track, but even then it was still a long trudge to the doctor's house.

'What the hell happened back there?' Travis asked at last. 'Who were those others?'

'I don't know, do I?' Arthur Culliford said belligerently. 'Nothing to do with me. I reckon 'tis they who've been taking your birds. I thought they might be around tonight, what with there being a good moon, so I went up to have a look.'

'Taking a *child* with you?'

'We were on our way home. Been over to see her gran after the rehearsal, hadn't us, Shirl? The old lady ain't been none too well so us took her over a bit of supper and I thought us might as well take a short cut through the woods on the way back.'

'Just happening to pass by my pheasants,' Furzey said, heavily sarcastic.

'And what if us did? There's a public footpath through these woods, as you very well know, Bill Furzey, and anyone got the right to use it. Anyway, I already told you, I reckoned there might be a few folk around that didn't oughter be, and I was right.'

'And they were nothing to do with you? You weren't hoping for a bird or two yourself, of course.'

'I ain't saying I wouldn't have picked one up if I found it laying on the path.'

'No, I bet you aren't!'

'But as it happened, there weren't, and you can search me if you like, you won't find nothing. Those others, they'm from Plymouth, I reckon, and they wouldn't take just one or two for the pot to feed a starving family, they'll fill up their van with birds and sell 'em in the market. But you won't do nothing about that, will you? You'd rather get after a poor bloke like me what's lived in the village all his life and has to struggle to make a living.'

'I don't see you struggling very hard,' Furzey snapped, but Travis cut in impatiently.

'That's enough. It's this child we've got to think of now. Look, we're closer to the Barton than we are to Dr Latimer's. We'll take her there. Hilary will make her comfortable and telephone the doctor, and he can come over. It'll be quicker than us taking her to him.'

'The Barton?' Arthur said suspiciously.

Furzey snorted. ''Tis easy to see why you don't want to go there! Only ever talked to the Squire across a magistrate's bench before.'

'I said, that's enough,' Travis said sharply. 'Culliford, don't be more stupid than you can help, this is your daughter and we're doing our best to help her. And before you say it's our fault she's hurt, just remember that you had no right to be up by the pens at this time of night, footpath or no footpath. Now, come on, both of you – there's a small gate in the hedge just here. It leads into the garden, quicker than going all the way round.'

The Barton was in darkness and once again Travis wondered at a father who would take his young daughter wandering the woods at this time of night. Keeping a careful hold of the makeshift stretcher, he and Furzey climbed the steps to the front door and he pulled the bell-hold. They heard a jangling somewhere inside and waited.

A window opened above them. 'Who's there?'

'Hilary!' Travis called out, relieved. 'Look, can you let us in? We've got the Culliford girl here, she's been hurt. We'll need to call the doctor.'

'*Shirley?*' Hilary leaned out. 'Why, whatever's happened? Who's that you've got with you?'

'Never mind that now. Just let us in, for pity's sake. She needs attention.'

Hilary disappeared and a few moments later the door opened. They staggered in, and she took a swift look at their burden and opened the door to the drawing room. Travis steered his fellow stretcher-bearer over to the sofa and they laid the injured child gently down.

'Phew,' Furzey said, rubbing his arms. 'I didn't think she weighed much when we started but she'm heavy enough now, for certain.'

'What on earth happened?' Hilary asked again. 'Shirley, are you all right?' She knelt beside the sofa, brushing the damp, straggly hair back from the white face.

'I'll call the doctor,' Travis said, making for the telephone. 'Don't move her. I think her arm's broken, but we don't know what other injuries there may be.'

'Well, I hope you were careful carrying her then,' Hilary retorted. 'How far have you come?'

'Top Cover,' Furzey said briefly, and she gave him a shocked glance.

'But that's right up at the head of the valley! What on earth were you doing there?'

'What do you think? Keeping an eye out for they poaching scum, of course. You'd be better asking this scoundrel what *he* were doing up there. And with a little maid, too.'

'I had every right,' Arthur retorted angrily. 'There's a right of way there. And 'tis my business where I takes my own children. I didn't expect to find a fool of a gamekeeper shooting a gun off in all directions.'

'Well, maybe you should have done. You knowed full well I had my pheasants up there, and by all accounts you knowed about they gangs from Plymouth too. 'Twas all a put-up job, if you ask me, and it's to be hoped Squire'll put you behind bars where you belongs, and keeps you out of the way of decent folk for a bit longer this time.'

Shirley began to cry and Hilary looked up furiously. 'For heaven's sake, stop that at once, both of you. Can't you see you're frightening this poor child? Haven't you done enough?' She turned back to the little girl. 'It's all right, Shirley. The doctor will be here soon and he'll look after you. You'd better get her mother too,' she added to the men. 'We'll sort all the rest out later, but Shirley's our first concern now.'

'She been my first concern all along,' Arthur muttered, glowering at the gamekeeper. 'I wouldn't never have taken her that way if I'd knowed he'd be there.'

Travis came back from the telephone. 'He'll be here in a few minutes. Now, let's have a look at that arm.'

'Shouldn't you leave it till the doctor gets here?' Hilary asked. She was wiping Shirley's grimy, tear-streaked face tenderly with a handkerchief. 'Look at her head. She's got a lump the size of an egg coming up on her forehead. She may have concussion. We don't know what else ... Oh, the poor child, the poor, poor little scrap.' Her voice trembled.

Travis looked at her properly for the first time and saw that she was wearing a dark blue woollen dressing-gown. Her hair was scraped back from her face, and she looked more like a young girl than the woman who seemed to fight him every inch of the way for control of the estate.

'Yes, you're probably right. We shouldn't try to do anything ourselves.' He rubbed his forehead, aware of a sudden weariness. The night was turning out very differently from what he had expected and a cloud of depression settled over him.

A sound made them all turn, and they saw Gilbert Napier in the doorway. He too was in a dressing-gown, but his was of brown camelhair and his thick mane of hair was tousled. He stared at them all.

'What the devil's going on here?'

We all seem to be asking that, Travis thought. No doubt Dr Latimer will, as well, but whether we'll ever get to the truth I've no idea. Wearily, he said, 'We seem to have got mixed up with poachers and this child's come off the worst. This was the nearest place to bring her. We're waiting for the doctor now.'

'*Child*? A *child* poaching?' He came closer. 'My God, it's

296

the Culliford girl.' He wheeled sharply and addressed her father. 'You ought to be ashamed of yourself, taking an innocent child, and a girl at that, out with you on your despicable—'

'That's right, that's right!' Arthur bellowed back. 'Take it for granted I'm the one at fault here! That's what happens to a bloke like me – always got to be the one in the wrong. Talk about giving a dog a bad name. Well, for your information, Squire, all I were doing was walking along a public right of way, minding me own business, when this fool of a gamekeeper come blundering along with a gun and knocked my little maid clean off her feet.'

'A gun?' Napier swung round on the others, his eyes blazing. 'What in hell's name were you doing?'

'Father, *please*. Not now. This child's hurt and frightened. She needs peace and quiet.' Hilary glared at the men and then returned her attentions to the little girl. 'All right, Shirley, don't you worry. The doctor will be here soon. He'll put you right.'

Shirley Culliford gazed up at her. Her enormous grey eyes were half-closed, filled with tears of pain and distress. She whispered something, and Hilary bent closer.

'What is it, lovey? What did you say?'

'Please, miss,' the small voice murmured, 'does this mean I won't be able to be in the pantomime?'

Chapter Twenty-Nine

'Poor little scrap,' Hilary said. 'All she's worried about is whether she'll be able to play her part in the pantomime. Stella says she's worked really hard at it, and she's very good.'

'I just hope her arm can be set properly,' Travis said. 'It took us a hell of a long time to bring her down. We had to be so careful and it was pitch-dark coming down the valley. I'm more worried about her head, though. I hope to God it's not serious.'

They were sitting in a narrow corridor at the hospital, waiting for news. Arthur and Maggie Culliford were in another room, and Shirley had been wheeled away on a trolley alone, her face as white as the hospital sheets.

'I don't understand what happened,' Hilary said again. 'What on earth were you all doing up there at that time of night?'

Travis sighed. 'My job. Helping Furzey apprehend poachers. At least, that was the idea. We didn't know Culliford was fool enough to take his daughter up there with him.'

'He says he wasn't poaching. He'd been over to see his mother and was taking a short-cut back.'

'And if you'll believe that,' Travis scoffed.

'I do believe it. Arthur's a bit of a rogue, but he'd never take his daughter out poaching. I can believe he might take one of the older boys,' she allowed. 'In fact, he probably has. But not Shirley.'

'Which could be exactly what he wants you to believe,' Travis said.

Hilary was silent for a moment. Then she spoke again, her voice taut with anger. 'You're determined to find him guilty.'

'Because he almost certainly is! Look, we've discussed this over and over again. You knew Furzey and I wanted to make an example of him.'

'You wanted to make a scapegoat of him!' she retorted. 'Didn't Bill Furzey say there were others there too, who got away?'

'We always knew there were too many birds disappearing for Culliford to be working on his own.'

'Yes, and that's another thing. *You* knew, Furzey knew – but neither of you thought it worth mentioning to me. Why not?'

'Didn't we?' he enquired. 'Maybe we didn't think it was necessary.'

'*I'll* be the one to decide what's necessary for me to know about,' she snapped illogically. 'All right, you needn't bother to explain. You didn't mention it because you wanted to go out and catch them all on your own and show Father what a big, brave boy you are, and what an efficient estate manager. And you'd made up your mind that Arthur was the ringleader and you thought if you could just catch him red-handed, that would be enough. Wasn't that it?'

'And suppose it was? You say yourself he's notorious around here. A bit of poaching, the odd bit of thieving – what's to say he hasn't got in with some real crooks? That's what happens, you know. People start small and work their way up. It's the same in the criminal world as in any other sort of career.'

'Oh, I give up!' she exclaimed in disgust. 'Look, Arthur Culliford's lived in Burracombe all his life. All right, he's a ne'er-do-well and a bit shifty, but he's not a hardened criminal. He works well enough when he's given a job he can do, like building a wall. And what poaching he does is just for his own pot or to sell at a few back doors around the village. He doesn't make much more than pocket money. Anyone coming

299

out from Plymouth is in it for big money, and they wouldn't be interested in small beer like Arthur.'

'Wouldn't they? Not even when he tells them he knows the covers like the back of his hand? There's nothing as valuable as local knowledge, Hilary.'

Hilary sighed. She knew that Travis could be right. Arthur could have got himself into deeper water than he was accustomed to. 'But I still don't understand why he took Shirley with him,' she said at last.

'I don't expect to understand people like Arthur Culliford,' Travis said grimly. 'They exist, more's the pity, and I have to deal with them. That's all there is to it.'

'And as a result,' she said coldly, 'an innocent little girl has been hurt.'

'You can't blame us for that!'

'Can't I? What were you *thinking* of – playing about with guns at night? Someone could have been killed!'

'Now that was definitely not my idea,' he said. 'I didn't even realise Furzey had a gun with him at first. I was furious when I did, but things happened too quickly then to do anything about it. But Shirley wasn't shot. Her arm was broken when she fell down.'

'She easily could have been shot,' Hilary said. 'I'm sorry, Travis, but I can't let you off that easily, and I don't think Father will either. You're the estate manager, as you're so keen to tell me, and you were in charge. You hadn't even let me know what you planned to do. If Shirley – or anyone else – had been shot, you would have had to take responsibility. As it is, she's got a broken arm and possible head injuries. And it's no good saying her father was responsible for her being there. I know he was, but that doesn't make it any better.'

Travis was silent for a while. Then he said, 'I suppose you want my resignation.'

'I don't know what I want,' Hilary said tiredly. 'All I know is that I want Shirley to get better. Just at the moment, I don't care what you do.'

'It's all I want, too,' Travis said. 'And I suggest we postpone this argument until later. This is neither the time nor the place to have a row.'

Hilary bit her lip. She knew he was right, but it didn't improve her mood. She felt close to tears – tears of anger, of fear and, most of all, of distress for the little girl who was now having a broken arm set.

Whose fault was it really, she wondered dispiritedly. Arthur must surely take the greater part of the blame, for taking the child with him. But as he'd pointed out, there was a public footpath close to that place and in law he had every right to walk there, at any time of day or night. Perhaps, for once, he was entirely innocent of any crime other than that of keeping his small daughter out too late.

Furzey had been there too, and carrying a gun as well. Yet that wasn't unusual, for a gamekeeper. He'd simply been doing his job, if over-zealously. He probably felt undressed without his gun under his arm.

There had apparently been at least two other men there too – the real poachers, who had got away. But even they could claim that it wasn't their fault a child had got hurt. Whatever their crimes, they wouldn't have expected children to be in the woods at night.

As for who had actually hurt Shirley, nobody seemed to know. There had been a scuffle, and she'd got in the way and been knocked to the ground. As far as that was concerned, it really was an accident.

She shouldn't have been there at all. That was what everyone would say, and the finger of blame would be pointed at her father. Yet, Hilary could remember many an occasion when she and her brothers had been taken out at night, to see the stars or to watch for owls, badgers or other nocturnal creatures. Like Arthur Culliford, she knew the woodland paths as well in the dark as in daylight. And if he had truly been taking a short-cut home from his mother's, he and his daughter ought to have been safe.

She drew in a deep, ragged sigh. It was all too complicated, and what did any of it really matter just now? She too was worried about Shirley's head. The lump seemed to have grown before her eyes, turning purple as she watched. Children's skulls were fragile – she might have more than concussion, she might have an actual fracture. Hilary felt the fear grow like a jagged lump in her own breast, catching at her breath. If the blow had been really hard ...

'Hey,' Travis said softly, catching her as she swayed. 'Don't go passing out on me.'

'I'm not. I was just thinking – suppose she's worse than we think. Suppose she doesn't recover.'

'Of course she's going to recover!' The sharpness in his voice betrayed his own fear. 'It's a broken arm, that's all.'

'And a nasty knock on the head,' she reminded him. 'That could be the worst part.'

'Oh God,' he said with a groan. 'How could he have been so stupid? Taking a child to a place like that so late at night.'

'He didn't know you were going to be there, with a gun. Or those other men.'

'I keep telling you, the gun wasn't mine. And how do we know he didn't – oh, don't let's start again.' He leaned forward, covering his eyes with one hand. 'It's happened, and there's nothing we can do about it. Except hope.'

'And pray,' she said quietly.

Travis looked at her. 'I'm not much of a churchgoer, and it always seems a bit dishonest to ask for things for myself when I don't bother the rest of the time. But in this case – yes, I'll try anything. I'll pray, if it will help that poor child in there.'

They sat quietly for a while. Travis's hand was still on Hilary's and she looked down at it, noticing the strong, blunt fingers. They felt warm and comforting, but even as she thought that, she snatched her own hand away. Whatever Travis said, he had been part of the cause of the accident, and her fear for Shirley overwhelmed all else.

At last a different doctor came along the corridor and approached them. They both leaped to their feet. 'Mr and Mrs Culliford?'

'No, they're in there.' Hilary indicated the room where Arthur and Maggie had gone with one of the nurses. 'How is she? Is she going to be all right?'

'I'm sorry,' he said, shaking his head, and her heart plummeted. 'I can't tell you anything. It's the parents I need to speak to. In there, you say?'

'Yes. But please, can't you even tell us ...' He moved away without replying and went through the door, closing it firmly behind him. Hilary turned and looked at Travis in dismay.

'Is she really bad? Oh, Travis!'

'Steady.' He put his arm around her shoulder and held her firmly. She forgot her previous reaction and leaned her head on his shoulder, her body trembling. 'He probably just meant that the Cullifords had a right to know first – whatever it is.'

Hilary sank back on to the hard wooden bench. 'I don't know how much more I can stand of this.'

'You can stand whatever you have to. We both can.' He sat down beside her, keeping his arm firmly round her shoulders. 'Look, I know this is hard but we mustn't quarrel over it. That's not going to help anyone.'

'I know.' She leaned against him, unexpectedly grateful for his strength. 'I just can't help thinking, suppose she's really badly hurt? That poor little girl. It was only last year that she really began to come into her own, you know. When she was made Festival Queen for the pageant. A lot of people didn't want her because of her family, but she looked so pretty on the day, she won everyone's hearts. And Stella says she's a bright little thing and should get into the grammar school. It'll be a tragedy if anything stops her now.'

'It won't. I'm sure it was just a bump on the head. And her arm will mend – children heal quickly.'

'I hope so,' she said miserably. 'Oh Travis, I do hope so …'

Chapter Thirty

The tension between Travis and Hilary, that had begun to soften slightly in the hospital, was as taut as ever next morning.

When she finally reached her bedroom, in the early hours of the morning, Hilary wanted nothing more than to fall into bed and into a deep sleep, but as soon as her head touched the pillow she found herself wide awake, her mind going over and over all the events of the night, from the startled moment of shock when she had leaned out of her bedroom window to see the strange little group on the drive below, to the moment when Travis had finally said goodnight to her at the front door.

Thank goodness they had managed to persuade her father to go back to bed once Charles had arrived and decided that Shirley must be taken straight to hospital. He had put her into his own car, and Hilary had gone with him while Travis took Arthur Culliford to fetch his wife. By the time they all met at the hospital, Shirley and Charles had disappeared, and it was obvious to Hilary that the Cullifords and Travis had endured an acrimonious journey.

I can't waste any sympathy on him for that, she thought, all her anger returning as she turned over in bed, trying to find a more comfortable position. I know it was an accident, but it shouldn't have happened, and even though the gun wasn't part of it, it shouldn't have been there. It could have been even worse.

The thought of Shirley, or anyone else, for that matter, being shot – and, worse still, shot on Napier land – made her feel physically sick. Even as it was, she was sure the police would visit them. A little girl couldn't be hurt and end up in hospital without some repercussions. And if Arthur Culliford decided to press charges, it could even end in a prosecution.

She decided not to worry about that. The main thing was that Shirley wasn't too badly hurt; a broken arm and a bump on the head were bad enough, but it didn't appear to be any worse. She would recover. But it would take Hilary a long time to get the sight of her woebegone little face out of her mind, and that plaintive little whisper: 'Does this mean I won't be able to be in the pantomime?'

Hilary had reassured her at once, praying that she was right. Now, thankfully, she was confident that, even if she still had her arm in a sling, Shirley would still be able to appear on stage.

She turned over again, her head tight and aching with both the need for sleep and the impossibility of any rest with all these thoughts racing through her brain. Her eyes would not stay open, yet when she let them close they felt sore and gritty. She was hot and thirsty, but didn't have the energy either to throw off one of her blankets or fetch a drink. She lay staring hopelessly at the light patch of the window and then realised that it was brighter. Morning had arrived, and she must have slept after all.

It had only been a couple of hours, but she felt marginally better for it and pulled herself out of bed, her first thought for Shirley. It was just after seven – too early to ring the hospital – but she could at least start the day by getting her father's breakfast ready. Mrs Ellis didn't come in on Saturdays, and he would no doubt be up and about as usual despite his broken night, expecting the bacon and eggs that always started his day.

She was in the kitchen, making coffee, when he arrived,

wrapped in the same camel dressing-gown he had worn during the night. His mane of silver-grey hair was tousled and unbrushed.

'What happened, then? How's that child?'

'She's going to be all right.' It was seldom that Gilbert came to breakfast without having washed, shaved and dressed first, and she poured him a cup of coffee. 'Sit down, Dad, you look as if you've hardly slept.'

'Well, what d'you expect? Thing like that happening on my land. Can't imagine what Kellaway was thinking of. Inexcusable – a child injured. And what in heaven's name was Furzey doing, waving a shotgun about?'

'She wasn't shot, Dad.'

'Well, that's something to be thankful for, at least. Won't look good if it comes to court, though, I can tell you that.' He rubbed a hand over his big face. 'Is Culliford likely to press charges?'

'I don't know. I was wondering, myself.' She set a bowl of cornflakes in front of him. 'Let's eat here this morning – I can't be bothered with laying the table in the breakfast room. All I'm concerned about really though, is that poor little girl. What a dreadful thing to happen to her.'

'What the devil was she doing up there in the first place?' Gilbert demanded. 'That's what I can't understand. What was Culliford thinking of, taking his daughter poaching? It sounds to me as if the whole lot of them went stark, staring mad.'

Hilary was privately of the same opinion, but she said merely, 'I don't know much more than you do, Father, but I'm sure Travis will be here soon to tell you what happened. He said he'd come straight after breakfast.'

'Well, I'd better eat this and get myself ready, then. Can't talk to the fellow in my dressing-gown.' His tone was grim and Hilary noted with some unease that Travis had gone from being 'Kellaway' to 'the fellow' within a few short sentences. He was going to have his work cut out to convince the Squire that he was without blame in this matter – not that she was convinced of that herself. Whatever had happened up there in the woods, Travis was the estate manager and should have been in charge. The thought that a child had been injured, and could have been killed, was too horrific to let it go.

But surely Arthur Culliford must take most of the blame? Whatever he'd been doing up there, he shouldn't have had Shirley with him. Except ... except that there was a public footpath there, which he had every right to use at any time of day or night, and it was up to him what time he took his daughter home to bed.

Once again, the thoughts were whirling round in her brain. She laid down her spoon and rested her forehead on her palm.

'Come on, girl, eat up,' her father said gruffly. 'Got to keep up your strength. What time did you get home?'

'I don't know, about half-past three or four, I think.' She pushed her bowl away and got up to cook his bacon and eggs. 'I've hardly slept at all.'

'I can see that. Now then, when Kellaway gets here you'd better send him through into my study.'

'Just a moment, Father. I'll be there too.'

He shot her a look. 'Think that's wise?'

'Whyever not?'

'You've had an upsetting night,' he said. 'You didn't get much sleep and you're probably not feeling like a row.'

'Oh, I feel very much like a row,' Hilary said tightly, and then shook her head. 'No. Forget I said that. Why should there be a row, anyway? We've got to discuss this calmly.'

'Exactly. And that's why I think—'

'You don't think I could discuss it calmly,' Hilary said. 'You think I'd start shouting, or burst into tears or something.' She took a deep breath. 'I have to be there, Father. Travis and I have been working together and we have to sort this out together. And apart from anything else, I was the one who went to the hospital with Shirley. I have a personal interest in this.'

'Which may cloud your judgement,' he pointed out. She put his plate in front of him and they sat in silence as he ate, then he said, 'Very well. We'll discuss it together. Now I'm going up to get dressed, and I suggest you do the same.'

Hilary nodded and cleared away the breakfast things, then went to have a bath and put on fresh clothes. She felt better after that, but her anxiety over Shirley was still gnawing at her mind. Suppose that bump on the head had been more serious than they'd thought? Suppose she'd taken a turn for the worse? I wish we could ring the hospital, she thought, but they said not until nine. And what must her poor parents be going through, sent home without even being able to see their own daughter?

The grandfather clock in the hall was striking nine when Travis arrived. Hilary was already on the telephone to the hospital, but put it down as he came through the door, looking frustrated.

'They won't tell me anything. I'm not a relative.'

'For Pete's sake!' His face darkened. 'I was hoping you'd have news.' For a moment, he looked undecided, then he said, 'I'll go down to the Cullifords, and see if they've heard anything.'

'Don't be ridiculous! They're not on the phone. They'll have to use the kiosk by the Post Office. That's one of the reasons I wanted to phone from here, in case they had trouble getting through.'

The study door opened and Gilbert Napier came out. 'What the devil's all this chatter? Oh, you're here, Kellaway. I suppose you've come to put your case for what happened last night.'

Hilary glanced at Travis and saw the muscles of his jaw tighten and his eyes narrow. She groaned silently, hoping that this wasn't going to turn into the row her father was obviously anticipating, and followed the two men into the study.

'I was just trying to find out from the hospital how Shirley is,' she said as they took their seats.

'And how is she?'

'They won't say. The night staff have all gone home and it was a different nurse I spoke to. I'll have to go and see Mrs Culliford. If Shirley's allowed home today, they'll need transport.'

Gilbert nodded. 'You'd better see to that, then. Probably a good idea to slip along there now.'

Hilary felt the same irritation as she guessed Travis had felt a minute or two earlier. 'That would mean postponing this meeting,' she said evenly.

Her father shot her one of his looks. She met his eyes steadily, watching him weigh up the advantages or disadvantages of giving her a direct order which he knew she would disobey. Eventually, he sighed and said, 'Very well, let's get on with it. Your version, please, Kellaway.'

'Don't you think Arthur Culliford ought to be here too?' Hilary broke in. 'He's already feeling aggrieved. He'll be even more upset if he thinks Travis has put his side of the story first. And Furzey ought to be here as well.'

'He will be,' Travis said. 'I rang him when I got back earlier this morning and told him. He should be here at any minute.'

'Thank goodness someone's showing a bit of sense at last,' Gilbert said. 'As soon as he arrives, then.'

'But Arthur still won't be here, and he ought to be,' Hilary insisted. 'Shirley's his daughter. He has a right to be present.'

'The same right as he had to be lurking around my pheasants with her in the middle of the night?' her father demanded. 'I think Culliford has given up any "rights" he might have in this matter.'

'Don't be silly, Father! Of course he still has rights. And he had a right to be there, too – there's a public footpath nearby. It wasn't the middle of the night, anyway,' she finished. 'It wasn't much after ten. And he couldn't have been there long because rehearsal didn't finish until nine, and he came to collect Shirley from there.'

'That gives him a clear hour!'

'Part of which he spent at his mother's house. Which can, presumably, be corroborated.' Hilary could hear her voice rising and went on more quietly, 'Look, all we want is to get at the truth of what happened. But I do mean the truth – I don't want anyone made a scapegoat.' She met Travis's eyes briefly, aware that she was in danger of doing exactly this with him. 'And don't let's forget there were others there, too – the real poachers, who got away. They're the ones mostly to blame.'

Gilbert Napier sighed. 'Very well. We'll send Furzey to collect him as soon as he arrives.'

'No,' Hilary said. 'We'll send Crocker. Arthur won't come with either Furzey or Travis, and I'm not going to leave you two on your own.' Again, she met her father's eyes defiantly. 'I don't care if you do think I'm being a hysterical female, I'm staying here. Travis, would you mind going out to the stables? He'll be there now, mucking out after putting the horses in the fields.'

Travis glanced from her to Napier, who shrugged as if to say they would get no peace until the little woman had had her way. His lips pressed together, he got up and went out.

Hilary and her father looked at each other.

'Well,' he said, 'I hope you're satisfied. This whole business could have been cleared up in half an hour. Now it'll take most of the morning, and I doubt if we'll come to any proper conclusion then.'

'If that's the way you administer justice, Father,' she said coldly, 'I'm surprised you're still on the Bench.'

As soon as the words were out of her mouth, she regretted them. Her father was, she knew, a respected magistrate with a strong sense of justice. She bit her lip as she saw the mixture of shock and hurt on his face and said quickly, 'I'm sorry. I didn't mean that.'

Napier was silent for a moment, staring down at the blotting-pad on his desk, and Hilary looked at her hands, seeing them through a mist of tears. At last he lifted his head and said quietly, 'You're right. I'm not thinking straight. Of course we must have Culliford here, as well as Furzey, and it can't be swept under the carpet. We've got to get at the truth, however unpalatable it may be.'

They heard a door open and close, and Travis came back into the room. He glanced from one to the other, obviously realising that something had happened, and equally obviously deciding not to ask. He said merely, 'Crocker's gone to fetch Culliford in the Land Rover, and Furzey's just arrived.'

Napier nodded. 'We won't discuss this any further until we're all here, then.'

'Suppose Arthur doesn't come?' Hilary asked. 'He may be going to the hospital.'

'I told Crocker to make sure he's telephoned first, and take him there if necessary. He'll call in to tell us if that's the case,' Travis informed them.

'And if that happens, we'll postpone the meeting until he can be here,' Gilbert said. The doorbell jangled and Hilary made to get up, but Travis put out a hand to stop her.

'I'll go. It'll be Furzey. I told him to come to the front door, to be quicker.'

He went out and Hilary turned to her father. 'I really am sorry about what I said.'

'It's all right, girl. You were right. I'd forgotten myself for a moment.' He rubbed his face with that characteristic gesture of his. 'It's easy enough to administer justice when you're not involved – not so easy when it's close to home. An anxious business.' The door opened again and Travis ushered in the head gamekeeper. 'Ah, Furzey, thank you for coming. Have a chair.'

The gamekeeper remained standing. 'I just want to say,

Squire, that this weren't none of my wanting. I was just out to catch they poaching varmints. I'd never have hurt that little maid, not in a million years.'

'I know you wouldn't. Sit down. We're waiting for Culliford to arrive.'

'He's coming here? Well, I hope you'm going to take him on charge, Squire, and this time maybe you'll put him behind bars where he can't do no more damage. That man's caused enough trouble round here.'

'Furzey!' Hilary exclaimed, but her voice was drowned by her father's thunderous bellow, and she jumped back in her seat, startled.

'*That's enough!* We'll have no pre-judging of this matter. There's been enough of that, too.' The veins stood out on his forehead and Hilary glanced at him in alarm. He'll be having another heart-attack at this rate, she thought, and wished passionately that nobody had gone up into the woods last night. Or even that the poachers themselves had been left to go quietly about their criminal activities ... At this thought, she pulled herself up sharply. Of course they couldn't be ignored! Especially when it wasn't a case of the odd pheasant or salmon going home under Arthur Culliford's coat, but organised gangs coming out from Plymouth in vans to take game on a large scale.

At last the Land Rover drew up outside the door and before the bell could jangle again Travis and Hilary were both at the door. To their immense relief, Arthur Culliford climbed out of the passenger seat and stood in the drive, looking doubtfully up at the house. Hilary went forward quickly.

'Mr Culliford! How is she? Have you spoken to anyone?'

'Ah.' He took a step or two closer. 'She'm doing all right, no thanks to them as knocked her over.' He scowled at Travis. 'We can bring her home later on this morning. Go in on the bus.'

'Certainly not,' Hilary said warmly. 'You can't bring that

poor little mite home on the bus. I'll take you myself in the car. How's your wife? She must be very upset.'

'So her is. But Maggie's a good woman, she'm bearing up, and of course there's all the other little 'uns to look after. Our Shirl used to be a real help to her mum there. Dunno what her'll do without the little maid.'

'She'll still be able to do quite a bit,' Hilary said. 'It is just a broken arm, is it?'

'Ain't that enough?' he grumbled.

'The bump on her head isn't serious, I hope?' Hilary said anxiously. 'I was very worried about that – it came up like a huge egg.'

'She got to stay quiet for a couple of days, that's all,' he said reluctantly. 'They've X-rayed her and the skull ain't broke. No thanks to you lot,' he added belligerently, turning to Travis and Furzey, who had also come out to the door.

'Well, that's something to be thankful for,' Hilary said hastily. 'Now then, my father wants us all to sit down together and try to sort out exactly what happened. Will you come in, Mr Culliford?'

He shot them each a suspicious glance and heaved a sigh of resignation. 'S'pose I'll have to, if we'm going to get anywhere. At least you've had the decency to wait till I got here. Unless you've already decided 'twas all my fault,' he added as he wiped his boots on the doormat. 'Wouldn't surprise me.'

'I'll thank you to withdraw that remark,' Gilbert said brusquely as Hilary ushered them into the study. 'We're here to see justice done, not to cast blame. Now, I suggest you all sit down and we'll run this as a proper meeting. I'm chairman and all remarks must be addressed through me. Kellaway first. Let's go through exactly what happened.'

'Perhaps we ought to hear from Mr Culliford first,' Hilary suggested, seeing the angry colour already flooding into Arthur's face. 'He's obviously very upset and it is his daughter who's been hurt.'

'All right,' her father said after a moment's thought. 'We'll do it that way. Culliford? Now's your chance, man. And speak up – let's hear the truth.'

Chapter Thirty-One

The news of Shirley's injury ran like wildfire round the village. The shop was full of people discussing it that morning, and as usual opinions were strong.

"Tis just the daft sort of thing that fool would do,' George Sweet declared. 'Taking a little maid like her up in the woods at that time o' night. What was he thinking of?'

'Thinking of his stomach, like as not,' Norman Tozer said. 'Always was partial to a roast pheasant, was Arthur Culliford. Didn't ought to have took his kiddy up there with him, just the same.'

'Apparently he'd taken her over to see her grandmother and they were taking the short-cut back,' said Stella, who had just come in for the morning paper. 'Hilary Napier went to see Miss Kemp, after she came back from the hospital, and she popped in to tell me as well. Mr Culliford says he wasn't poaching at all, it was some people from Plymouth, with a van.'

'Tell that to the Marines!' Norman said scornfully, but Edie Pettifer looked thoughtful.

'I did hear tell there were a lot more birds being taken this year. And I don't think he's been selling more than usual – to folks who don't mind taking them,' she added, turning a little pink and opening the till hastily as if searching for change.

Norman grinned, but George Sweet wasn't so easily deflected. 'Never mind all that. The fact is that Arthur Culliford were up by Top Cover when he shouldn't have been, and had his little 'un with him, and somehow or other she ended up in hospital with her bones broke and a fractured skull, and might never walk or talk again. That's if her comes round at all,' he added.

Edie looked appalled. 'Is it that bad? Oh, the poor little flower. And after her did so well at the pageant last year, and now she'm hovering between life and death. It don't bear thinking about.' She felt for her handkerchief and Stella spoke quickly, before the story could be embellished further. No wonder gossip spread so quickly in a village, she thought.

'No, it isn't as bad as that. Hilary told me she's got a broken arm and a nasty bump on her head, but she's had an X-ray and there's no fracture. She'll probably be as right as rain by this time next week.'

'Her arm'll still be broke,' George pointed out.

'Yes, of course it will, but it's not a serious break and it won't take long to heal. She'll be asking everyone to sign their names on her plaster, I expect.'

'So what's going to be done about it?' Norman asked. Stella having spoken to Miss Kemp, who had received a visit from Hilary herself, they obviously expected her to know all about it. 'Someone ought to be charged over that. Kiddy hurt, and all.'

'I don't know. Nobody knows who knocked her over, or what really happened at all. It was an accident. And there were those other men there,' Stella finished doubtfully. 'It could have been one of them.'

'Best thing all round if 'twere,' George declared. 'Us don't want none of that sort of trouble in Burracombe.' He folded his newspaper and stuck it under his arm. 'I'd best be getting along, us got a wedding-cake to bake today for a Christmas wedding – that maid up to Spiney Farm and her young man. Suppose you'll be asking me to bake one for you one of these days,' he added to Stella as he left the shop.

Stella felt her face flame and Norman Tozer laughed. 'Don't you take no notice of he, maid. He'm just trying to drum up a

317

bit of trade. Mind you, we'm all expecting an announcement before too long, so don't you disappoint us, now.'

He went out after George and Stella drew a deep breath and turned to Edie. 'Is everyone talking about Felix and me?'

'Not more than they talk about everyone else,' the shop-keeper said. 'You don't want to worry yourself about that, maid. Mind you, we'm all *hoping*. It'd be a good match – you make a lovely couple. Did you want anything besides that paper, my flower?'

'No, thank you,' Stella said. She had intended to buy a small box of chocolates for Shirley, but decided to wait until she went into Tavistock on the bus later that morning. She could still feel the colour in her cheeks and didn't like the way Edie was looking at her. She'll be telling everyone I was blushing, she thought, making a hasty exit. And I don't suppose she'll stop at that, either. Goodness knows what the story will be before it's finished going round the village.

However, this time the village was too concerned with the accident to Shirley Culliford to bother much about the schoolteacher and the curate. Little Shirley was one of them, after all – Stella and Felix were both incomers. Edie didn't appear to have mentioned it when Stella joined the queue for the Saturday-morning bus an hour or so later, but everyone was talking about what had happened in the woods and, to her surprise, quite a few were more inclined to blame Travis Kellaway than Arthur Culliford.

''Tis always the way,' Mrs Purdy declared. 'A new broom always got to sweep clean. Everyone knows Arthur takes the odd bird or salmon, and he expects to be took up before the Bench once or twice in a season, but from what I heard, this new man wants to make an example of him and get Squire to send him to prison. What good's that going to do anyone, eh? Tell me that. What good's it going to do poor Maggie?'

'I think there were some other people there too,' Stella ventured. 'It wasn't just Mr Culliford.'

'No, but 'tis him that's got to carry the can, all the same,' Mrs Purdy said. 'It's not that I got much time for him in the usual way of things, but 'tis a shame when new folk come into the village and starts picking on us what have lived here all our lives, and I don't mind who hears me say it.' She glowered at Stella, who stared back in dismay, wondering if the last words were aimed at her as much as at Travis Kellaway. Is that what they really think of me, she wondered. A new broom, sweeping clean and picking on the villagers? On their children? Her eyes filled with tears and she turned away.

The bus arrived just then and they all clambered aboard, still talking amongst themselves. Stella found a seat at the back and sat looking out of the window, feeling miserable. She had known Mrs Purdy ever since her first day at the school, when the cleaner had complained about the muddy Wellington boots lined up in the lobby, and knew that she was inclined to be cantankerous, but she had never really thought that the ire was directed at her personally. In fact, the village as a whole had been so friendly towards her that she had felt warmed and liked from the moment she arrived. Now, she wondered if it were all a façade.

Maybe they don't like me at all, she thought. And what about Felix? How can he work as a vicar if people are only pretending to like his wife? Little Burracombe may not be the same village, but it's near enough and people all know each other. Most of the shops are here, so they come over quite a lot. Maybe it would be better if we were to move away. Or maybe he'd be better off without me …

The buzz of chatter went on all around her. The Saturday-morning bus was always full of people who couldn't get into town on Friday, the market day, and as it trundled round the lanes it picked up people from more remote farms and hamlets, all eager for the latest gossip. Today, of course, the great topic was Shirley Culliford, and Stella could feel the antagonism towards Travis Kellaway growing with every mile. By the time we reach Tavistock, she thought, they'll have completely forgotten there was anyone else involved. It will have been a straight fight between Travis and Arthur Culliford, with Shirley caught in the middle.

She got off the bus, feeling isolated, and walked slowly along the main street. It was as busy as usual with Saturday shoppers, but Stella didn't have much to do today. She had a few errands for Dottie, who was too busy sewing to make time to come in as she usually did, and she went to the library which was housed underneath the Town Hall, close to the pannier market. For some time now she had been reading the books written by the Dartmoor author Eden Philpotts, and she was pleased to see that there was one she'd been unable to find before. She took it to the desk.

'Stella! How nice to see you. Did you come in on the bus?'

She turned to find Grace Harvey at her elbow, a couple of books under her arm. 'Yes. I'm beginning to wish I hadn't, though. I've got hardly anything to do and it's quite a long wait before I go back.'

'Well, you must come back with us. Basil and I came in the car.'

'Oh no!' Stella exclaimed, horrified. 'I wasn't trying to beg a lift. I'm quite happy to wait.'

'I know you weren't, but you're welcome to one. We're meeting in the Bedford for a cup of coffee in ten minutes or so – why don't you join us? Tessa's there, too – you know, the doctor's daughter, you must have met her – so we'll be quite a jolly little party.'

'Yes, we're both in the pantomime,' Stella said, not quite as sure as the vicar's wife that the party would be particularly jolly. She had seen the way Tessa had looked at Felix a few times; but then, Tessa looked at all men in that way. 'It's all right, really. I don't mind waiting for the bus.'

'Oh, do come.' Grace handed her books over to be stamped and chuckled as Stella caught sight of their titles. 'I know – not the sort of thing you expect a vicar's wife to be borrowing, but Basil and I both love thrillers. Probably because things like that seldom happen in quiet little Burracombe!'

'Oh,' Stella said. 'You haven't heard, then?'

'About Shirley Culliford? Tessa told us. Poor little soul. A very nasty accident, but it could have been so much worse.'

'That's what everyone was saying on the bus.'

Grace glanced at her. 'It must be particularly upsetting for you, Shirley being one of your pupils.'

'Yes.' Stella hesitated. 'It's not just that, though. It's what everyone's saying. They're all taking it for granted it was Travis Kellaway's fault.'

'But why? Has Mr Culliford said so?' Grace took back her books and they made their way out.

'Not that I know of. It – well, it seems almost as if, because he's the stranger, it must automatically be his fault. As if they've closed ranks against all outsiders.'

Grace glanced at her again. 'Yes, I see. It's upset you rather, hasn't it? Well, I think you'd better come along with me and have that cup of coffee. And then we'll take you home. Village gossip can be a little harsh at times.'

'I've never noticed it before,' Stella said, her voice wobbly, and Grace took her arm and steered her across the square.

'It happens, from time to time. It's like a summer storm – it soon blows over. And it's not being directed at you, after all.'

'No, I suppose not,' Stella said, but inside she was not sure. When Mrs Purdy had spoken it was as if she'd been talking about outsiders in general. There had been something almost spiteful in her voice and in her eyes as she'd looked at Stella, something that had taken Stella back to her days in the orphanage when she had been taunted by other children. Something that she thought she'd put well and truly behind her, in the past.

They walked beside the low wall of the churchyard. The tall tower of St Eustachius loomed over them, and Grace paused to look at the remnant of the old Abbey cloisters, near the bus stop. There wasn't much left of the great Tavistock Abbey, just the church itself, this scrap of wall, Betsy Grimbal's Tower across the road and a further stretch by the river; but it had once covered almost half the present town and been a powerful landowner.

'Things must have been so different in those days,' she remarked. 'Tavistock's lands must have run right up to Buckland Abbey's, and almost over to Buckfastleigh. Only the worst land wasn't owned by the abbeys.'

'And then it was all smashed up,' Stella said thoughtfully. 'You know that poem "Hark, hark, the dogs do bark, the beggars are come to town"? Someone once told me that the beggars were actually monks, turned out of their homes by Henry the Eighth, wandering the countryside with no money and nowhere to go.'

'And in those days, "town" meant farm.' They crossed the road to the Bedford Hotel. 'And Tavistock was a dreadful place only a hundred or so years ago. I expect you know it was a stannary town, where ore mined on the moors was brought for assaying, but it was really nothing more than a collection of slums until the Duke of Bedford was persuaded to rebuild it as it is now. Most of these lovely buildings aren't old at all – not really.'

'I like the Bedford cottages,' Stella said. 'I wouldn't mind living in one of those, down by the river.'

Grace glanced at her. 'Really? I thought you might have something a little more substantial in mind.'

Stella blushed. 'I can't think what you mean.'

'Oh no?' They went up the steps into the hotel, both laughing. 'Well, at least it's put that lovely smile back on your face. And I don't mind telling you, in strict confidence of course, that Basil and I have much higher hopes for you than a Bedford cottage down by the river. Look, there he is already, and Tessa too. How nice.' She paused and looked at

Stella more seriously. 'Don't take any notice of village gossip, my dear. We all suffer from it at one time or another, and it passes. And don't worry too much about Shirley. I'm sure she'll be all right. In less than a week she'll be back at school, showing off her plaster and holding court over all those who wish they'd had adventures in the woods at night. Even Micky Coker won't be able to compete with that!'

'It was just like I told you,' Arthur Culliford began sullenly. 'I fetched Shirl from the practice at the village hall, and then I took her round to see me mother. She sent a message down to say she'd got one of her turns, so I thought I'd best see what I could do. Couldn't leave the poor old girl all night, could I?'

'Where does your mother live?' Travis asked, and Arthur cast him an unfriendly look.

'In one of they old places up to Burracombe Bourne. Everyone knows that.'

'It's a cluster of mining cottages at the top of the valley,' Hilary explained. 'I don't suppose you've ever had cause to go up there.' She turned back to Arthur. 'And how is your mother? I hope she's not really ill.'

He shook his head. 'No, 'tis just that she comes over a bit funny now and then. Angelica, the doctor calls it. To do with her heart. She got some tablets for it but she don't like being on her own when she takes 'em so she always sends one of the neighbours' tackers down to fetch me or Maggie.'

'So what happened next?' Gilbert asked. 'I take it she was well enough to leave.'

'After a bit, yes. Went off to sleep peaceful as a babby, so me and Shirl come away. And the quickest way back from there is that footpath that runs across Top Cover, and that's been used ever since I can remember. It was the way to the village from Wheal Betty, see, and anything that been used as long as that's a right of way.'

'That's right,' Hilary confirmed. 'And it would be the quickest way, during the day, anyway. I'm not so sure about at night.'

'Look, I knows those woods like the back of me hand,' Culliford said. 'Day or night.' He fell silent suddenly, no doubt realising what they would make of this remark. To Hilary's relief, nobody took him up on it although she could see that Furzey was tempted.

'Doesn't mean you didn't think of picking up something for your Sunday dinner on the way back,' he grunted.

'You knows as well as I do, I wasn't the only bloke up by those covers, and I don't reckon they were on their way back from their old mothers,' Arthur said. 'Why pick on me? Even if I did help meself to a bird – which I didn't – I'm not flogging them off by the cartload in Plymouth market.'

'It's all right, Arthur,' Hilary said. 'We're not trying to charge you with poaching.' She gave the three men a look which dared them to contradict her. 'We simply want to find out what happened.'

'And that's what I be trying to tell you. We took the short-cut through the woods and it weren't till we were nearly up by Top Cover that I realised there was someone else about. I thought it must be someone from the village, at first.' He stopped abruptly again, as if aware that he might be about to give away one or two of his own friends. 'Then I heard 'em talking and realised I didn't know them. And from what they said, I knew they were from Plymouth and they were out for rich pickings.'

'Why? What did they say?' Gilbert leaned forward across his desk.

'Why, they were going on about getting a net throwed over the young birds and how to get 'em down to the van, and taking 'em to market in the morning. Well, stands to reason it got to be Plymouth, don't it? Anyway, I reckoned it'd be a good idea for me and Shirl to get past without them knowing us was there. I've come across blokes like this before, and they ain't too friendly to the likes of me.'

'That's not what I've heard,' Furzey remarked to no one in particular. 'I've heard they like a bit of local knowledge. Chaps who know the woods like the backs of their hands, for instance.'

Arthur began to get to his feet, his fists clenched and his face darkening, and Hilary put out a hand. 'Please! Furzey, there's no need for that sort of remark. You're just making things worse.'

'And you might remember this,' Gilbert told the game-keeper sharply. 'When Culliford's finished telling us his side of the story, I'm going to be asking you what the hell you were doing, carrying a gun up there at night.'

'I always carries me gun—'

'Not *now*! Let Culliford finish first, for God's sake, or we'll be here all morning. Right, Culliford, get on with it.'

'Well, that's it, really,' Arthur said, sitting down again with some reluctance and still glowering at the gamekeeper. 'I was just figuring out how to get past them without them noticing and all hell broke loose. Bloody fool started firing his gun off in all directions and yelling at the top of his voice, the other blokes started stamping about and shouting back, and me and Shirl were caught in the middle of it all. I had hold of her hand up till then but she sort of jumped away from me and started screaming and crying and I couldn't find her again. And then someone shone a torch and I saw 'twas this pair of clowns here, and the others were charging through the trees like wild elephants, and my Shirl was laying on the ground with her arm broke. I tell you no lies, I thought she were a goner.' He wiped his face with his hand and added shakily, 'I did, really.'

There was a short silence. Hilary reached out her hand and touched the worn, grubby sleeve of his jacket. Until then, she had never felt anything other than distaste for Arthur

325

Culliford, but just at this moment her heart went out to him.

Gilbert cleared his throat. 'Well, that all seems plain enough. Furzey?'

'I told you, Squire,' the gamekeeper said. 'Mr Kellaway here said we'd got to put a stop to the poaching so we arranged to go up to Top Cover, around ten, and lay in wait for the buggers. Saving your presence, Miss Hilary,' he added. 'Only they were already there when us arrived, and so was this lunatic.'

'Here, you got no right to say that,' Arthur said furiously.

'No, you haven't,' Napier agreed. 'Take back that word, Furzey.'

The gamekeeper stared at him. 'What's going on here? Gone over to his side, I suppose, because it's his kiddy that's been hurt. Well, it wasn't me that done it, and I'm sorry if I can't look to you for a bit of support, Colonel Napier, after all the years I've served you. You know what Arthur Culliford's like, never been a bit of good, not since he were a little tacker, but if you'm going to support him against me I reckon maybe it's time for a parting of the ways. I'll give you me notice now.'

'For heaven's sake, man, don't be so ridiculous!' Gilbert snapped. 'I'm trying to find out what happened, that's all. Why were you carrying a gun?'

'I always takes me gun,' the gamekeeper said sullenly. 'Wouldn't feel right without it. You never know what you'm going to find.' He swivelled narrowed eyes at Arthur Culliford.

'But why did you fire it? You hadn't been threatened. You didn't know who might be there. You had no proof they were poachers – as Hilary says, there's a public footpath close by. Anyone could have been there, in all innocence.'

Furzey chewed his lip and glowered at the floor. Eventually, he said, 'I only fired it into the air. I never fired it *at* no one.'

Gilbert sighed. 'This is getting us nowhere. Have any of you any idea who might have knocked the child over?'

They all shook their heads. None of them, except Arthur, had been aware of a child's presence. Neither Travis nor Furzey remembered the feel of a small body during the uproar.

'I really think it must have been one of the others,' Travis said at last. 'And unless we can find out who they were ...'

Gilbert rubbed his face. 'I think you're right.' He turned to Arthur. 'Are you satisfied with that, Culliford? Do you want to press charges against either of these men? I have to warn you that without proof you probably wouldn't get far, but it is your right if you believe they hurt your daughter.'

Arthur pushed out his lips and scowled, and Hilary said hastily, 'That's not a threat, Arthur. My father really does care about what happened. If there were any way to find the people who hurt her, he'd do it.'

'I'll certainly inform the police that we've had suspected poachers from Plymouth out here,' Gilbert said. 'And I'll tell them a child was hurt. It's likely to mean a visit from them, I'm afraid,' he added. 'They'll want to know what happened, so we need to be prepared for that.'

'Get our stories right, you mean?' Culliford asked, and Hilary closed her eyes in exasperation.

'No!' Napier snapped. 'All I meant was, we need to be quite sure we know ourselves what happened. And I think we are, now.' He turned his gaze on Travis and Furzey. 'Are you two satisfied?'

The gamekeeper shrugged. 'About as much as us ever shall be, I reckon, Squire.' He shot a nasty look towards Arthur Culliford.

Travis cleared his throat. 'I'd just like to say that I take full responsibility. I knew Furzey had a gun and I should have stopped him from taking it. If anyone had been shot, I would have been to blame.'

Hilary glanced at him in surprise and felt her respect for him begin, albeit rather grudgingly, to return. He met her eyes for a moment and she looked away.

Her father nodded, evidently feeling the same. 'All right, then, we'll declare this meeting closed. Hilary, did you say you'd be taking Culliford and his wife to the hospital?'

'Yes. We'll go now, if you're ready, Arthur. We can pick up your wife on the way.'

'Us can't both go, not with all the little 'uns to think about. Someone got to stop with them.' He hesitated, clearly attracted by the idea of riding in Hilary's car. 'I suppose it had better be Maggie,' he said at last.

'I'll take you home then, and collect her.' She glanced coolly at the other men. 'I don't think this business is at an end, all the same. We need to draw up some ground rules about who goes out after poachers and how. And that goes for you too, Furzey. I'm sure my father agrees that carrying a gun at night is simply not to happen any more.'

Not waiting for an answer, she ushered Arthur out of the door, and followed him without a backward glance.

Chapter Thirty-Two

Jackie had decided to spend the whole day in Plymouth. Her interview was at eleven o'clock, but she caught the early bus so as to be there in good time and walk from the bus station to the Duke of Cornwall Hotel, which was at the other end of Royal Parade and up towards the Hoe. That meant walking past Spooner's and Dingle's, and she strolled slowly along, gazing in the big plate-glass windows and imagining herself walking here during her lunch-hours, or even during the evenings if she was offered the chance to live in.

Jackie had almost decided that this was what she would do. Her mother and father probably wouldn't like it, but she felt ready for a bit of independence. If she stayed at home, it would be another two years before she got the key of the door at twenty-one, and she felt grown up now. When you came to think about it, she'd already been through as much as most twenty-one year olds – more than a lot, she thought, remembering the scare she'd had after she and Roy had been up at the Standing Stones that time. Yes, she felt grown up, but she'd never prove it to her family as long as she stayed at home.

Look at her sister Val. She'd gone off as soon as she could once war had broken out, and she'd only been eighteen. And she'd gone all over the place – Portsmouth and Gosport first, and then Egypt. There'd been nobody then to tell her what to do or what time to come in, and she'd been all right. And she'd been thousands of miles away. Jackie would only be in Plymouth.

Besides, it was getting crowded at home. Val had moved out, but now Joanna and Tom had three children they'd be needing more room. It wasn't that Jackie didn't like the twins, but they weren't much fun at the moment, and they took up a lot of time and attention. She didn't really think anyone would notice all that much if she weren't there. It would probably be quite a relief.

As she sauntered along, she wondered vaguely what the gossip was that she'd heard about Shirley Culliford, when she was on the bus. There'd only been two other people from Burracombe going to Plymouth, and they were two women she didn't know very well and didn't like much, so she'd sat as far away as possible, but she hadn't been able to help hearing some of what they were whispering to each other. Something about an accident, up in the woods, in the middle of the night, she thought. But that didn't make sense. Shirley had been at the rehearsal last night and gone home with her father as soon as it had finished. The two women must have got it wrong. Jackie dismissed it from her mind and thought instead about the interview.

I hope I get the job, she thought. I really want it. I want to get away from home. And if Vic doesn't like it, that's just too bad. He doesn't own me, and we can meet in Plymouth if we want to. I might even meet someone nicer than him. Anyway, it doesn't matter if I don't. As Miss Hilary said, women have the right to get on in the world and make something of themselves. And that's what I want to do.

Miss Millington, the head housekeeper, who interviewed Jackie, seemed to agree with this. She looked in her late forties, smartly dressed in a black business suit, with her dark brown hair drawn back in a chignon and a single row of pearls at her throat. Jackie, who had been vaguely expecting someone like Mrs Ellis, but without the pinny, was startled and a bit intimidated, but she lifted her chin and answered the questions in a firm, quiet voice, as Hilary had advised her. Yes, she was working as a housemaid at Burracombe Barton, and Miss Napier knew she was coming here and was willing to give her a good reference. Yes, she had lived in the village all her life but now she wanted to branch out a little. No, she didn't have a regular boyfriend, and wasn't thinking of getting married in the near future. She wanted a career.

'You may change your mind about that, of course,' Miss Millington remarked. 'Young girls usually do. But if you're really thinking of a career in hotel work, you couldn't do better than start in a first-class place like the Duke of Cornwall. Do you think you'd want to stay here, or would you be looking to move on after two or three years?'

Jackie hesitated. To say she'd want to stay might look unambitious, but if she said she'd be moving on, the woman might not want to employ her. In the end, she said cautiously, 'I expect that would depend how happy I was here and what opportunities came up.'

'A good answer,' the housekeeper said. 'Well, I think that's all I need to know for now. Is there anything you'd like to ask me?'

Jackie hesitated again, and then asked, 'Would I be able to live in? Instead of going home every night?'

The woman seemed a little surprised. 'Why? It's not such a very long way to Burracombe, is it?'

'No. I just thought it might help me to feel more a part of the hotel. And it would be a good experience, after being in a village all my life.'

'I see.' The housekeeper looked at her thoughtfully, and Jackie's heart sank as she wondered if she had spoiled her chances. 'There's nothing wrong at home, is there? You've no special reason for wanting to leave?'

'No – we get along fine. I just want to be a bit more independent, that's all. It doesn't really make any difference,' she added in a rush. 'I mean, I'd still take the job – that's if you offered it to me – even if I couldn't live in. But my sister, who's a nurse, she went away during the war, she even went to Egypt, and I think she liked being away for a while. She's home again now – she's just got married – but she always says what good experience it was.'

'I'm afraid we can't compete with Egypt,' Miss Millington said with a smile, 'but we do have staff accommodation and we might be able to offer you a room, though possibly not straight away. It would probably be best for you to wait a while, to see how you get along. Anyway, we'll be in touch within a few days and let you know if you've got the job.' She rose to her feet and held out her hand. 'Thank you for coming, Miss Tozer.'

'Thank you,' Jackie murmured, taking the outstretched hand. 'Thank you very much.'

She went out and down the stairs to the foyer. The October air outside was fresh, with a taste of salt in the breeze, and she walked up to the Hoe. There, close to Smeaton's Tower, she bought herself an ice cream and sat on a bench to eat it, gazing out over the blue sparkling waters of the Sound.

It seemed a world away from tiny Burracombe with its narrow lanes, its cottages and its claustrophobic atmosphere. Everyone knows all about you there, she thought. Everyone's watching you and talking about you all the time. Here, not a soul knows me, and I can sit and enjoy an ice cream all by myself without thinking that someone's going to ask me what I'm doing.

'Well, by all the stars above us!' a familiar voice exclaimed close by. 'If it ain't young Jackie Tozer. What be you doing up here on the Hoe, then? All by yourself, are you?'

Jackie turned disbelievingly, and saw Jacob Prout standing just behind her with Jennifer Tucker at his side, her arm linked through his. They roared with laughter at her surprise and Jennifer said, 'I suppose you thought you were safe here, miles from home. Not that you're doing anything you shouldn't be, of course!'

It was so close to what Jackie had been thinking that she felt herself blush. 'I didn't expect to see anyone I knew,' she admitted. 'I've just been for an interview for a job.'

'A job?' Jennifer came and sat beside her. 'D'you mind if we sit with you for a bit? What sort of job?'

'At the Duke of Cornwall,' Jackie said shyly. 'As a trainee. I'll probably start off as a housemaid, like I am already, but if they think I'd be any good they might let me try reception. That's if I get a job at all,' she added, trying not to sound too hopeful.

'You *are* branching out,' Jennifer said. 'Good for you. You didn't think of coming to work at Dingle's, then? Or one of the other big stores?'

'Not really. I quite like the sort of work I've been doing. I'm not sure I'd like being in a shop.'

'So you'd be coming in on the bus every day, then,' Jacob said, sitting on the other side of Jennifer. ''Tis all right in the summer, but you got to get out to the main road and wait there for the Plymouth bus – not so good when it's raining and blowing or there's a bit of snow.'

'Well, I might be going to live in, if they can find a room for me,' Jackie said, making a note to remind her mother about the weather problems as a good reason for staying in Plymouth.

'And would you like that?' Jennifer asked. 'Being away from your family, and the village?'

'Yes, I would. I'd like to be a bit more independent. I have to be in at half-past ten at night, and tell them where I'm going and everything. Just like a child. I mean, some people are married at my age!' Jackie realised that her voice was rising indignantly. 'My mother was only a year older than me when she and Dad got married. It's daft.'

'You ain't of age till you'm twenty-one,' Jacob put in, but Jennifer nudged him hard and he fell silent, though not without giving her a surprised glance.

'When will you know if you've got the job?' she asked Jackie.

'In a few days. They've got other girls to interview as well.' Jackie felt suddenly depressed. 'I don't suppose I'll get it anyway, so there's not much point in worrying about where I'm going to live.'

'And in the meantime, you may as well enjoy your day in Plymouth,' Jennifer said bracingly. 'Jacob and I were going to go and have some dinner in Dingle's restaurant. Why don't you come too? My treat,' she added as Jackie opened her mouth to say she couldn't afford it. 'And then we could all go back on the bus together. Jacob just came in for the day, and I'm going back with him for the rest of the weekend.'

'Well, if you're sure you don't mind ...' Jackie said doubtfully, and Jennifer laughed.

'Of course we don't mind, do we, Jacob? It'll be nice to have your company. Now, would you like to walk down to the Barbican first? We like going that way, to look at the rock pools and the fishing-boats. I come down early sometimes and buy fish as they unload it – the sprats were lovely this year. Do you like sprats?'

'I don't know that I've ever had them,' Jackie said. 'Mum gets a piece of cod or haddock off the fish van sometimes of a Friday, or we might have plaice, but there's not much else.'

'There's plenty of fish in Plymouth,' Jennifer told her. 'Fresh mackerel, sea trout, pollock or coley, dabs – lots of different sorts. And all straight out of the sea. If you come to live here, you'll have to come over and have your tea with me sometimes. We could have fish then. That's if you'd like to.'

'Oh yes,' Jackie said, feeling warmed by her friendliness, and completely forgetting that one of the attractions of coming to Plymouth was that nobody would know her. 'I'd like that.'

They walked on together, along the top of the Hoe and down to the Barbican, and then back into the wide, bustling streets of the city. Jackie gazed around her at the white, square buildings with their big plate-glass windows and lifted her face to the October sun. I've had enough of village life, she thought. This is where I want to be.

'Live in?' Alice Tozer echoed that night when Jackie told the family about her plans. 'What do you want to do that for? It only takes half an hour to get out here on the bus.'

'Not if there's snow,' Jackie said. 'And it won't be much fun going out to the main road in the rain either. I know the village bus will take me out there, but I've still got to wait by the main road, and it'll be dark in winter, and windy too. You know how exposed it is.'

'I don't know why you got to go and work in Plymouth at all,' Ted grumbled. 'You got a perfectly good job at the Barton.'

'I don't want a "job". I want a career.'

'As housemaid in a swanky hotel? Being treated as a skivvy by all and sundry? At least the Napiers treat you right, you don't know what some of them snobby hotel guests'll be like. I dunno that I like this idea at all.' Ted put down the handbell he was working on and looked as if he were about to forbid her to have any more to do with the suggestion.

'Why can't you go to Tavistock instead?' Alice suggested. 'They might want someone at the Bedford. That'd be a nice place to work, and you know quite a few people in Tavistock, having been there to school and all.'

Which is exactly why I don't want to work there, Jackie thought, but instead of saying so, she said, 'They haven't got any vacancies at the Bedford.'

'Are you sure? Have you enquired?' Alice asked, but before Jackie could answer, which would have meant telling a fib, Ted broke in again.

'Have they actually offered you this job? You only had the interview today – I dare say they'd got others to see as well.'

'Miss Millington didn't exactly *say* I'd got it,' Jackie admitted, 'but she was very nice and I think she liked me. She said I gave good answers to her questions.'

'Well, so might the others,' Ted said, looking at his wife. 'I don't think you need worry about it too much, love.'

'Oh, I see, so you don't think I could have been good enough!' Jackie exclaimed hotly. 'You think everyone else is bound to be better than me. That's the way you've always been with me, isn't it. Just because I'm the youngest, I've always had to be the worst. The *baby*. Our Val could go off and be in the VADs and go to Egypt and do whatever she liked, but I've got to stay at home and be a housemaid all my life, just because *you* don't think I'd be any good at anything else. Well, it might surprise you to know that I *can* be good at things, all sorts of things, but I'm never going to be allowed to be if I stay at home, am I? That's why I want to go away – so that I can do the things I want to do and find out what I'm good at, without having you telling me where I can go and what time to come in. I'm fed up with it – do you hear me? *Fed up!*'

In tears by the time she finished, she turned and blundered her way out of the kitchen and up the stairs. They heard her feet stamping across the landing and then the slam of her bedroom door. A moment later, both the babies began to wail and Joanna came out of the room she and Tom used as a sitting room, looking exasperated.

'What on earth's going on? I'd just got them off to sleep.'

'I'm sorry, love,' Alice apologised. 'It was our Jackie getting in a tizzy over this job in Plymouth. She wants to live at the hotel.'

'Well, if she's going to rampage around the house like this, it'd probably be a good idea,' Joanna said irritably, and went up the stairs in her turn.

'Oh dear,' Alice sighed. 'Now she'm upset as well. I don't know why you can't handle our Jackie a bit better, Ted.'

'Me!' he exclaimed. 'It was you started it, saying her ought to go and work in Tavvy instead. All I did was say you didn't need to worry about it.'

'Because you didn't think she'd pass the interview,' Alice finished for him. 'That's what sparked her off, and no wonder. You got to use a bit of tact, that's all.'

'Tact,' he muttered, but Minnie, who had been sitting in her corner observing everything, decided it was time to put in her own word.

'I don't know what all the fuss be about anyway. 'Tisn't anything out of the ordinary for a girl to go into service, and, 'tis not often they can still live at home as long as Jackie's done anyway. When I was young, 'twas the common thing for a maid to go and live in, whether 'twas a hotel or a big house like the Barton. I did myself, over to Sampford Manor. And I were only fourteen. You did the same, Alice, when you first came here as dairymaid and met my Ted.'

'It was over seventy years ago when you went to Sampford Manor,' Ted said. 'Things were different then. You took it for granted you'd have to do as you were told and you were only allowed out one half-day a week. And you kept a pretty close eye on Alice, too. Her'd been here six months before you'd let us walk down the lane together. Our Jackie thinks she's going to be out every night, enjoying herself. Girls these days want too much freedom.'

'I don't reckon she'll find she's got that much freedom,' Minnie said. 'They work them pretty hard in those big hotels, and they keep the young ones on a tight leash too. What do you think she'm going to do, Ted, take herself down Union Street meeting sailors? Don't you trust her no more than that?'

'Of course I don't think that!' he said, turning red. 'And it's not a question of trust. You don't know who she'm going to run up against in a big hotel – there'll be men down from London on business, and all sorts, and even if they do keep an eye on them in the hotel, there's still no one there who really cares about her. And she won't have no friends there, neither.'

'She'd soon make friends,' Alice said, beginning to sound undecided. 'Our Jackie's never had no trouble getting along with people.'

'Yes, but what sort of friends? She won't have us there to see if they'm suitable or not. No, I'm sorry, Alice, but I don't like it and I won't have it. If she can't live at home, she can't take the job – if it's offered to her – and that's it and all about it.'

The two women were silent, recognising the flat, unequivocal tone of his voice. When Ted spoke like that, there was no further argument, and they looked at each other and sighed.

The kitchen door opened and Joanna came in, a baby cradled in each arm.

'Is it safe to come in now? I could hear your voices all over the house. Whatever is it all about?'

'I told you – our Jackie wants to leave home and go and live in a hotel in Plymouth. The Duke of Cornwall,' Alice added, as if Jackie had announced her intention of moving to Dartmoor Prison.

'Well, what's wrong with that? I left home at her age, and so did Val. Neither of us has gone to the bad, as far as I can see. Mind you, there's a bit of difference between this place and the Duke of Cornwall,' she added with a touch of mischief in her voice. She looked at Alice and saw the indecision in her face, and then the scowling resolve in Ted's and added more seriously, 'Look, why not get Val to have a word with her? Find out what she's got in mind? You've got to do something, or she'll just get more and more upset and she could end up leaving home anyway, and never coming back. Much better to sort things out in a friendly way.'

'That's just what I said to Ted,' Alice declared. 'A bit of tact, that's all that's needed.' She bit her lip and added in a worried tone, 'Do you really think her'd do that, Jo? Go off in a huff and never come back?'

'No, not really, but people do sometimes, and you don't

338

want to risk it. That sort of row can blow up out of all proportion.'

'She'm right,' Minnie agreed. 'There ain't nothing harder to heal than a family row. Think of poor Susan Hannaford, being sent away when her was expecting a babby. Never come back to the village again.'

'That was different,' Ted objected, but Alice was nodding her head in agreement.

'It might have been different circumstances, Ted, and old Abraham Hannaford were a bully, we knows that, but Joanna's right. These things can get out of hand and us don't want nothing like that in the family. Us got to have a proper talk about this, so us knows what to say to Jackie if she gets this job. And remember, even if she don't get this one, she's not going to stop looking. She've got the idea in her head now and it's not going to be shifted easy.' She thought for a moment. 'Joanna's right. Our Val's the one to talk to her now. I'll ask her tomorrow, when they come round for their Sunday dinner.'

Chapter Thirty-Three

At church next morning, Basil asked for prayers for Shirley Culliford, even though she was back at home now and not at death's door, and preached about forgiveness. It was strange, he thought, how often he found himself preaching about forgiveness, even in a village like Burracombe. Its inhabitants seemed contented enough on the surface, but there were all sorts of little grudges and feuds going on underneath, and every now and then one would break out, like a bubble rising on a pond, betraying the discord fermenting like rotting vegetation beneath.

What an unpleasant analogy, he thought as he waited at the door for his parishioners to file past him after the service, and not really a fair one. Burracombe was a happy place to live. People cared about each other; neighbours helped each other out; even lifelong bad blood like that between Jacob Prout and his neighbour Jed Fisher, often got sorted out in the end, although they had had to wait until Jed was on his deathbed to do it.

Gilbert Napier, who was always the first parishioner to shake his hand and compliment him on his sermon, interrupted his reverie. Today, Basil had been slightly nervous of the Squire's reaction, knowing how Shirley had come to be injured, but Gilbert simply nodded at him and said, in what was probably meant to be a murmur but came out as his familiar bellow, which everyone in the church could hear: 'Fine sermon, Vicar. Needed to be said. Call in for a drink before lunch, got something to discuss with you.'

He strode on, followed by Hilary who smiled and shook his hand, and then the rest of the congregation – Constance Bellamy, Joyce and Henry Warren, the Tozers, the Nethercotts (without Vic, who had only attended church once since his return home), the Friend sisters with Billy, and all the rest of the faces that were so familiar to him, and so dear.

I've been very fortunate to spend so long in such a pleasant place, he thought. The feuds and fusses that do go on are no worse than anywhere else and, on the whole, I think they're probably rather less. Even an accident such as the one that happened to poor little Shirley is a rarity, thank heaven.

He wondered what the Squire wanted to talk to him about and hoped it wasn't the accident. He'd already been to visit the family and talk to the little girl and, having asked for prayers and preached his sermon, felt there was little more for him to say. He certainly didn't want to become involved in the politics of gamekeeping, poaching and possible prosecution.

However, it was not the accident that Gilbert wanted to discuss, although naturally it couldn't be ignored. After a few commiserating murmurs, during which nothing of any real importance was said, Gilbert handed his guest a glass of sherry and said, 'I want to talk to you about young Copley.'

'Felix?' Basil lifted his silvery eyebrows in surprise. 'What's he been up to?'

'Nothing, as far as I know. Other than scorching round the lanes in that sports car of his and setting the village by the ears with this pantomime he's putting on. No, I want to talk to you about Little Burracombe. The Bishop's been in touch with me over the living there.'

'I see,' Basil said thoughtfully. 'It's in your gift, isn't it?'

'For what it's worth, yes. Must be a few generations since that actually meant anything, mind. I believe my grandfather had a hand in appointing a vicar here in Burracombe, but that was well before your time. Still, the Bishop does me the courtesy of asking my opinion, and since the young man in

341

question is here in Burracombe and pretty well-known to me, I ought to have something to say.'

'And what are you thinking of saying?' Basil asked cautiously.

'To tell you the truth, Basil, I'm not at all sure.' Gilbert looked faintly surprised, as if such a thing rarely happened to him. 'He's a good enough fellow, I've no doubt – used to come to the Barton quite a lot a year or so ago. Thought for a while he was getting keen on Hilary but nothing came of it. Anyway, the question is, will he make a good vicar?'

'Are you sure you ought to be asking me this?' Basil enquired. 'As his vicar at the moment ...'

'That's exactly why, man! You must know him better than anyone else. It's no different from asking an employer for a reference, surely, and I imagine the Bishop will be asking for your views, anyway.'

'Yes, he will,' Basil admitted, not mentioning that the Bishop already had.

'So what are they?' Gilbert demanded impatiently. 'Come on, Basil, you don't need to beat about the bush with me. Is he up to the job? I don't mind telling you I've got my doubts. A bit too frivolous, in my opinion.'

'That's just superficial,' Basil said. 'He's a very serious young man when it comes to important matters, and they think a lot of him in Little Burracombe. You know he's been taking services there for some time, while John Berry was ill.'

'So I've heard. But there's a difference between standing in for the odd service and being a good parish priest. Looking after people's souls, and all that sort of thing,' he finished in a rather embarrassed tone.

'I think Felix did quite a bit of that too,' Basil said, beginning to feel rather annoyed. 'He didn't simply pop over on a Sunday morning and then come home. He spent a lot of time in the village, visiting people and talking to them. All that racing about in the car his uncle gave him and starting up the Drama Club is for his spare time, which he's quite entitled to enjoy in his own way. It does, of course, help the village to bind together as well,' he added.

'So you think he could do it, do you?'

'I don't see why not,' Basil said. 'He comes from a very strong clerical background. The uncle who gave him the car is an archdeacon, his father is a bishop, and there are numerous other clergy in the family. I think you'll find he's well aware of what the job entails.'

'Hmph.' The Squire's grunt sounded unconvinced. 'Well, I'll give it some more thought. Don't suppose the Bishop will take much notice of me one way or the other, but I like to stick my oar in now and then.' The understatement of the year, Basil thought. 'As I say, he seems a decent enough young fellow, I just think he needs a bit more time to settle down. What's going on between him and that young schoolteacher, by the way?'

'I think they'd like to marry,' Basil said, feeling on more secure ground but hoping that he wasn't giving away any confidences. 'It would be a good match, and she'll make an excellent vicar's wife. They can't afford it on a curate's pay, of course, and it would be a loss to the village if they had to move away, but that will be something they'll have to deal with themselves. There's plenty of time; they're young yet.'

'Hm.' The grunt this time was non-committal. 'Another sherry, Basil?'

'Thank you, but no.' Basil began to get to his feet. 'I really ought to be going now. Grace will have lunch ready. So if that's all you wanted to discuss …?'

'Yes, yes, that's all.' The Squire seemed lost in thought. 'Well, thank you for dropping in, Basil. Been good to have this chat. I'll think it over and let the Bishop know.' He sighed. 'Got a lot on my plate at the moment, what with this accident in the woods, and Kellaway new here. Don't want to cause more trouble than we've got already.'

'No, indeed,' Basil agreed, and paused with his foot on the doorstep. 'Have you heard any more about Shirley's condition?'

'Back home, arm in plaster and enjoying the attention, from what I can make out. Hilary popped over after church and took her a few books and toys, and a cake Mrs Ellis baked yesterday. I just hope it doesn't give the parents ideas, that's all. You know what those people are like – give them an inch and they'll take a mile.'

Briefly, Basil considered taking up this issue, but decided against it. Better to go home and enjoy his Sunday lunch, he thought. Sometimes, it was best to let sleeping dogs lie.

'Well, since you ask, I think it's quite a good idea,' Val said, when the roast beef and Yorkshire pudding and treacle tart were all cleared away and the washing-up done. Ted, Luke and Tom had gone off to walk round the fields, with Robin tagging along behind his father, while Joanna had taken the twins round the lane in their pram and Vic Nethercott had called to invite Jackie to his parents' house for tea. That left just Val, her mother and grandmother sitting outside the farmhouse in the pale October sunshine.

'A good idea? For our Jackie to go off and live in Plymouth when she could get there on the bus?'

'Yes, why not? It's a good chance for her to see a different sort of life, and she'll be near enough to come home if she doesn't like it. It's time she grew up a bit, Mum,' Val went on, 'and you're never going to let her, as long as she's at home.'

Alice stared at her elder daughter in shock. 'I don't know what you mean! Of course I'll let her grow up. I just don't think she's grown up enough now to go away, that's all.'

'She's not very much younger than I was when I went away, and I went as a nurse, in wartime. I saw things you'd never believe, things I hope our Jackie will never have to see, but I was grown-up enough to cope with it and Jackie's grown-up enough to cope with living ten miles away. She just needs to be given the chance.'

'It was different in wartime,' Alice said, but Val shook her head.

'Girls weren't any different, Mum. I don't suppose they were any different when you were young, either – or Grandma, come to that,' she added with a glance at Minnie. 'If you think back, you'll know that you felt grown up at Jackie's age too, and probably thought your parents were holding you back.'

'I was engaged to your father by then, and I'd been out at service since I was fourteen,' Alice said, and Val smiled.

'There you are then.'

'But that was different! It was just like your grandma and me were saying yesterday – girls were looked after more then. There was no jaunting off in their spare time with nobody to account to.'

'You've just got to trust her to be sensible,' Val said, although with a little less confidence. Not all young women could be trusted to be sensible, as she knew to her own cost, and she also knew that Jackie didn't have to leave home to get into trouble. There had been that scare last summer with Roy Pettifer, which Alice knew nothing about ... But Val believed her sister had learned from that, and wasn't likely to take such a risk again.

Alice sighed. 'I don't know ... Your father's not keen on the idea at all.'

'Well, he wouldn't be, would he? Seeing his baby girl go off and not knowing what time she'll be in at night.' Val glanced sideways at mother and gave her a grin. 'Come on, Mum, you've been a young girl. You know what it's like. I bet you and Dad slipped away sometimes on your own.'

'That's not the point,' Alice said, and Val laughed.

'It is, though, isn't it. You can remember what you did and you're scared our Jackie might do the same! But you never did

345

anything really silly, did you? And neither will Jackie. She's got her head screwed on the right way – you don't have to worry about her.'

'Remember what us were saying last night,' Minnie piped up. 'You don't want a family row over this. When it comes down to it, there's not much you can do to stop her, if her've got her heart set on going, and 'twon't do no good if her goes off with bad feeling.'

'She's under twenty-one,' Alice said. 'She's still under her father and me's jurisdiction.'

'And what good does that do, when it comes to a fight?' the old woman asked. 'You can stop her getting married because she needs your signature, but she don't need that to go and get a job. The only way you can stop her is by going to court, and you don't want to do that. Her'd never forgive you.'

'No,' Val agreed. 'And there's another point, Mum. Jackie could go to court herself and get permission! I knew a girl in the VADs who did that to get married, and they took away all her parents' rights and said she could. Not that I think Jackie would go that far,' she added, 'but like Grandma says, there's not really much you can do to stop her.'

'Oh dear,' Alice said. 'I wish she'd never thought of it in the first place. It's not her working in the Duke of Cornwall that worries your father and me, you know, it's this idea of living in. It's come so sudden, us haven't had time to prepare ourselves for it.' She thought for a minute. 'I'll have a talk with him tonight. I don't know as it'll make any difference, but there's a lot to take into account and we don't want to be unfair to her. I know she's got to grow up sometime, but maybe you'm right – we've been treating her as the baby of the family and 'tis time to let go a bit.'

'Well, I should think so,' Val said with a grin. 'We've got enough babies in the family now.' She blushed and stopped suddenly, then said, 'Look, they're coming back – ready for a cup of tea, I expect. I'll go and put the kettle on.'

She went indoors and the two older women glanced at each other.

'What d'you reckon, Mother?' Alice said. 'Is she?'

'I wouldn't be surprised,' Minnie said. 'I wouldn't be surprised at all.'

Jackie's afternoon with Vic wasn't the success they'd both hoped.

'It's a smashing day,' Vic said as they strolled away from the farm. 'Let's walk along the river for a bit.'

Jackie nodded, and they went down to the bridge and along the footpath. The way led through ancient woods, with gnarled and twisted oak trees no more than twelve or fifteen feet tall whose roots twined and clung like writhing snakes about the moss-covered rocks. Grey wagtails danced along the banks and a dipper paused on a rock, flirting its tail and displaying its white breast before diving into the tumbling waters. On the far bank were pastures grazed close by sheep and dotted with gorse, showing glimpses of gold even in October.

'When gorse is out of season,' Vic said, stopping to pull Jackie into his arms, 'kissing's out of reason.'

She giggled and leaned against him. 'You always say that.'

'It's always true. There's always gorse out somewhere, even in the middle of winter, so kissing's never out of reason.' He nuzzled his lips down her neck. 'Mmm, you smell nice.'

'You always say that too,' she breathed, her heart beginning to thump.

'It's another thing that's always true. Oh, Jackie ...'

'Let's go a bit further,' she said, glancing nervously around. 'Someone might come along.'

'That sounds promising,' he said, tucking her hand in his. 'Are you going to let me have my wicked way with you today?'

'Wait and see,' she returned teasingly, and then added

a quick, 'No. No, I'm not. You know how I feel about that, Vic.'

'I know how you *think* you feel. I could make you feel different.'

'Please, Vic. Don't start that again.' She stopped. 'Maybe it's not a good idea to go too far.'

'Oh, I was hoping you'd go a lot further,' he said suggestively. 'All the way, in fact.' He slid his arm around her waist and held her tightly against him as he nuzzled her again. 'Come on, Jackie. We've been going out for ages now—'

'A couple of months. That's not ages.'

'It seems like it to me. Don't you realise what it's like for a man to have to wait? It's torture, Jackie.' He slid his hand down from her neck to her breast and his voice dropped to a throaty whisper. 'Isn't it torture for you too?'

'Vic, don't!' Jackie twisted away in panic. Vic knew quite well what he was doing, and what effect he was having on her, and she was terrified that she wouldn't be able to resist. Desperately, she cast about for a distraction. 'Don't you want to know how my interview went yesterday?'

Vic dropped his arm and turned away sulkily. He began to walk on along the narrow path and Jackie, feeling miserable, followed him.

'I suppose you'd better tell me. It's obviously the most important thing to you.'

Jackie felt even more disheartened. First her parents and now Vic. Her voice flat, she said, 'Well, it seemed to go all right. I think I've got a good chance of getting a job there.'

'And am I supposed to be pleased about that?'

'Well, you might try,' she retorted. 'If only because it's what I want.'

'And what I want doesn't matter, of course.'

'Yes, it does. Vic, I can't see why you're so against this. Just think, if I go to Plymouth we'll be able to see each other there. In our lunch-hours, perhaps.'

348

'I don't suppose they'll be at the same time. You'll probably be working then, waitressing or whatever you're going to be doing.'

'I'll be doing all sorts of jobs. I want to learn all about the hotel trade. There are some good opportunities for women.' Her voice was becoming more eager. 'I could end up as head receptionist – I really fancy that.'

'And getting off with all the swanky guests,' he sneered. 'You won't have time for your friends then. No wonder you're not interested in me.'

'I am! You know I am.'

'Do I?' He stopped abruptly and turned, so that she walked into him and he could grab her in his arms. 'Then why won't you let me love you properly?'

'Vic, *please*!' She twisted again, but this time he was ready for her and his grip tightened. 'Let me go!'

'Not until you give me a proper kiss.' His mouth was hard on hers. 'That's better.' His voice softened. 'Jackie, sweetheart, you know how I feel about you. I just don't like the idea of you in a posh hotel in Plymouth, meeting all sorts of other men. You're so lovely, they're all going to want to take you out. You'll forget all about me.' He nuzzled her again. 'What time would you be going in, in the mornings? I suppose we could at least go on the same bus. And home again in the evenings, perhaps. That way I'll be able to keep an eye on you.'

Jackie drew in a deep breath. 'I won't be going on the bus. I told you before, I want to live in.'

He dropped his arms again. 'You're not still on about that! It's a daft idea – you can be there in half an hour. Well, maybe more by the time you've gone out to the main road and then walked through town at the other end. You don't need to live in.'

'I want to,' she said stubbornly. 'Anyway, I won't be working regular hours so it'll be better, and Miss Millington—'

'Who's she?'

349

'The head housekeeper, the one who interviewed me. She said there might be a room available for me. She thinks it's a good idea.'

'Oh, she does, does she? I bet your mum and dad don't think so.'

'They'll come round,' Jackie said, unable to sound convinced.

He snorted. 'I can just see that. It's a stupid idea. The whole thing's stupid.'

'And I suppose I'm stupid too?' she demanded angrily.

'Yes, you are, if you want to know. Anyway, I don't suppose they'll have a room for you, so the situation won't arise and you'll have to come in on the bus with me.'

'I won't. I'll find somewhere else to stay. A hostel – the Girls' Friendly Society runs hostels, I bet there's one in Plymouth.'

'That won't be any better than living at home,' he said. 'Look, Jackie, you're the only person who thinks this is a good idea. Everyone else—'

'Everyone else wants me to do what *they* want,' she broke in. 'No one ever thinks of what *I* want.'

'Yes, they do.' He stroked her again. 'I can think of something you want.'

'Oh, for goodness sake!' She broke away and began to walk back along the path. 'There's only one thing you're thinking of, and I don't even believe it's because it's me. Any girl would do for you. Well, you'd better find yourself another girl, Vic Nethercott, and I wish you joy of her. Maybe you should try Tessa Latimer – she'll go out with anything in trousers.'

'Maybe I will, at that,' he retorted. 'At least she knows what it's all about. You're just a kid, Jackie Tozer. You're not even old enough to be out of your pram, let alone leaving your mummy to go and live in Plymouth. I tell you what, I'm glad found out in time. I was thinking of asking you to marry me.'

Jackie turned. 'You weren't!'

'I was,' he said sullenly. 'I thought it might be today, as

matter of fact. But now I know you're not interested ...'

Jackie stared at him. Her heart was beating fast. She looked at his face and saw the sulkiness there, and then the glint in his eye, and knew as surely as she knew her own name that he was lying.

'I don't believe you,' she said coldly. 'But as you say, there's no point in it now anyway. We've both found out in time.' And she turned and walked quickly away along the riverbank, back towards the village.

'But that's easy,' Jennifer Tucker said. 'She could come and stay with me.'

Val looked at her in astonishment. 'With you?'

They were strolling out towards the main road together, Jennifer to catch the Plymouth bus and Val to catch the one going in the opposite direction, towards Tavistock where she was doing an extra shift at the hospital. As they walked, Jennifer had naturally mentioned that she and Jacob had met Jackie in Plymouth the day before, and Val had told her about the trouble she was having persuading her parents to let her live at the hotel. 'If it wasn't for that,' she'd finished, 'I think they'd let her go. But they're really worried by the idea of her being in Plymouth all on her own.'

'I'd love to have her,' Jennifer said now. 'I thought yesterday what a nice girl she was. I've got a spare room – Jacob says he'll come and stay sometimes, now that he's got used to the idea, but it need only be when Jackie's at the farm, and I'd honestly rather come out to the village anyway. And I'd like the company.'

'It's an idea,' Val said slowly. 'But she might still think she'd rather be at the hotel.'

'Well, if she does, then that's it. But it could be a good compromise, you know. She'd be away from home and could have quite a bit of freedom, and at the same time she would be with someone your parents know.'

'D'you really think you'd want the responsibility? I mean, suppose something did go wrong – you wouldn't want the blame.'

'I wouldn't expect it,' Jennifer said frankly. 'It would have to be on the understanding that I'm no more responsible for her than any other landlady. But I would take care of her, all the same,' she added. 'As much as she'd let me, anyway!'

They walked in silence for a few minutes, each considering this new idea. By the time they reached the main road it was dark and they stood on the grass verge, still thinking it over.

'What do you reckon?' Jennifer asked at last.

'I think it's the best idea yet. I'll go round to the farm to-morrow and talk to them about it. And if they're agreeable, I'll let you know.' The lights of the Plymouth bus could be seen approaching in the distance. 'It'd probably be better if you suggested it to Jackie yourself, though. She's in such a contrary mood at the moment, if they do it she'll say no, just on principle! And I think she had a row with her boyfriend over it this afternoon. She came back early instead of staying to tea at his house, and she looked as if she'd lost a shilling and found threepence.'

Jennifer smiled sympathetically and Val flung her arms impulsively around her neck. 'You know, it was a good day for the Tozer family when you came to Burracombe. First you give me and Luke a home, and now it's Jackie. I don't know how we ever got along without you.'

'Don't be daft,' Jennifer said, and hugged Val back. 'I get a lot more from Burracombe than I'll ever be able to give in return. And don't forget, your mother was my mother's best friend, and your grandmother was my grandmother's. It's tradition, that's all.'

Just the same, she was glad that it was too dark for Val to see the tears in her eyes. And as she clambered aboard the bus and made her way to a seat, she felt a warmth enfold her body and her heart. It was true, she thought. Since that first day when she had arrived in Burracombe, the day the King had died, she had gained more than she had ever dared believe possible.

Chapter Thirty-Four

After the storms over Shirley's injury and Jackie's plans to leave home, Burracombe seemed to settle into a quiet period for a few weeks. Shirley's arm was mending fast and the lump on her head went down almost as quickly as it had come up, leaving a dramatic purple bruise that gradually faded to a greenish-yellow. Nothing more was discovered about the Plymouth poachers but Furzey had a long, private session with Gilbert Napier.

'You don't need to know what was said,' Napier told Hilary and Travis. 'I gave him a bit of a carpeting but he's a good game-keeper and I don't want to lose him. There's to be no more of this skulking around the woods at night with firearms, though.'

'He's probably done it for years,' Travis said. 'My father certainly did. But we don't want any more accidents, so it's just as well to have things clear. And what about Culliford?'

'What about him?' Hilary demanded at once. 'He wasn't doing anything illegal.'

The two men sighed. There would never be any agreement over this; they all knew that Arthur Culliford wouldn't have passed up the chance of a young bird picked up as he was going by the covers that night, but it wasn't organised poaching and the whole matter was best laid to rest.

'I've given Culliford some work on the estate,' Gilbert said. 'There's a lot of stone wall and some Devon banks that want repairing. He can get on with those. It'll give him a bit of income and make things easier for the family.'

'So he's done pretty well out of it, then,' Travis observed.

Hilary rounded on him at once. 'And why shouldn't he? His daughter was hurt, through no fault of his. We're lucky he didn't go to law over it.'

'Go to law – Culliford? He'd get laughed out of court.'

'It was on our land, and two of our employees were present,' she said curtly. 'I don't think we'd be the ones to be laughing.'

After that, their relationship had remained cool and businesslike. They met each morning, discussed what needed to be done on the estate, shared out the tasks with unnerving fairness and went and did them. If they could avoid meeting for the rest of the day, they did, and if they had to meet they were both scrupulously polite. There were no more early-morning rides or afternoon walks, and if Hilary, on Beau, noticed Travis in the distance on Sultan or Major, she turned and went the other way.

Worst of all, they were forced to meet at rehearsals and act together in the pantomime. Neither was prepared to give in over this, and both were determined to make the show a success, so they put all they knew into their acting and remained steadfastly apart the rest of the time.

It was all very, very civilised; and very painful.

'What on earth's the matter with Hilary these days?' Felix asked Stella just before the dress rehearsal in the middle of November. 'You could cut the atmosphere between her and Travis with a knife. It's like living on a glacier when those two are together.'

'I know. It's all because of Shirley, or because of her father. It's a shame because I thought they really liked each other to begin with. They seemed to get on so well.'

'Well, it's time they grew up,' Felix said tersely. 'The pantomime's supposed to be fun for everyone, and their attitude is beginning to rub off on other people. How they manage to work together beats me.'

'I think it's beginning to beat Hilary too,' Stella said. 'She looks really unhappy sometimes. I don't know how long she's going to be able to carry on like this. They've got problems in the house, too. Now that Jackie's left, they need more help and they don't seem able to find anyone.'

Jackie was now happily settled into the Duke of Cornwall Hotel and staying with Jennifer Tucker. Jennifer's suggestion had been met with relief all round. Jackie had been disappointed to find that there wouldn't, after all, be a room available at the hotel until she had worked there for at least six months and had been delighted with the idea of staying with Jennifer, while her parents had agreed that Miss Tucker was a person who could be trusted to keep an eye on their daughter.

'Not that I'm prepared to be totally responsible for her,' Jennifer had warned them. 'But at least I'll be there to help her if anything goes wrong and I can let you know if she needs you.'

'That's very good of you, Jennifer,' Alice said warmly. 'I'll sleep a lot easier in me bed knowing our Jackie's got someone to turn to. She'm a bit headstrong though, I warn you. But me and her father'll have a good straight talk with her beforehand.'

Jackie had listened to the straight talk without too much argument, satisfied that she was getting her own way, and when she arrived at Jennifer's house and was given her own door key she almost hugged herself with glee.

Instead, she hugged Jennifer. 'Thank you ever so much. I promise I won't let you down.'

'You'd better not,' Jennifer said good-humouredly. 'That key is simply to save me getting out of my chair to let you in. I'm not expecting you to come roistering home at three in the morning!'

Jackie giggled. 'I won't. But I can stay out after half-past ten, can't I?'

Jennifer looked at her seriously. 'You can decide for yourself when you come home. All I'll say is, that I expect you to be responsible about it. Let me know if you're going to be late, and don't do things you know are foolish. Your parents are good people and you know yourself how they expect you to behave. Don't let them down, and you won't let me down. Or yourself.'

Jackie nodded soberly. 'OK. You know, that's all I want – to be treated like a grown-up. Dad thinks I'm still a kid.'

'That's between you and your father – I don't want to get into discussions over it.' Jennifer gave her a quick hug. 'Right, now we've got that sorted out, I think we can have some fun together. How would you like to go to the pictures tonight? They're showing *Moulin Rouge* – I think you'll like that.'

Since then, even Ted Tozer was forced to admit that Jackie's new life suited her. She was a happier girl altogether, enjoying her job and the friends she was making, and the measure of independence that living with Jennifer gave her. She still came home two nights a week, for pantomime rehearsals, and at weekends, so on the whole it hardly seemed as if she'd left home at all. The biggest change seemed to be that she scarcely spoke to Vic Nethercott now, and if they got on the same bus, she sat as far away from him as possible.

'"Tis a shame, really,' Alice remarked to her mother-in-law. 'I thought they were well-suited. He's a nice-looking young fellow and got lovely manners.'

'Handsome is as handsome does,' Minnie said darkly. 'I always thought he were a bit on the smooth side, myself. And you don't know what ideas he got when he were in the Army.'

Val was pleased about Jackie's new life, too. 'I felt really sorry for her, having to stay at home and do what Dad told her,' she said to Luke as he painted scenery in the village hall. 'He's still living in the past, expecting her to be in by half-past ten every night, and never letting her decide for herself what to do. He'd have stopped her getting this job if he could, you know, and it's not that he's a bully – he really does think he knows what's best for her.'

'It must be a big responsibility, having a daughter,' Luke remarked, stepping back and narrowing his eyes to see the effect of his work. 'D'you think this dungeon looks grim enough? I thought I'd paint a couple of really starved-looking prisoners in chains on the wall, and maybe a torture weapon or two.'

Val walked to the back of the hall and regarded it thoughtfully. 'You could add a couple of rats at the bottom, perhaps, and a spider's web.'

'With a really big spider in it. Yes, I'll do that. I think there are going to be rats on stage, actually. Not real ones – stuffed ones, to be pulled across. Dottie's knitting them.'

Val giggled. 'This really is fun, isn't it. I've enjoyed the rehearsals. I just hope the performances go all right. I'm not sure we're even ready for the dress rehearsal on Sunday.'

'Shouldn't worry. They do say a bad dress rehearsal makes a good show.' Luke finished painting the silvery lines of a spider's web and began on a large, black spider in the middle. 'I hope this doesn't give anyone nightmares.'

'So do I. I must say, I like the greenwoods scenery best. It's a shame you can't sell it as a painting. It's really good.'

'Perhaps I'll get a few commissions for murals.' They were silent for a few minutes as he added eight long, black legs, and then he stood back and slipped his arm round her waist. 'My goodness, that's scaring even me! We might have to cover it up for the matinée.'

'I don't think Burracombe children are very frightened of spiders.' She leaned her head on his shoulder. 'It's been a good few months, hasn't it, Luke?'

'Very good,' he said, dropping a kiss on her hair. 'I can still hardly believe my life has worked out so well, you know. Coming to Burracombe and finding you, when I'd almost lost hope ... Not that I ever had much in the first place. I thought

358

by this time you'd be married with three or four children.' He stopped abruptly, then said, 'Val ...'

'No,' she said. 'Don't say it. Let me.' She turned to face him and he looked down at her face, half-puzzled, half-wary. 'It's all right, don't look so worried. I just want to say that I'm all right now. About children, I mean. I'd like us to start our family – that's if you're ready too.'

'Ready?' he said. 'Of course I'm ready! Oh Val, are you sure? There'll be no turning back, you know. Once it's begun ...'

'I know,' she said. 'I've just been so afraid that things might go wrong again. But I shouldn't think like that. We've got to take our chance, along with everyone else who ever wants to have a family. Jacob Prout showed me that.'

'Jacob?' he echoed in astonishment, and she laughed.

'I'll explain another time. But let's not wait any longer, Luke. Let's start straight away.'

'What – here?' he asked, looking round the empty hall. 'With those half-starved prisoners and that spider grinning down at us? Shouldn't we at least wait until we get home?'

Val laughed again and punched him on the arm. 'Put away your paints, you fool, and let's tidy up. And don't make any more idiotic jokes, or I may change my mind. If the baby takes after you, I'm not sure I could deal with two comedians in the family.'

Val was quite right to say that Hilary felt unhappy these days. She wasn't sure herself just why this was. The incident over Shirley had been upsetting, but it seemed to be more than that and she couldn't really understand why. She knew, though, that it had something to do with Travis.

I wish he'd never come here, she thought miserably the day before the dress rehearsal. I always knew it was a bad idea. We didn't need a manager. If only Father could have trusted me. If only he could bring himself to believe that this is the life I want ... If Henry had lived and we'd got married, it would

359

have been different, but he didn't. He got himself killed and that was the end of anything in that direction for me. This is all I have now – the estate and Burracombe. It's all I *want*. I don't need Travis Kellaway, or any other man, coming in and upsetting it all.

She went out into the stableyard after lunch, intending to saddle up Beau and go for a long ride, but to her dismay she saw that he was missing a shoe. He must have caught his hoof on a fence and pulled it off. There was nothing wrong with his foot, but until the farrier could come he couldn't be ridden. She turned away in disappointment.

It didn't mean she couldn't ride, of course. There were still two other horses, but when she looked down the fields she could only see Major. That meant that Travis had taken Sultan out. Hilary felt a pang of annoyance. She ought to be used to this by now, but it still seemed to her rather high-handed of Travis to take whichever horse he fancied without even mentioning it to her. Irritated, she called to her brother's horse and he came to her at once, hoping for a titbit. She gave him a windfall apple she'd picked up on the way through the orchard and slipped the collar over his head.

Fifteen minutes later, she was galloping over the moor, feeling the wind in her hair and the relief of being free from the estate, from Travis Kellaway, from her father and his demands. For the first time in a week, she felt like herself, and wondered why she went on with this, why she didn't simply tell her father that she was feeling more and more useless, that if he didn't need her help she would leave. I don't have to go to London, she thought. I could go to Canada or Australia. I could make my own way – I've got the money Mummy left me. I could make an entirely new life, away from Burracombe. Maybe Jackie Tozer's got the right idea. Women shouldn't be expected to stay at home. They can have careers. They can be free. *I* can be free. The world's my oyster.

Pausing at the top of the hill, beside the rocky tor, she gazed down at the valley and across the moor stretching into the distance beyond. Although she had been away to school and then during the war, this was the place that she had always known as home, and where her heart lay. Yet somehow, just lately, it had been spoiled. The deep involvement she felt with it all had been soured, and she thought she knew why.

Travis Kellaway.

A sudden wave of misery swept over her, bringing tears to her eyes. I feel like just riding away now, she thought, this very minute. I feel like asking Major to take me as far as he can, away into the night, where no one can find us. I feel like going and never coming back.

She brought one hand up to her head and rested the back of her wrist against her forehead, breathing deeply and swallowing. This is ridiculous, she told herself. I'm behaving like a stupid, spoiled child. All I have to do is work with this man, and if I can't, I'll have to talk to Father about it, quietly and sensibly. There's nothing to stop me leaving in a civilised manner if I want to. I don't have to start getting hysterical about it.

She turned Major's head and nudged him into a walk. Together, they went more soberly down the slope and then moved smoothly into a canter. Their ride for the rest of the afternoon was fast and exhilarating; and when she came back into the yard at last, just as the afternoon light was fading, she felt calmer and ready to face the long rehearsal next day.

Chapter Thirty-Five

'This is absolutely dreadful,' Joyce Warren said crossly as a large black spider, knitted by Dottie, fell from its web for the fourth time and landed on Hilary's head. 'And what on earth are those terrible groaning noises coming from backstage? Is someone ill?'

'We'm prisoners being tortured,' Micky Coker said, poking his head round one of the flats painted on one side as a dungeon wall and the other as part of the greenwood. Unfortunately, his appearance simply served to draw Joyce's attention to the fact that it had been placed the wrong way round. 'Me and Henry thought it'd make it seem more real.'

'Well, you'd better think again,' she said irritably. 'And someone turn that piece of scenery round, for goodness sake. I'm afraid the whole production has been just too ambitious,' she added to Felix who was sitting beside her. 'It's a pity you didn't take my advice in the first place.'

'What advice was that?' he enquired. 'You've given me so much.'

She gave him a suspicious look. 'About directing it, of course. I don't like to boast, but I do happen to have had quite a lot of experience in this field. And if you remember, I wanted to do *Cinderella*. Such a pretty pantomime.'

'Perhaps we'll do that another year,' he said, and raised his voice above the clatter of scenery being shifted behind Mrs Latimer's old velvet curtains which had been sewn together so that they very nearly reached the ground. 'We'll do the fight scene next. Are the horses ready?'

'Just finishing off their hay,' Tom Tozer called, and Joyce lifted her eyes to the ceiling. Through the gap at the bottom of the curtains, she could see feet traipsing back and forth until the cast were all in position for the grand fight between Robin Hood and the Black Knight. For some reason, it had been decided that this would be staged as a tournament, and Bill Tredicombe, who did most of the carpentry in the village, had spent several evenings in his workshop fashioning two 'horses', made mostly of plywood with long skirts (made from more old curtains), which could be fitted around the protagonists' waists. The skirts could be seen fluttering about as the two opponents jostled for position.

'Can we have the curtains drawn, please?' Felix asked after a moment, suspecting that the action had already begun. There was a muffled squeak from the side of the stage and the velvet parted somewhere near the middle and opened jerkily. Joyce sighed noisily.

'I *said* those curtains wouldn't be long enough. We'll have to sew something along the bottom and that will look dreadful.'

'They *are* long enough – it's just that the rail is too high.' Felix was having difficulty in keeping his own irritation in check, although in his case the annoyance was caused less by the problems on stage than by the criticism at his side. 'All right, let's start the scene.'

Grace Harvey, who had been prevailed upon to play the school piano, brought into the hall for this week only, began to thump out galloping music and the two plywood horses pranced across the stage, their riders aiming lances (made of billiard cues wrapped in silver paper saved from the entire village's chocolate ration for the past three months) at each other. They fenced with some enthusiasm until Robin Hood's horse fell apart and Val, taken by surprise, fell headlong on the stage.

'Oh, my goodness! Is she hurt?' Joyce was on her feet, but Felix was ahead of her. By the time he reached the stage, Val was sitting up, laughing and trying to extricate herself from the remains of her steed.

'It's all right. It's not broken – it just came apart. I think it needs stronger glue.'

'It'll have to go back to Mr Tredicombe,' Joyce said in exasperation. 'Really, this is the worst dress rehearsal I've ever been to!'

'You haven't been to as many as I have, then,' Felix said with a grin. 'All right, we'll do that scene without the horses. You'd better take yours off as well, Travis.'

At last the rehearsal came to an end and Val Ferris, looking very handsome in her green jerkin, tights and jaunty feathered hat, struck a pose at the front of the stage and declaimed the closing lines:

> 'And so we end our little tale.
> You've come through storm and frost and gale
> To see how Robin won fair Maid
> Marian in the greenwood glade.
> And conquered all those wicked blisters,
> The Sheriff, Black Knight and his sisters,
> And sent them all so far away
> They'll not be seen for many a day.
> So go in peace, all you who came
> To watch us in our merry game.
> Go now, with neither dread nor fear
> And come again another year!'

Henry Bennetts wound the handle that brought the curtain down and there was a spatter of applause from the scattered audience of helpers. Then he wound the curtain up again, Felix switched on the lights from the back of the hall, and the cast, gathered together on stage, gazed at him anxiously.

'It was awful, wasn't it,' Val said at last.

'Bits of it were, yes,' Felix admitted, coming forward. 'But once we've ironed those out ...'

'We haven't got *time* to iron them out!' Hilary exclaimed, pulling off her frothy blonde wig. 'We open on Thursday night, and we're only rehearsing once more. We'll never get it all together by then.'

'I'm sure we will.'

'I'm not,' she said, turning away despondently. 'We're going to be a laughing-stock.'

'Come on, Hilary,' Travis said, putting an arm clad in black-painted cardboard armour around her shoulder. 'It wasn't that bad. You know what they say about dress rehearsals.'

'I know, and I don't believe it.' She shook his arm off crossly. 'Felix, can't we put it off for another week or two?'

'Of course we can't! Look, Travis is right. It's only because you're not used to wearing the costumes. Everything seems different, but if we run through it again on Tuesday it'll be fine by the first night. You'll see.'

'Will I? Not if that great fat spider falls on my head again, I won't. And what about when all the Merry Men came charging on stage in the middle of Robin's love duet with Marian? It might not have mattered so much if they hadn't all tried to get off at once and fallen over in a heap. And even that wasn't as bad as when Val's plywood horse came to pieces ...'

'All that can be sorted out,' Felix said soothingly. 'That's what a dress rehearsal is for, to find out what can go wrong and make sure it doesn't. And if it does, the audience will enjoy it all the more. They love seeing things go wrong.'

''Tis no worse than any other dress rehearsal I've ever seen,' Dottie observed from her place in the audience. 'Even on the London stage they get things going wrong then.'

'There, you see?' Felix said. 'It'll be all right, Hilary. Anyway, the costumes and scenery in themselves are worth coming to see, thanks to Dottie and Luke and their helpers.

That dungeon scene is really gruesome, Luke.'

'I'm not sure it isn't *too* horrific for the little ones,' Joyce Warren began, but Stella interposed quickly.

'They'll love it. Anyway, we're going to drape some old net curtains over the skeletons and that big spider for the matinée, when the really small children come. They'll look just like cobwebs.'

At last the cast drifted back to the tiny room behind the stage which was all the dressing room they had. Bumping into each other, falling over and losing various items of apparel, they managed eventually to scramble back into their everyday clothes and went out into the night.

'Come back and have a cup of cocoa before you go home,' Val suggested to Hilary. 'You're all wound up. What's the matter? It's not just the pantomime, is it.'

'Oh, I don't know. I'm just a bit on edge lately. I'll be all right.' But Hilary sounded depressed and Val gave her an anxious glance.

She said no more until they were settled into the cottage living room with their cocoa and some of Minnie's home-made biscuits, then she said firmly, 'Right, then. Tell us all about it.'

Hilary hesitated and Luke said, 'I'll go upstairs if you like. Leave you two to your heart-to-heart.'

'No, it's all right, Luke. It's nothing private. I'm just a bit fed up, that's all. It's this arrangement with Travis – it's just not working.'

'Isn't it?' Val said in surprise. 'I thought things had been sorted out after Shirley's accident. Arthur Culliford seems to have settled down a lot, especially now he's got more work, and Maggie looks happier. She's even bought the children new winter coats. Well, new second-hand ones, anyway.'

'Maggie Culliford may be happier, but I'm not. I thought after that incident that my father would have the sense to see that we don't need an estate manager, but Travis seems to have wormed his way back in again and Dad hangs on his every word. They still let me sit in on their discussions, but that's all I'm doing. I throw in the odd word, but not much more. Well, maybe that's not entirely fair – I do make suggestions now and then, and they do take notice. But a lot of the time, it's Travis who does all the talking.'

'And don't you agree with what he says?'

'That's the annoying part,' Hilary said grumpily. 'I do. But that doesn't mean I wouldn't have said exactly the same if he hadn't been there to say it first.'

Val's mouth twitched. 'So you're not exactly at logger-heads.'

'Well, no. Not really. I just don't see that he's necessary!' Hilary burst out. 'There's no need for us both. And if we go on like this, I really think I'm going to leave. I've been thinking seriously about it, Val. I got out all that stuff Stephen collected about Canada the other day. There really is a lot of opportunity there. Or Australia. I'd like to see some of those places. Not to stay there, necessarily, just to see them. Maybe then Dad would realise how useful I can be,' she added woefully.

'So what you're saying is that you and Travis have more or less the same ideas,' Val suggested delicately.

'Well, yes, in a way, I suppose I am. But that's the whole point, you see. If we think the same way, there's no need for both of us, is there? I mean, if we were arguing all the time, one of us would be right and the other wrong, but as it is we're both ...' She stopped and looked at Val suspiciously. 'You wouldn't be laughing at me, would you?'

'Perish the thought!' Val said, her grin widening. 'Hilary, just what is the problem here? When your father first started to talk about getting in a manager, you were horrified. You thought he'd want to change things, that Burracombe estate wouldn't be yours any more, that nobody would take any notice of you and everything would be spoiled. Now you're complaining because you get along too well!'

'I'm not! Well, maybe I am … a bit,' Hilary admitted reluctantly. 'But that's the point, Val – we *don't* get along! We do see things regarding the estate in the same way, but on a personal level I can't stand the man.'

'Can't you?' Val enquired innocently, and Hilary threw her a baleful scowl.

'No, I can't.' She thought for a moment, staring into her cocoa. 'I did like him to begin with,' she confessed at last. 'And he was quite good when we were in the hospital when Shirley was hurt. But since then, everything he says seems to rub me up the wrong way.' She sighed. 'Oh well, there's nothing I can do about it now. We'll get this blessed pantomime out of the way, and Christmas, and then I'll think seriously about what I'm going to do. Because I do know that I can't carry on like this.' She put down her empty cup and stood up. 'I'd better go. I'm in a contrary mood tonight and nothing anyone says to me is going to be right.'

Val laughed and saw her out. When she came back, she looked at Luke and said, 'What d'you make of that, then?'

'Same as you, I reckon,' he said, and stood up, his head almost bumping the beams of the ceiling. 'The lady doth protest too much. I wonder what the gentleman thinks.'

'From the way he was looking at her tonight,' Val said, walking into his arms, 'much the same. That doesn't mean it'll work out well, though. I hope Hilary isn't going to get hurt. Maybe she's right, and it would be better for her to leave home.'

'You don't think they're suited, then? A bit too much like *Lady Chatterley's Lover* – the lady of the manor, and the gamekeeper?' He grinned wickedly. 'That would put the cat among the pigeons.'

'Luke!' Val pretended to be shocked. 'I don't know what you're talking about. I've never even read *Lady Chatterley's Lover.*'

'Not many people have, in this country anyway,' he said

'Too many rude words for English susceptibilities. Anyway, never mind that. It's time we went to bed. We've got a family to start, in case you've forgotten!'

Chapter Thirty-Six

Wednesday morning was dark and dismal, with low November cloud hanging over the village and a drizzle of rain. Hilary was in a worse state of nerves than ever. She found Travis in the office that morning, looking cheerful and relaxed, and almost turned on her heel and stormed out again. Instead, she forced herself to stay and go through the day's work with him, gritting her teeth. In the small office, crowded with a desk, two chairs, a wall full of shelves and two filing cabinets, there seemed barely room for the two of them and she was uncomfortably aware of his closeness as they pored over some maps of the estate he had spread out.

'These old field names are amazing,' he observed, apparently unaware of her discomfort. 'I suppose the old farmers had to be able to identify them, but look at this: Near Meadow, Far Meadow, Top Meadow, One Beyond, T'Other One – some of them sound perfectly reasonable but when I look at the others I think someone must be pulling my leg.'

'I don't think anyone would dare do that, do you?' she asked, aware of the edge in her voice. 'Look, this is all very interesting but I just—'

'It is, isn't it,' he agreed smoothly. 'I enjoy looking at old maps, don't you? There must be some really interesting ones of the estate.'

'Yes, there are,' Hilary said tersely. 'We'll get them all out one day and paper the walls with them so that you can sit and gaze at them to your heart's content. You wouldn't happen to have that information I got on Herdwick sheep, would you? Only if you can spare the time, of course.'

'The Lake District sheep? I thought Ken had given up that idea.'

'He's asked me to think about it again. He says if they're tough enough to stand up to Cumberland winters, they ought to be able to manage on Dartmoor, but I'm not so sure.'

'Nor am I,' Travis said. 'At least, I think he's probably right about that, but I'm not sure what use they'd be. Their meat's too tough, and their wool is more like barbed wire. I had some socks made of it once and they might as well have been knitted from brambles. Still, we can have a look.' He ferreted about amongst a pile of papers and came up with a small sheaf. 'Here you are. And how are you feeling about tomorrow night?'

'I'm trying not to think about it. Quite frankly, I wish I'd never agreed to be involved. We're going to look like nothing more than a bunch of amateurs.'

'Well, that's what we are.'

'Half of us don't know our lines,' she continued, 'and the other half don't know when they ought to be on stage. Henry Bennetts keeps getting the curtain wrong. It went down in the middle of my scene with the Sheriff the other night and left me on the outside, and another time he wound it up while Billy Friend and Luke were changing the scenery. If he doesn't get it right tonight, I'll strangle him.'

'I expect he will. He's only had a couple of rehearsals to learn when to do it, after all. And he's only a youngster.'

'He's got a list written up beside him,' Hilary said unforgivingly. 'I'll say that for Joyce Warren, she's been very efficient with her stage-management. There really isn't any excuse for anyone to get anything wrong at all.'

'Except that, as you say, we're really no more than a bunch of amateurs,' he pointed out. 'Come along, Hilary, try to relax. It's meant to be fun.' He smiled at her. 'Why not go for a ride this afternoon? Get some fresh air into your lungs, and forget about the pantomime and the estate and everything. That's what I'm thinking of doing.'

'Really?' Hilary said acidly. 'I'm surprised you haven't got too much work to do.'

'So am I,' he agreed cheerfully. 'But I expect I'll make it up sometime, if I haven't already. Anyway, I think you should stop worrying. You're very good in your part and I really like that bunch of candyfloss you wear on your head.'

Hilary laughed unwillingly. 'I know that's what it looks like. Do you really think it's going to be all right, Travis?'

'I really do.' He folded up the map. 'All right, let's get some work done. What are you planning for this morning, apart from talking to Ken about those Herdwicks ...?'

By afternoon, the fog had cleared, leaving a clear, pale sky. Hilary finished lunch and decided to do as Travis had suggested and go for a ride. She slipped out quickly, not wanting to encounter him, and took Beau, who was now wearing new shoes and eager for an outing.

The ride did, as Travis had said it would, clear her head and leave her feeling better. She was still nervous about the first performance next day but felt that she had got things into better proportion. It was just a village pantomime, after all, and nobody would expect London theatre standards. For heaven's sake, most of the audience would never have been to a proper theatre anyway! All they wanted was a good evening out and something to laugh at. Well, they'll get that for certain, she thought grimly, and pushed away the nerves that threatened to overtake her again.

As she had on Saturday, she reached home feeling calmer and put Beau back into the stable. Sultan and Major were in already, and she gave them a quick glance before rubbing Beau down and giving him his feed. As she ran her hands over his body, she noticed a long scratch along his flank and frowned at it. It looked as if a bramble had caught him, and she found some ointment and rubbed it on. I'd better come out later and have a look at that, she thought. It could turn nasty.

Indoors, she found Felix waiting for her, looking anxious.

'Hello, Felix. What's the matter?'

'It's Val. She's got a sore throat. She thinks she's got laryngitis.'

'Oh, no!' Hilary stared at him in dismay. 'Poor Val. But what about tomorrow?'

'That's just the problem. She may not be able to perform.' He rubbed his hand distractedly over his brown, wavy hair. 'I don't know what to do.'

'Has she seen Charles Latimer?'

'She was going round to his surgery when I left her. She said she wouldn't normally dream of bothering the doctor for a sore throat, but – Hilary, there's only one thing I can think of. Would you take her part?'

'*Me*?' Hilary's mouth fell open. 'But I've already got a part! And I don't know the lines.'

'One of the chorus could take on your part. Vic Nethercott's sister – she'd do it, I'm sure. And you've read in for Val several times when she hasn't been able to get to rehearsal, so you know the part pretty well. You could use your script – everyone would understand. It might only be for a night or two, if Val gets better quickly.'

'I suppose I could wear her costume all right,' Hilary said doubtfully. 'We're much of a size. But honestly, Felix, isn't there anyone else?'

'You suggest someone and I'll go and ask them,' he said gloomily, and Hilary had to admit that she couldn't think of anyone else, other than Stella, who was much slighter than Val and would need quite a few alterations to the costumes.

'Well, all right,' she said at last. 'But tell Val she's got to get better quickly! Fancy going down with laryngitis at this stage. Couldn't she have waited a week?'

'I'll pass on your sympathy,' he said with a grin. 'Thanks

a million, Hilary. I'll be your slave for ever. Now, I'll have to go – there are a thousand and one things to do and I've got some parish matters to see to as well. I should have asked Mr Harvey for a week's holiday – I will, next year.'

'That's if there is a next year,' Hilary said. 'I don't think I can go through all this again.'

Felix laughed. 'You'll really enjoy it once we get started. I'll see you tomorrow evening at the hall, then. Six o'clock sharp, mind, so that we can be sure to be ready in time, and you'll have a chance to run through some of Val's lines.'

'Maybe I won't need to. Val might be better by then.' But she didn't have any real hope. Laryngitis was a nasty thing, and unless Charles had some magic potions in his black bag, Hilary didn't see much chance of Val being better for at least a week. That means I'll have to play Robin for every performance, she thought, and I was nervous enough about playing the part I'd actually learned!

She spent the rest of the evening feverishly reading through the script, trying to memorise Robin Hood's lines and moves, and it wasn't until almost ten o'clock, when the words were dancing in front of her eyes and she was about to give up, that she remembered Beau and the scratch on his flank.

I'd better go and check that it's not infected, she thought, and went to pull on her boots and a warm jacket before going out to the stables. The November night was dark and cold, with a film of ice already forming on the puddles left by that morning's rain, but the sky was still clear and patterned with stars. This time tomorrow, she thought, the first performance will be just finishing. Oh, I hope Val's throat isn't too bad. I hope she can perform. She's so good as Robin Hood, and she's been looking forward to it so much. It *would* happen now!

She went into the stable. The horses were all in their boxes, behind the big wooden doors and the iron bars that had stood there for the past two or three hundred years, ever since the

Barton was built. There was supposed to be a ghost here, that of an old groom, Crocker said, who couldn't bear to leave his beloved stables and kept a fatherly eye on the horses. Hilary had never encountered him, but there was a friendly feel to the place and she loved being here at night, with the warmth of the big bodies and the gentle snuffling and scraping noises the horses made as they moved to welcome her.

She opened Beau's door and went inside, shining her torch on the smooth brown flank. The scratch was healing well, and she rubbed his nose and gave him one of the apples she had brought with her. His rubbery lips took it from her gently and his big teeth crunched with satisfaction.

Hilary closed his door and went to check on Major and Sultan, holding two more apples in her hand.

Sultan took his apple as if it were his right. Big and majestic, his dark body was almost invisible in the blackness of the stable. She rubbed his face and moved to the next box to look at Baden's horse, and then froze with dismay.

Major was on his back, with all four hooves pressed awkwardly against the wall. His body and neck were twisted and his eyes were rolling in pain. As Hilary stared at him in horror, he seemed to throw her a look of pleading desperation, begging her for help, and let out a strange, strangled cry, as if unable even to neigh properly. Shaking with fear, she thrust open the door and knelt beside him, her hands on the big head.

'Major! Major, whatever's happened?'

The question was purely rhetorical, bursting out of her own shock. She didn't need to ask what had happened. He was 'cast' and almost certainly had colic. He needed immediate attention to get him out of his awkward position, and Hilary knew she could not do it alone.

'I'm sorry, Major,' she panted, scrambling to her feet. 'I've got to leave you – I'll be back as soon as I can. Hold on, darling.' She slammed the door shut and ran out of the stable and across the yard to the cottage where Crocker lived.

Thank heaven there was still a light on; she banged hard on the door.

Mrs Crocker opened it and peered out. 'Miss Hilary! Whatever be the matter?'

'One of the horses is in trouble! I need help. Can your husband come, quickly?'

'Why, of course. And Mr Kellaway be here too.' She called over her shoulder but the inner door was already opening and the stableman coming out to see what the commotion was, with Travis close behind him. 'Miss Hilary says one of the horses is took bad.'

'What is it, Hilary? Which horse?' Travis pushed past and came to lay his hands on her shoulders. 'Take it easy now,' he urged as she gulped and caught her breath in her hurry to tell him. 'We'll come over straight away. Tell me as we go.'

'It's Major,' she gasped as they sprinted back across the yard, leaving Crocker dragging on his boots in the tiny hallway. 'He's cast and I think he's got colic. He looks awful – all twisted up and terrified. Oh Travis, if anything happens to him …'

'It won't. We'll sort him out.' They ran into the stable. The horse was just as she'd left him, still letting out that dreadful, strangled whinny and choking for breath. His legs and body were twisted and his struggles to get free were making it worse. Hilary knelt by his head and Travis said quickly, 'We've got to get him up. Stay with him while I get some ropes.'

Crocker stumbled in and took in the scene. 'There are some over in the corner, Mr Kellaway. I'll fetch 'em.'

Major's head jerked violently, almost knocking Hilary over, and Travis said tersely, 'You've got to stop him moving, Hilary. Kneel on his neck if necessary.'

'I'll choke him!'

'He'll die anyway if we don't get him up. Do it! If you don't, I will, and I'm needed at the other end.'

Tears streaming down her face, Hilary did as she was told.

She could see Major's eyes staring up at her, filled with pain and despair. 'I'm doing it to help you, old boy,' she told him. 'We all want to help you.'

Crocker brought the ropes across and Travis fastened them swiftly round the horse's legs, just above the foot, hobbling both fore and hind legs. The two men then began to ease the feet away from the wall and pull them steadily over the twisted body. Major shuddered and groaned, and Hilary whimpered as if she were sharing his pain. 'It's hurting him.'

'He's in pain anyway. There's definitely some colic there. Hold still, Hilary, it's the only way. Don't let him move his head.' They went on pulling, and at last the legs were over and the body began to turn. Carefully, they removed the ropes and helped the big horse to struggle to his feet. Travis examined him.

'It is colic, isn't it?' Hilary said, and he nodded.

'Has he had it before?'

'Once or twice, but not quite a while. I'm always extra careful with his feed. This is the worst I've seen him.' The horse was breathing with difficulty, his abdomen distended, and suddenly he sank back on his haunches, like a dog that has been told to sit.

'We'd better get the vet,' Travis said. 'Crocker – will you do that?'

'Use the phone in the house,' Hilary said. 'The back door's open and the phone is in the hall. Tell him to be quick.'

The stableman departed quickly and they turned their attention back to the distressed horse. 'We need to get him back on his feet,' Travis said. 'I'm not sure he hasn't already twisted his gut but we daren't let him roll again. Pull on that rope, Hilary, as hard as you can ... that's it. Up you come, old fellow, up you come ...'

They strained together, the horse's eyes rolling as he struggled against them, until finally they had him back on all four feet. Hilary's eyes filled with tears again.

'You can see how it's hurting him. Oh Major, poor old boy. Travis, if anything happens to him, it'll break Dad's heart. He's all we have left of Baden.'

'I know. It's all right, Hilary. We won't let him go. Once the vet's here, he'll be able to ease the pain and put in a stomach tube to relieve some of the gas. He'll probably use an anti-fermentation drug too. Major will be all right.'

'Have you ever seen that done before?' she asked, and he nodded.

'It's a good treatment. But until he comes, we'll keep him walking.' The horse was now up again and they led him outside. As they began to lead the suffering animal along the cobbled yard, Crocker came back, panting heavily.

'The vet's away on a call, all the way over to Notts Farm, out by Princetown.'

'Have you phoned there?' Travis asked, and he shook his head.

'They'm not on the phone. Vet's missus says he could be gone hours.'

'Where's the next nearest? Tavistock?'

'I've tried there too. They'm out as well. Looks like every animal in the county's down with summat tonight.'

Travis swore, then thought for a moment. 'Take the Land Rover, Crocker, and go over to Notts Farm. See if he'll come back with you. If he can't, get to the nearest phone and try every vet there is. He'll have a list. We'll keep the horse moving meanwhile, but for God's sake, get somebody!'

Crocker disappeared again and a minute or two later they heard the Land Rover's engine start up. The yard was swept by bright light and then plunged back into darkness again. Hilary and Travis continued their steady plodding up and down the stableyard, with Major between them, his head hanging.

'You know, I think his breathing's easing a bit,' Hilary said after a while.

'I think so too.' They looked at each other over his head

and Travis said tentatively, 'Hilary, I've been wanting to talk to you.'

'Oh?' Her voice was wary and she turned away slightly.

'About what happened up in the woods. About Shirley, I mean.'

'I think that's best put in the past, don't you?' she said immediately. 'Let's learn from it and forget it.'

'I'd like to, but I need to clear it in my mind first. And we need to clear the air.'

'Do we?'

'Yes,' he said. 'We do.'

There was a short silence, then she sighed and said, 'All right, then. Say whatever it is you want to say.'

'I just want to say I'm sorry,' he said, and she turned her head towards him in surprise. 'I acted wrongly. I ought to have told you what I intended to do. As joint estate manager, I had no right to make arrangements with Furzey behind your back.'

'Oh,' Hilary said blankly. She thought for a few minutes as they turned and began to walk the horse back along the yard. 'I don't suppose it would have made all that much difference if I had known. Arthur would still have been up there with Shirley.'

'You might have told me not to do it.'

'And would that have stopped you?' she asked wryly, and sensed his shrug.

'Maybe not. But at least we wouldn't have needed all that argument about who was in the wrong.'

Hilary sighed. 'I don't suppose I would have done that anyway. I know we've got to do something about the poaching – those city poachers are becoming a real nuisance. People like Arthur are very small beer in comparison.'

'Yes, but it was Culliford that Furzey and I were after. I can't use the city poachers as an excuse.'

Hilary was silent again. Then she said, 'It wasn't what you

did that upset me. Well, not entirely. It was the fact that you didn't discuss it with me first.'

'I know. That's what I'm apologising for.'

'You see, I thought we were beginning to work quite well together.'

'We were. We do. Even now, we work well together, when we allow ourselves to.'

'When *I* allow us to, you mean.'

'Well, perhaps,' he said, and she heard the smile in his voice.

'You see,' Hilary said again, 'in a small place like Burracombe, we all know each other. People like Arthur Culliford – well, there's at least one like him in every village. We just learn to get along with him. And we have to think of his family, too – Maggie, expecting another baby any time now, and all those other children. Shirley herself, a really bright little girl who's only come out of her shell in the past year or so. We have to weigh up the loss of an occasional pheasant against what prosecuting Arthur would do to the family.'

'I know. And we used to take the same view, more or less, in my own village. I suppose I was suffering from what you, or maybe someone else, called "new broom-it-is"!'

'I think perhaps we were both trying too hard to prove ourselves,' she said quietly.

They walked in silence for a few more minutes. Then Travis said, 'Shall we start again? I must admit, I've been thinking seriously during the past week or two about whether I should leave. I could see you were unhappy and it's seemed increasingly wrong for me to be here, in your home, making you miserable, when you can do the work perfectly well without me. In fact, if you want me to go, I will.'

Hilary turned to him in surprise. 'But I've been thinking just the same! That I'd have to leave, I mean. I've even been considering emigration.'

'Emigration?' he echoed, shocked. 'Hilary, you can't do

that. It would destroy your father if you were to go.'

'I don't think he'd care.'

'Of course he would,' he insisted. 'You're all he has now. Stephen's never going to come back here to live. And this old fellow,' he gave Major's neck a pat, 'he'll get through this crisis, but he won't live for ever. And a horse, even Baden's horse, can never make up for losing a daughter.'

Hilary said nothing. Her eyes stung and she too laid her hand on Major's neck, feeling the warmth of his body. His breathing was definitely easier, she thought, and a great wave of relief washed over her, though whether for the horse or herself she couldn't tell. She said, 'Perhaps neither of us needs to go.'

In the starlight, she saw the glimmer of Travis's eyes as he turned his head towards her. His voice was quiet as he said, 'Are you sure you mean that?'

'Well, it's as you said at the very beginning. If you leave, Father will be bound to find someone to take your place. Better the devil you know than the devil you don't.'

'And do you think you know this devil well enough now?' he asked, and she reached her hand across Major's neck towards him.

'I think I am beginning to know this devil very well.'

Travis clasped her hand in his. They stopped briefly, ready to turn and begin the walk back. At that moment, Major gave a grunt and a sigh and they released their clasp and looked at him in alarm. There was a rush of air, acrid and foul, followed by a surge of droppings from under his tail. The distended abdomen seemed to deflate like an enormous balloon and he staggered slightly and neighed. The stinking, slimy mass spattered over the cobbles and Hilary gave a cry of relief, and then an exclamation of dismay.

'It's all over me! Not that it matters − not that it matters a bit. He'll be all right now, won't he, Travis? He'll get over it?'

'I think so.' Headlights swept over the yard again and he turned thankfully. 'Here's the vet. He'll make sure there's no damage done. He could still have twisted something inside, but I'm pretty sure he hasn't. I think everything's going to be all right, Hilary.'

'Oh, thank goodness. Thank God.' As the vet leaped down from his vehicle, closely followed by Crocker in the Land Rover, she came round to Travis and leaned against him, sobbing with relief. 'Everything's going to be all right now – everything.' Then she straightened up and stared at him in horror. 'Oh! Except for one thing – I'd completely forgotten!'

'What? What else has gone wrong?'

'The pantomime,' she said. 'I'm going to have to play Robin Hood – and I haven't had a wink of sleep!'

Chapter Thirty-Seven

'Before we start on the food,' Felix said, climbing up on the stage and facing the crowded hall, 'I'd just like to say a few thank-yous. It would take rather a long time to thank everyone who's helped to make this production possible, so if I leave anyone out I hope you'll forgive me, but there are some people I just have to say a special word about.'

The cast of the pantomime, together with friends, relatives and other assorted hangers-on, gazed up at him. Some were still in costume, some had changed back to everyday or party clothes, some already had glasses in their hands, ready to start the last-night party. Bernie Nethercott had sent down a barrel of beer, several bottles of lemonade and squash, and even a bottle or two of port for those who enjoyed a port-and-lemon. The chairs had been cleared back to the sides of the hall and long trestle tables laid with clean white bedsheets and plates of food. There was an air of relief and festivity mixed with regret that, after all the rehearsing and hard work, the pantomime was over.

'First of all,' Felix said, 'I want to thank the entire cast who have worked so hard over the past two or three months. They've learned their words, they've sung the songs, they've even been on stage at approximately the right times,' everyone laughed, 'and I don't think it mattered at all when the Sheriff fell over the chains in the dungeon, or when Hangem and Floggem got caught up in the cobwebs. I think the audience thought it was meant to happen. And I was really impressed when the portcullis came down on top of Robin Hood and nearly cut off his head. It should have been in the script all along.'

'You may think so,' Val said, still a little husky from her laryngitis. 'As a cure for a sore throat, I thought it was a bit overdone!'

Felix grinned. 'That brings me to my first special thank-you – to Val Ferris, who has battled bravely through despite her illness and only missed the first performance. Well done, Val – you can have all day tomorrow in bed!'

The cast cheered and clapped, and after a moment or two Felix lifted his hands for silence.

'I also have to thank Hilary Napier, who stepped so nobly into the breach and played Robin on the first night, even more so as I understand she was up with a sick horse the night before and got hardly any sleep. How is Major now, Hilary?'

'He's fine, thanks,' Hilary said, and turned to smile at Travis. 'Thanks to the Black Knight here.' She moved a little closer to Travis and they clasped hands.

'There's another person who deserves our special thanks, too,' Felix went on, bending to draw Shirley Culliford forward and up on to the stage beside him. 'We were all very worried about this little girl when we heard about her accident, but she's a brave girl as well as a pretty one, and was determined to play her part, even if she still had her arm in plaster. As you can see, she didn't have to do that and I think you'll agree she made a very good Jailer's Daughter, helping Mother Hood and the others to escape. Thank you, Shirley.'

He went on through the list, thanking Dottie and her helpers for the wonderful costumes they had made, Luke for the scenery he had painted and the scene-shifters who had managed to get everything moved at more or less the right times, often into the right places, and only once put the dungeon backcloth into the middle of the greenwood. He thanked Henry Bennetts who had wrestled so manfully with the curtain when it refused to rise more than halfway, and Joyce for her efficient

384

stage-management and the lists she had carefully written out and pinned everywhere so that everyone knew exactly where they should be and when. 'It was just a pity they were all in such dark corners no one could read them,' he apologised. 'Next time, we'll make sure there's a light by them.'

'I could fix up a wandering lead,' Micky Coker offered. 'You could just have a torch bulb on the end. If us had one long flex, with lots of bits joined on, it could be plugged into that socket by the stage and there could be lights by all them notices. People would have to be careful they didn't trip over them, of course,' he added.

'Well, we'll bear that in mind for next year,' Felix said, imagining the chaos that would ensue, with at least one small child being electrocuted per evening. 'Now, who else must I thank? Miss Bellamy, of course, for playing the piano so well – I think nearly all the singers were together in that last song tonight, don't you, Miss Bellamy? And I must say a very special, personal thank you to someone you all know very well and without whom I just wouldn't have been able to do this.' He watched with a small grin as all eyes turned towards Stella, who was standing by the corner of the stage, turning scarlet. 'And that's our Vicar, Mr Harvey!' There was a murmur of surprise as they turned to look the other way. 'If Mr Harvey hadn't been so understanding and sympathetic in letting me spend such a lot of time on this, I simply wouldn't have been able to carry it through. And that brings me to the last thing I have to say to you – the last two things, actually.' He paused as the cluster of faces looked up at him again. 'I've had a wonderful time, producing this pantomime, and I've had a wonderful time here in Burracombe. Every day has brought me pleasure in some way – a smile, a cheering word, a tiny measure of acceptance. I've felt at home here and I've wanted for a long time to make it my home, if not for the rest of my life, then for a very long time to come.'

He paused. The hall was silent now, even the smallest

children recognising that something important was being said. He cast a small, swift glance towards Stella, and went on.

'Sadly, I'm afraid that isn't to be.' A gasp of consternation ran round the room as villagers turned to each other in dismay. 'I'm leaving Burracombe. The time has come for me to move on – and, I think, up. No, not quite as far up as that!' he grinned. 'Heaven isn't quite ready for me yet, I trust. But I've been offered a position as Vicar, and I hope you'll be pleased to learn that although I'm leaving Burracombe itself, I'm only moving a very short distance. Across the river, in fact, to our sister village and sometimes rival, Little Burracombe!'

There was a burst of cheering as the villagers clapped and congratulated Felix. He stood smiling, his fair face blushing a little, and after a minute or two held up his hands again.

'I think that's quite enough of that, but thank you all very much. Although I'm not quite sure whether you're pleased that I'm going to be so near, or just pleased that I'm going!' They laughed again. 'Anyway, I'm sure you all realise that I shall be rather busy in my new job, especially as I don't think I am going to have a curate to do all the hard work,' he grinned at Basil, who raised his hands and rolled his eyes, 'so I may not be able to devote quite as much time to our new Drama Club as I've managed to do in the past few months. But now that we've started, I hope we'll carry on, and I'd certainly like to be a part of it, if you'll allow me back over the river.'

'Us'll do that all right,' Alf Coker said. He had put on a wonderful act as the Dame, mincing about the stage in his elaborate costume, thrusting out his overflowing fake bosom and adlibbing outrageously whenever he forgot his words, and had been clapped and cheered at every performance. 'Now us got going again, us'll be keen to do more.'

'I'm very pleased to hear it,' Felix said. 'Perhaps we might think about a play for the summer ...' Basil gave a cough and he remembered what he was supposed to be doing. 'But we'll leave that for the time being. We all need to recover from this production first, and there's Christmas and the New Year to be thinking of. Have you all seen the new stamps with the Queen's head on, brought out just in time for the Christmas cards?' There were a few nods and murmurs from the philatelists in the audience. 'Anyway, I won't stand here chattering on and keeping you from your supper much longer. I have one more person to thank, and you all know who that is.'

He stretched his hand out and Stella, blushing again, stepped up on to the stage beside him. 'You all know Miss Simmons, our lovely schoolteacher, who came to Burracombe at around the same time as I did. She's given us a wonderful performance as Dawn, one of the Black Knight's sisters, and as you have probably noticed, I've become rather fond of her.' They laughed and he slipped his arm around Stella's waist and turned her to face him. 'I'm very proud and very, very happy to tell you all that this lovely lady has agreed to marry me.' There was a burst of cheering and Stella, taken completely by surprise, felt her face flame.

Felix lifted his free hand for silence and, when it was more or less accomplished, went on, 'We were going to announce our engagement at Christmas but it seemed to me that tonight, with all our friends around us, would be an even better time.' He felt in his pocket and pulled out a small box, opening it with one hand and offering it to Stella. 'Just to make it quite formal, my darling – will you wear this ring for me? Will you marry me?'

'Oh Felix,' she whispered, her eyes filling with tears. She looked down at the box and at the ring it contained – a tiny gold ring, small enough to fit her slender finger, with one sparkling diamond set in its centre. Felix removed his arm from around her waist and took the ring in one hand. Holding her hand with the other, he looked questioningly into her eyes and she nodded, speechlessly at first, and then found her voice. 'Yes. Yes, I will.'

Small as her whisper was, the hall was so quiet that everyone there could hear it, but as Felix slipped the ring on to her finger the audience broke into cheers, clapping and applauding as if they would never stop. Stella and Felix stood with their arms wound round each other's waists, smiling and blushing. The noise began to diminish only when Alf Coker stepped forward and raised his huge hands for silence.

'I reckon we'm all pleased by that bit o' news,' he declared, and they clapped again. 'We been waiting for it long enough,' he added, and there was a burst of laughter. 'But there's another side to it as well. When this young man goes over the river, he'll be taking his wife with him. And that means us'll be losing our schoolteacher as well as our curate.' He turned to Stella and Felix. 'So I hopes you won't take it amiss if I says, I'm real pleased to hear your news, but I hope the wedding won't be too soon. Us wants to keep Miss Simmons here as long as us can!'

Another cheer greeted these words, and Felix said, 'Thank you very much, Alf. We both appreciate that. And you may be pleased to know that we're not thinking of arranging a wedding for at least a year. I can't say I'm very pleased about it myself,' he added with a grin. 'I'd like it to be tomorrow. But even curates have to be sensible.'

Basil Harvey stepped forward. '*Especially* curates, I'd say,' he remarked severely, and then his face relaxed into a beaming smile. 'I'd just like to add my congratulations to this happy pair. I've thought for a long time how well-suited they are, and I'm very pleased for them. I'm also pleased for Felix in his new appointment, although he won't be leaving us just yet – there are still a few hoops to jump through before everything is settled. And I'm glad that they'll be so close, and still able to take part in the life of Burracombe. And now, I think we ought to start doing justice to this wonderful spread of food – and after that, I understand that the cast is going to sing once more, and for the very last time, every song they've been singing all week in *Robin Hood and His Merry Men*!'

*

'What a wonderful party,' Val said as they all sat round a trestle table, their plates filled with food. 'It's a lovely way to finish the pantomime.'

'Well, we couldn't just go off into the night as if nothing had happened,' Felix said. He and Stella were sitting as close as was both possible and still respectable enough for a curate and schoolteacher, both looking very flushed and happy. 'And I think we all deserve a party. Everyone's worked really hard.'

'It's been fun,' Val said. 'And we will do another one next year, won't we, Felix? You'll come back over the river and lick us into shape again.'

'That rather depends on my new parish. They may want their own Drama Club.'

'You couldn't!' Hilary exclaimed in horror. 'You couldn't abandon us in our hour of need – not when we've only just got going.'

'I'm sure I'll be involved, one way or another. But there are several people who could direct just as well as me. You could, for one – and so could Travis. He's already let me into the secret of his experience.'

'Travis?' Hilary echoed, turning to look at the man next to her. 'You didn't tell me you'd done amateur dramatics before.'

'Well, we've either had too much to talk about, or we've not been talking at all,' he returned with a grin. 'But I did do a bit, back at home. I've been in a few plays and a couple of pantos, and I've directed one or two – so yes, I'd probably be ready to do it again. But like Felix, it rather depends on whether I stay here or not.'

'Oh, you'll stay,' Val declared, getting up from her chair. 'I'm going back for seconds – anyone else want anything while I'm there?'

'I'll come too,' Luke said, and both Felix and Stella followed them to the long table. They moved along it slowly, refilling their plates with Dottie's sausage rolls, Joyce Warren's cheese flans, Jessie Friend's tomato sandwiches and Minnie Tozer's flapjacks. Left alone for a moment, Hilary and Travis looked at each other.

'You are staying, aren't you?' she said quietly. 'Things are OK between us now, aren't they?'

'Do you think so?' he asked, meeting her eyes, and she nodded. 'Then, yes, I'm staying. There's quite a long way to go before we reach the place I'd like us to be, but I think we're on the right track now, after a pretty rocky start.'

'The place you want us to be?' she repeated softly. 'And just where is that?'

Travis smiled. His eyes were narrowed and lazy, and Hilary found her breath catching in her throat.

'You know that as well as I do,' he said. 'In Burracombe, of course.'

Janice Preston grew up in Wembley, North London, with a love of reading, writing stories and animals. In the past she has worked as a farmer, a police call-handler and a university administrator. She now lives in the West Midlands, with her husband and two cats, and has a part-time job as a weight management counsellor—vainly trying to control her own weight despite her love of chocolate!